Y0-BTE-439

Tales of the Shining Mountains

Book One
The Caves of Castleguard

Copyright © by Heather Pyrcz
and Borealis Press Ltd., 2016

*All rights reserved. No part of this book may be reproduced or used
in any form or by any means, electronic or mechanical,
including photocopying, recording, or any retrieval system,
without the prior written permission of the publisher or a
licence from the Canadian Copyright Licensing Agency
(Access Copyright). To contact Access Copyright, visit
www.accesscopyright.ca or call 1-800-893-5777.*

Canadä

*The Publishers acknowledge the financial assistance of the
Government of Canada through the Book Publishing Industry
Development Program (BPIDP) for our publishing activities.*

Library and Archives Canada Cataloguing in Publication

Pyrcz, Heather, 1951-, author
     The caves of Castleguard / Heather Pyrcz.

(Tales of the shining mountains) Issued in print and electronic formats.

ISBN 978-0-88887-661-4 (paperback).--ISBN 978-0-88887-662-1 (ebook)

     I. Title.

PS8581.Y73C39 2016   C813'.54   C2016-902706-6
                                               C2016-902707-4

ALSO AVAILABLE AS AN EBOOK (978-0-88887-662-1)

Printed and bound in Canada on acid free paper.

*Quote on page 88: David Young's translation of Duino Elegies by RM Rilke,
8th Elegy, WW Norton & Co, New York; 1978*

Tales of the Shining Mountains

Book One

The Caves of Castleguard

Heather Pyrcz

BOREALIS
BOOK PUBLISHERS
Borealis Press
Ottawa, Canada
2016

Acknowledgements

The Trilogy, *Tales of the Shining Mountains*, encompasses a fifteen-year journey with many companions and helpful guides. I would especially like to thank my loving and supportive family: Josh and Jennifer, who got me to the mountains and share my love of animals and the Parks; Tessa who has been an inspiration on the entire voyage, contributing exquisite photographs, reading drafts; her husband, Cameron, to whom she read later drafts, both giving brilliant suggestions; and Greg, husband, best friend and constant supporter whose editing has made the trilogy so much better. I would like to thank Alec Hamilton, Peter Hamilton and Robin Colyer who read early drafts, contributed photographs of Yellowstone and made invaluable suggestions; Jacquelin and Jim Fowler who ferried me in their camper to the wild places of the Yukon and taught me so much; Dianne MacPhee who read drafts and always gave me encouragement in the doubting times; to the many young people, especially Madeleine Ahern, and the students of the WITS program in Nova Scotia, with whom it was such a delight to discuss the book. I would like to thank Frank and David Tierney of Borealis Press who are the best of publishers—open, considerate, kind—my talented editor Janet Shorten, and all those at the press who helped in the publishing process. A giant bear hug to all!

Table of Contents

Cathedral

Once upon a time, long ago, there was a mountain called Cathedral that belonged to the Mountains of the Source. These colossal peaks encircled a vast Icefield: cold, remote, where time was old and days fell as quietly as ripe pine cones to the forest floor. Beneath the Icefield lay a sacred trust. Melancholia, the Spirit of Mount Cathedral, dwelt in the mountain with a race of grizzly bears bred by the old gods to protect what lay hidden beneath the ice—ancient ice, so deep you could tie six great totem poles one to another, lower them down, and still not reach bottom. For eons the grizzles had watched and protected, guided by the Spirit, daughter of Gaia.

Melancholia had known many Keepers, for she had known all the ages of Cathedral since its tumultuous beginning, but none she admired more than the newest Keeper, Grundel. Many moons ago, Grundel's sire, Rakor, inexplicably disappeared. He was born into the line of Keepers, but deserted the way of truth for the path of power. His desertion caused a fog to descend on Melancholia's sight, obscuring her vision. Now, nothing was safe. The mammoth blanket of ice that had protected her charge for millennia was receding. She must conceive

*a plan for Grundel to implement before Rakor secured
the power he desired, and for which he sacrificed so much*

IT WAS spring in the mountains; melt-water gurgled happily, carving channels through the crusted snow. Marmo, a grizzled marmot, was basking in the sun on the scree slopes above Furtive Folk Valley. He heard the noise from a long way off, many feet scrambling slowly, breathing hard, but he pretended to doze until the party of small animals stood before him.

Oldest and wisest of the hoary marmots, Marmo was leader of the Furtive Folk, but he didn't always relish the role. Marmo was pretty sure he knew what the ground squirrels had climbed all this way to ask him. He also knew what it took for them to

Marmo

climb his mountain just after they had emerged from their winter sleep. It was a scrawny, hungry looking group. They hummed and hawed to get his attention.

"Marmo?" He opened one eye, then two, and gave them all a stern glare. The largest one spoke. "Sorry to interrupt your sleep, but we have a request."

"Go on." He sat up.

"I think—that is, we think, that is—,"

"Spit it out Uro, or we'll be here until the leaves fall."

"There are more disappearances. You have to ask The Keeper for help." Uro shuffled and gave a little nervous giggle.

"You think I should ask The Keeper's help, again?"

Uro nodded. "Yes, we need help."

"I see." He surveyed the group of young squirrels all smiling and nodding, as if it was an everyday thing to plead with The Keeper.

"Well, you go get him and then I'll ask," he said and closed his eyes, pretending to return to his nap.

"Me?" gasped Uro. Marmo opened his eyes again.

"Why not? You've got legs and a brain."

"We-we thought you should go." Uro looked around at the other ground squirrels, who were nodding.

"Hmmmm," said Marmo deliberately, "you think I should climb down off my safe and comfortable mountain where I have so many places to hide from enemies, cross the meadow to the river—the *river*," he emphasized, staring at all of them. "Have any of you crossed the river?" They shook their heads. "And will I have reached The Keeper?" Again, they shook their heads. "No. Then, you think, I should hike all the way to Entrance, climb three icefalls, trek across the largest field of ice you can imagine. Can you even imagine the Icefield?" They shook their heads.

"Look," replied Uro, "all we're—"

"Am I speaking?"

Uro nodded, "Sorry."

"Then you think I should cross a treacherous ice-bridge and climb Mount Cathedral to face The Keeper and who knows how many other grizzles. Have you ever faced even one grizzly?" They all shook their heads vigorously.

"So, we're clear. This is what you are asking of me?" Marmo gave them a long, hard stare. The ground squirrels exchanged embarrassed looks.

The older animal sighed and said, "Of course I'll go to The Keeper. I had reached the same conclusion. But just so we're clear about what I am about to do."

"We are grateful, Marmo," said Uro.

"I know. But I don't need gratitude, just your respect."

"You have that," Uro exclaimed. All the squirrels noisily agreed, standing taller with relief.

The next day dawned clear with a light wind. Marmo had started early, even before the birds sang, scrambling down the mountain, following his valley stream to the point where it joined the Sunwapta River. As the sun rose, a feast of scents engulfed him—the glowing pines with their lime-green tips, spring beauties blooming at the edge of the river, emerald green mosses laced with fragrant morels—all the rich, spicy earth smells released from their winter sleep. By noon, he reached the scattering of large rocks that served as stepping stones across the river, stopping to rest under a bush before he scanned for dangers above. This was a vulnerable spot, where cunning predators hidden in the high branches knew the small animals had to cross. He scanned the sky and trees carefully, but for the moment, all looked quiet. Quickly he darted out, leaping heavily from rock to rock. He caught his breath on the other side, then raced through the open meadow, slowing only when he reached the deep forest with its long shadows. He didn't like being off his mountain with its slippery slopes and many hiding places. Didn't like being out here at all, but he persevered.

It was another long day before he reached the glacier that spilled down from an unseen plateau. *Entrance! Finally*, he thought. Marmo scrambled up the lower end of the glacier, the rough ice bruising the pads of his feet. As night fell, he could see a grove of spruce trees off to his right; he scurried off the glacier, and bowed to a gnarly old tree in the midst of the ancient wood. Suddenly, the tree swirled and whorled and opened. Cold and exhausted, Marmo darted inside, found a warm, dark corner and slept soundly. He woke the next morning, and spoke briefly.

"Thanks, Nagi!"

Any time, my pleasure, answered a deep voice from inside his head. The tree swirled and Marmo found himself outside. He took a deep breath in the dazzling sunlight and scrambled over to the three high icefalls of the glacier that led to the upper plateau of snow-covered ice. Marmo was a good climber, but still, he made his way up the ice carefully. It was a maze of pitfalls. When he arrived, breathless, at the top, he stopped. Behind him were the icefalls; before him was a vast field of snow-covered ice.

From his low vantage point, the Icefield appeared not as a smooth field, but as an undulating mass of blue shadows, vales and peaks of new snow covering ancient ice. He knew not to go near the shadows where the snow could cave in, where he would fall to a lonely death. Gazing across this vast ocean of ice, every cell in his body screamed, *do not go there*! He took a deep breath of icy air, feeling it run cold through his nose, throat, through his body. He shuddered. It would be a long day, *so cold*, cold from the inside out. He thought of the safety of his mountain, the warmth of his home, and cringed looking across the ice. Then before he changed his mind, he shook himself—he had done it before. He could do this. Still, his body froze, refusing to budge.

"If not me, who?" he yelled to the wind, and slowly his body released and he stepped onto the Icefield. He had deliberately chosen a sunny day so that the snow would offer a crust to scamper across, instead of soft, billowy snow through which he would have had to wade. But he would pay for this decision with snow blindness. As the sun glittered, Marmo wished he was a polar bear with that protective eye membrane Grundel had told him about. But he wasn't; he was just a foolish old marmot who would end the day with sore, red watery eyes and a blinding headache—if he was lucky. He sighed and scurried forward—praying he didn't fall through a hidden crevasse— keeping one eye on the ground and one eye on the skies above. With no cover from eyes of hungry eagles, no food, no respite from the achingly bitter wind or the blinding snow, he constantly fought turning back. *I have to stop the disappearances*, he muttered repeatedly; *I have to find Whistler*. Feet numb, heart pounding, he scurried on.

In late afternoon, the marmot stopped and gazed around. He figured he must now be in the sight-line of The Keeper and so safer. The mountains surrounding him were white and silent, rising above the Icefield like phantoms. He trudged on. Closer to the mountain, a large black bird swooped down and circled above him; he froze in panic, but it was just Raven, who cawed loudly and returned to The Keeper.

Finally, Marmo arrived at the foot of Mount Cathedral and gazed stoically up the steep climb to the pinnacle where The Keeper watched. The long rays of the sun dancing off the ice crystals dazzled his aching eyes. He ignored the headache. Before he could tackle the mountain's difficult ascent, he had to cross the narrow, slippery ice bridge that lay before him. Chanting the ancient words of safe passage, he nervously crept across it, trying not to look down into the deep crevasse. Once across, he paused to drink at the edge of Spirit Lake. He wanted to scramble up the side of the mountain, away from the chilling winds blowing off the ice, an easier climb up bedrock, but he knew he would lose respect in the eyes of the bears unless he scaled the Face of Fakara.

"Well," he said to the mountain, "I'll tackle you tomorrow." Tucking himself into a large crack in an outcrop of rock, Marmo curled into a tight ball of fur and tried to sleep.

The next morning, he shook out his aches and pains and gazed up at the mountain, still dreading the vertical climb of Fakara. Marmo was a good climber, but he was accustomed to scree slopes, not this icy rock. However, there was nothing for it but to begin; so up he went, beginning with the lower sediments, clinging to the mountain when he needed a rest, climbing ever higher. Meanwhile, informed by Raven that Marmo was approaching, two great grizzlies lumbered out on the ledge to watch the small animal's final ascent, admiring his courage and perseverance. They were large bears, even for grizzlies, the two largest of the Brothers who kept watch.

Grundel and Gorath, both a cinnamon brown colour with silvery fur ends, had flat, dish shaped faces, pointed muzzles, and a prominent shoulder hump of massive yet elegant strength. As he approached their ledge, Marmo stopped to catch his breath, warily eyeing the long ivory claws that protruded beyond their foot fur. *One swipe*, he shuddered, *one swipe and wham—gone.* He halted. As leader of the Furtive Folk, Marmo knew he was safe on the sacred mountain, no matter how hungry the bears were. But instinct had a mind of its own and right now it was telling him loudly, wildly, to run.

He took a deep breath and scrambled up onto the ledge. Sometimes you just had to do what needed to be done.

It was a very large ledge, large enough for a dozen grizzlies. He ducked as an enormous raven swooped over his head, flying back to his perch on top of one of the two seracs carved in the shape of a grizzly, flanking the entrance to the Keeper's Cave. Standing in front of Grundel, he declined an invitation to enter the grizzlies' cave, shifted uneasily—forcing himself to stand firm—and made his plea.

Grundel grunted now and then, listening carefully, but Gorath looked sceptical. Marmo, he knew, was usually easygoing, but lately he exaggerated every danger: if a heavy snowfall was imminent, he feared a blizzard; a heavy rain and he feared flooding; a dry spell could only mean forest fire. Grundel tried to be tactful.

"Perhaps it's a new predator?" he said when the small animal stopped for breath.

"A new family of owls?" added Gorath, exchanging an arch glance with Grundel.

The marmot sighed, finding their remarks condescending. He just shook his head. "I'm not exaggerating. There are too many animals disappearing. It's been going on for too long— something's not right—it's not—*natural*. We can't figure it out, Grundel—please—help us!" Marmo was quite near the edge of the ledge, his small body quaking with agitation. But suddenly he froze; a figure, like a dazzling ice crystal, a shimmering crucible of light, had stepped out of the cave.

An ancient spirit—born with the mountain—Melancholia had been created by the old gods to watch over the Icefield. Inside the cave she was tall and imposing, with a pale face dominated by two large dark eyes and long hair flowing like a river of silver. But outside, in daylight, one could barely see her; just her outline glowed as the air around her vibrated. Marmo could hardly look at her without collapsing in awe. She nodded to him benignly, and when Grundel looked to her, she briefly nodded.

"All right," agreed Grundel, "we'll look into it." Marmo thanked them, bowed gratefully, before turning to make a hasty exit.

"Wait!" thundered Gorath as Marmo darted off. "Where are you going?"

"Home," said Marmo, muttering, "where else?"

"But you must eat; there's nothing for you on the ice. And it's getting late. When you're done, one of the other Brothers will take you down the Spiral and across the Icefield." Marmo looked nervously from one to the other. As frightening as clinging to a bear might be, it was not as fearful as travelling across the ice alone. He accepted their offer. Grundel nodded, then called for Raven, who was listening just inside the entrance of the cave.

"Has Piotr left?" Grundel asked.

"Not yet," said Raven, cocking his head and eyeing Marmo.

"Good. Tell him to take Marmo home after he has rested and fed."

"Follow me," said Raven, waddling into the cave, suddenly full of self-importance.

"Thank you," replied the marmot, bowing to Grundel, again showing his respect to The Keeper.

As they disappeared into the cave, Gorath grinned, "You can't help liking that one; he has courage."

LATER THAT DAY, The Keeper eased his massive body down near Gorath who was resting in the main cavern and called Raven who appeared, fluttering above their heads; then he summoned Melancholia.

"Let's take the problems one at a time," said Melancholia, "starting with Marmo."

"What's that about—all those disappearances?" mused Grundel. Then he sat up abruptly. "Do you think it has anything to do with Rakor's disappearance?"

Melancholia shimmered. "I hope not. Let's start with a search party."

"We should draft Bighorn and his herd," replied Gorath. "They cover a lot of ground."

"Yes, and Monk, in case it's hunters," said Grundel.

"That man needs something to do," added Gorath. "He's wasting away at the Weeping Wall."

"And the eagles from Chaba," piped Raven, "though, if you listen to Bighorn, Aquila can't be trusted."

"Don't judge Aquila too quickly," said Melancholia, "you don't always know another's responsibilities."

Raven eyed her quizzically and then continued, flapping his wings excitedly. "Well, don't forget you have me!"

"No," chuckled Gorath, "how could we?"

"That should do for now," said Mel. "Remember that Tuktu is on her way from the Barrenlands, Grundel. Someone will have to meet her."

"It will be good to see Took again!" Raven chimed in, then, dropping to the ground, added more thoughtfully, "I hope she thinks so."

"Well, then you must meet her, Raven," said Mel. "Once Tuktu arrives, gather everyone at the base of Entrance. Hopefully travelling to Cathedral together, they'll forge a bond—it may prove necessary." She paused, thinking, and then added, "I'll take care of that."

"Don't reveal too much, Mel," Grundel cautioned. "They don't need to know everything yet."

The Spirit nodded, "I agree." Then shimmering, she disappeared.

"Raven, I want you to fly over to Furtive Folk Valley and find out who's missing, when, where—get as much detail as you can. Speak to Mustela. Get help from the Chaba ravens if you need it."

"Mustela was taken last summer," replied Raven.

Grundel growled, "What? Why wasn't I told?" Raven shrugged in reply.

"I'll go speak to Bighorn," grunted Gorath, rising.

From Cathedral, Grundel could gaze out over the Icefield at the towering peaks cloaked in glaciers. To the northeast, the snow cap on the South Twin glistened in the sunshine. Further east, he knew the bighorn sheep were keeping watch on Snow Dome. To the south, over at Castleguard, all seemed quiet. Cloud shadows on the immense Icefield played in subtle hues of blue and violet. He sighed and entered his cave.

A FEW DAYS later, Raven flew into the cave, landed and hopped about in excitement.

"Mel," he squawked, "It's Tuktu—she's coming! They're in the river valley!"

"Good," replied Melancholia. "Is Aquila with her?" Raven nodded. "Then we must begin. Collect Bighorn and Marmo, then wait for me at Entrance. I'll get Monk." Monk, she knew, would be difficult to persuade.

The young man was camped near the Weeping Wall. He had built a snug home from a canvas tent stretched on a wooden frame set on a sturdy platform. A pot belly stove, whose pipe exited through a hole in the top of the tent, kept him warm. Around the stove were a simple wood table with two chairs and a cozy cot draped with a homespun quilt.

Melancholia found him outside, lounging on a low sling

of canvas, his long legs stretched out in front of him, hat pushed back, gazing peacefully at the river. Monk was strong and wiry; he wore his dark hair long, pulled back in a braid, under a worn, red woollen toque. His deep blue eyes were the colour of lupines, and his ready smile revealed dimples. The animals recognized him by his easy gait and the Hudson's Bay plaid wool jacket he wore through spring, summer and fall. They trusted him; he had never done any of them harm. Well, at least, no intended harm.

With its back to the Weeping Wall, Monk's make-shift home faced west across the flats—shallow streams that meandered through a wide, coarse gravel bed—to the high snow-capped mountains of the main range. Coursing north through the central valley Corridor, the river would soon gather together all its streams, and merge with other tributaries, surging north to the Arctic Ocean.

It was a glorious May morning; the mountain air heightened the contrast between verdant green new leaves and snowy peaks. The Weeping Wall was at its full flush; glistening rivulets streamed down its face. The icy water contacting the warm valley air created a misty veil, shrouding the wall in mystery. For a time, Melancholia studied Monk, trying to gauge how he was faring since his family's tragic accident. She noticed his body had relaxed in the spring warmth, something it had not done even in the height of last summer's heat. She was pleased to find him, if not happy, then at least at ease.

Squinting at the sudden radiance in front of him, Monk slowly realized what he was seeing. He groaned.

"You are needed at Cathedral," the spirit announced. "Come, there isn't much time. Grundel waits."

"No, Melancholia, not now, no." He waved her off, but she remained resolute. Finally, he stammered, "You have the

View from Weeping Wall

wrong man, Mel—the wrong man—*propter metum mortis!*"

"Remember death, indeed," countered Melancholia and waved his protest away with her own dismissive gesture. She turned, a dazzling spiral, expecting him to follow, but Monk only sank deeper into his chair.

"Wait, Mel! What does Grundel want? I'm waiting for Bighorn," he added, lamely. She swirled back, turning searing eyes on him.

"You would deny him this request?" she asked, in disbelief.

"No. No! Of course not. But can't you tell me what it's about?"

"Inexplicable disappearances—he fears Rakor."

"He fears nothing," retorted Monk.

"Come. I have others waiting—including Bighorn. You can talk with him at Entrance." She looked around. "Where is your horse?"

"Still at Hilda's," he replied.

"Well, come along then, it will be a long walk."

Monk sighed, knowing he could not resist the combined force of Melancholia and Grundel. Reluctantly, he entered the tent and picked up his few belongings—goggles, pick axe, a couple of books, a compass—stuffing them into his pack with a few clothes, some dried food, and a small first aid kit. He strapped his snowshoes and crampons to the outside of his knapsack, where he could get to them easily—he would need them soon, and slung rope over his shoulder. For a while, Monk trudged behind Melancholia sullen and silent, trying to hide behind a façade of bad humour. Perhaps it was the azure sky, or the first Fairy Slippers sprouting in the wooded edges of the meadow softening under his feet, or the mountain air pulsing through his lungs, but it wasn't long before he was smiling and calling out to his companion, floating in front of him like a mirage, a silver river of hope.

"What are you thinking, Mel? You're awfully quiet." The spirit turned, smiling wryly.

"I am thinking like a glacier," she answered in her slow, deliberate way. "Imagining myself as a wilful, capricious, unstoppable glacier."

Monk laughed, "Why?"

"It slows me down, puts things in perspective. After all, a glacier moves about two kilometres every 250 years." She arched her eyebrows and gave him a piercing look. "It helps me accept what humans *can* do." Monk grimaced—Melancholia was often sardonic; perhaps that's what happens to you when you exist as long as she had. He tried to increase his pace.

They passed narrow waterfalls that plunged down mountain runnels; they followed engorged spring rivers; they navigated forests shimmering with new growth and aspen leaves glisten-

ing, an almost transparent lightness of being. They had reached
the Sunwapta valley, part of the main Corridor running north
and south through the length of the Shining Mountains, which
provided the main route for the migrating and territorial animals, when suddenly Raven appeared, croaking loudly.

"Hurry Monk, you must hurry," said Mel. "Raven says the
others are about to disperse."

"What others?"

"Come. You'll see."

They arrived at Entrance as the sun threw long shadows
across the mountains. Bighorn, leader of the sheep that watched
over Snow Dome, was pacing, tossing his great rack in irritation;
Tuktu was attempting to graze, but her head would rise every
few minutes as if she heard something; Aquila, the golden
eagle, looked as if she was ready to leap into flight. They all
stilled when they saw Melancholia. Then Bighorn noticed
Monk and butted him from behind, sending him flying.

"Monk! You old goat! Why are you here?"

Monk grinned, his dimples deepening, but Mel interrupted.

"Where's Marmo?" she asked, looking around.

At the sound of her voice, the marmot scrambled out of the
brush. He'd had another long, cold trip and had nervously
waited for Melancholia, silently. The eagle sat haughtily on her
perch, looking down disdainfully at him. "Hiding, Marmo? Was
that necessary? I'm not about to eat you." Marmo threw the
eagle a wary look.

"Perhaps not, though there are others who would beg to
differ."

Aquila sniffed. "Everyone has to feed," she retorted, then
turned her attention to Raven who was staring intently at the
caribou.

Raven knew he had to act now or the moment would pass.

He flew awkwardly over to Tuktu and mumbled an apology.

"It's all right," replied Took. "That's all in the past and forgiven." Monk threw Bighorn a puzzled look; neither had ever seen Raven so humble or relieved.

"What's that all about?" he asked. The mountain sheep just shrugged.

"No idea," he whispered back. They turned to Melancholia, hoping for an explanation, but she was plainly in no mood for such questions.

"We'll bed here and proceed with first light," she announced. The others did not argue; they heard the wisdom of eons resonating in her voice. The animals found boughs, nudged them into a pile and lay down; the birds perched quietly on nearby branches; Monk lit a fire then wrapped himself tightly in his blanket, gazing up the mountain. But no one could sleep. Finally, Tuktu summoned her courage, her curiosity getting the better of her.

"Melancholia," she pleaded in her soft velvet voice, "could you tell us why The Keeper has summoned us—what the problem is?" It was hard to deny her; the gentle caribou had come a great distance, never once doubting Grundel's need. Melancholia slowly surveyed the expectant faces watching her intently.

"Grundel will tell you when he is ready," she replied, but when they all showed disappointment, she sighed and added, "Well, I suppose it wouldn't hurt for you to share your thoughts. Together you may know more than you think you do."

"Good idea," said Bighorn, perking up. "We'll tell you our stories first, Tuktu, since you don't know them. Then you can tell us yours—I know I'm curious!" The others nodded in agreement.

"But I think I should start," said Marmo, "because part of the reason you're here is to help me." And he told the others of the unnatural disappearances of the young burrowing animals in the Furtive Folk Valley and his request for Grundel's help as The Keeper.

"It's been so long," he concluded, "a bitter time, never knowing who would be next. And nothing, not a trace of anyone who disappeared. Whistler has been gone a full cycle of seasons. I know I should mourn and let him go, but I can't because none of this feels right." The animals sat quietly thoughtful after Marmo's account, until Bighorn shook his great rack.

"You go next Monk, you're the storyteller—it will give the rest of us time to think. But land sakes, none of your Gregorian chants or fancy sidestepping!" When Aquila flew down closer to the fire to listen, Bighorn leaped up, moving away from her. The golden eagle rolled her eyes.

"Well, all right." said Monk, "but it is a story I'm going to tell, Bighorn, so I'll use whatever I need to hold your attention." He grinned, unable to resist teasing, just a little. "This is a simple story, a recounting of facts—that is, if we *ever* just recount facts, if we ever tell anything other than stories. Then again, perhaps this will be a chant—who knows what the priests say behind the mask: *sed haec omitto; ad illa quae me magis moverunt respondeo...*"

Bighorn jumped up and stamped his foot. "Now cut that out, Monk, and get on with it!" Then, settling once again, he added, "You might as well get it over with." Monk's smile evaporated at the thought of what lay ahead of him. He stoked the fire and gazed intensely at the others, drawing them in.

Monk's Tale

"WHY, you might ask, would Grundel send for me—a mere man—with him lord of the mountains? Better still, why did I come? Well, the truth is that I owe him a debt, the largest of debts: he saved my life." Tuktu's brown eyes widened.

"Me too!" she whispered, not wanting to break the spell, "And Raven." Nodding, Raven stole a look over at the golden eagle on his other side to see what she would say, knowing she too had been saved by those at Cathedral. But Aquila sat haughtily on her perch, her great curved beak clamped shut. Bighorn coughed and pawed the ground.

"Go on Monk," urged Took. "How did he save you?"

"As some of you know, for many years I've been a guide in these mountains. For a long time, my wife Rachel and I were the only guides to brave the glaciers. We were good. But it's dangerous to be told that you're the best, if it creates too much pride and something more deadly in the mountains—." Took looked at him quizzically. "Carelessness," he answered. Monk stopped and shook his head. "I know these mountains—I've spent so much time in them—with Rachel, with Koko." He paused again, sighing. "But not on the Icefield; the Icefield was taboo. Only a few Elders knew of it. When they discovered the Icefield, long ago, a map was drawn, partly from memory, partly from dream—for those who saw it had many dreams—."

"What kind of dreams?" prodded Aquila.

"Dreams full of secret trails, labyrinth caves, blinding light, of betrayal and death and strange awakenings." Monk paused, remembering the stories he had been told, then continued.

"The dream map, covered with these markings, was folded tightly and never opened again, as is the proper way with dream maps. The Icefield was decreed a sacred and perilous place, to be left alone, unnamed."

Bighorn snorted and nudged him with his rack. "Come on, Monk, you're sidestepping the story."

"I'm getting there, Bighorn," he said, shifting uncomfortably. "Many years ago, before our daughter Koko was born, the Elders decided to give the map to my wife to keep safe because Rachel and I were exploring and guiding on the glaciers, and the Elders wanted to warn us away from the Icefield. But the more they told us to stay away, the more I had to see it. Finally, Rachel took me to the top of Entrance, but she would go no further—she felt the Icefield's peril. We told no one. But it haunted my dreams. A few years later..." He stopped, but Bighorn nudged him again. "A few years later, the one time I convinced her to go further, against her good sense, was—a terrible, terrible error in judgement." He paused and drew a deep breath, avoiding the others' eyes.

"It was late spring and the run-off had started. We should never have been on that glacier; run-off is dangerous and unpredictable, but I just had to get a glimpse of the Icefield. We took a short cut across a glacier to the Castleguard meadows. We had come over a peak into a small alpine valley, very remote, with a tarn shimmering in the sunlight. Koko, who was five then and swam like a fish, wanted to go swimming, but I said the water was too cold. She protested and refused to budge so I picked her up and carried her on my shoulders—she's a little slip of a thing, but with a fierce, stubborn will." He tried to steady his emotions, but tears were beginning to well.

"Well, we know who she got that from!" retorted Bighorn. Monk winced, then continued, "We were near the Icefield when, without warning, a torrent of rushing water swept us up and into a bergschrund."

"A what?" interrupted Tuktu.

"A crevasse," Bighorn answered, but Took still looked puzzled. "Where the upper end of a glacier lies against a rock wall, the glacier can pull away from it, creating deep, deep ragged crevasses—when we cross the ice bridge to Cathedral, you'll see one up close. Go on Monk."

Monk paused, his flow broken. For a few moments he was lost in thought as he found his way back to that dreadful day. The others watched his face begin to crumble with anguish. Eventually he continued, "We were wrenched apart in the fall—Koko was torn from my shoulders. The crevasse narrowed as I fell feet first, finally coming to a scraping halt, my body too wide to descend any further. No sound but the steady drip of water." He halted again.

"What's it like—inside a crevasse?" prompted Took.

"Inside, the ice is a rich turquoise; blue light-waves dance like trapped Northern Lights—and it's bone-chilling cold."

"And he was trapped!" added Bighorn, trying to get Monk back to the story.

"Yes, I was wedged in a narrow well of ice. Suddenly, I realized I was alone. No Koko, no Rachel. I yelled and yelled, but no sound came back, nothing, nothing at all. At first, my body felt like it had been dragged by horses, then I could feel my clothes sopping up the icy water, then my body slowly going numb. I don't know how much time passed; I drifted in and out of consciousness. I was slowly freezing to death, when I heard deep guttural growls above me, and a rough rope swung down in front of my face. I knew I couldn't hold on with my numb hands, so with the last of my strength, I looped the rope around my waist, tied a knot through my belt, and tugged above

Weeping Wall

my head to signal that I was ready. I couldn't imagine who was up there; who would have the strength to pull me out of my grave. You can imagine my surprise!

"That's how I first met Grundel, and two of his Brothers, Boris and Gorath. They searched long into the night for any signs of my family, but found nothing. My wife and little girl were gone, swept away without a trace."

"Just like Whistler," sighed Marmo, but no one paid him any attention.

"When Grundel brought you to Cathedral, you were out of your mind with grief," said Melancholia, who had been listening carefully not just to their words, but to the state of their emotions. A lot hung on the courage of this group.

"I wanted to die," muttered Monk, swiping angrily at his tears. "My stupidity, my *arrogance* destroyed the two people I love most." Bighorn butted Monk roughly, trying to jar him from this memory. Monk swatted at him then continued.

"I'll admit that I'm afraid, especially with the raging run-off and the spiral wells reeking of death. I dread going to Cathedral. I know Grundel's waiting and I fear what he will ask of me. I'm not like him; I can't match his courage or his strength. I've finally found a kind of contentment at the Weeping Wall, comforting others in despair—but Grundel saved my life; he needs me, so I'll do what I can."

A long pause followed before Tuktu muttered, "But then what happened? How did you end up at the Weeping Wall?"

When Monk didn't respond, Bighorn said, "Shall I pick up the story?" Monk just nodded, lost in remorse.

BIGHORN stepped forward, turning to face the others. He was a powerful animal, a mottled tan colour with a white rump and muzzle, and massive backward curling horns revealing his age. Able to survive the arctic winter awake, he was one of the toughest creatures on Earth. But it was his deep brown eyes that caught and captivated his listeners.

"As you'll see when we get there, Took, near the peak, Mount Cathedral has a wide granite ledge from which The Keeper watches over the Icefield—well, actually, the bears can't see all that far. Their eyesight, like Monk's, is quite poor in the grand scheme of things, but the Chaba ravens keep watch with Grundel. And we bighorns watch Entrance from Snow Dome. Not much escapes our notice!"

When Raven squawked in protest, Bighorn quickly added, "Oh, and Raven, of course! It was actually Raven who noticed the family sliding into the bergschrund. That night the bears brought Monk back to the Keeper's Cave. Monk holed up there the rest of the spring and most of the summer, shunning not

Bighorn

only the summer sun, but any warmth anyone offered him. His sleep was filled with nightmares; his days with loneliness and scourging self-reproach. He whipped himself endlessly with blame. He convinced himself that he was weak and useless and without hope of redemption. We couldn't stop him; couldn't help him." Tuktu followed Bighorn's gaze over to where Monk, who had risen to stoke the fire, had sunk down on his haunches, one hand cradling his drooping head.

"We all tried, but only Boris, Grundel's twin, could reach him. Boris was—well—one of those old, gentle souls."

"Was?" asked Tuktu.

"That's another story," replied Bighorn. Monk groaned.

"Eventually, Boris convinced Monk to go foraging out on

Boris

the meadows. In the evenings, Grundel and Boris and other
Brothers who were home would gather and tell Monk stories,
trying to draw him back into the world of the living.

"I didn't have much time to spend there. I was busy that
summer with my own brood—darting up and down the mountains, traversing rock cliffs, teaching our young to climb to
places our enemies cannot follow. On the highest slopes our
only fear is the cougar and there weren't many that year. We
were fancy free—at least that's what we thought—we didn't
know what was waiting for us at Wicked River. The only humans
we saw regularly were Mikaila, her mother Faida, Monk,
Rachel and Koko, and none of them were threatening. Our
rocky domain is so high and remote that few dangerous men
had ever come near our terrain—until Malenger."

"Must I listen to this again?" moaned Monk, clamping his hands over his ears. Bighorn stopped, looked away and then said, "Ok. Another time. But we've had a few fine adventures, eh Monk? Like the time we rescued Aquila—"

Aquila, giving a quick sharp *whit whit whit* and flapping her ruffled wings, interrupted him. "I believe that's my story," she said haughtily.

"I suppose so," replied Bighorn, scowling at her. "But my duty is to Cathedral and The Keeper and that's why I'm here." Tuktu was about to say something, but before she could speak, Aquila swooped onto a branch of a fallen pine tree, drawing everyone's attention. Her powerful golden feet with their ebony talons revealed her immense, elegant strength. Her gleaming black eyes pierced the darkness that had fallen. It was hard to imagine a golden eagle like Aquila ever needing to be rescued. She arched, stretching her magnificent wings for effect, and then settled back on the log. Bighorn, however, turned his head away, methodically chewing his cud.

Aquila's Tale

Aquila

"THAT wretched fall passed slowly for all of us. An early, heavy snow buried not only Bighorn's greens, but also our food source. The rodents were able to hide easily, tunnelling deep under the snow; they were rarely seen on the surface."

Marmo grunted and Aquila, throwing him a contemptuous look, said, "We have to eat, Marmo," then continued. "We nearly starved. We should have migrated, but we didn't think the snow would last; it was too early. Without paying attention to it, our weakness crept up on us.

"I had birthed two eaglets and Winda was still with me from the previous year—even at the height of summer's bounty my mate and I were hard pressed to keep them fed. With the onslaught of an early winter, other eagles were extending their territories, ranging into ours, high-jacking what little food there was. The situation became intolerable. Then one day, Winda decided to venture out beyond our territory to see what she could find. She had developed quickly in size and courage, but we still begged her not to go. Weak with hunger, it was too dangerous, but she left anyway. They're foolish at that age, pushing limits—listening to no one." Begrudgingly, Bighorn grunted in agreement.

"My mate followed her surreptitiously. You need to give them their wings; you can't hold them back, but you try to protect them. I wept when they left—they were both so scrawny—their beautiful feathers had lost their brilliant gloss. I could barely face the anguish in my youngsters' eyes—they were so hungry their bodies couldn't produce heat. I settled between them, trying to share what little warmth I had left. But when Winda and her father were gone too long, I told them to stay put, and flew off in the direction that Winda had taken. It wasn't long before I heard a racket. There were Winda and my mate locked in battle with two large eagles. I watched from above as they fought fiercely over a stash of ground squirrels that Winda, I discovered later, had uncovered. I looked carefully to make sure the eagles weren't mine from an earlier season, but they weren't, and it was clear that they meant to steal the food. I looked at the stash longingly, surprised by my own deep hunger and rising aggression."

Marmo snorted loudly, breaking her spell. Aquila shrugged, "Honestly Marmo, must you?" Then continued, "I had no real strength. I descended with a blood-curdling screech, but it was all show. Even three of us were no match for two healthier adults. We were soon fighting for our lives, and losing.

"Thankfully Bighorn and Monk were in the vicinity, heard my screech, and came running. Bighorn with his rack and Monk, brandishing a heavy branch, drove off the two strangers. Winda and my mate were near death. They carried us back to Cathedral, and then fetched the younger ones from the Heights of Chaba." Bighorn gave her a hard stare across the fire, one which she chose to ignore. "The bears had just entered their Long Sleep. Melancholia sheltered us, allowing us time to recover—all except my mate who did not survive. For the rest of the winter we remained in the Keeper's Cave. Monk made us fires; we slept like bears; sharing Raven's food—carrion he and Chaba ravens brought back to the cave and for which we will always be grateful." She nodded to Raven, who grinned broadly.

"It was our pleasure," said Raven.

"Gradually, we recovered, the snow began to recede, and we were again able to hunt. About that time the bears began to stir, so we returned to the Heights."

"And yet," said Bighorn, angrily, "when Grundel asked for your help at Wicked River, you refused!"

"Yes, Bighorn, and you'll just have to accept that I had my reasons. I owe Melancholia and Monk and I owe you. I came because Melancholia needs me and if she needs Winda, she will also come. We repay our debts." Her golden beak clamped back shut.

Melancholia sighed deeply, watching the two. If only Aquila would open up a little. But the great eagle preferred to go her own way, alone in her austere heights; it was difficult for her to reveal any weakness, even to gain sympathy or understanding. And that would be fine, thought Mel, if Bighorn had not lost his trust in her. The defences of the Icefield were weakened by this rift between them. Still, the eagle was here; she was a powerful ally and they needed her. Only Melancholia knew just how much.

Soon attention turned to Tuktu. The others were familiar with these first stories. They were participants in some, which, of course, is the best kind of story to be told, and had heard them many times before, never tiring of their details. But Tuktu was a mystery, a newcomer, a source of new stories. They resettled themselves, stretching a leg, a wing, an arm, turning intently in her direction, curious to know what could have brought a Barrenlands caribou so far from home. All they knew was that she was from the Barrenlands, the great northern plain north east of the Shining Mountains. The caribou was tall, tan coloured with a lighter underbelly, and still carried a rack of antlers because it was before calving season. The others eyed her curiously, but her alert brown eyes were turned on Raven.

"So, how well do you know Raven?" she asked, smiling mischievously. They all looked at Raven who had become unusually silent.

Now he squawked indignantly, flapping his wings in protest.

"No, no Raven. It's all right. It's time," said Tuktu. She turned back to the others, dismissing Raven's protest. "Do you know where he came from—or why? Did you inquire when he first arrived?"

The others cast back in their memories, thinking about Raven's arrival.

"Well," said Aquila, "we noticed him, of course. Any newcomer is noticed. But we would hardly question Grundel's decision to include him in our community."

"But surely you could ask who Raven was?"

"Well—we were told he was from the Barrenlands. But

that's all," answered Aquila, thinking back. "We didn't ask Grundel for more information."

"It's true," replied Bighorn, remembering. "Grundel had the look that said 'do not push this matter any further.' When he has that look, you don't ask."

"Curious. And have there been others who just appear, who are unknown, unexplained?" As the others paused, thinking hard, Tuktu looked pointedly at Melancholia.

"Now don't go lumping me in with that lot," said Melancholia. "Believe me, I didn't 'just appear' and the ones here know very well who I am." She looked around, but no one leapt to her defence. "Bighorn, you've known me all your life. I was there at your birth. Tell Tuktu who I am."

"She's—she's Melancholia of Cathedral. She was here before our birth, and will be here long after we're gone. Right?" He tilted his head at Mel. Tuktu snorted.

"All right," replied Mel, deigning to smile. "Let's just say, they know of my existence. It is allowed. They know I am from Gaia; that I work with Grundel to protect the Icefield. But, you must all remember: Although I possess many skills, I cannot change what will be."

"Now I'm puzzled," said Tuktu, frowning.

"You will come to understand," Melancholia replied, her eyes darkening. Just then her head snapped up as if she had been called. The others searched the air, but saw nothing, heard nothing.

"Wait here," Melancholia said, rising on the wind, and disappeared.

"Where does she go?" asked Tuktu, searching the empty sky. The others shrugged. "Could you explain—is she—an angel?"

"She's a bit of a puzzle," answered Monk. "I think she goes back to Gaia." The others nodded. "But Mel isn't an angel; she's a spirit. I think of her like music in church—she takes form, but it's not really substance. She needs the bears to act for her."

"And usually she can see the future," added Raven.

"Usually she can see everything!" declared Bighorn.

"Usually?" asked Tuktu.

"Her vision has been clouded ever since Rakor left. He just disappeared. No one knows why he left or where he went," continued Monk.

"Rakor is Grundel's sire?" asked Tuktu.

"Yes, the last Keeper, the one who betrayed Melancholia."

"Betrayed?"

"Mel can see the future, but only if the bears stay true," said Bighorn. "When Rakor left, Mel went virtually blind."

"Ah," said Tuktu, tucking away the information for later. But before she could start her story, Melancholia reappeared.

"The night is passing. You'd better get some sleep. You have a long, hard climb tomorrow and the night is half gone."

"I can tell my story another time," agreed Took, giving Mel a long look.

"Or not!" said Raven.

The animals, realizing how tired they were, soon fell asleep.

THE PALE DAWN comes softly in the mountains, still, cold and silent until the strength of the sun's rays penetrates the sleeping birds and, ruffling themselves awake, they begin the morning chorus. The animals rose early, licking the dew frozen on the first early leaves of the cinquefoil. Tuktu, not finding anything familiar, tasted the leaves, but spit them out. Bighorn laughed his infectious laugh, breaking the stillness.

"Kind of tough and woody, eh Took? I'll show you where to find some lichen—unless you want to share this new sedge—not bad, really."

The Sisters at Entrance

"A fine time to tell me!" Tuktu groaned.

"Look!" exclaimed Raven, pointing to the ground. "White bark pinecones—let's take them for Grundel!" Both Raven and Bighorn laughed.

"What's so funny?" asked Took.

"Wait till you see! Will you carry them, Monk?" Monk nodded, tucking them into his pack. They got under way quickly, Melancholia preoccupied, driving them forward.

Suddenly Monk looked up and halted—before him rose a sweep of glacier. A river of ice, it flowed from the ridge of a high plateau, between snow-capped mountains, The Sisters on one side, an outcropping of Snow Dome on the other: Entrance. Near the top, a series of three icefalls spilled down from the unseen Icefield. The mountains and wind-carved snow of the ridge framed a startling blue sky. Just over the high ridge, Monk knew, lay all he dreaded and loved.

He looked up at the virgin snow and the glaringly truthful sky.

"Putting on your gear?" asked Melancholia, gently prodding.

Monk nodded, bent down, and attached the ice-gripping spikes of the crampons to the soles of his worn boots. He took out his ice pick, and stood back up, adjusting first his goggles and then his pack. Mel said, "Ready?"

"I guess so," replied Monk, setting his sights on the plateau above the glacier: The Icefield—an immense bowl of ice, cradled between some of the highest peaks in the spine of mountains that formed the Continental Divide.

Between the mountains, the Icefield spilled over its edge, forming six outlet glaciers flowing down to broad valleys. The small group made its way up the Entrance glacier, a dangerous climb filled with deep crevasses carved by melt-water. Aquila and Melancholia flew in front of them, while Raven hovered above them, encouragingly. Just after passing the lower terminus of the glacier, they spotted the Ancient Wood to their far right—a grove of small, hardy spruce trees, dwarfed and twisted by fierce winds off the Icefield. Melancholia bid them wait, flew over and then bowed formally in front of one of the trees. She waited as it suddenly transformed into a large spiralling cone, and she disappeared inside.

"How did she do that? What is she doing in those trees?" whispered Tuktu.

"Those trees are five hundred years old! And that's not just any tree, that's Toholinagi," replied Bighorn.

"Who?" Tuktu's eyes widened.

"Toholinagi—the spirit whose wisdom is as deep as its roots that feed the layers of time—at least, that's what Mel says," Bighorn whispered back. "Why are we whispering?"

"This feels like allirnaqtuq," replied Tuktu.

"What's that?"

"A sacred place."

"Ah."

Once Melancholia returned, they continued up the glacier, travelling slowly at Monk's pace, until the sun was high overhead.

Glacial stream

From a distance the glacier looked like a smooth climb, but on closer inspection the ice was filled with great gashes and ruts and rushing streams that whorled into gurgling mill wells. It was rough, unstable and unpredictable. Monk hiked cautiously in his crampons, using a walking stick to test the ground in front of him. Snow covered the crevasses, forming insubstantial bridges that collapsed easily under pressure. He took his lead from Bighorn, but he was wet and cold and sore when they finally ascended the three icefalls to the head wall that culminated at the edge of the Icefield. What lay before them was the immense, bleak expanse of ice. A bitter wind blew. Mel took one look at Monk and decided they should stop and rest. Monk nodded gratefully; every muscle screeched a protest. He filled his canteen with glacier water from a stream, sat down on his pack and drank slowly, gazing out over the Icefield—remote, magical, but deadly. He tried to take his mind off his heart-breaking memories. He listened to the gurgling of melt-water as it splashed like surf, the clatter of ice as chunks broke off and shattered down the icefalls, and the creaks and moans of the shifting ice. It was a rare, clear sky of astonishing blue.

After a short time, Melancholia roused them, starting the long trek across the ice to the base of Mount Cathedral.

Having changed to his snowshoes, Monk fell into a steady pace, but still found it hard to keep up with the others. Even little Marmo stayed in front of him, padding along behind Tuktu. The animals kept a sharp lookout for trouble. As the day progressed and they made their way across the ice, all seemed safe. They were shouting back words of encouragement to Monk when, suddenly, Tuktu felt her back legs giving way. She leapt ahead, dragging her hind legs, out-leaping the caving snow. But Marmo, who was trailing behind her, was caught in the collapse and, with a frantic squeal, disappeared in a flurry of snow.

Tuktu gasped. Mel turned. Monk, who had run to catch up, was already on his knees, unravelling his length of sturdy rope. Lying flat on the ice to distribute his weight, Monk pulled himself to the edge of the hole and called out, but for an interminable time there was only the crackling noise of ice falling. Aquila flew to the hole's edge, flapped her wings screeching, until Monk shifted out of the way, then cocked her head and peered into the gloom. They all waited for the snow to settle, peering silently into the crevasse. Monk's heart ached for his family. Like that time, he could hear nothing, see nothing; the fathomless pit had swallowed Marmo whole.

"Do you want me to see if I can get in there?" asked the golden eagle.

Shaking himself, Monk said, "No, we don't want you trapped down there too. The crack's too deep. And anyway, you'd probably give him a heart attack—if he's still conscious." Aquila peered once more into the hole. The others waited, fearing the worst.

Above them Raven hovered. "Do you need The Keeper?" he asked.

"Perhaps," said Melancholia. "Here comes—"

"Wait, I can see him!" squawked Aquila.

"Marmo!" bellowed Monk. "I'm sending down a rope. Hang on and I'll pull you up." There was no reply. Aquila gave a piercing screech and, after a long moment, a muffled, high whistle floated back. Monk sent down the rope and waited for a sign, a tug, a weight that said something was on the other end. But he felt nothing. He sent down more length and waited. Finally, he looked to Mel.

"Do you think the rope's too thick for him to hold?"

"Haul it up now," she said. Puzzled, Monk pulled the rope gently, as if there was a marmot on the other end, but he could feel only the rope's weight.

"There's nothing there," he said.

"Still," replied Mel, "haul it up slowly."

Not until the rope was more than halfway up did he begin to feel extra weight.

"Ok! I think I have him!" He looked up for a moment and caught Bighorn's encouraging grin.

Suddenly Marmo appeared, shaky and covered in ice crystals.

"Are you injured?" asked Melancholia. The marmot crawled onto the safe surface of the ice, untangling his claws from the rope, shook himself, then turned and looked back at the hole.

"No, I'm all right. Bruised is all." Another raven cawed above them and Raven answered.

"Here," said Monk, putting out his hand, remembering his own fall. "Jump on my pack." The marmot nodded wordlessly and slowly climbed up.

They trudged on in silence, but as hard as he tried, Monk fell further and further behind. The others tried to be patient—Raven fluttering above his head, Bighorn cheerfully jogging back to see how Marmo was doing, his boundless energy just getting on Monk's already stretched nerves.

"Honestly, Bighorn, must you make my inadequacies so painfully obvious?" Bighorn gave him a friendly butt and trotted off. Later in the afternoon, when the sun slanted between the peaks and began to cast long, bruising shadows, the wind increased and Monk, bent double into it, sat down with a resounding groan. Marmo fell off. Melancholia, who had been appearing and disappearing, materialized again in front of him. Monk eyed her ruefully.

"I know we don't have far to go, but that's all I can do. This should be easy for me, but this is an inhuman pace, and I'm done."

Melancholia scrutinized him, assessing the limits of his endurance. "We've been patient with you, but we must go on. You can't camp in the middle of the Icefield."

"I know. But I need a rest."

By this time, Bighorn and Tuktu had trotted back to find out what was wrong. Monk marvelled at their stamina. They seemed oblivious to the wind and cold.

"Here," said Tuktu, bending her forelegs, "climb on."

"Absolutely not," said Monk. "You're already carrying wood for me!"

"You won't tire me," snorted Tuktu, "The Throng travel far greater distances at much faster speeds. It's only this unfamiliar ground slowing me down. I'm not tired, and when I am, I'll tell you." Deeply grateful, Monk climbed on her back and they started up again. But he had a hard time staying on when Tuktu stumbled on the rough ice. When Marmo fell off Monk's pack again, Bighorn burst out laughing.

"You'd better come with me, Marmo," he said, still chuckling.

"You can laugh, but you don't know my humiliation," groaned Monk, rummaging in his rucksack.

"Then do what you do best—tell one of your stories."

"Haven't we exhausted them?"

"Well," said Tuktu, "I still haven't heard what happened at Wicked River."

Monk fell silent and even Bighorn looked away.

"Not something you wish to talk about?"

"Monk doesn't," Bighorn replied, gently, "but you should know the whole story, so I'll tell you. Ok, Monk?"

"Suit yourself," he muttered, munching on chocolate as they moved along.

The Wicked River

Bighorn

"WELL," said Bighorn, finding Tuktu's pace and keeping abreast, "the following summer, after Monk's accident on the bergschrund, when he was finally getting better, and starting to see Cathedral as home, a strange thing happened. One morning Raven came back from feeding, terribly distressed, barely able to speak."

"Well, you would be too if you had seen what I did!" squawked Raven.

"Yes, of course. That wasn't an insult!"

"Every time you tell this story you make me sound like a coward!" groaned Raven.

"Oh for Gaia's sake, Raven, just let me tell the story, alright?"

"Then please make me sound more like the hero I was!"

Bighorn rolled his eyes and continued. "Anyway, finally he managed to say that there was something horrible on Sheep Mountain—something that Grundel needed to see, and me too. Monk said he'd come. On the trip over, Grundel probed Raven for more details.

"Raven replied, 'There are three full grown male sheep on the mountain—all—dead,' but then he glanced over at Grundel nervously, knowing that what he was about to say next would enrage him, so he dropped his voice and muttered, 'and their heads are gone.' Well, Grundel reared up on his hind legs, and gave a mighty roar."

"What do you mean?" asked Tuktu, stumbling heavily so that Monk had to grab onto her neck to keep from falling. Marmo was glad he was on Bighorn's back.

"I'm coming to that," said Bighorn, "but that wasn't all. Raven said that there was a young woman, perched on the ledge near the carcasses, but she didn't have a weapon and he could hardly believe that she had done this. Monk asked for a description and realized it was probably Mikaila, a young botanist who lives near Angel Lake. When we arrived, he said he would go talk to her first, so we wouldn't frighten her. He made a lot of noise scrambling up to the ledge so that she was on her feet, prepared for his approach. Monk knew her slightly, so she wasn't alarmed. Rachel, Monk's wife, had visited Mikaila's cabin a couple of times when Koko, their little girl, was ill. Anyway, Monk found Mikaila horrified.

"'I saw them do this,' she gasped, 'a group of men led by a guide.'

"'White?' asked Monk. She nodded. 'He brought them up the river in a freighter canoe, brought them up here, practically held the guns for them, bagged the heads and took them back down. I heard them say something about Wicked River. I'm so sorry—I couldn't stop them. They just laughed at me.'" Bighorn paused in his story until Took prodded him to continue.

"Grundel, unable to contain his rage when faced with the useless slaughter, reared up again and roared even more savagely. Mikaila fell back; Monk reached out for her, afraid she might leap off the ledge, and explained that they were all there to help. She nodded to Grundel, claiming not to be afraid, just taken by surprise, and said she had heard much about him. Curious, Grundel dropped down on all fours. It turned out that she knew Marmo—right, Marmo?"

The marmot nodded vigorously and Bighorn continued.

"When Grundel introduced Raven and me, Mikaila said: 'This—this is such a sacrilege. We must do something.'

"I was in shock at this point—so Grundel stepped in and told Raven to fly over to the river to see if the hunters were camped there. Raven leapt off the ledge and disappeared into the sun's glare. Mikaila and Monk offered to move the bodies down to the valley floor to bury them, but that is not our way. I was too traumatized to perform the ritual, so Grundel spoke the words of passage, and we left them to feed others their strength and courage. When we were done, Grundel turned to Monk. 'Now, we do something,' he said.

"We could see the anger flickering in Grundel's eyes. We felt the great restraint he was imposing on himself. Monk thought carefully. 'I believe you could scare them off, Grundel,' he said but Mikaila cried, 'they have guns—they'll just shoot him!' But Monk thought otherwise; he figured he could sneak into camp while they were asleep and take the rifles, and then

Grundel and Boris could scare the men—scare them so badly they'd leave. One unarmed look at Grundel and Boris in a rage, he thought, and they'd never come back." Monk groaned again. Bighorn coughed, but continued.

"At first Grundel was not convinced. We all suspected that Monk wanted to redeem himself for teaching that scumbag—Malenger—the secrets of the glaciers. You see, it was Monk who taught Malenger how to survive on the glaciers—how to avoid the dangers, how to spot us, how to track us. He thought Malenger wanted to be a guide—and he did—but not one like Monk or Rachel—not to observe and learn from us, to show others how to live peacefully with us.

"None of the animals trusted the newcomer, as we had instinctively trusted Monk, Rachel and Mikaila, but none of us, including Monk, understood at the time what Malenger really wanted. He had no interest in coming to know us; he only learned enough for his own vile purposes. He wanted just the bare facts—how we could be found, tracked, when and where—hunters' queries. But Monk didn't suspect anything. Malenger is cunning at getting what he wants. He acted as if he had no intention of killing."

"What does he look like?" interrupted Tuktu. "Is he still around?"

"He hasn't been seen for about a year."

"Well, that's a relief. Please continue."

"Correct me if I'm wrong, Monk, but some of us thought you mentored Malenger because you felt you should atone for deserting the priesthood—by helping another human come to know and love nature." Monk shrugged silently. "At any rate, when Malenger learned everything he needed to know, he started guiding head hunters—men who wanted only to kill us for sport. Something Monk and Rachel had always refused to do. Fortunately, most head hunters don't want to come this far, the trail is too primitive for them and it's hard to get a guide. At least, until Malenger offered to guide.

"Anyway," Bighorn continued, "after Monk's suggestion to scare them off, Grundel remained quiet for a while, thinking through a strategy. And, I suspect, disciplining his desire for a quick and savage revenge. At least, I know I wanted one. When Raven returned, Grundel instructed him to fetch Aquila. Raven was obviously annoyed, insisting we didn't need her."

"I did not!" squawked Raven, glancing awkwardly over at Aquila.

"You did!" grinned Bighorn. "Grundel explained that although Raven had many respected talents, we needed Aquila's eyes. He wouldn't send Monk into that camp before knowing exactly where the rifles were hidden."

"Well, in the end we didn't need her for that, did we?" said Raven.

"No, we certainly did not!" snorted Bighorn.

"Now who's side tracking?" said Monk. "Tell the story, Bighorn."

"All right. I remember Mikaila spoke up asking who Aquila was. When we told her a golden eagle, she shook her head. 'If they're trophy hunters,' she argued, 'a golden eagle would make a fine prize.' Grundel agreed, but noted that Aquila was very clever, and could be evasive and discreet. 'If she doesn't want to be seen, you'll not see her,' he said."

"A wise leader," interjected Aquila, dipping low to gaze into Bighorn's eyes. Bighorn ignored her.

"Then he told Raven to go and fetch her. Well, you all know what happened." The sheep paused, finally glaring at the golden eagle, "Aquila refused."

"And as I have told you many times," Aquila answered in a

diffident tone, "I had my reasons."

"Which you have never explained!" retorted Bighorn, his natural good humour darkening over this tension between them.

"Please," said Tuktu, gently, trying to break the tension, "won't you continue, Bighorn?" Bighorn tore his eyes away from Aquila, and turned back to Tuktu.

"It was Raven who sat in the tall spruce all day, inspecting the camp, waiting patiently to see where each rifle was stowed for the night. He didn't have Aquila's keen eyes, but he could move more freely without causing suspicion, pretending to dive for scraps of food, flying right into camp to get a better look. All was ready, and darkness had crept across the camp, when Monk, Grundel and Boris stole into the wood beside the river. Raven kept watch in the tree above them.

"The men had drunk heavily, sitting around their fire, bragging grossly of their kills. When they fell into sleeping bags in their flimsy tents and started to snore, Monk crept into camp, stealthily gathering the rifles. There was a wild gleam in his eye as he deposited them at Grundel's feet.

"'Now we teach these men a lesson,' Grundel growled. I wanted to stay," Bighorn lamented, "to seek my revenge, but Grundel sent me back to Snow Dome with Mikaila to be with my herd, to help them accept what had happened. His youngest brother, Boris, had been reluctant to join Grundel on this particular task. He had spent the previous day helping Mikaila collect flowers. She's documenting the flora of the Icefield area; Boris showed her treasures she had never seen. This was Boris' nature—one alien to violence," continued Bighorn. "But Boris was the only other bear at Cathedral at that time, and when Grundel needs the Brothers, they never fail him."

The golden eagle gave Bighorn a stony stare across the ice. "Is that a dig, Bighorn? Am I supposed to feel guilty because I failed Grundel?"

"You said it, Aquila, not—!"

"Get on with it, Bighorn," Monk interrupted brusquely. The memory of that terrible night on Wicked River was beginning to tell on everyone. Tuktu began to regret raising it, but now that the story was begun, she needed to hear the ending. She knew that whatever had happened had driven Monk away—away from Cathedral to his nether world of the Weeping Wall.

"It gets worse," said Bighorn, looking over to where Tuktu was lying. "Are you sure you want to hear the rest?"

"Yes," replied Took, hoarsely, avoiding Monk's eyes which were becoming increasingly bleak.

Bighorn continued. "Well, after insisting 'No Killing!' Grundel and Boris roared into camp, ripping open the tents, leaping over the men, thundering into their drunken slumber. The men woke with a start and shouted uselessly at one another, grasping wildly for rifles that weren't there. The three greenhorns leapt down to the dark river in their long underwear, hoping to escape by canoe—Grundel roared after them. But Boris—Boris—"

"Ah, gentle Boris," Melancholia said, letting Bighorn compose himself, "this is the part that makes me who I am." They all looked over at her, glittering in the moonlight, pulled by the melancholy in her voice, caught for a moment in her ageless eyes. "Go on, Bighorn," she prodded. He shook his great rack, pawed the ground and took a deep breath.

"Boris reared up on his hind legs to frighten the guide, not knowing, no, not suspecting even for a moment that Malenger had a hand gun stashed under his sleeping bag. The terrorized man shot; Boris staggered, shocked, and the guide reloaded, shot again and again until Boris lay in a ragged heap in front of him. Raven dived at his head, trying to stop him, but the man was oblivious. He turned towards the beach and Grundel. Monk, who had been standing at the edge of the trees, trying to figure out what to do without a weapon, raged into camp, leapt up behind Malenger, jumped on his back and threw him to the ground, the gun flying, clattering, lost among the rocks. They struggled. Monk fell, hit his head on the rocks, and lay unconscious. Malenger tried to find his gun but Raven harassed him until he retreated into the woods, deserting his three clients to Grundel's wrath.

"Now, you might think that Grundel would destroy them, but this is not the Keeper's way. He let the three men escape, although he chased them in the water, swimming after the canoe to make sure they would never return. When he got back to the beach, he found Monk, then Boris lying motionless on the ground. Raven swooped down and explained what had happened—how quickly the two had fallen. Grundel carried Monk back to Cathedral, grieving silently as a bear does for his twin." Slowly, Bighorn glanced over at Monk, secretly hoping he had fallen asleep and so escape the pain of the telling. But Monk stared back at him, painfully alert.

"And Monk?" Tuktu probed.

"Well, when Monk came to, he blamed himself. Partly because it was his plan, partly because he felt he had again failed those he loved best. He's good at that—blaming himself. He packed up his few belongings and left the Icefield. We couldn't convince him to stay. Boris' death was the last straw.

"Mikaila also returned to her solitary life. Raven sees her occasionally, as do we from time to time, methodically collecting flowers over at Castleguard Meadows." Bighorn fell silent, the birds flew off, and Tuktu trudged on wondering what Monk was thinking.

WHEN they reached the bottom of Mount Cathedral, Melancholia asked if they wanted to push to the top to complete their journey. Monk groaned. Even Bighorn frowned. It was dangerous to cross the ice bridge and then climb the mountain tired. They probably had just enough sunlight left, but it had been a long day and it was still a four-hour ascent to the Keeper's Cave.

"Then this will have to do for tonight. We'll camp here," said Mel. The others looked around. It was a bleak spot, nothing to protect them from the icy wind, no boughs with which to make a bed, nothing to eat. Monk dug a snow trench for all of them and pulled out his tarp to help ward off the bitter wind's penetrating cold. He started to unload the wood that Took had carried, to make a fire to warm soup, but the others shook their heads.

"Don't cook on the Icefield," Melancholia said, without explaining. Monk had heard the stories from Rachel about not cooking with grease on glaciers, but he had heard nothing about this before. He turned to Bighorn who added obliquely, "You don't offend it with strong smells."

Monk did not question them; he put back his things quietly, getting out instead some previously cooked bannock and dried fruit. He had carried a little food for each of them and they ate watching the sun descend, the darkness a curtain closing the radiant day. As it grew colder, they listened to the roar of meltwater torrents quieting, then ceasing altogether. At one point, Bighorn leapt up.

"Oh no! Look! Spirit Lake is disappearing!" Tuktu stood to watch the small lake across the ice bridge—it was slowly vanishing before their very eyes.

"How is that possible?" asked Tuktu astonished.

"I don't know—it's as if spirits are drinking it dry!"

"S-Spirits?" Tuktu gasped, ready to believe anything in this mystical place. Bighorn nodded solemnly.

"It's happened before. Terrible things follow."

Tuktu looked around fearfully, "Monk do—do you have any protection?"

From his bedroll, Monk chuckled, "Relax, Took. Bighorn's just pulling your leg."

"What? Bighorn!" she scolded.

"Sorry!" Bighorn guffawed. Tuktu gave him a wry smile. Always curious, she couldn't help asking, "So what *is* happening?"

"Ah, well, during the day, the sun melts the top layer of ice and the water collects in that depression where you see the lake. When the sun goes down and cold night air descends, the water freezes again, and presto! Spirit Lake disappears."

When they were as comfortable as they were going to get, with Monk surrounded by the warm animal bodies, everyone fell silent for a time, thinking once again about Boris, letting the story resonate in the deep and hidden places of the mind. As they settled down again Tuktu, in her straightforward manner, asked, "Then what happened?"

"No, no," Melancholia interrupted, always astounded by their capacity for storytelling, "enough stories. We will have a devil of a time keeping Monk on his feet tomorrow as it is." They snorted, murmuring their agreement, and settled to sleep.

When morning arrived, they were all stiff from the cold. It was the last leg of their journey—a long, difficult climb up Mount Cathedral. Monk packed his snowshoes and took out his crampons and ice pick. Facing them was a deep, wicked bergschrund, crossed in one spot by a precarious, narrow bridge of ice.

"We have to cross that?" asked Tuktu, staring down the deep

crevasse on both sides. "I don't think I can."

Melancholia came up beside her.

"It's all right, Took, I'm going to teach you the word, the ancient word of safe passage—we will say it together as we cross. Now, repeat after me: da·sa."

"da·sa," Tuktu repeated, warily.

"da·sa· biv·san."

The others joined in. "da·sa· biv·san."

"mun·liv·zu."

"mun·liv·zu."

"Now altogether: da sa biv san mun liv zu. Dasabivsan-munlivzu. All right Bighorn, you first."

They followed the sheep, chanting their way across. When the caribou was tempted to look down Mel whispered in her ear, "Not now," so she kept a steady gaze on Monk in front of her and concentrated on the word. Once they were across, she glanced back, grateful there weren't bergschrunds where she lived on the Barrenlands. Tuktu scanned the flat face of the rock wall—icy, treacherous. It was a formidable sight.

"I've done pretty well so far, but do you expect me to climb that?" she asked.

"Took's right, Mel, she'll never scale the Face of Fakara," said Bighorn.

"Face of Fakara?" asked Tuktu.

"That rock wall you're staring at," said Monk.

"Come," said Melancholia to Tuktu, "he's right. We'd better take another route."

RELIEVED, TUKTU followed Melancholia around the side of the mountain. The caribou tried to persuade Monk to join her—he looked exhausted—but he declined; it was a matter of honour, to scale Fakara. They stopped for a drink at Spirit Lake.

The sparkling pool that had disappeared the night before was now refilling with melt-water released by the warm sun. Monk refilled his canteen and began the climb up the sediments confidently, finding his own path, secure in his experienced judgement and skilled use of crampons and ice pick. But when they reached the rock face and it became unreadable, Monk followed Bighorn, stepping where he stepped, mimicking his gestures, trusting the sheep's judgement. Aquila flew up, waiting on a narrow ledge above the face, keeping watch for danger. The sun shone on the regal golden mantle of her crown and her feathered feet with their daggered claws. Raven fluttered about making suggestions, explaining what was ahead, trying hard to be useful.

"Careful, Monk," Raven cautioned, "go to your right, you'll find footing there, and it will lead to strong handholds for the next lag." Monk was out of shape; his arms ached; he had been sitting for too long at the Weeping Wall. Distracted from Bighorn's lead, he tried to turn the way Raven suggested but his right foot on the ice—slick from the scouring wind— slipped, and he had hardly enough strength to hold on. Then his shifting weight pulled his left foot away and for an awful moment he hung just by his hands, praying his handholds would not release. Aquila let out a screech and Bighorn turned just in time to scramble below him, buttressing the man against the cliff face until he was able to catch his crampon in a firm foothold. Monk hugged the mountain, breathing heavily. Bighorn, moving up ahead of him said, "Follow me."

Raven landed lightly beside him and chattered, giving Monk time to catch his breath without losing face "Take heart Monk, if I fly up just a tad, I can see the Keeper's ledge. You won't have Bighorn's white butt in your face for much longer."

"Dear God, don't make me laugh, Raven," pleaded Monk.

When they reached Aquila's narrow ledge, they rested huddled together, gazing over the splendour of the Icefield and the majestic peaks that surrounded it. After he recovered his breath, Monk sent out a chant in his pure tenor voice, and it echoed off South Twin and returned subdued, polyphonic, in a lower register, like the voice of angels.

The sun was just reaching its zenith as they reached the cave entrance with its two seracs—great pillars of ice carved into grizzlies with the faces of Arctos and Ursula. Grundel was waiting for them.

"Come in my worthy friends! You honour me with your presence. I was watching your ascent. Welcome back, Marmo. Well done, Bighorn, ever the leader! Monk, my man, you look like death—what have you been eating? We need to fatten you and get some glacial air back in those lungs. Thank you for coming Aquila, I appreciate your quick response. Good job, Raven. Come in all of you—there's much to talk about, but first we need to feed you."

The exhausted group fell into Grundel's hospitable cave. For a moment, Monk was blinded, partly by the change of light, partly by the tears welling up in his eyes. How he loved this cave—the sweet smelling pine boughs, the old armchair that he and the bears had found and dragged all the way from the settlement dump, the side Den with its ancient map drawn in the sand and kept by Grundel and Boris. Boris.

A deep depression crept over Monk, which he tried to shake off. Keenly aware, Grundel gave him a friendly clap on the back which knocked Monk off his feet and started everyone chuckling. Tuktu and Melancholia arrived and they turned their attention to the waiting feast—fresh picked corms, sweet roots and wild onion bulbs, last year's nuts, glacier water in wooden bowls Monk had carved, lichens and sedges for Tuktu and

Bighorn. But Monk had no appetite. When Raven nudged him, Monk, remembering, pulled out the white bark pine cones that Raven had spotted, and handed them to Grundel who received them with his jovial belly laugh.

"Want the show do you, Raven?" It was always worth bringing the grizzlies pine cones just to watch their amazing dexterity. "Here we go, then." Grundel rolled a cone in his claws then plucked the scales off with his lip, spun the cone once more and expertly licked up the fat rich seeds. It was a delicate operation, precisely performed, unexpected from such a massive animal. Raven flapped his wings, while Tuktu stamped her hooves in applause.

"How do you do that?" laughed Monk, clapping.

"Your lips are connected to your gums right? Ours aren't. Watch again." Grundel picked up the second cone and repeated the process with a flourish. The merriment helped Monk through the first difficult moments of his return, as Raven hoped it would. Show over, everyone hungrily dug into the food. Grundel quietly gave Raven an appreciative nod.

The Listening Mountains

Mountain glacier

"Now," said Grundel, lounging, scratching his belly, "any reports from your journey here?" The others looked at one another and then burst out laughing.

"What's so funny?" The grizzly sat up, searching each face.

"Oh Grundel, we were so busy telling one another stories we barely noticed anything other than where we put our feet. I'm afraid we weren't very good scouts!" replied Bighorn.

"Even you, Monk—a guide?"

"Especially me—I had my hands full just trying to keep up!"

"Well—some good you lot are. I can see we'll have to start from scratch."

"Yes, but start what?" asked Tuktu, hoping at last to have the mysterious mission out in the open and understood.

"Ah, Took! Well, first things first. The situation is serious. Marmo has brought to our attention that animals are disappearing all around the Icefield, and apparently have been for a while. I've sent the Brothers out, but they haven't found traps or any strange prints—it doesn't seem to be harvesting—there are no remains, so we don't think it's head-hunters or fur hunters." Grundel paused, thoughtfully, then continued. "Nothing remains, not even bones—they're just vanishing. I've been asked by the Furtive Folk to lead a rescue. Although, to be honest Marmo, we don't know if those who have gone missing are alive or dead. Still, don't be discouraged, look at my team—the best!"

"Sounds like we're going to have to come up with something quickly. How many animals are missing?" asked Bighorn.

"Sixty-five that we know of," replied Marmo.

"Sixty-five!" Bighorn whistled through his teeth.

"As far as we know smaller animals—marmots, voles, ground squirrels—mainly from Furtive Folk Valley are missing," Grundel added.

"Any pattern?" asked Aquila.

"Mostly healthy young males and females of mating age," said Marmo.

"A regular Noah's Ark," mused Monk.

"What's that Monk—a regular what?" asked Grundel.

"Noah's Ark—it's an ancient Biblical story—the world is about to be flooded because it is seen as evil and corrupt. But two animals of each kind are led onto an ark by Noah, saving them from the flood, so they could start a new and better world."

Tuktu nodded thoughtfully, "You think that whoever's doing this needs animals to breed—but why?" Trying to fit together the few pieces that they had of the puzzle, the others began to get lost in their own thoughts.

Rousing them, Grundel said, "Speak your thoughts!"

"How could we have not noticed?" sighed Bighorn, perplexed. "Sixty-five disappearances!"

"We must not be looking in the right direction," said Aquila. "Where have we not been looking? Where do we regularly not look?"

"If they are not killing them—where are they taking them that we haven't noticed?" added Raven.

"And who?" asked Tuktu. "Sometimes things appear normal, even when they're happening right under our noses."

"But why," said Marmo. "What for?"

There was silence for a few minutes before Grundel said, "A good start. We should have this solved in no time. First, we need to set up a close watch for strangers or unusual movement. Let's get a good night's rest and start our investigations first thing in the morning."

They all agreed, found comfortable spots in the sweet smelling boughs on the large cavern floor, and fell into a sleep peppered with strange dreams. All except Melancholia who watched over them; she found herself surprisingly fond of this group. And Grundel, who was often up late with other problems needing to be solved.

As the days progressed—off to the right of the main cavern in the Map Den, the grizzlies and Tuktu were involved in a related problem; one that was not discussed with Monk and the other animals.

And so began their long summer. Grundel's Brothers returned regularly, one or two at a time—all, Grundel noticed, except Rakor's twin, Vang, who stayed away as much as possible. Upon their return the bears would sequester with Tuktu in the Map Den. The others, planning or resting quietly by the fire, could hear the muffled growling of their voices, rising and falling in argument, and underneath, Tuktu's steady voice, questioning them. The bears talked and planned late into each evening, well after the others had turned in. Though the others were curious, they respected The Keeper's decision not to share the reason for and meaning of these talks. They trusted that whatever the bears were discussing would be revealed to them in time, if it was deemed necessary.

At dawn, the bears were usually up and out, foraging where berries were ripening or upturning logs for caches of insects. They were all busy during the day. A watch had been organized, and a Council with a representative from each area met every few days late in the afternoon, to report any findings.

MARMO, again, was the first to notice. The cave was filling up, noisy with chatter. When Grundel entered the Keeper's Cave, the others all sat or lay down. He brought the meeting to order and asked for reports of sightings of any kind.

"Has anyone noticed increased activity by owls?" asked Marmo, from the top of the rock slab that acted as a low table. He was sitting up as tall as possible, to be seen and so heard. He knew he wasn't always heard.

"Yesterday," said Aquila, eyeing him. "We were watching at night and we noticed a flurry of activity by the great grey owls, but we weren't sure if the numbers were unusual or whether it was just one very busy owl. We were going to give ourselves a few nights of surveillance before we raised it."

"In our area," added Marmo, "there is definitely an increase of night activity."

"Well that could explain why we haven't noticed—owls taking rodents at night is pretty normal," said Tuktu.

Marmo's fur bristled. "Not that many!"

"Sorry Marmo, I meant no disrespect."

"Was anyone able to follow them?" queried Grundel.

"We couldn't," said Marmo. "Did you, Aquila?"

"Not yet. We don't want them to suspect anything and won't track them until we have a more surreptitious way of following them. We don't want to tip them off, lose our advantage."

"All right, that's our next priority—ideas?" asked Grundel. They mapped out a strategy, the meeting lasting until the sun's dwindling rays sent them out of the cave to feed before dark.

"Grundel," Melancholia said the next morning, noting the sun's position in the sky, "you should visit The Ursula." Insuring that The Keeper's line remained strong and healthy was one of her tasks.

"I don't have time for that now," answered Grundel, from the Map Den. "I have too many things on my mind right now."

"As for that, we will have to bring the others into the search for Rakor soon."

"I'd rather not, at least until we solve the Furtive Folk disappearances. I think we're close—don't you agree?"

"Perhaps."

Grundel looked up surprised. "That's tentative. Do you know something I don't? Is your vision improving?"

"No, my vision is still fractured. But back to my initial point: shouldn't you visit The Ursula?"

"Yes, I suppose so—when I get a minute."

Melancholia decided to go visit Ursula herself.

THE URSULA, Alethia, a golden grizzly, Grundel's mother and Rakor's mate, watched as Kyna, a younger female, plunged her elegant snout into the river, drinking deeply. Alethia imagined the icy water surging through her own body, awaking each cell just as it had every spring she could remember. She had been observing Kyna's body carefully since they had emerged from their dens, waiting for the scent of that particular musk that she had finally detected today. Yes, the young bear was fully mature. It was time to call the Sunados—to decide who would become The Keeper's mate and next Ursula. She had narrowed the contest to two females—Kyna and Tasmira. Alethia sighed. It would be difficult to give up her role—to become merely an advisor, like Inyx. She wondered if it had been hard for Inyx to give up leadership—she had not thought about that when she became Ursula. Most often The Keeper and The Ursula grew old together, but both Inyx and Alethia had lost their mates early and were compelled to surrender their role in the prime of their lives.

Alethia wondered why Grundel had not come—all that business about the disappearances. Well, she had her own problem to solve—deciding between Kyna and Tasmira. She had almost sent Kyna as the female representative to the latest Council, to stand in when The Ursula couldn't be there, but she had reconsidered and sent Tasmira instead, even though she knew the choice to be risky. After Kyna, Tasmira was the smartest of the mature female grizzlies. She had matured faster and was quicker than Kyna. She would do a good job. The Ursula had to admit that she was also curious as to Grundel's reaction to the younger female.

Would Tasmira be the best choice as Grundel's mate and the new Ursula? The young female was hungry for change, and power would satisfy her—she tried so hard, but too hard Alethia realized, to please, in order to be chosen. The young bear had an ambitious streak that she worked hard to conceal. Instinct whispered that power could be dangerous in Tasmira's control. The only female who could learn to control Tasmira was Kyna. And there were other reasons for choosing Kyna—her innate wisdom, her strength of character, her ability to keep her own counsel—traits worthy of the next Ursula. All spring Alethia had been testing them both, and Kyna had not faltered.

Grundel had not shown any interest in mating last season, but he could not afford to ignore mating this season. Alethia was thinking, as was Melancholia, that it was time—so she wasn't surprised when the spirit appeared in a shimmering of light. Mel found the grizzly foraging beside the milky, glacier-fed river.

"Hello Melancholia," greeted Alethia, lifting her great head from where she was rooting in the soil, uncovering sweet spring corms.

"Ursula," Melancholia replied, her gaze sweeping the lovely valley—The Valley of the Twins—with its swift flowing river. Afternoon light radiated that dangerous glow just before a storm.

"You've come about Grundel." Alethia often surprised others, easily reading what they were thinking.

"Yes."

"What's keeping him this year?"

"The times."

"I suppose he has a lot on his mind what with trying to find Rakor and the increasing problem of the Corridor and now these disappearances. I don't know how we're going to solve the problem of humans encroaching on the Corridor. The stories coming out of Yellowstone are horrific."

"You, Grundel and the others will think of something. I'm more concerned right now about the disappearances."

"And Rakor?" Alethia threw the spirit a challenging look.

"And Rakor. However, we must get on with the business at hand here in the Valley."

"The Sunados—the Keeper's mating. Yes," agreed Alethia.

They both fell into thoughtful silence. The grizzly upturned a log and the spirit waited for her to feed.

"Have you chosen?" Melancholia finally asked.

"Almost."

Alethia sat down and faced Melancholia, grunting loudly. "I know Kyna would be the sensible choice, but Tasmira wants it more, and she has strengths—she learns fast, she thinks creatively and she's a real beauty, but she could cause a lot of grief. It's not an easy choice." Melancholia nodded, not wanting to influence The Ursula's decision either way. "Couldn't we let Grundel choose?" asked Alethia, munching on a tuber.

"You know we can't for two good reasons: desire could cloud his judgement, and there should be no contest between The Keeper and his Brothers. If The Ursula chooses, the Brothers accept the choice more readily, especially when they desire that female."

"But what if I choose Kyna and Grundel desires Tasmira?"

"Grundel trusts you. He knows why you must choose. Many years ago Ursula Galina tried to please her son's desire and we got Rakor." Alethia growled.

"Don't be angry, Alethia. Rakor is your mate, but you have to admit it looks like he has betrayed us—why else would my vision be fractured?"

Alethia turned away to control her emotion. She hated to hear any criticism of Rakor, but she couldn't stay angry at Mel when she herself was in doubt about Rakor's actions. Lately she had spent a lot of time thinking over the lineage; wondering if Galina's choice of Inyx for Einar's mate had somehow upset the natural progression. Rakor had been full of surprises, his defection from Cathedral among them.

"But didn't Galina make a good choice—Inyx made a good Ursula," she said, turning back to Melancholia.

"But she was not the obvious choice. Still, let that be. You need now to prod Grundel. Whomever you choose, he must mate this season," she insisted.

"I know. Are you sure you don't want to make a nomination?" Alethia asked, cocking her head.

Mel smiled at the bear's diplomacy, but shook her head. "Sorry, my dear, it is your decision."

Changing the subject Alethia asked, "How's Tasmira doing at Cathedral?"

"An admirable job."

"Has Grundel noticed her?"

"Grundel is locked in his problem-solving mode. All he seeks now are solutions."

"Then, I suppose, we must get him away from his problems, even briefly, and have him mate."

Mel smiled. "My thoughts exactly."

AFTER Melancholia disappeared, Alethia left to seek Inyx, the oldest Ursula, finding her on a hillside, lazily stretched on a mat of mountain heather, dozing in the heat of the early afternoon. Alethia watched, hating to wake her; Inyx was aging. She had been in her prime when Einar, The Keeper and her mate, had been challenged by Dagur, seemingly in a fit of rage, and both had fallen from the ledge, down the Face of Fakara to their deaths. But that was a long time ago now—before Rakor's betrayal, before Rakor became Keeper.

Over a year ago now, when Rakor deserted Cathedral, both females—mother and mate—had gone through a terrible time not understanding, but knowing deep within that something had been at work for some time. They had both felt the subtle changes in Rakor prior to his leaving. They had felt immense guilt that they had not been able to stop Rakor or warn the others. Melancholia had counselled them for long hours, revealing that she too should have known, should have seen what was coming. She convinced them that there must be more to this than any of them could have anticipated—more than any of them could understand. But this was little comfort and Alethia in particular fell into deep depression. For a while, Melancholia feared she would lose both her Keeper and her Ursula. Finally, necessity and her loyalty to duty pulled Alethia out of depression, but only to replace it with a new despair.

Alethia shook herself out of her memories. It was time to plan the Sunados. With the lengthening days the solstice would soon be upon them, and this season The Keeper must mate. There had not been a Sunados for many seasons; this time the Ursulas would insist. Grundel could not ignore the drum.

Alethia gently prodded Inyx.

"Are you awake?"

Inyx grunted. "I am now."

"It's Grundel."

"Harrumph," Inyx pushed her arthritic body into a sitting position and squinted her little eyes against the glare of the sun. "Now what?"

"He's avoiding the Valley."

"So it would seem. I doubt, however, that this is deliberate. He's busy."

"Yes. But he's ignoring his duties here."

Inyx let out a hearty chortle. "My dear sow, mating is not a duty—it's a pleasure!"

"You know what I mean, Inyx." Alethia sat down in frustration.

"Yes, yes. I suppose it's time to pry him away from his maps and his problems."

"We need to announce the Sunados."

"You've chosen then?"

"Almost. Was it this difficult for you?" Alethia shifted uncomfortably.

Inyx replied, "There is always a Tasmira."

"Do you think I'll make the right choice?"

The old bear put her paw sympathetically over Alethia's. "Only time will tell."

Suddenly Alethia felt a cold chill and a dark shadow fell across the hillside. She looked up to a massive black cloud, racing towards them.

"C'mon," she said, heading downhill, "we'd better find cover, storm's here and it looks like snow!"

"Oh, I hope not," groaned Inyx, "I'm finally dry and warm." The two lumbered towards a dense alder hell that swallowed them whole.

THE NEXT NIGHT the drumming began. Just at dusk when the crepuscular sky glimmered and shadows roamed freely, it could be heard rumbling thunderously through the valleys. The Brothers heard it as they were falling asleep on the hillsides; Grundel heard it as he foraged leagues from Cathedral on one of his night treks; Monk heard it in the Keeper's Cave. At first, he thought it must be a continuation of last night's storm, which had been swift and severe. But something was different. He sat up, looked outside at the starry night, stoked the fire and waited for Grundel.

"What *is* that?" asked Monk, after Grundel had returned

and was stretched out in front of the fire. Grundel sat back up with a grunt.

"Drumming. They're calling for the Sunados in the Listening Mountains—the Ursulas are reminding me of my duty in the Valley of the Twins."

"It's rather—."

"Unsettling?"

"To put it mildly!" They listened together, feeling the vibrations through their bodies, playing every nerve. They felt their heartbeats race to catch up.

"What exactly is a Sunados?" asked Monk.

"Oh—a kind of—celebration," replied Grundel, distractedly.

"Really—who's going?"

Grundel let out a deep belly laugh that reverberated through the cave.

"Sorry Monk—you're not invited!"

"Why not? Couldn't I just observe?"

"No, my man, trust me—bears only. This ritual brings out the aggression in us. The Sunados is volatile and unpredictable."

"What kind of ritual?"

"Mating, Monk."

Monk started to say, "Mating—I thought—?" but Grundel interrupted.

"Listen. It's different for the Keepers. The Ursula searches to find the best candidates—females from other regions—to mate with the Brothers. Any offspring born from these pairings are eligible to be chosen as a Brother. After intensive training two females are chosen for further instruction; finally, one is chosen as mate of the Keeper and she becomes the dominant Ursula."

"You don't choose your own mate?!" scoffed Monk. At this careless remark, the bear growled deep in his throat, an angry, menacing growl. When Grundel refused to make eye contact, Monk realized that he had crossed a line and was sharply reminded of the power of a grizzly, how easily he now took their relationship for granted, how privileged he truly was. This magnificent animal—lord of the mountains—had saved him, befriended him, treated him with nothing but kindness. He must not repay him with rudeness and disrespect.

"My deepest apologies, Grundel. That was rude and thoughtless. May I rephrase that?" Grundel nodded curtly, not one to hold a grudge. "Why don't you choose your mate yourself?"

"There can be no breach between The Keeper and his Brothers. We depend too much on one another. This prevents jealousy, envy—emotions that can divide us." He sighed and looked away and Monk wondered what he was thinking about. Then the bear turned back and added, "It is the Way."

"There are never contests, challenges?" asked Monk.

Grundel gave a little grimace. "Oh, there are physical contests between Brothers! And I have to continually defend my superior skills! But no challenge of authority between The Keeper and his Brothers." He paused and then said, "Well, almost never." When Monk raised an eyebrow, Grundel added, "Except if a Brother challenges The Keeper's position."

"Has that ever happened?" asked Monk.

"Yes," replied Grundel, "once when The Keeper's courage failed. And once, not so long ago, Inyx's mate Einar was challenged, but it was a bizarre challenge that happened too quickly out of rage and in an inappropriate location out there on the ledge; both fell from the ledge to their deaths. It's why Inyx is alone. But we've never understood Dagur's rage or why it happened. It was so out of character."

"Then who chooses your mate?"

"The Ursula."

The drumming had become more intense.

"And the drumming?"

"The drumming announces a special Sunados—the Keeper's mating. The Ursulas are summoning me." He paced the cave's floor, restlessly.

"They can do that?"

"Oh yes." Grundel let out a sigh, and lay back down. "But I will obey in my own time."

GORATH lay in a deep hollow at the base of an Engelmann, not sleeping, aroused by the drum, brooding again as he brooded so often. He always believed he would have made a great Keeper. He was often annoyed at Grundel's cautious nature, his deliberations, what seemed to Gorath as his plodding mind. Now the Sunados had arrived and Grundel would get the best mate. It didn't seem fair, especially if Alethia's choice was Tasmira. Well, he thought, he would make Tasmira his own this Sunados, even if he had to challenge Grundel for her! He knew that Kyna was also a contender for Ursula. He hoped for the sake of them all that Alethia would choose her.

Tasmira, too, lay awake, listening to the drumming. So it had begun. She wondered what was in store for her. She wondered if her deepest longing would be realized. She realized that Kyna was probably the front-runner, but the final test was still to come, and she believed, like Iynx before her, that the decision in her favour would be decisive. She had believed this from birth.

Grundel lay listening, trying to avoid thinking about the Sunados. How could mating possibly help at this point, he wondered? There were so many problems, too many tasks. He was worried about Melancholia, worried about the way she was retreating into herself. Mel could not fully explain her state since Rakor left; she said it was like seeing all possibilities at once, not just past, present, future—but all the permutations, where not one asserted itself as the truth. It was overwhelming, and she could just barely contain herself.

Monk meanwhile was half asleep in his armchair, his book having fallen closed on his lap. The sun had finally set, a red flaming ball, igniting the tops of the peaks, when Gorath lumbered in. At first, Monk thought it was Grundel—the two Brothers looked so alike—but Gorath's voice was deeper, sharper, more insistent. When Gorath called out to him, Monk sat up, momentarily disoriented.

"Sorry to startle you," said Gorath, "were you sleeping?"

"Not really—just dozing," Monk replied. Gorath paced around the cavern, lying down, then jumping up to pace again. Monk lit a candle and waited patiently in his armchair, accustomed to the bears' pacing. Suddenly Gorath stopped right in front of him.

"This might sound absurd to you, but I need your help," he said, bluntly. "I need something to help me win Tasmira at the Sunados. If I get the chance," he added, as an afterthought.

"I thought the Brothers competed physically for females," he said, giving himself time to think.

"We do," said Gorath. "I have the strength—I'm not worried about the challenge, but that's not the final test—the final test is a gift."

"Oh," said Monk, smiling.

"It's not funny, Monk! You need something unique to convince a female like Tasmira, who could have anyone. The gift can decide a draw."

"I'm not smiling the way you think, Gorath—honestly. I just think it's kind of sweet."

"Well, the question is—would you have any brilliant ideas?"

"What are the traditional gifts?"

"Creature comforts like a woven mat or delicacies to eat." Monk thought for a while, his fingers drumming the armchair. He looked down at the book on his lap.

"Poetry," he said suddenly.

"What?"

"Poetry—it's a human thing—you can seduce her with words!"

"Words! I'm no good with words!" wailed Gorath. "Never mind, sorry I asked, it was a crazy idea."

"No, no. Listen. This can work. We'll do a little artful translation—I'll teach you what to say. We'll use something short and simple, but true and compelling."

"And you think this will work—this—poetry?" asked Gorath, unconvinced.

"Like a charm," said Monk. "Mind you—you have to believe the words, and you must do it with heart, with passion. She'll know right away if you are just posturing. How much time do we have?"

"A day or two at the most," said Gorath.

"C'mon then, we need to find a private meadow where you can practise." He leapt up, Gorath trotting behind him. Watching them go, Mel shook her head at the machinations of the living.

"I WISH I could go to the Sunados," said Monk. He was passing the time with Melancholia while she waited for Grundel to return from feeding. "I wish I could just materialize there!" Melancholia said nothing.

"Mel, the way you come and go," he said, suddenly sitting up on the edge of his chair. Melancholia nodded, she had a pretty good idea what was coming. "Can you go—anywhere? I know I can't understand all the dimensions, but say, in my reality, can you go anywhere? Appear anywhere?"

"No, I am of Cathedral."

"But what does that mean?"

"It means I exist purely for the mountain, the Icefield and its needs. I am its spirit. I exist in all its dimensions simultaneously."

"How far does that extend?"

Mel let out a rare tinkling laugh. "You are thinking too much in time and space. As I said, I extend the full range of the Mountains of the Source's influence and need." Monk was silent for a few minutes.

"Are there other spirits?" he asked.

"Indeed, at all the sacred sites. There are more here—like Toholinagi."

"Why can I see you and Nagi when I can't see the others?"

"Because you lack doubt with us, and because we allow it. Besides, there aren't many left."

Monk sank back down into the deep folds of the armchair and took a deep breath. "I have one more question," he said.

"Go on."

"Do you have any idea what happened to Koko and Rachel?" It was hardly a whisper. It was a question that had haunted him since the accident; a question he hadn't the strength to ask until now. Melancholia had been expecting it for some time.

"Yes."

Monk sucked in his breath and waited, but Melancholia didn't continue. "Are you going to tell me?"

"No." She gazed unwaveringly into his eyes.

"But why not!" Monk wailed, turning away from that gaze.

"Because my vision is fractured. I can no longer see clearly even what I once knew, and I can't see the future at all."

"What's that got to do with it?" he moaned.

"Monk, you asked me if I had any idea; if you had asked me *if I knew*, I would have answered as honestly—no, I don't know. I can't be certain if what I'm seeing is true. I'm mostly going on instinct these days and it's very—unsettling. I can't separate this reality from others; I can't separate images in time; I can't separate your destiny from Cathedral's. Until we find Rakor, I'll be uncertain of everything. I do know that things must unfold naturally, so I'm leaving a lot of it up to Grundel, as I must."

"But that's not fair—and it might be dangerous for us not to know."

"I realize that."

Just then, Grundel trooped in with a cadre of his Brothers. Noticing the painful look on Monk's face, he quickly guessed its cause. Only Grundel really understood the nature of Melancholia's new blindness. She was seeing all possibilities at once. Somewhere in the plethora of possibilities was the one that Monk wanted to hear—that they were alive. It was there, but so were many others, and since Rakor's betrayal, Melancholia could no longer tell their truth. They were working through all the possibilities, searching for Rachel and Koko, as they were searching for Rakor, but there were so many possibilities. Grundel and Mel had decided it would be cruel to give Monk false hope. They both knew that he would have died if the bears had not rescued him—how could Rachel and Koko have survived? So they told him nothing for the time being. But all of this was taking its toll on Melancholia who was making too many trips between dimensions; and each time she re-entered Earth, she was having more trouble emerging.

"Are you ok?" he asked. Melancholia was shimmering, losing form.

"I've been better," she said.

Grundel looked around the room. "Where's Tasmira, Monk?"

"She returned to the Valley," Monk replied, sullenly

"Good," he said. "Are you ok?"

"No," snapped Monk and lurched out of the cavern, hurt and confused. The bear turned back to Mel.

"He'll be all right, but we need to find Rakor soon; everyone's nerves are fraying to the breaking point." The bears growled in agreement.

"I agree; so should I stay? I thought you wanted me to go to the Sunados?"

"Right—first things first. Go and mate," she said. When he looked confused, she repeated, "Go."

Before he left, the massive grizzly spoke quietly to Tuktu and Bighorn who were back from feeding. "I'm leaving things with you. I won't be gone long. Watch Monk—he's had some bad news and isn't taking it well. And I'm worried about Melancholia—she's having a hard time maintaining her shape. Don't let her retreat so far into herself that we can't reach her. We need her."

"Will do—but try to enjoy yourself, Grundel!" said Tuktu.

"Yes, we'll be fine," echoed Bighorn.

"Let me know if there is the least change—send Raven," said Grundel, casting a worried eye around the room. His Brothers called urgently from outside, and he left.

Melancholia watched them go thinking this, at least, felt right. She hoped Alethia would make the right choice, and that she would take into account Tagore's choice. The White Wolf had seldom been wrong. They all needed a strong level-headed Ursula for what lay surely ahead.

Monk eventually wandered back into the main cavern and

slumped back into his armchair. "Where do they go?" he asked, settling in.

"No one knows," said Bighorn, "well, except Mel."

"There's a Sunados Canyon over by—" began Monk.

Bighorn shook his great rack of horns. "No Monk. The bears' mating is private. It originated at Sunados Canyon, but it moves around now, somewhere in the Listening Mountains. And I know that look! I wouldn't go poking around if I were you."

"Why not?" asked Monk.

"Because last time someone did, they ended up dead," replied Bighorn. Monk looked over at Melancholia for confirmation.

"You forget at your peril the power of these creatures," she said.

"Besides, the Watchers wouldn't let you through anyway," added Bighorn.

Monk didn't respond; he slid back into himself, as if he had lost interest in the conversation, letting his own dark thoughts wash over him. Melancholia wondered what she could do to keep Monk's mind more usefully occupied. She was exhausted and needed to return to Gaia.

"Tuktu, why don't you tell your story now? Monk and Bighorn never got a chance to hear it." Tuktu nodded, understanding. She and Bighorn were also troubled by Monk's state of mind.

"Good idea," agreed Bighorn, "I'm always ready for a story—aren't you, Monk?" Monk nodded absently from the depths of his armchair. Tuktu looked questioningly at Melancholia who nodded to go ahead.

"All right," began Took, "we were talking about Raven." Hearing his name, Raven flew in from the outside ledge and slumped on a perch, looking very uncomfortable; he had hoped to avoid this moment. As Tuktu began, Monk raised his head, drawn in by her velvet voice, not noticing that Melancholia was dissolving out of vision.

Tuktu's Tale

"WHERE I come from, Raven is well known. You know we're both from the Barrenlands?" The others nodded. "But even there, Raven was someone the rest of us couldn't predict. One day he would be generous and helpful, the next—mischievous, even—cruel." Monk and the others snuck a look at Raven who was hanging his head. "His antics continually got him into trouble, not only with us, but also with the humans who live there—the Ihalmiut and the white men who call us La Foule or The Throng.

"We live out beyond white man habitation, beyond the trees, on an immense plain called the Barrenlands, where we travel en masse, hundreds of thousands of us, a living brown river half a mile wide and a length that for others is hardly imaginable. If you sat and watched us, just the does passing would take half a day. Picture a place without trees, without your mountains, simply a vast plain flowing with caribou.

"I met Grundel out on that plain. Grundel was a surprise to us. We know grizzlies, but up at the inlet, at the calving grounds, there are just polar bears. We took him to be a spirit—but I'm jumping ahead. It was spring; my mother had run with the does from the winter grounds in the forest to the Chosen Ground on the northern inlet where the fawns, where I, would be born. Their urgency drove them faster than the others, faster than the elderly, the stragglers, even the buck herds who were far behind them. They follow an ancient trail, so old that it is worn into solid rock.

"We are born swift—within an hour we can outrun the fastest man, or even wolves, for a while. The night I was born,

Raven was with the does. He was in a cruel mood, taunting and ridiculing them in their labour." The others threw Raven surprised looks—this was not the Raven they knew. Raven just hung his head not meeting their eyes. Tuktu continued. "My mother angrily drove him from her, demanding he not return that night or there would be severe consequences. But after I was born, Raven came back in stealth. As I stood, shaky and trembling, he lured me away from my mother who was resting. He drew me away from the herd, drew me into the shadows, and then deserted me. I had no idea where I was, or where my mother rested. I believe Raven just meant to prove to my mother that he had powers she shouldn't mock. He never meant to do anything but frighten her.

"But in the darkness, I ran away from the herd thinking I ran towards them, until I didn't know what to do but lie down and wait for my mother. While I was lost on the Barrens, a pack of wolves hunting around the edges found me. Although I was lying down, huddled against the loneliness, I smelled them and instinct told me to flee. I ran and ran, trying to outrun them, but they kept coming with a fierce, terrifying determination. Just when I thought my lungs would burst, when I could feel their fiery breath on my back, I practically ran headlong into Grundel who snatched me up and set me behind him, so he could turn to face the wolves. A grizzly is a fearsome sight, particularly to a pack of wolves who were not expecting him. He gave them a terrifying roar and they stopped abruptly, bumping into and falling over one another, then turned and fled howling.

"For many long days, Grundel tried to find my mother. Can you imagine trying to find an individual in that throng, that living, sweating brown river? Grundel was also waiting to speak to the Caribou Conclave—but it only forms when it is called upon to perform a duty. Since he was not of The Throng, Grundel could not call a Conclave. He could cause an incident so that the caribou would call one, but he loathed doing this. He needed their cooperation, and he didn't want to damage the relationship by an act of manipulation. And so the Conclave remained invisible and seemingly powerless.

"But, word spreads. Grundel, as you can imagine, caused a great stir wherever he went. The first ray of hope we had was when we heard there was to be a Conclave about Raven. He had been last seen with me and so had been detained, waiting my return. When there was no more hope of finding me, my mother demanded a Conclave to judge his role in my disappearance.

"We saw the Great Circle well before we were in range of hearing. Walking ahead of me, Grundel effortlessly divided the crowd, creating a path for us. We cautiously approached the circle of elders. Grundel wanted to hear what was going on before he made his move. My mother was speaking, explaining what had happened that night. I wanted to run to her, but Grundel motioned for me to be patient a little while longer.

"'And so,' my mother concluded, 'I ask for Raven's punishment.'

"An aged doe stood up and faced Raven. Her voice rang out through the herd waiting and listening. 'What do you have to say in your defence, Raven? This is not the first time your cruel tricks have caused havoc among The Throng. We have been lenient, but you should know that we grow weary of the complaints lodged against you. And this is a serious charge—it calls for permanent banishment.'

"Raven looked fearfully around at the hard faces staring back at him. He started to cajole, but saw the faces grow stonier. He tried remorse, but no one believed him. He realized his usual defences would be useless; he had used them carelessly too many times.

"'You're right,' he said finally. 'I have no excuse. I drove the little one into the night.'

"Then the Elder asked, 'Well, before we pronounce judgement, is there anyone to speak on Raven's behalf?'

"Raven looked around wildly, but dropped his eyes when all he met were accusatory looks. Only when he had given up on these pleas did Grundel step forward.

"'I will speak in Raven's defence.' There was a gasp as the Council leapt up and started to back away.

"'Do not fear me. I mean you no harm. Come.' He waved me in front of him and another gasp spread through the Conclave. My mother leapt to my side nuzzling me. Grundel continued, 'I found Took being chased by wolves. She is very fast, very brave. And we have been searching for her mother ever since.'

"'But,' my mother broke in, 'despite Took's return, I am not prepared to let Raven go unpunished.' Her voice was filled with both relief and anger. Murmurs of agreement rippled through the herd.

"'If you will permit me,' said Grundel, bowing low to her and then the elders, 'I have come a long way to speak with the Conclave on a serious matter that involves us all. I would like to speak on Raven's behalf, but first, I need to speak to the elders in private.'

"The Circle huddled together for a few minutes, and then agreed. The rest of us were dismissed, and it wasn't until the next day that rumours started flying about what had been discussed. Of course, they were all rumours because only the elders knew and they weren't talking. My mother knew because Raven's future was involved, but all she told me was that Grundel was very wise and we had all better listen to what he was saying. Finally, it was agreed that Raven was to be banished to

Grundel's home where he would act as the Keeper's messenger. If, in time, he paid his dues for what he had done, he would be allowed to return.

"The night before Grundel and Raven were to leave, Raven came to me. He apologized for what he had done. He said that no one was more relieved than he, when I stepped into the Conclave Circle. He had spent a miserable time after my disappearance, whether the others had believed him or not. He was grateful for the second chance. He said Grundel seemed a very interesting fellow and they were on an important mission.

"This is what Grundel understood about Raven—that he needed to be involved in a great plan to engage all his lively skills—to keep him out of trouble!"

Tuktu turned to Raven. "Right, Raven? So what have you and Grundel been up to?"

Raven began slowly, embarrassed at being exposed, but grateful for not being excluded.

"Have you ever seen the map in the Map Den?" he asked, forgetting his embarrassment and enjoying the rapt attention. His black, penetrating eyes searched the others.

"No, none of us," replied Bighorn, "have you?" Before Raven could answer, Melancholia reappeared.

"Not yet, Raven—not yet."

Piotr's Revelation

Piotr

SUDDENLY, Piotr, the youngest of the Brothers, burst into the cavern. Everyone looked up in surprise. A tall, young woman trailed in behind Piotr, shaking off snow; Mel nodded to her. Monk raised a hand in greeting and patted the wooden chair he had just recently made, then turned to the grizzly. Piotr was the youngest and smallest of the Brothers. When Alethia had her last set of twins, Carth, a large, brawny cub was born first, then Piotr, a scrawny undersized cub. During their first spring, Alethia taught Carth to protect Piotr. Given his diminutive size, she was afraid Piotr would not survive the season, but she underestimated him. Piotr was small in size, but not in intellect. What he couldn't do using physical strength, he accomplished by mental strength. Even Grundel had learned to depend on his quick, problem-solving ability. Carth was fiercely protective and loyal to his twin. They were seldom apart, unless Piotr was sent on a special mission.

"Shouldn't you be at the Sunados?" asked Monk.

"Oh that. Where's Mel! I've news," said Piotr, ignoring him and turning to Melancholia, who was having difficulty re-emerging.

"Can it wait for Grundel?" she asked, not wanting to have to make decisions in her state.

"No!" replied Piotr, barely able to contain his excitement. Melancholia looked around; Raven, Took, Bighorn, Monk and Mikaila were all watching her. Silently, she cursed her blindness.

"Go ahead, then," she said, hoping she was not making a decision that she would later regret.

"Here?" Piotr gestured to the others.

"Yes. It's time."

"Well—ok—but it's about Rakor." He paused then, but Melancholia just nodded to go ahead. "He—he's in the Castleguard Caves!" There was a sharp, collective intake of breath. "Are you going to get Grundel?" prodded Piotr after a few moments.

Melancholia hesitated—hesitation seeming her lot in life lately. She gazed into the kaleidoscope of her realities, insisting one emerge, one clear vision, but nothing formed.

"No, not until the mating is completed." She could tell that Piotr had more to say, but gave him a look to indicate that he should wait. "But while Grundel is away, I'm going to take this opportunity to explain to all of you in the room what the grizzlies have been doing. We have a series of problems that appear to be related—but be patient, all will be revealed in time."

There was another moment of stunned silence, followed by a rush of rippling excitement.

"The disappearances from the Furtive Folk Valley you already know about. As you must have surmised, we have also been searching for Rakor. In the Den is a map which represents the area we have been covering in our search. Each Brother has a designated area for which he is responsible, and reports to us regularly. We have been working methodically in ever widening circles. But Piotr believed that Rakor was closer to home, so as the others widened their scope, he stayed near the Icefield, resurveying that ground. He is very intuitive in his thinking." Melancholia nodded to Piotr who ducked his head in modesty. "It appears that your instincts were good, Piotr."

"Well—it was something Mikaila told me," said Piotr, "that finally gave me the clue I've been waiting for."

"Me?" said Mikaila.

"Yes, remember when you said that sitting on the ground in the Castleguard Meadows, you felt a rumbling, thought it might be an earthquake, but nothing of the sort happened that day. The rumblings appeared to be very localized. That's when I started to suspect that someone was up to something in the caves."

"Rakor in the Caves of Castleguard!" interrupted Bighorn. "But why? They're dangerous, unmapped, forbidden! What could Rakor possibly want—why would he be in those caves all this time?"

"I suspect because he is searching for something." Melancholia paused and gazed around the room—each creature had a little knowledge of the complicated problems facing Cathedral. It was difficult to decide how much they should all know—how much would put them in jeopardy. Raven flapped his wings and hopped up and down in agitation and excitement. Monk and Mikaila leaned forward in their chairs. Bighorn looked over at Tuktu, wondering how she fit into all this. As Melancholia continued, he turned his attention back to her.

"A long time ago, in the beginning, when the mountains were thrusting up out of the chaos of formation, something was placed here in my keeping; something that was later covered by the glacier, held in stasis for millennia." Melancholia paused again, wondering how to express the mystery in a way they would understand.

"What? What was placed under the Icefield?" prodded Monk.

"The essence of what you call life—the Quintessence." There was silence in the room as the others tried to take this in.

"When the earth had evolved enough to support mammals such as yourselves, I needed help—actors in the world, to help protect, and to intercede when necessary. This is when the bears became the Keepers. Our lives were inexorably linked together from that day. My vision was tied to their loyalty."

"But how?" asked Monk.

"Well, when I told the old gods that I needed help, they asked me to describe what I needed. I told them someone strong and fearless, with an incorruptible heart. The gods chose Ursula from the Valley of the Twins," the spirit continued, "and came to her in the form of a bear, Arctos, with whom she begat the line of Keepers. And until Rakor, the bears have stayed true to this cause. Even Rakor, I must believe, has a role to play— although if I once was shown it, I do not remember. The Quintessence is buried under the Icefield; it is Earth's life force, but I fear that Rakor has decided to claim this for himself—to gain the power of immortality. If this be true, he does not understand that to steal this is to take the breath from the planet."

"Then nothing will live," said Tuktu, horrified, "surely he understands that."

"The quest for power has done stranger things," replied the spirit.

Melancholia decided that she had said enough for the time being, though there was more to be told, so she sat back and waited for questions, but the others fell into deep thought. She waited, but no questions came—each one had too much to ponder. After a time, Bighorn and Tuktu excused themselves and left with Raven to feed. Mikaila fell asleep in her armchair, having travelled a great distance, which left only Monk awake. Melancholia motioned for Piotr to join her in the Map Den. Monk, lost in thought, didn't notice that Piotr, following Mel, was practically dancing, barely able to contain his excitement.

The Map Den was the heart of the Keeper's Caves. It was medium sized, longer than it was wide, with a domed roof. In one corner was a small pool fed by a warm spring. All around the edge of the cave there was a rock pathway about four feet wide. In the centre, in a large flat bed of sand, was a carefully drawn map of the Shining Mountains' Corridor from the northern territory to the newly formed Yellowstone Park in the south, an intricate map with designated areas, symbols, and markers.

"I gather there is more to your story," Melancholia said quietly.

"Oh yes!" said Piotr. "Just wait—this is hard to believe!" He was pacing wildly back and forth on the rock path, making her dizzy.

"Stop pacing and get to the point, Piotr. And please, lower your voice." The unfamiliarity of not knowing what he was going to say was more than frustrating; it was unnerving. Piotr noticed that Mel was again shimmering so he tried to calm down.

"Rakor is in the caves all right, but do you know why I haven't been able to find him?" She shook her head. "He's changing shape—like in the old stories! I got talking to Mikaila in the meadows and she suggested we stake out the Rivergate one night, make what she called a blind so we could hide and watch the entrance. Well, we did and a great grey owl flew out of the cave early in the evening, which we didn't pay much attention to, until it returned; then, just at the entrance, at the Rivergate, which we could see quite clearly, he changed back into bear form! I know, I know, this sounds fantastic, but it's true. And there's some kind of enchantment on the Rivergate which must be why we never paid any attention to the spot. He walked towered the cave and just disappeared! Honest! Ask Mikaila."

"I believe you," Mel soothed. "But we are going to keep this information between the three of us until Grundel gets back. Do you understand?" Piotr nodded his head in agreement. "Explain to Mikaila, but first tell me everything again, slowly and from the start, everything you've seen and heard. Try not to leave out any detail, no matter how small."

A while later, Melancholia and Piotr heard the others re-entering the cave and stepped out to join them. Monk was still in his armchair, not even a book open in his lap, staring into the fire. Bighorn greeted Melancholia and then bobbed his rack towards Monk.

"Don't mind him," she answered, "he's brooding."

Monk raised his head, giving her a long look. She could see a question forming, but it was not one she expected.

"Why did the gods make bears the Keepers?" he asked.

"You mean, why not humans?"

"I guess so," said Monk, sheepishly, realizing his conceit.

"Because you insist that the mind be in control."

"Isn't that a good thing—reason over passion?"

"No. The mind should be the servant of the spirit and of the heart."

"And bears?"

"Know this instinctively."

"But that's plainly not all?" He was beginning to read her, as Grundel could.

"No," Mel hesitated.

"What else?" he pressed.

"It's difficult to explain. Let me just say that unlike humans, *a bear looks out at the Open with its whole gaze.*"

"The Open?"

She fell silent for a few minutes, while the others waited with interest, then she quoted but not from any book Monk had read: "… his being is infinite to him/ incomprehensible and without a sense of condition/ pure as his gaze/ and where you see the future/ he sees everything/ and himself in everything/ healed and whole/ forever."

"What is that?" Monk asked. But Melancholia just shook her head. "And you're saying this is Grundel?"

"Yes."

"Isn't that a bit of a stretch?" Melancholia responded with a severe look. "Well, he's not perfect," Monk muttered.

The spirit held the look until Monk turned away, still muttering sullenly and glaring into the fire. He was still angry with Melancholia and by extension with Grundel for not giving him the answers he needed. Melancholia understood this so she let it go, in the hope that his black mood would soon pass. For the moment, there was really nothing she could tell him about Rachel or Koko.

The Sunados

Into the Listening Mountains

While Melancholia had begun slowly to reveal aspects of Cathedral's complex problem to the others, Grundel was lumbering after Gorath, who had chosen this year's Sunados location. They met up with the other Brothers and climbed steadily up an old trail worn to bedrock west of Cathedral, into the Listening Mountains. Gorath was watching for the appearance of the hoodoos and the waterfall that hid the entrance to the Hot Springs. It was a warm evening and the sun, reluctant to set, rolled lazily across the tops of the peaks. They soon came over a rise and the Watchers' Hoodoos loomed tall and proud, silent sentinels in the gathering dusk. The strange formations formed great columns of rock, like church steeples, which stood out from the mountain walls. Near these limestone columns a magnificent waterfall cascaded into a dark pool that spilled over into a noisy stream. As they approached the hoodoos, the bears halted. The first stars revealed themselves as dusk deepened.

Out of a dark cavern high in one of the hoodoos glided two terrible angels, beautiful and menacing with their long spears. They were almost seven feet tall and their bodies were muscular. The bears, however, showed no fear. For millennia the animals of the Icefield had lived with these two Watchers who had once heralded from Paradisi¤. The animals had never asked why the angels had left their homeland, but had made them welcome in their own. In exchange, the angels taught the animals their wisdom, and performed many rituals for them including this one—insuring the bears' privacy during the purification, by protecting this exclusive entrance to the Hot Springs. Armaros and Semjaza flew to the bears and landed lightly, standing in front of Grundel and Gorath.

"Greetings, Keeper," said Semjaza in his honey smooth voice. Like Armaros beside him, Semjaza wore a short leather skirt and vest of thin, shimmering mail. An acute scent like lemon verbena and mint accompanied them.

"Greetings, Watchers. We come to request your protection for our Sunados."

"So be it," replied Semjaza and the two angels swept over the bears, pointing the way, and took up their positions in front of the waterfall. The bears lumbered behind the falls' veil, through a deep limestone slash in the rock wall. They had to enter on hind legs so narrow was the break; their paws on the wall felt the soft slick moss lining the dark, dank interior. Gorath felt his heart racing and wondered what this Sunados would hold. Coming through to the other side, they followed an ancient stream bed between high rocky cliffs to the Hot Springs—a mineral spring that bubbled out of the depths of the earth, hot and sulphuric. Its constant motion had formed a large basin in which the bears now eased their massive bodies. Vang splashed Gorath, hitting the water with his giant paw, dousing the bear's head with an avalanche of water.

"Don't look so glum!" he roared. "You're not the sorriest bear among us—you'll mate someone!" That started a free for all, a little warm up to what lay in store.

Meanwhile, as the pale full moon rose and the northern lights danced overhead, Alethia and Inyx gathered the females in the chosen canyon. These were the candidates that Alethia had chosen during her search for matching mates. They had trained together, competed together, until finally Tasmira and Kyna had been chosen for the final Ursula contest. The other females would be paired with the Brothers.

Earlier, the females too had been through the Hot Springs, and were now posed in a circle with their drums in their laps, simple drums made of skins scraped, stretched over a circle of bone, then dried as Melancholia had taught them. Here in the

Sunados their dead were thought to be with them, preserving voices of the past. The females began deep rhythmic drumming—that slowly increased in tempo and intensity. Back at the Springs, the males heard the drumbeat echoing off the hills, rising in the night air, and their desire intensified with it. Alethia swept her gaze over all the young females. As always, there were more males than females; the competition would be fierce; she would have to keep her wits about her. Only the two final candidates sat without drums, preparing themselves for what lay ahead.

In the spidery moonlight, Kyna stole a sideways glance at Inyx and Alethia. Inyx, as she expected, was calm and smiling, enjoying the ritual, intent on drumming. Alethia was tense, serious, controlling the beat; much rested on her shoulders this Sunados. All the drummers found it hard, initially, to surrender their private thoughts; but eventually the drumming took over, sweeping their minds clean of everything—everything but the heartbeat. Alethia began the Bjorn Chant warding off darkness and its spirits, and the others joined in: na-mu-am-id-a-but-su, namuamidabutsu, namuamidabutsu…

Just before dawn, Gorath led the males to the canyon. The females remained in their trance-like state until Alethia became aware of the males taking their places in a larger circle surrounding them.

She rose, as the sun rose. She raised her massive head to dawn's glorious rays and then pointed. A young female stood and four male challengers jumped to their feet. They paired off and soon there were roars not only between the fighting bears, but amongst their Brothers who roared their encouragement. The females continued drumming, taking their lead from the nature of the struggle, slowing when the bears circled, intensifying as they attacked, and beating frantically at the climax of their struggle. The winner, already battered and bloody, faced the next challenger. When his last competitor finally resigned, the winner turned to the female. She bowed and waited for the gift he offered. Another bear rose from the circle handing pine nuts wrapped in a large soft leaf to his twin. The male then offered it to the female. Accepting it, she sat down with him in the circle, sharing the succulent gift.

One by one young females rose and faced the males. Challengers rose with them, and great battles rocked the canyon. As the day passed, Grundel stole a look at Gorath, wondering why he wasn't challenging, wondering for whom he was waiting. He knew Gorath coveted his role, but tried not to let that affect the way he saw his Brother. Gorath knew he was taking a chance, not challenging for any of these females. The Brothers usually challenged early, to give themselves plenty of chances to win a female. The Sunados came seldom and these females were the strongest and smartest in the extended region, all candidates The Ursula had chosen. They were trained together, though only two were chosen for the last stage of the contest. At the end of the day there would be only Kyna and Tasmira, and one of them would be Grundel's. The other would be the mate of Grundel's second in command. From these two couples' offspring Melancholia was likely to choose the next Keeper.

Gorath was also looking around—to see who else was waiting as he was. He noticed some of the larger, older, more experienced males—Kedar, Lunt, Vang—all waiting. Vang nodded to him with a grim smile. Gorath knew that he could end up with no mate, but he didn't care. It was a gamble he was willing to take. In fact, he was prepared to challenge Grundel for Tasmira if he must.

Grundel tried not look at Tasmira, intent not to let his desire play with his emotions, diverting him from his role as

Keeper. He had recognized Tasmira when he first entered the circle, the female representative on the Council—a good candidate, she was strong willed, intelligent, sure of herself. But who was the other one with the dark eyes that Ursula had chosen? She was a stranger to him. He tried not to dwell on this new interest.

Alethia rose again and all were silent. She gestured for Kyna and Tasmira to also rise. Now the time had come to prove their ability to provide, to lead.

"Kyna and Tasmira, now is your final test." Alethia's voice rang out for all to hear. "You must each provide a kill for the Sunados. After you each bring one to us, we will wait for Tagore to appear. Whichever heart she chooses to eat will help in my deliberation of who the next Ursula will be."

A female white wolf had been the original Ursula's constant companion on the candidate quests, and her descendants had taken part in the mating rituals ever since. The white wolf's influence on The Ursula was strong; her instincts valued. This was Tasmira's secret knowledge, why she was so certain she would be chosen. The White Wolf had appeared at her birth, had dug out the mouth of the cave where she slept alone—her mother had gone foraging. The wolf had looked at her long and intently, but left her unharmed. Her mother had taken this as an omen. When Tagore and Alethia had arrived on the candidate quest, Tasmira was sure the wolf had recognized her, had come for her.

The kill was Tasmira's last hurdle and she had been practising for this all her life. She threw a look over her shoulder at Kyna loping away. No one doubted Kyna's strength, but The Ursula, Tasmira knew, needed more than strength. Remembering everything her mother had taught her, her senses honed, enhanced by her intense desire to win, she moved through the valleys, determined, confident. Still, it took her longer than she expected to find a suitable kill; she had gone further than she intended, and it was late afternoon when she dragged the large caribou doe back to the drums and the waiting bears. Kyna had already returned, standing over an impressive stag. For a raw moment, a dark shadow clouded Tasmira's confidence, but she quickly shook it off, proudly dropping the doe in front of Grundel, who nodded solemnly. Gorath, standing off to one side, smiled encouragingly at her. Perhaps he saw the doubt in her eyes. She looked down at the smaller doe, then again over to Kyna's impressive stag.

The sharp smell of blood in the air fed the bears' hunger, and they were restless by the time the White Wolf appeared. She came stealthily out of the pine woods and circled around them — large, wary. The bears lumbered to their feet and opened a path, closing it behind her. The white wolf stopped first at Tasmira's kill sniffing at it and then, without hesitation, went straight for Kyna's kill, tore the stag open and ate the heart. Tasmira gasped. A muffled roar of rage escaped her. Tagore gave her a long look, then nodded to Alethia, and turned back to the Brothers. They stepped aside to let her pass, and she disappeared into the woods.

Grundel and Alethia exchanged glances. Alethia motioned for Tasmira to come forward. This, Tasmira knew, was her last chance. The Ursula had the final say. Galina, she remembered, had ignored the White Wolf and chosen Inyx to please Einar; Alethia could do the same. Tasmira looked over shyly to Grundel who watched her closely. Alethia motioned for Tasmira to stand at her side, and for a moment Tasmira's heart leapt wildly, but then Alethia gestured to Kyna.

"I give you Kyna, your new Ursula!" she announced in a stirring voice that resolutely echoed off the canyon walls. A roar overtook the echo as Grundel stepped forward to receive his mate. The bears parted, and The Keeper and the new Ursula left the Circle. The bears watched them until they disappeared into the forest, but in the semi-darkness of the evergreens, Grundel gestured to Kyna to stop for a moment, undetected; he wanted to assess Tasmira's reaction.

"Tasmira," Alethia said, "you now have the choice of mating or declining this season. Which do you choose?"

Tasmira looked warily around the Circle. She had been so certain of becoming the next Ursula that she had not paid attention to the mating, nor noticed who had waited, who held back. Gorath watched her carefully, and her indecision prompted him to rise and challenge, prompting her with a flourish. Vang too leapt to his feet with a few others.

"Sit down Gorath, Vang," said Alethia testily, "you are acting in haste." She turned to Tasmira. "Take your time," she said kindly.

Tasmira fought back her bitter disappointment, and tried to decide what was best, while her emotions played havoc. She glanced at Inyx who subtly nodded her head. Tasmira turned to Alethia. Standing upright, she threw her head back proudly, her golden, silky fur gleaming.

"I am ready to mate," she answered, her voice ringing clearly through the Circle. Immediately, Gorath, Vang and a few other Brothers leapt up and paired off. This was the final contest, the most important pairing, next to The Keeper's. Whoever mated Tasmira would be second in command. The canyon echoed the male roars, overpowering even the drumming. The older, veteran bears were expert fighters and fierce competitors. They drove one another back and forth in titan struggles. Two, three times Gorath held off his competitor until, finally, he found himself head to head with Vang, Rakor's twin, his final competitor. Rearing up on their hind legs, they were instantly locked in a test of towering strength. Although Vang was slightly smaller, he had years of experience over Gorath. At first, he out manoeuvred Gorath, tripping him, slashing him behind the knee so he fell heavily, but the younger bear's strength was enhanced by his intense desire, and each time he was thrown, he struggled back up. He was running out of ideas as to how to outsmart Vang when Kaare, his twin, roared at him. He gave him a quick glance and Kaare hugged himself and roared again. In order to win, Gorath realized, he had to use all his strength—his younger, rawer, brute force. He lunged at Vang, pulling him into a massive hug, and, although Vang broke free, Gorath could see that the older bear was struggling for breath. Before Gorath could do it again, Vang took him by surprise and Gorath fell hard, again scrambling back up before the older bear could do more damage. As the struggle swayed first one way then the other, their roars thundered through the canyon; their long claws swiped great red gouges down the sides of the other's body. The Brothers were hoarse from cheering, the drummers exhausted, but Vang and Gorath were in a violent, unrelenting deadlock. Finally, Tasmira's voice pierced the night.

"Enough," she roared, surprising even Alethia with her command. "Vang and Gorath may present their offering to me and I will choose." The males stopped, confused for a moment, then turned to Alethia, who nodded.

Vang turned to a Brother who handed him an intricately woven mat. It was a traditional sleeping mat both soft and strong, woven of muted marsh grasses in elaborate designs—a skill passed down through the generations. As Vang placed it in front of Tasmira, her eyes glowed in appreciation.

"It's beautiful, Vang," she said, "I am pleased." Vang had

the easy charm of his brother and mother, and he bowed low to her, with an intimate smile. Tasmira by then had regained her composure and was now carefully weighing the consequences of choosing one suitor over the other. Vang, Rakor's twin, had always been close to power, had been Rakor's second; he was older, wiser, more experienced, but Tasmira already felt a strong attraction to Gorath. The younger bear radiated energy, confidence and initiative. And he was close to the new leader.

"What do you offer, Gorath?" she asked, looking around, but no one passed him anything, and he stood empty handed. Gorath was dreading this moment. Suddenly Monk's idea seemed foolish beyond belief, and he cursed himself for not bringing a traditional gift. But now he had no choice; Tasmira would be deeply insulted if he offered nothing. And he would seem unprepared or arrogant. He surveyed his Brothers who looked around in embarrassment. They liked Gorath, knew how much he wanted Tasmira, and hated to see him fail the final test. Only Kaare, who was dubious, knew his plan. He shifted uneasily and looked around him. When he saw the doubt on everyone's face, especially Gorath's, he growled, snapping Gorath out of his thoughts and back to the moment at hand; then he nodded encouragingly to his twin.

"I bring the gift of words," Gorath said, lamely.

Tasmira looked at him in disbelief. "You mock me?"

"No, please hear me out. I bring the gift of poetry."

"Poetry—what's poetry?" the female asked haughtily. As a snicker ran through the Circle, and Alethia prepared to intercede, Gorath remembered Monk's admonishment: the only way to pull this off was to believe passionately—to speak from your heart. Gorath braced himself and let his desire for Tasmira fill his mind.

"If you will allow me," he said, "I will show you."

Tasmira nodded her head, bewildered. Risking not only the embarrassment but the searing mockery of his Brothers, Gorath stood and took a deep breath, letting his voice ring out clear and full and passionate.

"To Tasmira:
I know her by her wildness rare
Her snow white bands, her golden hair,
I know her by her rich silk dress,
And her perfect loveliness."

There was dead silence for a few moments, while Gorath bowed holding his breath. Suddenly, the bears roared their approval, laughing and slapping one another's back. Blushing, Tasmira turned to the Ursulas for advice, but they gave her blank stares, waiting for her reaction. In a moment of sheer brilliance, Tasmira rose to the occasion. The two Brothers stood facing her as she decided.

"I thank you, Vang, for your attentions and your lovely gift. You have fought long and hard and you honour me." Desolate, Gorath turned his eyes on Kaare, to avoid looking into Tasmira's, but then she went on. "But my choice is Gorath." A second roar went up. Vang bowed gallantly and stepped aside. Stunned, Gorath froze for a moment, until Kaare jumped up, slapped him on the back, and gave him a push towards Tasmira.

Food was brought out, the drumming recommenced, joyful now, lively and light-hearted. From the edge of the forest, after seeing Tasmira's disbelief and then her profound disappointment, Grundel saw also the swiftness of her decision, her generosity to Vang, her ability to open herself to Gorath's unusual yet compelling gift.

"As I thought," he said quietly. Kyna looked at him, but remained silent, and the two left.

The Keeper led his Ursula to a small cave in the mountain

where he had already laid a delicious meal. Kyna smiled when she saw it and thanked him. They lay in the mouth of the cave, learning to be at ease with one another, watching the moon's path throw patterns of ghostly light across the valley floor.

"I thought Alethia would choose Tasmira," said Kyna shyly, breaking the silence. Grundel smiled down at her.

"No," he replied gently. "The Ursula would not have chosen Tasmira tonight—even if you hadn't been such a strong obvious choice."

"Why do you say that? She's so smart and beautiful and confident. Alethia chose her to represent us on the Council. I figured then my chances were slim."

"Alethia chose her for the Council because she wanted to engage Tasmira in something positive, a taste for power that is measured by responsibility. And she shows great promise. But, for all her confidence, intelligence and, I must add generosity, her spirit is not pure enough to be Ursula."

"But she is quick and fearless."

"I don't doubt that, but she is too quick to rage."

"Sometimes rage gives us strength to do what we must do."

"Yes, but it can also blind us. However, she will make an excellent mate for Gorath. Now you—you have the heart of an Ursula!"

"How could you possibly know that already!" said Kyna, smiling shyly.

"Because Ursula thinks so, and she is never wrong."

"Your respect honours her," said Kyna thoughtfully, "I hope I will be able to deserve such respect."

THE DAYS passed peacefully. Grundel, enjoying himself immensely, put aside Cathedral and its pressing problems. He realized that he had not felt this free since Boris had died. It was the first time since his twin's death that he had talked this way—completely open. There was no need to hold back anything from Kyna; she needed to know everything he knew, just as he needed to know everything she knew. Their lives were intrinsically linked now. They were one. But it was not just their bond that made him feel so at ease. Kyna reminded him of Boris, gentle but forthright, open and inquisitive, especially about others. He felt totally at home, totally himself around her and hated to think of leaving this quiet, secluded spot, where they indulged their desires. But eventually both of them knew that it was time to return. Only Tagore, ranging across the hillside at dusk witnessed their last joyful romp, play fighting, rolling down the hills like two cubs, greedily feeding, then making their way back to the cave. The White Wolf trotted off, pleased with her choice.

The morning sun, peeking into the mouth of the cave, found the bears gone.

Finding Gulo

Kyna

GRUNDEL was not expecting the rush of excitement when he entered the main cavern. Piotr leapt to his feet. Vang, Gorath and his twin Kaare were also there, along with Monk and Mikaila, awaiting Grundel's return.

"Finally Grundel, you're back!"

"Ho there Piotr—what are you doing here? Why weren't you at the Sunados?" Grundel nudged him with his snout affectionately; Piotr was a favourite of his.

"Just wait till you hear! Call Mel first!" Piotr said, dancing about in anticipation.

"I'm here," Melancholia said, reappearing, but shimmering

in and out of vision for a few minutes. Grundel looked at her with a growing disquiet, but she waved his concern aside, turning to the younger bear. "Calm yourself Piotr—let's ask Grundel about the Sunados first."

"Oh, I'm sure that went fine," said Piotr, dismissing the subject, "it's just mating."

"Indeed," said Grundel, his smile returning, "one day soon, you will sing a different tune. If—."

"Tell him, Mel," interrupted Piotr, "or shall I?"

"Tell me what," asked Grundel, his smile fading. "What has happened?"

"We've found Rakor!" blurted Piotr, unable to restrain himself.

Grundel sighed deeply—Cathedral called again. He glanced around the cave, scowling, noting the odd look of confusion that crossed Vang's face.

"It's alright," Melancholia said, noticing his concern that Piotr had blurted out something he should have kept more private, "I have informed the others. It's time to take action."

"Ah," said Grundel, "good." After the others told Grundel all they knew, Melancholia nodded for Piotr to reveal the fact of Rakor's shape-shifting.

"Shape-shifting! I thought that was just legend," grunted Grundel. Murmurs and growls followed from every corner of the cave.

"No, not just legend, but it hasn't happened for eons," said Mel. "Mikaila and Piotr have witnessed Rakor's transformation, Grundel." When Grundel looked at her, Mikaila nodded. "They're pretty sure there are others with Rakor in the caves, but so far they've seen only him leave the cave, in the form of a great grey owl. I'll need to consult the Watchers to find out how this is possible," she added, absentmindedly, the event clearly troubling her. How could Rakor be shape-shifting? How had he remembered something she thought had been lost to the Keepers, if not the Ursulas, ages ago?

"In the meantime," added Grundel, "we'd better call a Council meeting and plan a strategy for infiltrating the Castle-guard Caves. We need to know who is with Rakor, and what he's doing." Melancholia agreed, heading off to the hoodoos for her own inquiries. There was more at stake than she was willing to share with the others, even Grundel.

THE COUNCIL MEETING was not going well. Everyone had a different idea about who should be sent to explore the cave; fear was feeding dissension; the atmosphere was thick and unpleasant, as if some evil presence was bending its dark wings invisibly over their shoulders, breathing its fiery breath, stoking trouble. Tasmira raised her commanding voice over the hubbub of the others.

"You know who we should get to explore the caves," she said, turning to Grundel, making a declaration rather than posing a question.

"Who?" challenged Aquila, haughtily.

"It's obvious," Tasmira continued, "Gulo."

"Who's Gulo?" whispered Monk to Bighorn.

"A very clever wolverine," he replied.

"And how might we do that?" scoffed Aquila, flapping her wings in agitation. "First you'd have to find him, which is almost impossible, then you'd have to persuade him to do something for the good of the community," she laughed scornfully. A ripple of sardonic laughter moved through the room. "And then you'd have to trust him! I think not."

"It's the right choice, Grundel," said Tasmira, ignoring Aquila. "Who would be better to pass undetected in the area and in the caves? Nobody sees Gulo if he doesn't want to be seen. Even if Rakor spotted him, he wouldn't suspect anything; Gulo is nocturnal, always exploring—he's one of the few who could actually manage the caves—he would be perfect."

"She's right about that," agreed Bighorn.

Grundel snorted, and sat back, considering.

"But Aquila has a point," Kaare interceded. "Who could approach and persuade Gulo—even if we could find him?"

Grundel nodded. He looked around the room, but every face was blank, shoulders shrugged; Gulo had few friends in this company. Vang, he noticed, looked away when he caught his eye. This troubled The Keeper, but he set it aside for now. No one seemed to have an answer; they were all familiar with Gulo's reticence, his desire for anonymity, his insistence on being left alone. They just couldn't see him helping, but neither could they come up with a better choice. They recognized the brilliance of Tasmira's suggestion. The meeting went silent as everyone considered how to tackle this immediate problem. Grundel was on the verge of breaking up the meeting when Mikaila finally spoke up.

"Perhaps," she said quietly, "I could."

"Really," said Aquila, dismissively, "how so?"

"Well, Gulo might think he's in my debt."

"How extraordinary!" replied the golden eagle, sizing the woman up and down with her piercing eyes. "Why would he think that?"

"Well, not long ago, I was working in the meadows when I heard a distress call. I followed the cry and soon came upon a trap, an iron cage. There were two young wolverine kits in it. Gulo suddenly appeared, also drawn by the distress call of the frantic mother. He didn't say anything, just looked at me most distrustfully, but he didn't disappear. I motioned towards the cage, and the mother nodded her head. It was a complex mechanism, but one I had seen before, so I was able to release the youngsters. They took off like a flash, but Gulo stopped, and looking over his shoulder, thanked me."

"But even if Mikaila could persuade him, can we trust him!" Aquila blurted out.

"She's a fine one to talk!" whispered Bighorn to Monk. Aquila whirled to face him.

"Not only do I see well—I also hear well, Bighorn. Do you have a problem?" The eagle was bristling with barely contained anger, her yellow eyes blazing.

"Well," snorted Bighorn, his own anger flaring, "trust isn't something you should judge in others, Aquila! Remember your reaction when Grundel asked for your help at Wicked River!"

"Not now, Bighorn," interrupted Grundel, "we have pressing matters. Let that be, for goodness sake. Mikaila, I think this is worth trying."

"One more thing, Grundel," added Mikaila, "the trap that caught the wolverine kits was the kind to keep animals alive and unharmed."

"Indeed," said Grundel, pausing thoughtfully and quickly seeing its significance. "Aquila, we will need you to spot Gulo. We need to get into the caves undetected—and soon."

"Fine, expect the impossible from me by all means," Aquila said, ruffling her wings and glaring at Bighorn.

"All right, let's get on this," Grundel declared, rising; he nodded dismissal and everyone dispersed.

"Vang," said Tasmira as she was leaving, "you're to come with me. The Ursulas need you." Grundel looked up surprised; it was the first he had heard of this. But when Vang looked to him, he just nodded.

Hoodoos

FOR HER PART, Melancholia left to contact Semjaza and Armaros at the hoodoos; something still troubled her, something that just didn't fit. The afternoon sun caught the tips of the limestone columns as she appeared on the front shelf of Semjaza's hoodoo.

He floated out to greet her, this time wearing a soft, white wool robe that rippled in the wind.

"Melancholia, always a pleasure," he said, raising his angel wings in respect. The Watchers had lived among the inhabitants of the Shining Mountains for millennia, ever since they had left their home-world to mate with the daughters of men. Melancholia gazed fondly at the younger Watcher. *How elegant he is,* she thought, *commanding yet open, terrifying yet exquisite. No wonder Earth women have fallen for him through the centuries.*

Just then, the older Watcher, Armaros, stepped out onto his ledge, raising his wings; Mel nodded in return and he flew over to Semjaza's ledge.

"What brings you to the Watchers? You are well I trust?" inquired Semjaza, smiling graciously.

"As well as can be expected," Melancholia answered, stepping over to make room for Armaros. The angels looked at one another and something passed between them. They communicated telepathically; although, they chose on Earth to speak aloud to others. Their speaking voices were rich yet subtle, full of complex tones; Melancholia often wondered what their silent speech must be like.

"Understandable," said Sem. "I don't envy your current state."

"Speaking of which—I've come about Rakor."

The angels waited for her to continue, as they seldom offered anything unasked. They had learned not to interfere with life on the Icefield, unless approached. Even then, they chose when and how to intercede carefully. They would not jeopardize their welcome in their adopted community.

"I just want to know how he is shape-shifting," Melancholia added, watching for their reactions. The angels exchanged inscrutable glances. "I've lost my sight, not my mind," she continued. "I suspect it has something to do with SaMäel. Am I right?" Again the response was a cool exchange of glances. But when she silently pleaded, her whole body shimmering with stress, Semjaza, the more compassionate of the two, nodded in accord.

"Will you offer anything else in the way of explanation?" Melancholia pleaded.

"No, I'm afraid that's not possible," said Armaros. "Now if you will be so good as to excuse me," and giving Semjaza a severe look, he returned to his hoodoo.

Semjaza folded his arms and waited patiently, but Mel didn't leave. Finally, he laughed and said, "Oh, all right—come in," and ushered Melancholia into his home. Inside the hoodoo was a warm, golden glow; soft silks billowed on invisible currents of warm sea air; there were pillows to recline on, a low table with crystal filled with ephemeral liquids and elegant manuscripts; and the room hummed softly with a chorus of angelic voices. It was a rare gift to be invited; Melancholia settled down into a pile of plush cushions.

"I feel so lost, Sem. I hate this sort of blindness, this not knowing. Please tell me anything about Rakor that will help me direct The Keeper."

Semjaza gave her a long look, then expelled a deep breath. "You have me at a disadvantage," he said, grinning. "Armaros will not be amused, but I cannot resist a beautiful woman, even a spiritual one, although, as you well know, I prefer Earth's daughters." Mel waved this aside. "Oh, all right, as you suspected, it is SaMäel. Rakor and he have made some sort of pact. Mind you, I don't have the whole story."

"So SaMäel taught him how to shape-shift?"

"It appears so, yes."

"Is SaMäel here—is he watching us?"

Semjaza said, "Not to my knowledge. He was, but he got what he wanted, and he's back in Abadon."

"What did he want?" she asked, alarmed.

Semjaza shook his head, unconsciously looking around for Armaros. "I fear I have given you too much information already. And to be frank, I really don't know."

"You wouldn't care to find out for me, would you?" she asked.

Semjaza laughed lightly in response. "No, sorry, I don't go to Abadon unless I'm desperate. I'm not fond of fire."

As Mel knew, Abadon—home planet of SaMäel—was a fiery realm, full of seething passions and lustful abandon; a realm bubbling with volcanic energy. After SaMäel's fall, the Watchers had helped him heal. In gratitude, the dark angel had invited them to Abadon. But they kindly and wisely declined his invitation, explaining that they wished to remain near their Earth mates. Their relationship with the dark angel was made more tenuous as SaMäel was insulted at their refusal, although he understood their reason. Currently, neither angel had an Earth mate. They were hoping SaMäel would not notice. Semjaza did not want to bring attention to himself by visiting Abadon.

"I understand," Mel replied. "But if a few of us need an enchantment to get us into Abadon, would you teach one?"

"I might," answered Semjaza, "but you must promise not to get caught and tell SaMäel who taught you."

"Then it will have to be a very good enchantment," countered Melancholia.

"I'll start working on it right away," he answered, smiling ruefully.

Mel thanked him and returned to Cathedral somewhat comforted.

THE BROTHERS, out on their rounds, were not expected back to Cathedral any time soon, so The Ursula, who had been in conference with The Keeper, was surprised when Kaare entered the Keeper's Cave, scruffy, bleeding, with great tufts of hair missing.

"What happened to you?" gasped Kyna, exiting the Map Den. Grundel followed her.

"A rogue—a brute," answered Kaare, dropping to the floor of the cave. Kyna rummaged around for a compress of moss, dipping it into the spring water.

"Where?'

"Near Angel Lake."

"Angel Lake! Is Mikaila there?'

"No," interrupted Grundel, "she's working at the Meadows. But Raven said that while out feeding he saw Monk there, fishing for their supper. Which direction did the rogue come from, Kaare?"

"Piotr saw him in the south west quadrant a couple of days ago. I was checking it out. I found him further north in Ravenwood, but when I confronted him and told him to keep moving, he attacked."

"With so little provocation?" asked Kyna, swabbing Kaare's wounds.

"Like I said—a real brute."

"Are you well enough to return?" asked Grundel. Kaare nodded. "Gorath is nearest. Raven!" Raven glided into the cave. "Find Gorath—he's in the Listening Mountains near the Hoodoos. Quickly. Tell him to meet Kaare at Ravenwood. There's a rogue."

MONK, meanwhile, was fishing in a quiet spot where the Chaba River ran into Angel Lake. After making his way downstream, lured by the shadows in the dark pools, hoping to find a bountiful supply of rainbow trout for their supper, he had stopped where the forest was pushed back revealing a small green opening; the spring sun shone brighter there. He now sat on a large worn rock at the river's edge, the current curving into a lodgepole forest in the distance. The sun shone warm on his face. Beside him an ancient pine leaned into the water as if reaching for the fat trout just below the glittering surface. Monk had a respectable catch beside him, but decided that he would try for one more trout before heading back to the cabin. It was peaceful

by the river, with the birds chirping and insects humming—
and the fishing distracted him from depressing thoughts.

Monk was so still that Gulo, coming out of the forest into
the opening, didn't notice him at first, despite his sharp eyes.
Wolverines move swiftly, but Gulo went from full stride to a
dead stop when Monk shifted positions. His low growl startled
Monk, who looked up. When he realized it was Gulo, he smiled
broadly; one did not often get to see the wolverine so close.

"Care for a fish?" Monk offered, hoping he could keep
Gulo from disappearing, to invite him to speak to Grundel.
Gulo eyed him suspiciously. In his experience there were two
kinds of humans: one gentle and generous, the other cruel and
dangerous. "I don't know if fish appeals to you today—but it's
all I have," added Monk. Gulo nodded. He wasn't picky with
his food and a free meal was always appreciated. Monk threw
him a fish, but it landed just short of where Gulo stood. The
wolverine hesitated. He recognized Monk as the human who
was sometimes with Grundel and sometimes with Mikaila,
both of whom he trusted. He decided to take a chance, and
grabbing the fish he sat down on his haunches to eat it, cautiously eyeing Monk. Suddenly, from behind Monk, a bear
appeared out of the forest. Gulo looked up and leapt to his feet,
but didn't back away. The bear snorted loudly.

"You may have one too," called Monk over his shoulder,
keeping his eyes on Gulo. "But only one, I'm treating Mikaila
tonight. Look who I—." As he turned to toss the grizzly a fish,
he realized that this was no Keeper. The Brothers were large,
healthy, with rich heavy fur bred for the Icefield. This bear was
scruffy and gaunt, his matted fur from which large tufts were
missing was clotted with dry blood. He had a hard wildness
indifferent to anything but raw hunger, now focused intensely
on Monk.

The bear rose, clacking his teeth and pawing the air. Then, dropping down, it slung its head low and with ears cocked, and the hair of his ruff standing on end, he lunged at Monk. Mesmerized by the brute force, the raw unleashed power, Monk froze. His legs went numb; his mind, cold, blank. The only thought that he could retrieve was one of fear: that this was the end—this was how death came.

But, before the rogue could reach him, Gulo hurled himself in front of Monk, blocking the bear's access, growling ferociously. The rogue veered wildly at the last moment. Terrified, Monk watched both wolverine and bear circling one another. He stood up and frantically threw a fish at the bear.

"Here—take this. Take it all. Just let us get out of your way." The bear paused, then grabbed the fish, stuffing it into his mouth, spitting out spine. Monk threw him another one. Gulo growled menacingly, showing his teeth. Slowly backing away from the bear and the river's edge, Monk looked around for an escape route. But although the wilderness closed in on all sides, he could not see even a decent tree to climb. He realized how careless he had become—acting like he was part of the wilderness, forgetting that, even more than this rogue bear, he was an intruder, an outsider who was about to pay for his carelessness and presumption.

Fish gone, the bear pawed the ground, eyeing Gulo, then eyeing Monk behind him.

"There's fish in the river and insects under that log. You don't need us," Monk gestured wildly. Trying to gain some control, he slowly drew a knife out of his belt. "Let's not make this necessary."

When the bear's ears perked up, Monk knew he was in trouble. The bear roared a warning challenge, then paused. Unexpectedly, Gulo wheeled around, turning his back on the rogue. Confused, Monk spun too—behind him Kaare and

Gorath had bounded into the clearing. The Brothers reared, roaring an answer to the rogue's challenge. Monk could see that the rogue was considering taking on both Brothers—reckless and aberrant behaviour; he inched back slowly, out of the line of attack. After a long moment of eyeing the two healthy bears, the rogue dropped on all fours and lumbered off, turning repeatedly to protest his displeasure. Monk turned to thank Gulo, but the wolverine had gone.

"Get to the cabin and stay there until we get back," Gorath called, over his shoulder to Monk, as the Brothers loped after the stranger. When the rogue realized the Brothers were following, he stopped, stood his full height, and roared his anger. But the Brothers were unmoved. As the rogue dropped back on all fours and headed north, the Brothers picked up their pace, steadily driving him out of the territory. Monk turned upriver, still shaken, trying to convince himself that perhaps he could continue his fishing in closer proximity to the cabin, and still rescue Mikaila's supper.

Gulo's Tale

THE NEXT DAY began clear and bright; a cool wind blew off the ice. Torrents of melt-water roared happily through the channels in the ice, emerging many miles away as a rushing stream at the toe of a glacier. The roan mare, Equus, who had been with Mikaila since she was a little girl, had just dropped her and Monk at Cathedral's ledge. Mikaila stroked the small, powerful horse, thanking her. Long ago, Armaros had brought the horse from Xeni, west of the mountains. Equus was the strongest and fastest of the Cayuse ponies. He could travel any terrain sure-footed, which was what Armaros had wanted for the women. Semjaza, to his credit, had added a few enchantments, giving the horse the ability to fly.

Monk knocked the snow off his boots from habit; Mikaila nodded to Aquila who was sitting in Raven's spot on the lip of the cave's entrance.

"I wonder which direction that melt-water will take," mused Mikaila, gazing over the dazzling Icefield, "and where it will end up?" She was pointing to the water glistening at its source on the summit of Snow Dome. "What a journey it has just started! That water could end up in any of three great oceans!"

"How so?" asked Monk. "I thought watersheds only ran in two directions."

"Not Snow Dome's — its water runs in three directions — east, west or north."

"Huh," grunted Monk as he went inside.

"It's so raw, so true up here," added Mikaila.

"But still you prefer your green meadows?" murmured

Aquila, keeping her sharp eyes scanning the Icefield.

"Not necessarily, the Icefield has a majestic beauty—enticing, enchanting. But I admit the meadows are more hospitable for humans."

Just then Raven flew over, landing beside Aquila. Mikaila had to smile; he was obviously trying awfully hard to befriend the eagle.

"May I help you look for Gulo, Aquila?" he asked, hopefully.

"Perhaps," Aquila replied coolly, continuing to survey the area. "Are you familiar with Gulo and his habits?"

"No," replied Raven, bluntly but honestly.

"Then you wouldn't be much help, would you!" she declared, rolling her eyes at Mikaila. Raven was not put off so easily.

"Come on, Aquila. I can be useful. No one pays much attention to me—I'm the perfect spy."

Aquila eyed him thoughtfully. "Perhaps you are. Very well, follow me, but keep up. I don't have time to coddle you." Before Raven could protest, Aquila continued, "I have a pretty good idea where Gulo will be today. You will return to Mikaila after I spot him. I won't be able to take my eyes off him for a second. If he thinks we're tracking him, he'll go underbrush and then we'll never find him." With a great sweep of her wings, Aquila launched herself off the ledge effortlessly, with Raven scrambling behind.

"Stay here Mikaila; Raven will come for you," Aquila called back on the wind.

Just as Mikaila was wondering how she would get down off the mountain quickly, if she should call back Equus, Grundel joined her on the ledge.

"I'll take you," he said, reading her thoughts. "I could use the run. Sitting waiting isn't the easiest thing for me to do either. Too many things on my mind, I guess." He looked worried.

"What's up?"

"I'm not sure—I'm worried about Vang. He looks gaunt these days, like something is eating away at him. But he won't talk. And he's seldom here." Grundel turned towards her, shaking off his thoughts. "But that's not your concern and I don't mean to burden you with mine. Aquila won't take long. The rest of us would have a hard time finding Gulo, but she has plenty of knowledge that she keeps to herself. And there isn't much she misses from her lofty perspective!" Grundel added.

They stood in comfortable silence for a while, watching the dazzling light refract off the ice. It danced and bobbed, appearing and disappearing, as if it were alive.

"I knew your mother—Faida wasn't it?" said Grundel, out of the blue. "Well, at least, we spoke a few times. I liked her."

Mikaila nodded, "I know. She told me. That's why I wasn't frightened on Snow Dome."

"She was from one of the great islands, wasn't she? How did she ever end up here?"

"It's a long story but eventually a biologist from Switzerland rescued her from a hard life on Iceland. He was an adventurer who travelled the world collecting specimens for museums. My mother had always been interested in flora and had an extensive collection when he arrived in her community. Eighteen, bold, with little to lose—she approached him one day when they were both out on the same meadow. When she revealed her knowledge of the place and showed him her collection, he was impressed. They worked together for months before he decided to move on—he wanted to see the Shining Mountains if he could get to them. She asked to go with him. He managed to get her aboard the ship as cook's helper. They worked here for a few years until he wanted to move on again. She didn't. She said she had formed too many ties to this place—she wanted to stay. So she remained at Angel Lake in the cabin and workshop they had built together."

"Your home."

"Yes."

Mikaila fell silent, remembering when she was sixteen and her mother had told her this story. She had asked, then, if he was her father, but her mother had said no. It had taken courage to ask—who then?

"It's not yet time to tell you," was all her mother would say.

"But why not?" she had whispered.

"Because you are not yet old enough to understand." Mikaila was puzzled, disappointed, and even a little angry at the time. Her mother, Faida, had tried to soften the harsh truth. "I'll tell you on your 18th birthday, Mika, I promise." She had reached out her arms and asked Mikaila not to let this come between them. Mikaila went to her willingly—their companionship was too important to risk conflict.

Growing up, there weren't many humans in Mikaila's life— her mother was a recluse. Periodically they would go to Hilda Creek to trade for supplies and Mikaila would speak to Hilda, the owner of the outfitter and trading post, whom she liked. But her mother always hurried back to Angel Lake before Mikaila had a chance to get to know the few children of the guides, like Rachel. As a child, Mikaila didn't find this reclusiveness strange because it was all she knew. Her companions were the small animals and birds that she befriended, and her mother.

Even as a small child she had loved to watch the ravens playing, watching them dropping twigs or feathers from a great height and then retrieving them after about 12 metres, doing this over and over. She would watch patiently, laughing and clapping, until the ravens got to know and trust her. Then they allowed her to slide down snowbanks with them. The birds going first, feet first, all of them squealing. In the summer, after the small animals had emerged from their winter homes, she had no lack of companions.

She and her mother lived simply, rising with the sun, collecting the flora during the summer months, and then documenting their findings during the long winter. Days were filled with gardening, studying, preparing food, and many crafts to enhance their survival. A couple of times they took a trip east to a city where her mother visited the museum she worked for and delivered their findings; although they kept a second set of records and specimens for themselves. These trips were highlights in Mikaila's simple life, filled with excitement, stimulation, learning. But as much as she loved them, like her mother, she couldn't wait to get back to the peace of the mountains.

Mikaila could not help feeling a thrill of anticipation as her 18th birthday approached. It was May and although the mountains were still snow covered, the valleys were lush with new green growth. The two women had decided to make a day of it—to follow the river to see what blossoming spring flowers they could find this year along its bank. They had been unusually silent for a while and Mikaila wondered if now her mother would tell her—something was obviously weighing heavily on her mind. But before Faida had a chance to speak, the fragile ice she had been standing on broke from the shore's edge; Faida, in a shocking second, was swept into a swiftly moving channel—terrified, she had yelled "Armaros" as she lost her balance, fell and disappeared under the ice floes. Mikaila had frantically whistled for Equus hoping to fetch Armaros to save her, but it was already too late.

Grundel broke into her memories. "When she was here alone, was she never lonely? Don't humans need one another?"

"I was born not long after the biologist left. She said I was all she needed."

"You two seemed at peace." Mikaila shook off the lethargy brought on by despair that always accompanied the memory of her mother's death.

"We were content. We had one another and our work. I miss her." Mikaila stopped, fighting back tears. "I almost left after she died, but really, where would I go? This is my home. And I wanted to continue the work we had shared for so many years."

"I would be interested in seeing your collection, Mikaila."

"Certainly, Grundel, anytime—it would be my pleasure. As I said, we kept two records—one for the museum and one for ourselves. Were you aware that once in a while Boris helped Mother? After her death he would sometimes visit me. I remember talking about the delicate mats of River Beauty, one of my favourites, and our shared amazement at how it survives here. He found glacier lilies for me and rare lichen."

"I didn't know," replied Grundel, "but it doesn't surprise me." For a while, they again fell silent.

"Mother and I," mused Mikaila, "would go months without seeing other people. In winter, we hardly ever went to the settlement. Sometimes I thought she preferred angels to people—we saw more of the Watchers than any human. Mother even avoided Monk and his family, although I was very curious about them. But she was always sociable with the animals, when they let her. Oh look—is that Raven coming back?" She pointed to a black dot quickly growing bigger.

"Probably," said Grundel, whose eyesight, no better but no worse than hers, prevented him from seeing it in detail. "You have to admire someone who could converse with Armaros—he's one tough hide!'

Mikaila chuckled, "I know what you mean, but we saw a

side of Armaros most never see. He can be very considerate, kind, generous. I don't think we would have survived here, in the beginning, without him. He taught us so much."

"Like enchantments?" chuckled Grundel.

"Oh no!" laughed Mikaila, "Mother had no interest in that—she was all practical scientist. Besides, it's Semjaza who teaches enchantments; Armaros teaches how to disenchant—which was probably why he and Mother got along. She liked things in their natural state."

"What about you—" began Grundel, but he was interrupted by Raven who, having braked too late, over-flew the ledge and crashed into the grizzly.

"Whoops," said Raven, dusting off his satin black wings, "sorry Grundel, not used to this speed. Aquila has spotted Gulo—he's sleeping in Wild Wood. I'll meet you at the log bridge." And he flew off again at breakneck speed.

"Hop on Mikaila, and hang on. I'm going to take you down the back. I know a short cut to the Wood." As Grundel knelt, Mikaila climbed onto his broad back gingerly, not sure what to grasp.

"Just sink your hands into the fur on my neck ridge—you can't hurt me. How do you stay on Equus?"

"Basically, I just use pressure from my knees to hold on."

"Good, same thing here. Are you settled? You're as light as a feather."

Mikaila grabbed hold of Grundel's coarse, long neck hair hoping she wasn't hurting him, and he took off at a loping gait, a pace he kept all the way down the mountain. They made good time across the meadows. Away from the Icefield, the summer heat intensified, releasing the fragrance of wild flowers, juniper, mixed with Grundel's musty scent. Mikaila's body began to relax into Grundel's rhythm.

Raven joined them at the bridge. "He's still there. He's sleeping in the north east corner. This way," said Raven excitedly. It was a pine wood; a forest floor cushioned with a deep layer of decaying needles and cones. They made their way silently, stepping carefully over the fallen spruces' grey spiky limbs. Gulo—who had killed, gorged himself and stashed the rest, covering it with his musk so no one would take it—was sleeping in the heat of the midday sun, tucked under a rotting log that rested against an outcropping of granite. As they approached, the wolverine leapt to his feet. His brown fur shimmered in the sun; its golden streaks down his sides and across his brow gilded his small but powerful body, now poised to leap into flight or stand and fight.

"Wait!" screeched Aquila from her perch. Gulo, startled, glanced up, wary of both the golden eagle above him and the approaching footfalls. "They need to talk to you, Gulo. Don't disappear—it's important."

"Perhaps to them, but I doubt it's important to me," growled Gulo.

"Look," said Aquila, "it's Mikaila. You trust her don't you? She saved your little ones, didn't she?" Gulo was already slinking off, but he turned to see if Aquila was telling the truth.

"C'mon Gulo—you owe her. That's The Keeper with her."

Gulo jumped up onto the rock to get a better look and to be eye level with Grundel, Aquila thought, admiring the quick thinking. Standing on top of the outcrop, the wolverine was a small version of the grizzly—similar shape, colouring and bright intelligence.

"Good afternoon, Gulo," Mikaila began, formally. Gulo nodded, wary of Grundel who had bent down to let Mikaila slip off his back, then remained crouched to appear less fearsome. "Grundel and I were hoping to speak with you."

"What about?" asked Gulo suspiciously, casting furtive glances from one to the other.

"We've come to ask you a favour," Mikaila replied, squatting cross-legged on the moss.

"I make no allies," grumbled Gulo, and he began to slink backwards off the rock.

"We're not asking you to, Gulo," replied Grundel, raising his voice slightly and adding a note of authority, "you are free to say no, but listen first. This involves all of us."

Gulo hesitated, his instincts telling him to leave now, but his sense of fairness making him reluctant to turn his back on Mikaila. "I'll listen, but no promises. I stay only because of her."

"Understood," replied Grundel.

THE SUN was rimming the mountains, shedding a soft alpenglow, melding from copper to bronze by the time Mikaila and Grundel finished recounting the problems facing Cathedral. The golden eagle perched silently throughout, still sceptical about trusting the wolverine. Raven, hopping about on a low branch, couldn't help noticing Gulo's powerful chest and front legs—he wouldn't want to meet him in a dark cave. The wolverine was also silent throughout, just nodding periodically to let them know that he understood. Finally, he spoke.

"So, basically, you want me to investigate the Castleguard Caves, even though they're forbidden, and see what Rakor's up to—is that it?"

Mikaila looked at Grundel then back to Gulo. "Yes," she replied.

"What makes you so sure I'd go into the caves?" There was an awkward silence. Gulo snorted roughly. "What's in it for me?"

Aquila guffawed from her perch. "I told you so," she said haughtily. Grundel glared at her.

But Gulo was unruffled. "Word has it, you're pretty self-interested yourself, Aquila. I repeat, what's in it for me?"

"To be truthful," said Grundel, "I can't think of a thing, except the knowledge that we all respect your talents."

"And the fact that we need you," piped Raven, who liked to be needed.

"And think of all the creatures—powerful creatures—who will be in your debt," added Mikaila. That hit home with Gulo; he paused, thinking. When he looked up, he caught Mikaila's gaze, steady and believing. He could almost see a kind of shadow around her. He snorted loudly. Turning to Grundel, he announced, "I won't make this a habit—and you must not tell anyone!"

"There can be no secrets amongst us—there're a lot of creatures involved. But I'll not go out of my way to say what you've done. Is that still a yes?"

Gulo drew a deep breath, releasing it slowly. He was surprising even himself. "All right, but nothing long term—just in and out."

"Agreed," said Grundel. "Thank you."

"Don't thank me yet—you might not like what I find in Castleguard."

Aquila and Raven exchanged glances, wondering if the wolverine already knew something they didn't.

Gulo decided to get the job done before he regretted his decision. *She's a clever one, that Mikaila*, he thought, trotting along the edge of the wood, just inside its shadows to travel unnoticed. *But there's something odd about her.* He let this thought go, promising himself to return to it later. He already knew that Rakor was in the caves, which is why he had avoided them lately. You don't mess with grizzlies in confined spaces. He realized

Rakor was up to something when he saw him shape-shifting, but Gulo tended his own business.

The Castleguard Caves were ghostly places at the best of times, a network of underground passages carved out of lime-stone by surging melt-water. One and a half million years old, the caves were capable of great violence at any moment when runoff swept through the chambers drowning anything in its path. They were dark and rank smelling at the best of times. Usually Gulo didn't have to worry about anyone else; the taboo that hung over the caves was firmly rooted, passed on to each generation for as long as anyone could remember. But Gulo's line had always explored the caves, making the damp darkness their own, charting the labyrinthine pathways, burying all sorts of things in their depths. Over the years, some of them had died in flash floods in the caves, but even this did not stop the wolver-ines from entering.

What Gulo also knew, that the others apparently did not, was that a human named Malenger was also coming and going secretively from the caves. On a nightly prowl, Gulo had entered what he thought was an empty entrance, to discover as he passed through an invisible veil that there were traces of humans in the cave's entrance. He had quickly backed up, only to see an empty cave again. Passing through the veil a number of times, he realized that there was an enchantment in front of the caves' entrance, the Rivergate. From the outside, everything seemed normal, the entrance empty. Only once he crossed the enchantment's threshold could he see what was actually there. He didn't like the smell of humans, nor the underlying smell of bear. For a while after that, he had avoided the caves.

Now, waiting patiently in the wood to the left of the River-gate, he saw Malenger slip out. He growled quietly, deep in his throat. He despised Malenger for the chaos he inflicted with his traps, for all the fear and death. Gulo often tracked Malenger, watching while the man set his traps. Wolverine fur was especially desirable to men because of its resistance to freezing, its lushness and glossy colour. Wanting to observe how Malenger set the trap, he watched carefully so he could spring it later, but he wasn't always successful and numerous times he almost trapped himself. Too often he came across wolverines and other animals trapped and dying, but could not figure out how to free them because Malenger had devised another cunning alteration, staying one step ahead of Gulo's best efforts.

It was, in fact, Malenger's involvement that had prompted Gulo, finally, to agree to help—he wanted revenge for all of Malenger's killings, but he was not about to tell the others. *Let them think I've become pathetically altruistic*, thought Gulo, grinning. *What do they know? Let them be in my debt.*

The wolverine lay in a hollow, sheltered by a tangle of brush and a canopy of branches, waiting for night to deepen. He waited patiently until he saw Rakor leave the cave and transmute into a great grey owl. He assumed that this was how Rakor was feeding and estimated that he would have enough time to make a quick appraisal of the caves. Malenger, he knew, after laying traps in Furtive Folk Valley, would most likely spend the night in his cabin.

Gulo entered Castleguard's Caves slowly, not wanting any surprises. The entrance cavity was large and a glacial stream trickled down its centre. The limestone walls were pocked with ice formations. Some light filtered in here, but a tunnel led deeper into darkness. Gulo waited for his eyesight to adjust. The tunnel had bear paw, owl and foot prints in the wet sand. Gulo took it. It was dark and musty; he heard the sound of running water, but he could also hear an unfamiliar sound, a faint chink, chink of metal on stone from deep within. He hesitated, wondering if he was falling into a trap, but went on determinedly, noting the smaller side tunnels he could use later if necessary. Expecting darkness, Gulo was surprised to discover that someone had created lanterns to light the way. He studied them, but could not fathom their device. Suddenly he heard voices and darted into a side tunnel, flattening himself on the rocky floor. Two men carrying rifles slung over their backs passed by without a glance in his direction.

Greenhorns, thought Gulo, *if they hadn't been smoking, they would have smelled me.* He crawled to the entrance and watched their backs disappearing. He could still hear their high, rasping voices.

One of them said, "We better hurry and git back to the entrance. Malenger'll have a fit if we're not there when he gits back."

The other drawled, "Ah—there ain't no rush—he'll stay overnight at the cabin. I'm tired of sitting there with nothing to do but shoot at anything that moves. Nobody said we couldn't explore the caves a little and see if there's anything in them. Maybe we'll find gold, eh?"

After that, Gulo lost the words. He hurried forward, wondering what lay ahead and how he was going to get past those two on the way out. There were two entrances to the caves— this southern entrance and a north facing one, but it had great, gushing springs of freezing water, and the water level never receded. In fact, Gulo knew, this was the only way out. He had a long way to go. He'd been climbing steadily, but suddenly the tunnel ended at a vertical shaft about eight metres deep, the first of the obstacles that kept others out. Gulo climbed carefully, remembering the footholds he had been taught. Further on, the ceiling dropped drastically with overhanging ice so that he had to crawl under it—the Ice Crawl his mother had called it.

Two kilometres in he came to another vertical shaft, The Drop, only this one was even higher, but here too he knew the footholds. He was now entering the central part of the cave system. It was warmer and safer here because the groundwater that had once carved this system now flowed on a lower level. He picked up speed in The Eye, a circular tunnel that ran straight as an arrow for five hundred metres. At the end he met one of the toughest obstacles in the caves, The Fissure—a long, deep canyon whose narrow floor was so broken up that Gulo had to traverse its sloping walls or leap from block to block of wedged, fallen rock. The walls of the canyon were rough and damaged the pads of his feet as he slipped and clung to its side.

By this time Gulo was tiring, but he still had a difficult section to traverse before he reached his destination. He stopped to catch his breath, eyeing The Trench ahead—a wickedly deep trench with only steep columns of clay to use as stepping stones across it. He had to leap from clay column to clay column, knowing only his forward momentum would keep him from falling down, down into the muddy trench far below. It was his least favourite part of the caves—as a youngster he had almost lost his life here, slipping on the slick clay. Only his mother's quick thinking and immense strength had saved him. He looked up at a waterfall that entered the trench through an overhead shaft, creating a thunderous shower, and took his first mighty leap.

Finally, he stood at an entrance to another large cavern, the loveliest part of the caves, The Grotto—a vaulted cave with pure white dazzling calcite deposits on the ceiling and walls, like sleek, hanging straws. There were four tunnels radiating from the cavern. Deep cuts in the limestone formed shelves on the walls, and overhead stalactites hung like crystal pointed swords. There was a large slab of rock balanced on stacks of flat rocks and used as a table in the centre, covered haphazardly with maps and drawings and figures. A small girl, a short haired ermine, and a young marmot were kneeling on the table, all filthy and scrawny, bent over the maps, whispering quietly but fervently to each other. Gulo could hear the chink, chink of metal on stone much louder now, more insistent, but still deeper in the tunnels. There was a putrid smell in the room and the floor was littered with bones and decaying carcasses of small animals. As he moved into the cavity, the three looked up, startled.

"*Quiquahach!*" gasped the little girl, and she clutched the two animals into her protective arms. "Get out!" she yelled. "Go! Go away! Get!" The ermine tried to say something but her voice was muffled as her head was squashed up against the child's body. Gulo ignored the girl's yelling and spoke directly to the ermine.

"Tell her to relax, Mustela. I'm not hunting. I come from Cathedral."

The little girl looked down at Mustela who nodded her head.

"Gulo! What do you want?" said Mustela, shaking herself out. She hesitated for only a moment, and then jumped lightly off the table.

"Get back to your post, Whistler," she said, "we've been careless." The young marmot eyed the wolverine warily, then jumped down and circled slowly around to the entrance of the Grotto.

"How did you get in? Are those men gone?" asked the child, left alone on the table and trembling. She was thin and sickly. Her raven black hair hung in limp, unkempt strands and her dirty brown skin had a greyish hue. Gulo could smell death hovering around her.

"No," he replied, "I slipped passed them."

"They're so dumb," said Mustela, the ermine, flicking her tail, "they couldn't see a moose if it stood in front of them."

"Unless it moved," added Whistler.

"Yes," replied Mustela, "watch yourself because they've been told to shoot anything that moves. And believe me, they do."

"And they take a lot of pleasure doing it!' barked Whistler, from the entrance.

"I don't have much time, Mustela. I come from Grundel— tell me quickly what's happening here."

"Grundel?" asked Mustela, looking Gulo over carefully, "You?"

"It's a long story that I'm sure you'll hear later—numerous times."

"That should prove entertaining! Now—Rakor—."

"We know," said Gulo, "What's he doing?"

"Digging for something." Mustela hesitated. "He has us all trapped here, digging for him in these tunnels."

"All?" said Gulo, looking around.

"There are about twenty of us left now, I think—Malenger live-trapped some and Rakor caught others. You know about his shape-shifting?" she asked. Gulo nodded. "Look here on the map." She jumped back on the table. "Four small tunnels, only the Furtive Folk fit into them—marmots, ground squirrels, a few weasels, Whistler and me. We have the largest tunnel. It's terrible work. There's been so much death."

"Why are they using animals? Why are they working so slowly?"

She hesitated again. "Rakor says that it's work of an arch-archaeological nature—whatever that means—it has to be slow and deliberate and carefully executed. We are to report any-thing—*anything* we find. We're trapped here, Gulo. Some of us have been here forever. The two men at the entrance shoot anyone who tries to escape—not that there's much hope of that. The child, here—" she broke off as the marmot gave a high whistle and ran back from the entrance. Mustela shuffled the maps and then leapt off the table.

"Quickly," she said, "to the tunnel!" As the child began to climb weakly down, Mustela called to her urgently. The ermine hesitated then turned back to Gulo. "You'd better come with us." The wolverine looked around and then leapt onto a ledge.

"No," he called, "I can't afford to get trapped deeper in the cave. Go. I can look after myself."

"Gulo," called Mustela, fearful that she wouldn't have another chance, "tell Grundel—no one else mind you—that we found it." There was no time for questions; it was clear from the sound that something was close to the Grotto's mouth. With powerful leaps, Gulo was soon near the top of the high wall, where he flattened himself at the back of a shelf, out of sight.

SUDDENLY a great grey owl with a bear's strength flew into the cavern and dropped a man onto the floor. Picking himself up gingerly, the man threw the owl a dirty look.

"Will you get the two from the entrance?" he said, brushing himself off. "I need to frighten them a little. Give me a few minutes with them alone."

The great owl eyed him carefully for a moment, and then flew out. When the man turned around to pace, Gulo had to stop himself from growling—it was Malenger—a stocky, muscular man, with a broad face, deep set brown eyes and full lips. Obviously trying to control his temper, the man was muttering to himself. A little while later, the owl flew in with the two men from the entrance, dropping them unceremoniously, and then disappeared out the passage again.

"What—?" began the shorter man, looking around.

"Shut up!" growled Malenger.

"What's wrong?" said the taller one, eyeing Malenger, who had a nasty temper.

"Just smell it in here!"

"What? It smells like it always smells—gawd awful." He pushed back the cowboy hat on his head and thrust his hands deep into his pockets.

"What?" roared Malenger. "It friggin' reeks of wolverine! You're supposed to be keeping everything out." He reached out and grabbed the cigar from the man's mouth and threw it on the ground, crushing it with his foot. On his high perch, Gulo held his breath. "If you stopped smoking for five seconds, you might be able to do your job!"

The two men stepped back to avoid Malenger's blows. The taller man, Slank, was better looking than Malenger—with a mass of dark hair and a physique that attracted women—broad in the shoulders, trimmer in the hips. But his good looks were undermined by shifty eyes and a large droopy moustache that pulled down his finer features. Only in those rare moments when he was relaxed and smiling would you notice his good looks. He was a restless bundle of energy; a man with a fierce determination that all his life had found nothing on which to focus. His inability to grasp onto anything of significance embittered him. He was hoping that at last, with Malenger's help, he had found something of value, something that would make him rich, make him someone to reckon with. So he took the occasional blow without retaliating.

The other man, Payne, was Slank's opposite, a day dreamer who lacked even dreams. He was average height, but so skinny it looked like his baggy pants would fall off if it weren't for his suspenders. He had large ears and a rapidly receding hairline so he always wore a knitted toque, and he had a habit of scratching his head with the toque when he was puzzled or confused, which was often. He followed others mindlessly, content to have someone else think for him. Back home they called him Mongrel because he was always sniffing around what others had, like a mangy, lost dog. Now, he cowered at the expected blows and pushed his small cap nervously back and forth over his short hair, slinking behind Slank for protection. He had latched onto Slank in a bar in a rail town and had followed him into the mountains, never questioning what they were doing there. It hadn't taken Slank long to hitch up with Malenger.

"Honest, Malenger, nothing came into the caves," whined Payne, looking over Slank's shoulder.

"Right, that's why I can smell it in here."

"I don't know how you can smell anything in here with all the stinking animals," said Slank. The obvious attempt at distraction was transparent; Malenger glowered at him. He regretted pulling Slank into this business. Payne was easily manipulated, but Slank was different, more cunning and harder to control.

"Maybe the scent is coming in on the wind," Payne suggested.

"And maybe you're just an idiot!" retorted Malenger. "I thought I told you to put out that stinking cigar. Get back to the entrance and do your job! What am I paying you for anyway?"

"How?" asked Payne, horrified, glancing back at the tunnel. "You don't expect us to climb back to the entrance on our own do you?" Payne prodded Slank from behind.

Just as Slank began to join in the protest, there was a loud whooshing noise and a great flutter of grey white wings entered the cave. The great owl landed on the floor, dropped a ground squirrel from his talons and again transmuted into a huge, dark grizzly. The two men scurried to the back of the cavern.

"Look at them run with their tails between their legs! They're still terrified of you," scoffed Malenger.

"They should be," said Rakor offhandedly. "So should you."

"They need a lift," said Malenger. Rakor shifted shapes again with a snort, and swooping down on the cringing men lifted them effortlessly in outstretched talons.

When he returned, Rakor in grizzly form sat down pensively on the cavern floor. Malenger looked up from the maps on the table, into Rakor's stony face, shuffling nervously. The man was strong and had fought his way out of many tight spots with his fists, but Rakor made him feel small and vulnerable. He hitched his thumbs into the suspenders that he wore over a black shirt tucked into black wool pants, and set his wide brim hat further back on his head.

"Do you smell wolverine?" he asked, to divert Rakor's attention.

"As a matter of fact, yes," Rakor eyed the perimeter of the cave carefully. Gulo crouched even lower on his shelf.

"Should we be concerned?" Malenger looked up from the maps.

"That the two idiots you employed can't seem to do their job?" asked Rakor wryly.

"That something is in the caves," replied Malenger, ignoring the jibe.

"It's probably Gulo. He frequents these caves. When he spots those two at the entrance, he won't stick around. Gulo minds his own business."

"Well then, shall we get down to ours? Are you finally prepared to tell me what we're digging for?" asked Malenger, rubbing his hands together.

"Treasure, I told you," replied Rakor, mildly.

"Don't take me for a fool, Rakor. Bears don't dig for treasure."

A dark scowl crossed Malenger's already dour face.

"And what do you know about bears?" Rakor gave the man another stony look. Malenger bit back the words on his tongue, wondering what Rakor would do if he knew that Malenger had shot and killed Boris.

"I know enough to be certain that you're not interested in money—of any kind. What would you do with treasure?"

"Maybe it's not that kind of treasure," snapped Rakor, instantly regretting his careless remark. He eyed the rim of the cavern again.

"Really," drawled Malenger, rubbing his beard, "then why would I be interested? SaMäel did say I would be very interested."

SaMäel! thought the wolverine from his hidden perch. *Grundel won't like the sound of that.*

"Because I am infinitely knowledgeable about men—particularly your sort."

"How would you know anything about men?' replied Malenger, again ignoring the slur.

"You forget that I was educated by immortal spirits."

"So you say. But I see little evidence of that, except for SaMäel who seems to be no friend of yours."

"Yes—it's a pity you cannot see the other spirits—you have such limited perception. Why do you think that is? Some humans do see them." Rakor paused, "You did see someone disappear though, didn't you?"

"Yes—no—I don't know what I saw that day!" exclaimed Malenger. The conversation was getting away from him; Rakor could always talk rings around him, keeping him in his place, avoiding the real issues. Rakor's shape-shifting was also unnerving. Malenger was uncertain how many forms Rakor could take—did Rakor spy on him in another shape?

"Look, I just want to know if all this work is worthwhile—

is that so much to ask?"

"And I have assured you it is. Be patient. SaMäel will reveal all in time."

Rakor knew his familiar answer was no longer satisfying Malenger, who slunk away, retreating to the maps, and brooding. Malenger was dangerous in that mood; he had a mean streak that was never far from the surface. The bear wondered what SaMäel had in store for the men. Their greed was blinding them to SaMäel's manipulations. Rakor knew that SaMäel would never share the Quintessence with humans; they were going to be very, very angry. SaMäel, of course, had no fear of them. It would be Rakor that they would punish. Was this SaMäel's plan—to have them destroy each other? Rakor shook off these dark thoughts. SaMäel wouldn't let that happen to him—they were partners. He just had to manage Malenger until the job was done. What SaMäel did with the men was no concern of his.

"It won't be long now. We need to have the maps up to date. We're getting close—we must be. Get Mustela, we need to map her group's progress. It seems to me that they have slowed down considerably. We might have to punish them."

"It's the child. She's getting so thin you can practically see through her. The others are trying to protect her. She's so useless we ought to get rid of her. What is SaMäel planning to do with her and the others when you find this—treasure?" Malenger asked, sneeringly.

"That won't involve you," Rakor said absentmindedly, intent on the maps.

"Why—are you going to eat them?" drawled Malenger, trying to get a rise out of the grizzly. Rakor knew this mood— Malenger would goad him until he hit a nerve and the bear lost his temper. He decided to end it quickly.

"No, but I do feel like ripping your eyes out!" he roared, shape-shifting into a giant golden eagle with dagger-like talons. He flew at Malenger, who collapsed on the floor, cowering, his hands over his head. Rakor hovered above him.

"Ok! Ok," Malenger yelped, "I get the point!"

"Good," said Rakor, resuming his shape and his even temper, "remember it. Now get Mustela, and take that squirrel to her while you're at it." The young ground squirrel, huddled in a corner of the cavern, was shaking uncontrollably from both his night ride in Rakor's claws and the scene he had just witnessed. Malenger picked him up roughly and threw him towards a tunnel.

THE TUNNEL they started down began large enough for Malenger to enter, but quickly became smaller and narrower, until it was just large enough for the Furtive Folk. At this point, Malenger had to send a runner to fetch Mustela. In the tunnels groups of workers—ground squirrels, badgers, moles, marmots, minks— were carving out passageways, ferrying buckets of earth, chipped stone and ice out to the exchange point where Malenger gathered the waste. He and Rakor moved it out of the way higher in the next cavern. Each day the teams of diggers were expected to progress a certain distance; at the end of the day, they brought a length of string to show how far they had progressed, and the distance was logged onto the maps. The diggers were fed lightly in the evening and given water at sunrise and midday. If progress was not fast enough, they were not fed. Each group was managed by a badger or ermine, who was told to terrorize the others into working. But in some of the tunnels these natural enemies had found more in common with each other than with their cruel masters, and were working together to survive.

Some of the more rebellious animals had starved to death or were simply killed, replaced by new workers from Malenger's traps or Rakor's hunting, their bodies left to rot in the cavern as a reminder to the others. It was fairly easy to supply food for the diggers; except for the child. Without proper food, coupled with a lack of fresh air and sunshine, she was wasting away. Malenger was all for getting it over quickly and disposing of her, as he resented the time he spent collecting food for her. It seemed pointless. Who was she anyway? All he knew was that SaMäel had found her almost dead, seemingly abandoned. But it wasn't like SaMäel to care for others. Why was he bothering to keep her alive? Malenger turned back to the cavern shaking his head. Whether SaMäel liked it or not, the kid would soon be dead.

Gulo waited until the man disappeared down the tunnel. When Rakor lay down on the ground for a quick nap, the wolverine grabbed his chance. He crawled along the ledge, high above Rakor, leapt powerfully onto a lower ledge, then another and another, waiting between each one to see if Rakor stirred, but the bear had his back to him and was snoring. As he leapt to the floor, Rakor spoke up. Gulo froze.

"Leave before he shoots you," Rakor said, keeping his back to the wolverine, "this does not concern you." Gulo dashed out, just as he heard Malenger returning. Further down the tunnel, he stopped to listen for anyone following him, but he heard nothing. Now all he had to do was get past the two idiots at the caves' entrance.

Gulo crouched in a side tunnel near the opening of the Rivergate, watching the men while they squatted, new cigars hanging from their lips, whittling away on small pieces of wood. It was dawn; their breakfast fire was still burning. Gulo pondered over how he could divert their attention. He had tried throwing a handful of large stones deeper into the tunnel, but only one man ventured back to check it out, rifle cocked. Gulo knew he had to make a move, but he didn't know if he had the nerve to try to slink past those two waiting rifles.

The wolverine watched for a long time, hoping the men would go out to collect food for the diggers, but the two men just continued to sit and smoke, flicking their cigar butts over their shoulders into the damp cave, near to where he was hiding, the embers glowing red for a few minutes before extinguishing. Suddenly Slank sniffed loudly and said, "I think I actually smell wolverine. Can you?"

"Ya," drawled Payne, also sniffing the air, "what a stinker!" They laughed loudly, glancing back into the cave, trying to make a dent in the darkness.

"Though small, they're supposed to be extremely fierce," said Slank, uneasily.

Got that right, growled Gulo to himself.

"Ever see one?" asked Payne.

"Na, hard to spot—real loners."

"Well, that's good. Just think if they roamed in packs!" They laughed again, but there was a thin, hollow ring to the laughter.

Suddenly Gulo knew what he had to do.

Marmo's Ire

BACK AT CATHEDRAL, Monk remained distant and brooding. Hating to see him like that, Grundel spoke to Melancholia, hoping she could help. When she appeared in front of him, Monk barely acknowledged her presence, but she stood there patiently, solid yet fluid as a glacier. Finally, he spoke.

"I suppose you're about to say that I should cheer up; live in the present moment, try to enjoy what there is to enjoy." Melancholia chose not to reply, waiting. He muttered something Mel didn't hear and then said, "Well, how *do* they live in the present moment? What happened to us? Where did we screw up?" He sat up, still diffident, but obviously wanting an answer. Melancholia decided to humour him.

"Let's just say that all sentient life has four selves to keep in balance: the physical, emotional, intellectual and spiritual selves."

"And I suppose humans messed up the balance. How?"

"Well, from my perspective: humans take your physical life for granted and abuse it; you indulge in the lesser emotions that ought to be controlled, while demeaning the emotions that ought to be your guides to truth and value; you think too much about the future and how to satisfy your desires instead of enjoying the present moment; and you lost your spiritual life when you organized religion and allowed the desire for power to corrupt spirituality."

"That all?" asked Monk sarcastically, slumping back into his chair. After a few moments he sat up again. "Sorry, indulging my lower emotions there for a moment. How can you have a spiritual life without some form of organized religion? I don't go to church but I follow the precepts."

"I'm not saying they are exclusive—if they remain uncor-
rupted. But look around you, Monk; these animals have a deep
spiritual life. They are one with all things; they understand
themselves as part of a sacred unity. Isn't that what you were
after, when you left the church?" When he started to protest,
she put up an elegant hand. "I'm not saying they're perfect.
They also get caught up in their emotions and their desires—
but they can let them go more easily, returning to their authen-
tic nature. Perhaps their desires are less convoluted than human
desires; in any case, their spiritual life reminds them daily of
the truth and beauty in the world, even in the face of their
adversity. They draw immense strength from this awareness."

"How does this help them live in the present moment?"

"Truth is the purity of the moment—seeing clearly. Beauty
is the afternoon light gilding a mountain top. Why would they
want to live anywhere else or any other way? There is no need
to live in the future—it comes in its own time with its own
beauty. Nor do they long for the past—they have already lived
there fully, and take with them its revelations."

"Did you teach them that?"

"No, I just remind them once in a while."

Monk fell silent, but Grundel, watching from across the
cave, thought the man looked more thoughtful than morose
and hoped it was a good sign.

GRUNDEL had been in the Map Den with Took and Gorath all
night, when Aquila and Raven entered the Keeper's Cave.
Grundel came out to greet them.

"Any news?" he asked, looking around for Gulo.

"Gulo is waiting with Toholinagi in the Ancient Wood,"
replied Aquila.

"Good," said Grundel, "I'm on my way. Fetch the others." The massive grizzly lumbered down the mountain, over the ice bridge, and crossed the Icefield. It was a clear day, the sky a bright turquoise. Grundel filled his lungs with the rejuvenating energy of the cold, fresh air. Halfway down the entrance glacier, he cut across to the grove of gnarled trees. He had made this journey many times. All Keepers turned to Toholinagi in the Ancient Wood for counsel and guidance. The portal's knowledge was different from Melancholia's or the Watchers'. Toholinagi had a long, detailed memory; his wisdom was derived from making astute connections between his many careful observations. Long ago the old gods had created spirits like Melancholia to aid Gaia, the spirit of Earth, and then created the portals to allow easy communication between Gaia's sacred places. Now there were few portals left—human encroachment, often unwittingly, had destroyed most. The grand days of the portals had ended. The old gods had grown old and silent. But here at the Icefield, so far isolated from man's destruction, Toholinagi flourished.

When he reached the ancient portal, Grundel noticed Toholinagi trembling with laughter. Then he heard the tree's voice in his head.

Welcome! Gulo has just been relating his tale of adventure. You're going to enjoy this, Grundel. Once the portal had spun its cone shape to admit Grundel and he was settled comfortably, Gulo began again.

"So how did you get out of the caves?" asked Grundel, when Gulo had neared the end of his tale.

You'll like this part! chuckled Toholinagi.

"Well, I couldn't get them both away from the entrance at the same time, so I knew that I had to come up with something more elaborate, some diversion that would take both of them, something they both feared; so, when I saw them flicking their cigarette butts back into the cave, I crept back into the recesses and collected every bit of brittle grass, twig and dead leaf that had blown in—and some damp ones so there would be a lot of smoke. When I had a heaping pile, I snuck up and grabbed the lighted butt ends they had just thrown. It didn't take very long before the pile was on fire and the smoke drifted out to the entrance. The skinny one yelped and the taller one jumped up and shoved a bottle into the skinny one's hand—told him to get some water from the pool outside the cave. They were terrified that Malenger or Rakor would smell fire. When the big one ran past me, I darted out and was in the wood before the other one had filled the bottle!"

Well done, said Toholinagi again, admiringly. Grundel smiled absentmindedly, quietly working through the implications of the situation, and then said, "Do you think the men suspected it was you?" Gulo shrugged.

That's the pure genius of it, replied Toholinagi, *they would think they had started the fire by their own carelessness!*

"What about Rakor? Do you think he'll say anything?"

"No," answered the wolverine. "If he didn't give me away then, I can't see him saying anything later. What would be the point?"

"Did you get a chance to see those maps on the table?"

"I did get a quick look. Mustela showed me four tunnels all leading towards the centre of the Icefield. Whatever they're after is old, ancient, and well buried."

"And, in the cave, you say there's Rakor, Malenger, two other armed men, and the diggers?"

"Yes. Oh—and a human girl child."

"A child?" He paused and then asked, "Did Mustela use her name?"

"Just to call her as they left, but she's a starveling, Grundel. She won't live long, and they have disposed of other animals. There are bones and skeletons littering the cavern floor."

"What did Mustela call her?"

"Let me think—Koko? Something like that."

"How old?"

"Young—maybe five seasons. She's so scrawny it's hard to tell."

Grundel turned to Toholinagi, "Should I tell Monk? He'll be beside himself with anger."

Toholinagi said, *He won't forgive you if you keep this from him even for a day.*

"But he can be rash and could spoil everything. There's so much at stake."

He's made mistakes in the past, but he won't let you down. Grundel slowly nodded; he trusted Toholinagi. Boris used to say it was like hearing your innermost voice—the one that always knows the truth, but the one we seldom listen for— jumping at the first voice that tells us what we want to hear.

Not one to put off a task, Grundel thanked Gulo, left him with Toholinagi, and started back to Cathedral. When he reached the Keeper's Cave, Grundel found Monk sitting peacefully reading his *Vade Mecum*.

Will this man's life never settle? thought Grundel, hating to interrupt him with his disturbing news. "Reading poetry?"

Monk looked up, began to say something, and then read the look in Grundel's eyes.

"Something has happened," Monk said, flatly. Grundel lowered his huge body to sit in front of Monk, but he didn't say anything for a few minutes, collecting his thoughts. Monk's uneasiness grew.

"Just say it, Grundel. Whatever it is, tell me. I can handle it," he said.

"I hope so, because much hangs on it. You understand that we can't afford any rash, independent actions." Monk, confused by the unexpected answer, became even more distraught.

"For God's sake, Grundel, what is it?"

"We think—*think* mind you—that Koko is in the Castleguard Caves."

"What? Koko?" Monk's mind reeled. "Alive?" The bear nodded. Monk turned ashen white. "I have to sit down."

Grundel put a huge paw on the man's knee, which seemed to ground him. "You are sitting down. Understand, Monk, that Gulo has seen a small girl child in the caves. We only surmise that it's Koko."

Monk stared through the bear, his mind filled with wildly clashing images of his little girl alone in the caves—then Koko with Rakor. But why? He desperately tried to control his colliding, terrifying thoughts. When his mind settled a little—he leapt to his feet. Instantly, Grundel was ahead of him, blocking the entrance. He held out a giant paw and said mildly, "What are you doing?"

"Getting her, of course! Out of my way, for heaven's sake!"

Grundel didn't move. "This is what I meant, Monk—rash, independent action. Please sit down; I've sent Raven for the others. We will decide what to do, together."

"What? Get out of my way! You can do whatever you bloody well want, but I'm getting my daughter!" Monk threw himself at Grundel, to plough his way through if he had to. Grundel stood up on his hind legs, picked up the flailing man, walked him over to the armchair and dropped him in it.

"Calm down," Grundel said, patiently. "We're waiting for the others."

Hearing the raised voices, Tuktu came out of the Map Den with a couple of Brothers. As Monk eyed the entrance, first Bighorn, then Tasmira, Gorath and a number of other Brothers began to troop in, with Marmo scurrying not to get trampled underfoot. Melancholia appeared, then Mikaila. Aquila flew through the opening, landing gracefully on the slab table, with Raven in her wake. They waited a while longer, then Monk watched three more bears enter, with Vang.

"Females," said Gorath in Monk's ear. "The Ursulas." Suddenly Monk realized the significance of the gathering and tried to settle down, to be patient, to trust Grundel. Gulo entered last, very reluctantly, staying close to the cave's entrance.

"Here's our problem," Grundel began. "As you now know, Melancholia and the Keepers are here to protect the Quintessence that's buried under the Icefield. The ice is receding—we knew that eventually we'd have to relocate the life force—find another protected home for it. Since our last meeting, Gulo has explored the Castleguard Caves to find out what Rakor is doing." He paused as a hushed *ahhh* swept the room. "It's as we feared—he's digging for something. And he's not alone. There are three other armed men." He paused again, looking at Mel who nodded her head. "More troubling, SaMäel is involved." A low rumble swept through the bears. "Rakor and SaMäel are getting so close to discovering the Quintessence— we need to move it—now."

"SaMäel? Who's SaMäel," demanded Monk. "And what does this have to do with Koko?'

"SaMäel is a fallen angel, Monk, like the Watchers, but dangerous. We believe that he wants the life force for vile purposes, even though, by taking it, he could destroy the planet and every living thing on it. Malenger and Rakor are probably under his spell—they're organizing a dig. Koko is one of the diggers."

"What!" gasped Monk. "She's been digging in the caves since our accident—that's where she's been?"

"That we don't know. We just know that she's there now."

"So how are we getting her out?"

"It's complicated. We can't just barge in and snatch her. We will, of course, rescue her, but we must locate the Quintessence before they do, and then relocate it—all without SaMäel's knowledge. And without jeopardizing the lives of the other diggers."

There were anxious murmurings from all around the cave.

"I know such a task sounds immense, but we mustn't lose heart. You are all here because you understand that this affects all of us; in fact, it affects all living things. We need to pull together if we're to succeed. Gulo has spoken to Mustela and Whistler in the caves." The others gave Gulo appreciative looks, but, embarrassed by their attention, he looked away. Marmo's ears had perked up at the sound of Whistler's name. He tried to intercede but no one noticed him except Kyna who hushed him.

"The child," Grundel continued, "might or might NOT be Koko, Monk's daughter. Gulo says she's in very bad shape—we will have to act quickly to save her." Gorath put a paw out to keep Monk from rising.

"We will save her. You must trust us," he said quietly. Monk clenched his fists, so great was his effort not to barge out of the cave after her. Grundel continued.

"Our challenge is complex. It has at least four parts: locating the Quintessence, relocating it, distracting SaMäel, and saving everyone in the caves."

"Grundel," added Gorath, thoughtfully, "perhaps the first thing we need to do is to disenchant Rakor—and get him back."

"Maybe Armaros would help," piped Piotr, "he knows how to disenchant."

"Ordinarily, yes," replied Melancholia, "but this is no ordinary enchantment. What you must remember is that SaMäel is a powerful angel who can be wantonly destructive. But he can only do something to any of you with your permission or through intermediaries."

"You mean someone doing his dirty work for him?" asked Piotr.

"Precisely," said Mel. "He has many resources; he need only beat his dark wings and an evil wind stirs up trouble. Make no mistake; he will try to come between us, to set us one against another, to instil doubt, anger and mistrust. This is what he did to Rakor. He must have told him about the Quintessence, told him it would make him immortal, made him feel that I was deliberately keeping it from him, and convinced him it was there for the taking."

Melancholia noticed how Gorath's eyes were shining in the darkness of the cave.

"And would it?" Gorath whispered hoarsely.

Melancholia turned to him. "Would what?"

"Make him immortal?"

The ancient spirit sent a withering look around the room. "It is imperative that all of you understand two things: first, the Quintessence was placed there by the gods for the planet, not for individuals. Without it, the planet will die. And if the planet dies; you all die. Second, the Quintessence is far too powerful for any earthly living thing to use, except Earth herself."

"What would happen if Rakor tried to take it?" asked Tuktu, irrepressibly inquisitive.

"It has never happened—though I suspect that just to look upon a fraction of it would cause immediate and painful blindness. Any more would certainly be death."

"Then how could anyone relocate it?" asked Took.

"It is contained."

"But you haven't said why we can't just disenchant Rakor," interrupted Piotr.

"Well, to put it simply, you can't disenchant someone who has chosen to be the way they are. SaMäel did not enchant Rakor with a spell—first he manipulated him into believing that what Rakor is doing is in his own best interest. The only way to reclaim Rakor is to show him the error in his thinking."

"You mean to show him he was brainwashed," said Alethia, growling in anger.

"Exactly," replied Melancholia, "a much more difficult task."

"And Malenger?" asked Bighorn, bitterly remembering his dead.

"A lost cause," spat Monk, "irredeemable—the man's evil to his core." The others agreed silently.

"Those men are not our concern," replied Mel coldly, "they can be left to their fates."

Grundel said, "But whether we can win Rakor back or not, the first thing we need to do is to rescue the child and any other creatures in immediate peril. Until we relocate the Quintessence everything must remain as undisturbed as possible, so as not to alert SaMäel, but we do not want nor will we tolerate any more deaths. Suggestions?"

Monk jumped to his feet. "The dream map! I can get the dream map; it's in Rachel's pack in our cabin. It has the caves on it and tunnels, I'm sure of it. And, and all sorts of symbols that maybe someone will be able to decipher. It could help us!" As he started for the opening, Grundel motioned for Mikaila to accompany him. Gleaning his thought, she sprang into action, whistling for Equus.

While they waited, Marmo stood up impatiently, trying to

get noticed, but Kyna rose at the same time and everyone's attention turned to her.

"Grundel, this is a task for the Ursulas." Grundel opened his mouth to protest, thinking of the danger, thinking of Rakor's power, especially if it was enhanced by SaMäel, but then reconsidered. She was right. The three Ursulas had more power and magic then all the rest of the bears in the cave put together. One was Rakor's mother, another his mate and the third the current Ursula—if anyone could persuade and control Rakor, they could.

Alethia rose beside her. "Yes," she said, "we will free Rakor and the child first."

Inyx rose. "We'll need some of you to waylay Malenger and draw out the men. Leave the rest to us." Tasmira watched the Ursulas with bright eyes; she could almost hear them thinking together, and she immediately sensed what they were going to do. She longed to join the trio.

Gulo squirmed in his seat. He felt the heat of the Ursulas' stares. He had not yet told Grundel what Mustela had said just before she disappeared into her tunnel. He had thought it might be useful information to trade, if Grundel kept information from him. But this gathering made Gulo realize this was not the time for bargaining, or for artful silences—too much was at stake; and after all, Grundel had included him, trusted him. If Mikaila could step outside her kind to help others, then perhaps he could too.

Alerted by the Ursulas, Grundel was now watching Gulo.

"Is there something you would like to say, Gulo?" Grundel asked, interrupting the wolverine's thoughts. Gulo growled, guttural and hoarse, swept his eyes around the crowded cave, and spoke.

"As she left, Mustela said something that wasn't clear to me then, but is beginning to make sense now, though she said to tell you in private."

"As you can see, there's little point in secrecy now. You may speak freely, here," replied Grundel emphasizing *here*.

"Alright," he conceded uneasily. "Mustela said: *Tell Grundel we found it.*"

"It?" repeated Tasmira. There were gasps around the room.

"That's all she had time to say," said Gulo.

"Do you think she meant the life force?" asked Tasmira. "Does she know about it?"

"I don't think so, but she might have figured it out," surmised Grundel. "All we can do is to assume, for now, that Mustela meant the Quintessence. If this is right, it relieves our burden of finding it. You all have your tasks. In the meantime, remember, no one is to mention the word Quintessence outside this room. Understood? Our lives depend upon it."

Kyna turned to Vang, who had been silent for a long time. "Vang, we will need you as well. We know what you have been doing and why. It was ill judged. If you love your twin, you must take direction from us now."

Puzzled, Grundel scrutinized Vang, and then turned to Kyna for an explanation.

"We have discovered that Vang has been meeting with Rakor outside the caves," she revealed.

"What?!" roared Piotr, leaping to his feet and turning on Vang who instinctively leapt up to meet the challenge. "You knew he was in the caves? You knew and let us—?"

"No!" Vang growled and shook his massive head. "Believe me Piotr—I didn't know he was in the caves until you found him. We met outside at different locations. He said he was doing something important and he was almost finished—he'd be home soon. He just wanted to know how everyone was doing—

what was happening. I never told him you'd found him. I didn't know what to believe—who to believe." Vang rose, turning to the Ursulas. "Alethia," he began, but Grundel interrupted. Standing suddenly, with a great swipe of his paw he knocked Vang off his feet, then dropped down on all fours and headed towards the back chambers.

"Come with me," he demanded, his anger barely contained. Vang wrenched his gaze away from Alethia, got up slowly and followed him.

"Don't be too hard on him, Grundel," pleaded Inyx as he passed her. "Remember that Rakor's his twin." Grundel ignored her and passed through to the deeper chambers. Inyx glanced at the other bears all of whom were looking away. To be a twin was a profound and unbreakable bond. They could understand why Vang would need to speak to Rakor—he had been without his other half for a long time, unable to mourn, not knowing if Rakor were alive or dead. But to keep that information secret, not to tell Grundel, was unthinkable. Their sole purpose was to protect the Icefield, to serve Melancholia. Inyx sighed—what was happening to her offspring?

BEHIND the Keeper's Cave, deeper into the mountain, was a labyrinth of chambers for the bears, used for the Long Sleep. And a shaft—a long, spiral tunnel just wide and high enough for a bear to sit up, which the bears used, sliding on their rumps to the bottom of the mountain. The spiral tunnel was a fast, wild ride, but it got the bears off the mountain in a hurry when necessary.

No one passed beyond the Keeper's Cave into these back chambers—and never into the tunnel—except the grizzlies.

Grundel took Vang deep into the mountain. At first, the others waited patiently, chatting, some coming and going to feed, if only briefly.

When Monk and Mikaila returned to the cave with the dream map, they were told what had happened. Monk slumped in his chair. Waiting was unbearable. A cold wind rose in the afternoon, blowing in through the cave's entrance. Monk draped his tarp over it and made a small fire. It disturbed the others to see Melancholia showing signs of stress, shimmering in and out of their vision; but they all felt the same anxiety. Loyalty was a primary principle with the Keepers; it was Grundel's responsibility to maintain loyalty. If Vang defected, the Brothers would challenge Grundel as Keeper and control could pass out of Melancholia's hands for a period, as a Brother not chosen by her took command. There was more than one covert look thrown in Gorath's direction.

Just before the meeting, Tasmira had revealed to Gorath the truth of Vang's divided loyalty. Gorath's mind was racing at the possibility of a challenge. Could Grundel convince Vang to desert his twin? If Grundel could not persuade Vang to break with Rakor until they could trust the defector again, then no one would object to Gorath's challenge. In fact, it would be expected of him as second in command. But could he defeat Grundel? They were matched in size, strength and endurance. Gorath searched his own heart—did he really want to challenge Grundel?

Others in the cave were also searching their hearts—with so many problems unravelling, the very air seemed to be disintegrating, growing foul. As time passed and everyone became restless, the Ursulas began to pace the length of the cave. The others had to move to make room for them. Back and forth, back and forth, slowly, deliberately. At first Mikaila found it distracting, but she soon realized there was a rhythm and a purpose to their pacing—as if they were weaving a net, mending the fabric that held them all together.

When the clouds turned a final crimson, and the sun sank behind the mountain, Vang entered the Keeper's Cave, Grundel behind him. Vang's face had lightened; he had lost the haunted look he had worn lately. Whatever understanding they had reached, he and Grundel were comfortable with it. There was a concert of sighs in the room. Everyone sat up and began chattering more freely, relief on all their faces. Tasmira and Gorath eyed one another, but Kyna, watching, could not read the message in the exchange.

Marmo, who had been waiting for Grundel and an opportunity, finally, to speak, jumped up, but before he could, the Ursulas stood and began to leave.

"Tasmira, you're with us," Kyna indicated. Tasmira's heart leapt as Inyx and Alethia nodded their heads towards the entrance. Marmo sighed heavily, and, realizing that he wasn't going to get anyone's attention today, padded out behind the Ursulas. The others watched him curiously. Kyna heard a few snickers and, puzzled and annoyed, turned quickly, almost stepping on the small animal.

When Kyna shot Grundel a look, The Keeper called to the marmot, "What are you doing, Marmo?"

"I'm going with them," the marmot replied, matter-of-factly.

"No, I think it best you stay here with us. The Ursulas have their own methods," he smiled tolerantly.

"Don't be absurd, of course I'm going!" Marmo stood up to his full height, indignant and outraged. "Whistler's in there and Grub and Mustela and hopefully all the other animals we lost. Who else will go down those small tunnels to talk to them? Bears? Not likely!" There was a ripple of laughter around the room. Marmo glared. "Didn't you just say you needed things to remain the same—who's going to tell those animals that they have to remain there after all the suffering they must have endured already? Who will have more authority to ask this of them?" Marmo's body shook with indignation. In the Furtive Folk Valley, no one contradicted him. He was tired of the bears' condescending attitude. Grundel, taken aback, realized the truth of Marmo's words, as did Kyna.

"He's right, Grundel. We will need him." She turned to the irate marmot. "Your services will be much appreciated. My apologies for overlooking you, and those in your care. It was negligent and arrogant on our part. Forgive us."

"I accept your apology," he answered, placated. He graciously extended a paw, "After you."

"Wait!" called Monk, "won't this help?" he said, offering The Keeper the dream map, but Grundel refused it.

"Dream maps are full of power, and dangerous. I don't know if you even have the right to show it to me." He hesitated, looking to Kyna.

"It might help," she said.

"All right. Show it to Kyna so they can study it, but then put it back." Monk looked down at the map in his hand, then held it out to Kyna who took it silently and spread it out on the table, beckoning Alethia and Inyx. The three Ursulas stood over it, memorizing its details, speaking quietly, intoning a language none of the others had ever heard. At last they gave Grundel a brief nod and, with Marmo and Tasmira, left the cave. Monk folded the map carefully and put it back in his shirt pocket.

With everyone dispersed, Monk was left alone with Grundel for the night. He tried to sleep, but couldn't control his racing thoughts—what was Koko doing now? How could the Ursulas save her? Should he leave matters in their hands? He stepped outside to clear his head and was surprised by a squall of hard rain, biting crystals that pierced and stung his face and hands. The sky was grey, overcast; he crouched, turned his back on the driving wind, and gazed out through the veil in the direction of Castleguard. His body shook, but not from the cold. Then Grundel was beside him, sheltering him from the wicked wind, the rain and his dark thoughts.

IN THE CASTLEGUARD CAVES, night had fallen. Not that it made a difference; it was always night in the caves. SaMäel had magically lit the cavern, turning large white stalactites into gleaming lanterns that radiated both light and heat, but still the Grotto was damp and fusty. Rakor and Malenger sat at the slab table, hardly noticing the air which reeked of decay.

"There's something wrong," said Rakor, studying the map and the lengths of string. "We should have found it by now."

"Found what?" asked Malenger. Rakor gave him an intimidating look; he was tiring of Malenger's constant prodding. "Okay—then, *why* do you think they should have found *it*," sneered Malenger.

"By SaMäel's calculations, we just should have. Something's wrong." Whistler was hiding at the end of their tunnel, listening fearfully.

"Then what?" asked Malenger. "You think they're pulling a fast one on us, keeping it for themselves?" He laughed crudely. "Them dumb little animals?"

Rakor ignored him. Tension simmered between them until suddenly, with a rush of hot air, SaMäel appeared. Whistler instinctively flattened himself against the tunnel wall. Malenger retreated a few steps, back into the recesses. The angel alighted gracefully, his powerful aura of danger filling the grotto. He strolled around the cavern, and then leaned lightly against a rock wall, crossing his arms and eyeing them carefully.

"Any progress?" he asked, mildly. But Rakor felt the suppressed anger.

"I think we might have miscalculated," said Rakor.

"Oh?" drawled SaMäel, "I don't miscalculate." A hard metallic edge crept into his voice.

"Well—" snickered Malenger, "except that once."

"Be careful human; I don't like you; you are at best useful," replied SaMäel, gazing piercingly into the man's eyes. "As useful as say—a bat," and with a flourish, SaMäel waved his arms and Malenger began acting like a bat.

The dark angel laughed crudely. "That's too easy," he said, then shook his head and turned back to the grizzly bear. "It should be any time now, Rakor. My patience thins. Get this done."

"Do you think the Furtive Folk could be lying to us?" asked Rakor hesitantly, his eyes drawn to Malenger's bat antics.

"No," interrupted SaMäel, "that's very unlikely. It's not in their natures. Besides, my ancient source, devious creature that he was, stated clearly that the Q will instantly kill anyone who looks upon it. It used to be contained in some kind of shell, but is no longer. The fool wouldn't tell me more, so now he can't tell anyone," SaMäel added absently, then continued. "Convenient actually, as the animals will be killed when they find it. One evening a group will not return and we will know which tunnel to excavate. Anyway, get this done." Rakor nodded. He was thinking about what Mustela had told them about the accident. SaMäel was about to leave when Rakor pointed to Malenger agitatedly flapping his arms.

"Oh, very well," muttered SaMäel, "though I'm beginning to doubt the humans are worth the bother." With a sweeping gesture, he spoke a few words and the man fell to the ground heavily; then the dark angel vanished. Malenger lay on the floor of the cave as if he had fallen from the ceiling, groaning, rubbing his sore muscles, straining to recover his eyesight. Rakor looked at him in disgust. He knew that it was all illusion, that SaMäel could not change Malenger into anything if the man had any strength of will, if he realized that it was mainly the power of suggestion that SaMäel was using. SaMäel, the magician. He reached out a paw to help the man up.

"Why goad the creature? Do you want to be a bat permanently?"

Malenger shook off the hypnosis. It was not the first time SaMäel had done that to him, but the terror of it never lessened. "Ya, well, I don't like him either. It wasn't my fault he was thrown off his world—isn't that what you told me? What arrogance to say he never miscalculates!" Malenger turned and spat on the floor.

"Are you blind to his power, or the force and consequences of his anger?"

"And what do I have in the face of that power except my ability to get under his skin?"

"Trust me, you don't want to get under that skin—under that skin is pure fire. Go get Mustela. I don't have to put the fear of SaMäel in her; she knows better," said Rakor, turning back to the maps. "I might have to check out the tunnels myself," he added, more to himself.

When Whistler heard that, he raced back down the tunnel to safety.

Malenger headed into the tunnel and gave a screeching whistle as the tunnel quickly became too small for him to continue. Whistler hesitated, then ran back to where Malenger was crouched, staying well out of kicking range.

"Get Mustela," drawled Malenger haughtily. Wordlessly, Whistler turned and disappeared. Malenger sat down with a thump; he was still shaken by SaMäel's actions. Trying to remember what had happened during the hypnosis, he could

Whistler

only recall the feeling of terror as he lost himself in a dark void. He had no recollection of being a bat, only Rakor's word for it. If he were not convinced that these two were onto something big, something that would change his life forever, he'd leave, but his greed and morbid curiosity kept him patient, for now. He rubbed his hands together imagining the riches he had coming to him.

Whistler hurried back to Mustela, who was digging with Sandy and Grub, two large ground squirrels. Their tawny peppered coats had lost their sheen and they were thin and worn out. Koko lay on the floor behind them, sleeping, her breath coming short and fast. Whistler gave her a look of concern on his way past.

"Mustela!" cried Whistler. She tensed, in fearful anticipation. "They want you. SaMäel's been there. He wants to know why we haven't found it."

"Well team—this is it. Any words of advice?" asked Mustela, breathing deeply, summoning her courage. Koko roused herself.

"Mustela," she said weakly, "don't—don't—don't," but she couldn't finish.

"She means don't sacrifice yourself," said Whistler. Koko got up with difficulty and wrapped her arms around Mustela. The ground squirrels tweeped in alarm and looked at her in pity, not expecting the ermine to return. How could she outwit Rakor, let alone SaMäel?

"Keep digging," said Mustela hoarsely, "and Koko," she said, loosening the child's grip and laying her back down, "get some rest. I'll be back." They watched her march down the tunnel, her beautiful black-tipped tail held high. The tunnel seemed a place of comfort compared to where she was going. After a few minutes, Whistler jumped up.

"I'm going after her. She shouldn't have to do this alone," he said.

Mustela's Tale

MUSTELA was dreaming of winter, of rose hips and clean, wide open spaces, but she shook off these thoughts and grimly rehearsed her story as she scurried through the tunnel. She knew what the summons meant—SaMäel and Rakor were becoming suspicious. If she couldn't convince them that all was normal, one of them would shape-shift and come down the tunnel—something that must not happen—not when Gulo said Grundel was so close to rescuing them.

Could she deceive her captors a bit longer? A fortnight ago, the animals had discovered what they believed Rakor and SaMäel had them digging for. A young ground squirrel, in the day's lead position, suddenly broke off a small chunk of lime-stone and a sliver of light coming from deeper in the tunnel instantly blinded him. The animals quickly and carefully filled in the fissure, but a second ground squirrel was blinded in the process. The two animals were filled with a strange euphoria. They were only aware of one another; their faces were ecstatic; they held hands and danced; their bodies seemed so ephemeral, so filled with light, they seemed to float. But after a short while, they started shivering; they called out that everything was black and cold, then their small bodies rocked with massive agonizing spasms, until finally they fell quiet, then lifeless. The others were horrified by what had happened. At first, Mustela did not know how to shake them out of their shock and terror. They had raced away and wouldn't go near the end of the tunnel. Mustela had sunk to the floor, mystified. She lay there thinking, Whistler watching her. Snatches of an old song, sung to her as an infant by her mother, came to her and she sang it out loud:

...Deep in the caves of Castleguard
Deep in the waves of Castleguard
The ever breath, the foil of death
The light at the end of the tunnel...

"Whistler," she asked, "do you know this song?" Whistler nodded.

"I do. There's a warning—right? Something about not opening a gilded lid, something about—the Keepers?"

"Yes, that's it—something in the caves that belongs to the Keepers," added Grub, rejoining them. His curiosity overtaking his fear.

"No, not belonged, something else," replied Mustela, thinking deeply. "What they—protect." In a flash of intuition, she realized what they had stumbled upon.

"Oh dear," said Whistler as the full impact dawned on him. "If it's what the Keepers protect—it's probably what SaMäel wants—what we've been digging for?"

Mustela nodded glumly. "We have a difficult choice."

"What choice?" piped Grub.

"To tell or not to tell." The animals, now crowding around, looked at her in disbelief.

"I don't understand everything," she said, "but I do know that Grundel is to be trusted, and that SaMäel is not." How Rakor played into all of this, she couldn't tell, but for some reason he was with SaMäel and if she had to choose whom to trust—she would choose Grundel. "Whatever we've found must not fall into the hands of SaMäel, not if we can prevent it."

"But how," gasped Whistler, shaking his head, "how can we possibly deceive SaMäel? What about the string? What about the buckets of earth we have to produce?"

"Well," offered Mustela, "we could dig around the light."

"That's so dangerous. What if we hit it again?"

"It's a chance we have to take. We'll veer away from it, that way the string continues to get longer and the earth continues to be mined out of the tunnel."

"Change courses?" asked Whistler, horrified. "Not go in the direction SaMäel has plotted?"

"Yes. I think that's our best plan."

"Won't they know or at least suspect our diversion?" asked Grub.

"I can't see how," countered Mustela. "They're not in the tunnel."

"But what happens to us if they do find out? Rakor or SaMäel could shape-shift and come down here at any time," said Whistler.

"If they weren't so afraid of us attacking them," sneered Grub. "Which I would!"

"Don't get too cocky," said Whistler. "Be thankful they haven't come for whatever reason."

"Look—don't you think we owe Grundel this risk?" said Mustela. "If SaMäel wants it, it must be important. I suspect we could use our 'ignorance' to cover ourselves—they think of us as so dumb. They tell us so all the time—right?"

"True," they muttered, nodding their heads in agreement.

"We could say we must have gone off course without realizing it."

"But it's so dangerous, Mustela. SaMäel would have Malenger kill us instantly if he knew we deceived him. Hasn't there been enough death?" asked Sandy. They were all silent for a while, thinking.

"We each need to think about it. I, for one, believe we will be rescued and that it's our best chance for survival. But, each of you must choose. Then we'll decide what to do."

Mustela looked around at the others. "Agreed?" They nodded, nervously.

"Wait a minute! Wait a minute," said Grub, "if we tell them, then we can go home! Home! No more digging or starving or beatings. No more darkness and cold. No more death. Surely we don't owe Grundel our lives?"

Whistler struggled with himself. Should he tell them what SaMäel had said—that they were all going to die anyway? He feared the blunt truth would be too debilitating, would undermine their fragile hope, so he just hinted at it. "Do you really think Samäel will just let us go?" he asked. "Just walk out of here with the knowledge we have?"

In the end, all the animals, even Grub, realized that Mustela and Whistler were right. They all owed Grundel and the bears; they all trusted The Keeper, who had rescued many of them at one time or another. Besides, even if they told SaMäel the truth, they knew in their hearts that there was little chance he would set them free.

"But we must not tell them about the two deaths," said Mustela. "We need to leave the bodies here. We don't want their deaths to signal a clue that something is amiss."

"But won't they know when feeding time comes around? And we'll need more help—there're not enough of us now. If we don't get help we won't get enough work done and they won't feed us. We'll starve," argued Grub.

"I'll have to convince them that's there's been an accident, two animals buried under falling rubble. We'll bury them in rubble and that way SaMäel won't see them and recognize the manner of their deaths."

"And replacements?" prodded Grub.

"No! No more. We'll just have to work harder."

Grub gazed over to the sleeping child, muttering to Sandy.

"It could be any one of us," said Whistler, frowning at them. The squirrels hung their heads.

Mustela did not know how long the animals in the tunnel could deceive a spirit as powerful as SaMäel, but she knew that SaMäel did not think much of them, and that gave them an advantage. He simply would not suspect them capable of deception. What she had to do today, then, was to continue to convince SaMäel and Rakor that all was normal and proceeding as to their plan.

THE SLEEK ERMINE, arriving at the mouth of the tunnel, paused to steel her courage. Rakor and Malenger were still poring over the maps, but looked up when she entered the Grotto.

"Ah, Mustela," said Rakor, "and how are things in the tunnel, today? Any more accidental deaths?" She didn't care for the new tone in Rakor's voice and braced herself for what was coming.

"Everything's fine," she replied, trying to keep her voice light and matter-of-fact.

"No, in fact, it's not," Rakor growled menacingly. "SaMäel is not pleased. We should have reached something by now. You're not hiding anything from us, are you?"

Both Rakor and Malenger measured Mustela's reaction carefully. Inwardly she trembled, but outwardly she managed not to let it show.

"Like what?" she answered. "I don't know what you mean." She kept very still as Malenger slunk towards her. Suddenly, when he was in reach of her, he kicked her savagely, sending her flying. She landed heavily against the rock wall, banging her head and scraping all down her right side.

"Fool!" boomed Malenger, "you think we're idiots! Don't play games with us!"

Whistler, hiding in the tunnel, hissed angrily, but only

Rakor heard him. The marmot was just about to run into the cave in Mustela's defence, when Rakor lumbered over and picked up Malenger by the scruff of his neck.

"Stop this," he said, shaking Malenger, and dropping him unceremoniously on the cavern floor. Then he trotted over and picked up Mustela, gently.

"Anything broken?" he asked. Mustela shook her head which throbbed painfully. Rakor laid her carefully on the table, giving Malenger a scathing look, and then he turned back to the ermine. "Malenger's not the only one doubting your word, Mustela. SaMäel is also angry. He's not one you want angry. Perhaps there's something, anything you can tell me?"

"Rakor, we're doing your bidding. We're dying in there trying to find what you want! All we have found so far is dirt and stone and ice. Don't you think I would tell you if we found something, anything? All we want is our freedom."

"You will get nothing until you find what we're looking for. And if it takes too long, I'll not be responsible for SaMäel's wrath." Mustela sat up slowly, testing her muscles and bones.

"How's the child?" Rakor asked, unexpectedly.

"Fine," she said, rubbing her head still pounding from the fall.

"We don't keep anyone who's not pulling their weight. She looks ill. Is she doing her share?" asked Malenger.

"Of course she's ill!" Mustela burst out, no longer able to keep her feelings hidden. "She's a child who has had no sun, no decent food, no care. What do you expect from her or any of us? It's a miracle we're still alive. Those caves are wet and dark and the work is backbreaking." Mustela took a deep breath, controlling her anger. "But she's doing her share." *She keeps us going*, Mustela added to herself. *We keep digging for her. We would do anything to bring back her infectious laugh, her kind acts.* Mustela thought of the child lying in the cold tunnel.

"Maybe you'd better send her out here to me," said Rakor, remembering that SaMäel had told him to keep the child alive.

"Why?" asked Mustela, fearfully.

"We ask the questions, here," roared Malenger. "You just do as he says."

Rakor gave him a withering look. "I'll find something for her to do out here where it's warmer and the air is better, and I can feed her more regularly. Give her some time in the sun. There's no need for any more death. For now," he said pointedly. "But the rest of you need to work harder. Do you need more help?"

"No," answered Mustela, quickly. She didn't want any more animals trapped and brought into the caves. "There's no more room in the tunnel," she added.

"Perhaps I should come get the child and see your progress," Rakor added.

"If you like, but it's not necessary; it's very cramped in there," replied Mustela, trying to keep her voice from trembling. Rakor hesitated. He did not want to enter the tunnels; he would have to shape-shift into something small and he might be vulnerable in so confined a place, with so many creatures who hated him. But he did not completely trust the ermine either; her answers were too quick, too glib. Mustela stayed very still, her fear almost revealing itself. In the tunnel, Whistler held his breath.

"All right. I'll get you someone from the other tunnels— you're three short. In the meantime, send out the child. But put the fear of SaMäel in the rest of them; your time is running out."

Mustela nodded, jumped painfully from the table and limped back into the tunnel. When she saw Whistler, she collapsed against him; her body, no longer able to hide its shock, trembled uncontrollably. He helped her back towards the tunnel's end.

"I don't like it," she said weakly. "They've never cared for the child before. What do they want from Koko?"

"I don't know," replied Whistler, thinking. "You didn't give him anything; maybe Rakor thinks she'll be more easily intimidated."

"How can one so young not break down and tell them what they want to know?"

"Because she's Koko—she's no ordinary young," said Whistler, mustering all the confidence he could.

"Remember at the beginning?" whispered Mustela, near tears. "Malenger set me against all of you. I was put in the tunnel to terrorize you—I was to kill if you didn't listen to me—I forced you to work harder, faster or I wouldn't be fed. It was all fear and suspicion."

"How could I forget?"

"Then Koko came. She was so full of life, so kind, petting and singing to the stricken animals, keeping up our hopes that we would be rescued. We all began to have hope—"

"Until no one came," said Whistler.

"Yes, and her homesickness began to overwhelm her," added Mustela, remembering. "She came to find me in the night, weeping pitifully curling up beside me, stroking my fur. I didn't know how to comfort her."

"But you did, just by being there," he said.

"Oh, Whistler! How can we just desert her to those wretched creatures?"

"We don't have any choice, but we will stay close, and we won't let them harm her!" Mustela looked over at the tiny animal; he had stretched to his full height and puffed out his chest;

but he was no match for a grizzly or a mighty angel. She smiled sadly, knowing his heart was larger, greater than either of theirs.

Whistler helped her back to the end of the tunnel, where the others were waiting. Koko gave a cry of relief when she saw them coming—too many animals had disappeared down the tunnel and never returned. Mustela sat down beside the child, who put her arms around her.

"Koko, we have what we hope will be good news," Mustela said. The child's eyes lightened. "Rakor is going to take you into the cavern, away from this miserable tunnel so you can get better." Koko's eyes darkened again. "He will feed you, let you out in the sunshine; it will be better for you."

"No, I want to stay here." Whistler gave Mustela a troubled look.

"You can't, dear," she said, "we have to do what Rakor says."

"I don't like him." Koko's voice rose in alarm.

"Listen to me very carefully, there's not much time," said Mustela. "We have to depend on you. Think of the blanket your mother has sent you. Remember Gulo—help is coming. We just have to wait patiently. It will better for you in the cavern. You can get decent food, better air—you'll be warmer. And you won't have to dig to exhaustion."

"Why is Rakor doing this for me? I thought he hated us," asked Koko, suspiciously.

"Good question," said Whistler, "we figure he thinks he can get information out of you that he couldn't get out of Mustela."

"What information?"

"Like whether or not we found something. Can you hide that fact? Can you pretend that we have found nothing?" Whistler looked at Mustela who nodded.

"Yes," said Koko, resolutely.

"You can answer all his other questions truthfully," said

Mustela. "But do not tell him about the light or how the squir-rels died. Do you understand?"

"The light and the deaths," Whistler pressed.

"The light and the deaths," Koko repeated, nodding. Sud-denly they heard Malenger roaring at the other end of the tunnel.

"Be quick now. You must go. We promise we will be close by."

"You won't let Malenger hurt me?" she asked, clinging to Mustela.

"No, we won't let him hurt you. Follow Whistler, I will be along when I catch my breath."

Vang's Tale

Grundel broke up the Council and sent everyone off except Tuktu and Monk who had taken out the dream map to study. But it just reminded him of Rachel and made him feel more miserable, so he put it away again. Tuktu tried to divert Monk's attention with idle chatter; she lay down near him on a bed of pine branches, searching for something to talk about.

"Why do they call you Monk?" she asked lightly. She had been out feeding and now chewed her cud contentedly. Monk looked over at her and slowly sat upright, trying to pull himself out of his misery, trying to be sociable.

"A nickname—I studied to be a priest."

"Priest? Like shaman?"

"Yes."

"Before you became a guide?" Monk nodded. Tuktu tried again. "Why a priest?"

"Hard to remember now—my upbringing I suppose. I had the romantic notion that a cloistered life would be uncluttered, so I could devote myself to one place, one purpose." There was an unaccustomed bitterness in Monk's voice.

"What happened? Did you become a priest?"

"No. Rumpled reality is never the same as one's dreams. I had no trouble with the vows of poverty and chastity, but I couldn't take one of obedience. It wasn't in me. So I didn't last. But I loved the study, the simplicity—"

"The singing?" interrupted Tuktu, smiling.

"Especially the singing. But I hadn't factored in the number of rules and regulations, or the loss of freedom. Eventually I left, started guiding and then came out here to the mountains hoping to find a life as austere, without all the rules. Really expecting loneliness, and finding Rachel instead. Rachel gave me the nickname." Monk shuffled uneasily in his chair.

"How did you meet her?" The question was out before Took realized she was putting Monk on dangerous ground.

"We met when I joined Hilda's outfit. Rachel had grown up there and knew every rock in every valley, every icefall on the glaciers. I thought I knew something about trail guiding, but beside her I knew nothing—nothing of these mountains anyway. Hilda, who runs the business, sent her out with me to teach me the lay of the land. At first I was insulted that Hilda would send me out with a young woman—barely out of her teens—when there were men, older guides, her uncles that I could have travelled with and learned from. It was embarrassing. But Rachel was an incredible teacher. I remember when we arrived back at the settlement after our first outing. Hilda was grinning from ear to ear, knowing I would have to eat humble pie. Rachel's father, a Stoney Indian who also worked for Hilda, had taught her well." Monk fell silent. Tuktu leapt to the next question, carelessly, her curiosity piqued.

"Then what?"

Monk shifted again, cleared his throat, hesitated, but continued. "Eventually we became a team and, well, one thing led to another and we were married. We continued to work for Hilda until Koko was born, and then Rachel wanted to stay home and look after her." Monk put his head in his hands and suddenly shook it violently. "I could be so stubborn, even when I knew I should listen to her. Stupid male pride. That day, that terrible day," Monk choked, "she told me we shouldn't go. She had had a dream the night before, said it was an omen. But I didn't listen. I didn't—I—" Monk jumped up and bolted for the mouth of the cave again.

"Oh no! Grundel!" Tuktu gave a loud snort. Grundel poked his snout out of the Map Den. "I never know when to stop!" wailed Tuktu, rising from her mat of pine branches. "Monk has bolted. What should I do?"

Grundel just shook his head. "Don't worry, Took. He'll be back. He has to let it out; the whole thing has festered inside him for too long. Humans are like that—they have to talk it through in order to let it go. What just happened isn't necessarily a bad thing."

"But the timing is terrible!" said Tuktu. Grundel said nothing; his thoughts were elsewhere. He was waiting for Kyna to appear.

THE URSULAS with Tasmira, Marmo, Raven, Vang and a couple of Brothers were planning their strategy not far from the Rivergate, the mouth of the Castleguard Caves. They were in a meadow, near a small tributary of the river where their noise would be covered by the babbling brook. Vang looked very uneasy.

"You can do this, Vang—you must do it," repeated Inyx. "You must replace Rakor in the caves, so we can recover him. We must take him back to the Valley; it would be too dangerous to leave him here to fall back under SaMäel's hold."

"But what's to say that I won't fall under SaMäel's spell?"

"We explained that," said Alethia, growing impatient. "Listen to us, Vang. You're letting your fear dominate you. Semjaza will be here momentarily to give you the power to shapeshift. When you come out of the caves as an owl to feed and hunt, you will come to us first. We will counteract anything SaMäel has tried to do to you."

"And where will we be first?" asked Kyna, gently. Vang looked at her, gratefully.

"There," he said, turning and looking up at Watchman Peak, breathing deeply, regaining his composure, his courage.

Suddenly Semjaza appeared in a burst of light. The animals instinctively cowered, all except the Ursulas, who held their heads high.

"Ready?" asked Semjaza, lightly, hovering above them. Vang nodded mutely, not knowing what to expect. With their agreement, Semjaza first put an enchantment on the others, so he could elongate time. Then, murmuring words Vang neither heard completely nor understood, the angel held out his spear and thrust it into Vang's heart. Shocked, Vang gasped and staggered as the spear entered, and again as Semjaza tore it out. But there was no blood. Vang's eyes clouded, then cleared and he sensed a new knowledge inside him.

"Whoa!" cried Vang.

Semjaza smiled. "Now all you have to do is to think like a great grey owl. Care to try it?" Vang nodded mutely, closed his eyes and thought of the owl, thought of its hooked beak, its killing talons, thought of its majestic wings. Suddenly, with a gasp, he realized he *was* a great grey owl. His first reaction was to flap his wings, and suddenly he was gaining height. Once airborne, Vang had no idea how to manipulate his wings and he careened wildly around the meadow. Semjaza chuckled at his wild attempt, but when Vang started to nose-dive, Semjaza called out to him.

"Think like an owl, Vang—you're thinking like a bear!" With the very thought of bears, Vang spiralled and crashed to the ground, returning to his bear shape.

"This is too hard! It will take me days to master!" wailed Vang. "I don't have time to learn this!"

"It's all right. Take your time—take as much time as you need," said Semjaza, settling himself on a small hillock to wait. "I've put time on hold for the moment."

Vang practised; he had no idea for how long. Semjaza gave him a few pointers, but mostly he let Vang discover his own way. First Vang noticed how acute his hearing had become and how his vision had increased, although he had to swivel his head to see anything at the side. He looked down at his heavily feathered feet with their dangerous black claws. He tried hissing and barking and snapping his bill. He spread his vast wings and felt their power. Slowly Vang mastered leaping into the air, stroking his wings, gliding silently. He began to enjoy the new perspective and yearned to fly higher, further. He even felt a new over-whelming urge when he noticed a mouse running across the meadow, but it took him many tries before he could capture it. He almost gave up, arguing he didn't plan to kill. But Semjaza insisted he practise until he could catch anything quickly.

"We can't have you starve to death. You will need to feed on at least eight mice a day, as an owl."

"Well, I do not intend to hunt for food in my owl form. I will shape-shift to feed. Although," mused Vang, "it will be easier to find summer berries and the like when I'm flying." He liked the idea of that.

"But," Semjaza lazily replied from the ground where he lounged, "you also have to capture workers for the caves, for SaMäel. Remember that's why he taught Rakor to shape-shift in the first place." So Vang practised, letting the terrified animal go after he had swooped down upon it successfully.

Once he had mastered the necessary skills, Semjaza disen-chanted the others. What felt like hours, to Vang, was experienced by the others as only moments.

"Show me," said Kyna frowning. Vang transmuted and flew

around the meadow.

"Hey," said Raven, bomb diving around Vang, "you look pretty good for a bird, although you could use a few lessons!"

"Careful," replied Vang swiping a large wing at him, "I'm still bigger than you are!" After Vang resumed his bear shape, Kyna gave the final directions and headed for the Caves, with the others trailing her and Marmo running to keep up.

Piotr and Carth, Piotr's twin, had been chosen to distract the men at the Rivergate. Carth was the opposite of Piotr. Where Piotr was quick, small, and clever, Carth was slow in movement and thought, but massive, almost as large as Grundel. And no one had more heart, more courage. Carth understood his own limitations and was happy to follow the instructions of those he trusted, as he always did with Piotr. The plan was not complicated; they were to lure the men out of the cave, then draw them into a hunt, always staying just far enough ahead of them to give the men the hope of a kill. It was simple, but dangerous. To give the Ursulas the maximum amount of time, Piotr and Carth were to confuse the men, so they lost their sense of direction, and could not return quickly. This would be Piotr's responsibility, for no one had a better mental map of the territory than he.

As the bears approached the caves, they could not see nor hear anything unusual, in fact, the Rivergate looked distinctly empty, but Gulo had warned them about the enchanted veil. From her cover, Kyna nodded to Piotr. Carth motioned for Piotr to stay hidden, stepped out of the woods, picked up some small stones and threw them into the mouth of the cave. Nothing happened. He picked up heftier stones and threw them further into the cave. A head poked out through the veil, and a tall, muscular man stepped out.

"Rakor?" said the man. Carth dropped back down and

growled a low deep growl. "Is that you Rakor?" No response. The man shifted nervously.

"Come here, Payne. What do you make of this?" called Slank, dashing into the cave to grab his rifle and pushing another man outside. As Payne stepped out beyond the veil, Piotr lumbered out to join Carth.

"Jeesus!" said Payne. "Who are they?"

"They ain't Rakor, that's for sure! Now what?"

"Well, they're moving, and we're to shoot anything moving, right?"

"Right!" agreed Slank, "and wouldn't I like one of them hides!" He raised and cocked his rifle.

"Me too," answered Payne, scrambling back inside to grab his rifle. The bears dropped back down on all fours and edged further into the woods as Slank raised his weapon. They dropped flat as the first shot rang out.

"OOOeeee—did I get it? I must've got it!" yelled Slank, running towards the bears.

"Slank, wait!" roared Payne.

"Why? We gotta go after it."

"What about the other one?"

"It's taken off! C'mon!" When they reached the spot where the dead bear should have been, the ground was empty.

"Crap. Now what? Maybe we should go back," said Payne, fearfully, looking all around.

"Don't be such a greenhorn! I'm sure I hit him, and I probably injured him, which means I gotta go after him!" Slank looked wildly around; the bears stood up just out of range. "Look, there they are. Shoot—shoot!" The bears galloped off, with the men in pursuit. The Ursulas watched grimly, and then entered the cave. They left Vang, acting as if he were Rakor, with Raven at the cave's entrance. It was Raven's job to warn the Ursulas of any unannounced appearances of the men, and Vang's to stop the men from re-entering the cave should they return suddenly.

"What about SaMäel?" wailed Vang. "How do I stop him?" Vang was not at all sure any of this was a good plan.

"Get a grip!" barked Inyx. "You're a Keeper, act like one!" Vang hung his head and then shook himself.

"Yes. Of course."

"Are you ready?" asked Alethia, more gently. Vang nodded. The females followed the footprints in the cave's sand, as Gulo had, making their way silently to the inner tunnel. When they reached the first shaft, they shifted their shapes into owls.

EARLIER, Rakor and Malenger had been interrogating Koko, but when Malenger became aggressive, badgering the child, Rakor had sent him out to find some decent food for her.

"You'll have to go to the settlement," Rakor told him. "You need to get something more nourishing—milk Koko said, eggs, apples—whatever children eat." Malenger stared at him, enraged that he had to go instead of Slank or Payne, but Rakor insisted, wanting the man to wear off some of his pent up energy.

"Well, at least give me some money for the food."

"I have no money," replied Rakor.

"I need to be recompensed."

"You can deal with SaMäel for that."

Malenger swore savagely, furious about having to go all the way to Hilda's trading post to spend his hard earned money on a worthless kid.

The outfitting camp, Malenger knew, consisted of just a few families that had settled around the trading post near the confluence of two rivers. Hilda Van Buren, whom her Stoney guides called Yahe-Weha—Mountain Woman—had come to the Shining Mountains with her husband, Joe Van Buren, nearly fifteen years earlier. Joe had been convinced by Lewis, an outfitter at Jasper House, that an outfitting depot was needed halfway between Banff and Jasper House on the Stoney Trail. He believed that it wouldn't be long before this part of the country was opened up and the man who had the first foothold would do well.

The Van Burens were enthralled by the glaciers and had set up camp near the Sunwapta Pass, but quickly found the weather too unpredictable, especially the snow in summer. They moved a little further south to a warmer valley at a lower altitude where there was enough grazing land for their animals. After her husband died of pneumonia in their fifth winter, Hilda decided to stay. She kept supplies of all sorts for anyone using the trail, although there weren't many that came north of Banff. Mainly she traded with the Stoney and sold in Banff.

Malenger stuffed his pack angrily, gave the child a scathing look and left in a huff. Hilda Creek was a long, tiresome ride by horse from Castleguard, even if he used the shortcut across one of the Icefield's outwash glaciers.

Sometime after Malenger had left, Koko, lying on her straw mattress, heard rifle shots echoing through the caves and wondered who had tried to escape. Rakor was now using the shots to increase her fear—he was learning from SaMäel.

"There's no escaping, Koko," threatened Rakor. "But I could make things easier for you, if you give me some information." Rakor eyed the trembling child; he knew that what he was doing was wrong. Many nights he had lain in the cavern, horrified at his own actions, the unnecessary deaths, but then a dark wave of pleasure would rush over him, a wave of power and ambition. SaMäel had promised so much; how could he refuse? And if he had to do these things, these small dark acts that SaMäel said made so little difference in the grand scheme of things, wasn't it worth it? He could live with himself—SaMäel said you get used to it—it gets easy. But something deeper in his soul knew that he would pay; an inner voice told him that his actions wouldn't be easy to live with, whatever the outcome. He angrily silenced that voice, calling it other names, like fear.

"I know that you've found something," he cajoled, lying, testing a theory. "All you have to do is tell me about it, and then I'll let you go." Rakor smiled charmingly. For a moment, he almost convinced her with those magic words: *I'll let you go.* Koko's heart opened wildly to the sun, the sky, the green grass. But then Rakor pushed the lie too far.

"You could go back to your father."

"My papa is dead!" Koko shouted angrily.

Impatient, Rakor rose from where he had been lying down, and started pacing the cavern. The small child shook in fear of the massive animal and his suppressed anger.

"What have you found?" he growled, turning on her.

"Dirt, rock, stone, ice."

"What else?"

"What do you mean, that's what we found!" Koko took deep breaths, trying to master her fear. She dare not turn her head towards the tunnel where Mustela and Whistler were holding their breaths.

"You know what I mean; we both know there's more. Just tell me and we can take you to your mother."

Tears welled up in her eyes, but she knew he was lying, so she just put her head down. Rakor waited. Koko closed her eyes, remembering what Mustela had told her, to answer truthfully in everything—everything but the light and the deaths— and said nothing.

"What else!" Rakor had not anticipated such stubborn resistance.

"Nothing! Don't be such a bully!" she shouted at him, backing into a corner. Rakor snorted loudly in frustration and was bounding over to her when Inyx roared his name.

The bear stopped dead in his tracks and twisted towards the entrance. Before he could get his bearings, the four females leapt into the cavern, and instantly surrounded him. He roared his anger, twisting and turning, flailing out his wicked claws, trying to wreak havoc, to create an opening for escape. He shape-shifted into an elk with a heavy rack, but the Ursulas, to Rakor's surprise, shape-shifted with him. He became a moose, meaning to plough his way through, but there was no budging the females who held together, forming a barrier. Finally, he tried his owl shape, trying to fly up out of their reach, but they closed the circle too quickly and clawed him down. He turned back into his own powerful form, but even in his rage, Rakor was no fool; he knew he would never overpower four females, especially Ursulas. The females waited for his show of strength to subside.

"I am The Keeper!" roared Rakor, in one last desperate attempt, "Out of my way!"

"You *were* The Keeper," said Inyx icily. "How could you do this, Rakor?" Although his mother's words cut deeply, Rakor feared Alethia more. He searched their faces until his gaze finally settled on Alethia, his mate. It was to her he spoke.

THE BEARS had been talking for a long time. At first, Koko crouched, trembling in a corner, wanting to run to Mustela and Whistler. As Rakor calmed down and all the bears resumed their bear shape, Koko began to watch and listen intensely. Was this the rescue? Mustela and Whistler too hoped, clinging to one another. But if it was, it was a slow process. Rakor clung desperately to SaMäel's logic. The females probed Rakor's answers, wearing him down, making small chinks in his armour, until Rakor finally revealed SaMäel's promise of immortality, when they found the Quintessence. Throughout, he had been standing upright, brazen, clinging stubbornly to SaMäel's false promises.

"Mel has immortality—why should she keep it to herself? What harm is there in my having it? I won't take all of it! I just want a little bit of it!"

"The Quintessence isn't Mel's, nor does she have it; it belongs to Earth, to Gaia. You know full well Mel just protects it as we do," Alethia responded.

"Why should she be the only one who knows where it is?" roared Rakor. "I should know where it is! I am The Keeper!"

"I think this situation, this horrible predicament you have put us all in, is a very good answer to your question," said Inyx, sardonically. "Your new knowledge of the Quintessence isn't helping anyone—except SaMäel." Rakor squirmed, feeling caged in body and thought.

"Well, why shouldn't The Keeper have the right to immortality?" he repeated lamely, for the umpteenth time.

"Rakor, you're not listening," said Kyna wearily. "SaMäel has deceived you. The Quintessence was made for Gaia only. Without it Earth dies. If Earth dies, *where* will you exist, and with whom? What good would immortality be then?"

"Even if you could withstand its power—which you couldn't!" snapped Alethia.

"And Rakor," added Inyx, tightening the screw of their argument, "did it not occur to you to think what SaMäel might do with this kind of power?"

"What's it to him—he already has immortality! He doesn't care—he's doing this for me!"

"Really?" said Inyx. "Except that he would also have Earth's death to hold over our heads—to get anything he wants. Is this worth it, Rakor? Do you want to ransom your home, our home, to SaMäel?"

"Ransom? You mean—I'm—" In a deadening flash, Rakor dropped down on all fours, feeling SaMäel's magic draining out of him.

"He wasn't doing this for me," he said flatly, hanging his head.

"No," replied Alethia.

"And I couldn't bear the power of it even if I did find it."

"That's right. We are not gods," said Alethia, gaining heart. "But we are the protectors of all that's sacred. That's what The Ursula taught you, what she teaches all of us. We are the Keepers." Slowly she drew near to him. "Cathedral still needs you."

The Ursulas, Koko and Marmo all held their breath— would it be enough? Finally, Rakor looked up at Inyx and then into Alethia's eyes.

"I've missed you," he said.

"And I you," she replied, stepping forward, to nuzzle him.

MARMO had been quietly entering each of the tunnels and had just re-emerged, when Kyna gestured to him. After speaking softly to her, Marmo entered the tunnel where Mustela and Whistler were waiting breathlessly. Kyna waited until she heard them scampering down the tunnel.

"What happens now?" asked Rakor, dreading what he had to tell them.

"You're coming with us. We have Vang outside ready to take your place," replied Kyna.

"Vang? But he can't shape-shift! SaMäel will know right away!"

"You'd be surprised what Vang can do. Leave the details to us, Rakor," smiled Inyx.

"Right, now, come with us." Kyna turned to the child who was still huddled in a corner, and asked gently, "Are you Koko, daughter of Monk and Rachel?"

"Yes," she whispered.

Kyna looked at her kindly and said, "Don't be afraid." The child was filthy; her long black hair a mass of knots and tangles, her skin raw in places, scabbed and bruised in others. Her knees were purple with old bruises and callused, as were her hands. And she was so scrawny that her ribs showed through her rags.

"Come," Kyna said gently. "We're going to take you back to Monk."

"Papa?" the child asked, her large eyes widening. "My papa is dead," she whispered.

"No, Monk is alive," Kyna replied, "and anxiously waiting for you." Koko started to cry, softly at first, and then sobbing wildly, great heaves wracking her weak body. Mustela came tearing out of the cave.

"It's all right, Mustela; it's all right. We just told her we're taking her home," smiled Kyna.

"He's alive, Mustela," cried the child, running to her. "Papa's alive! We're being rescued!"

Kyna exchanged looks with Alethia and then asked, "Has Marmo explained everything to you, Mustela?" Mustela nodded. "Can you do this? We know what we're asking of all of you."

"What?" asked Koko, stopping midstride, looking frantically between Kyna and Mustela who was not smiling. "What are you asking of them?" From the other tunnels, the small animals traipsed into the cavern and stood around Marmo who was glaring at Rakor. Mustela turned to him. Marmo had to drag his eyes away from Rakor to address Kyna.

"These animals," said Marmo, drawing himself up to his full height, "are unequalled in their courage. They have all agreed to stay, to keep things seemingly as normal as possible; to go on deceiving SaMäel; and to suffer his wrath, if discovered."

"No!' cried Koko. "You must rescue all of us!"

Marmo gestured to Mustela to calm the child. Then he bowed to Kyna. "And with your permission, I will stay here with them." Kyna, looking around, realized how much these creatures needed Marmo to give them strength. She nodded.

"We will do everything in our power to get all of you out of here as soon as possible," said Kyna. Koko started to protest again, but Mustela spoke quietly to her. Suddenly, they heard Raven cawing in the tunnel, then appearing in the entrance.

"It's Malenger. He's coming back. He'll be here soon. Vang will distract him from entering, but come, be quick. What are the other two men's names again?"

"Slank and Payne," answered Rakor.

"Thanks," cried Raven as he careened out of the Grotto and back to Vang.

Kyna spoke briefly to Marmo, and told Koko to climb on her back. Koko hesitated, shaking her head. Kyna exchanged glances with Mustela. They were out of time.

"We need you out there, Koko," said Mustela. "You know better than anyone what's happening here. What we need." The others animals nodded vigorously. "Go with Kyna. Help rescue all of us." The child rushed to Mustela and clung to her.

"There's no time. You must go." Mustela gently unfastened the child's arms and encouraged her to climb onto Kyna's back. With tears streaming down her face, Koko tried to be brave.

"Hold on tightly, child," said Kyna, "I'm going to change shape. Are you ready?"

"Yes," she whispered. A loud gasp echoed through the cave as Koko found herself clinging desperately to an owl's neck.

Kyna looked over to Inyx. "Is she secure?"

"She's fine, as long as she doesn't strangle you!"

"Oh, sorry!" wailed Koko. "What should I hold onto?"

"We're fine," said Kyna. "Don't mind Inyx. She's teasing. Just hold on tightly." She leapt into the air and flew out of the Grotto, the others following.

They had just reached the Rivergate when Malenger came into the meadow in front of the caves; they transmuted, dropped down flat, pressed to the cold hard stone. Koko's heart raced wildly as she lifted her head slightly to watch and see what Vang would do. The bear went out to meet the man, directing Malenger's attention away from the caves' entrance.

"Malenger, thank heavens you're back! Slank and Payne are chasing bears, but they have no idea what they're doing. They're going to get themselves killed. You'd better go after them."

"Bears?" asked Malenger, looking at Vang oddly. "What bears?"

"I don't know—I didn't see; I just heard them. I was just coming out, but there was definitely more than one. I thought the men would be all right—after all, they were the ones with the rifles. But they've been gone much too long." The bears in the cave snickered; the two men were no match for Piotr, they thought.

"Which way did they go? Will I be able to find them?" Malenger asked, sounding doubtful, looking longingly towards the caves.

"That way," said Vang, pointing to the north. "You'd better try. Hurry!" Vang moved and stood obstinately in his way, blocking Malenger's view of the caves, leaving him no option.

"Bloody fools," said Malenger. "Here," he said angrily and thrust a hemp bag at Vang.

"What's this?" asked Vang, confused.

"Her food, of course! Jeesus!" And Malenger jammed his rifle into the saddle pocket, remounted his horse and headed off into the woods. Kyna and the others jumped up, exiting the caves.

"It's for Koko," said Rakor, taking the food bag from Vang, as he left.

"And how am I to explain both Koko *and* her food disappearing?" Vang asked to Rakor's retreating back.

Tasmira, flashing him a radiant smile as she lumbered past, said, "You'll think of something, Vang. I know you will." Vang gestured back weakly. Just before they turned out of sight, Rakor looked back to see Vang sitting in the meadow outside the caves, dejected, head in his great paws. "Are you sure Vang will be ok?" Rakor asked Inyx. She drew a deep breath. "He comes from a very smart line," she said smiling, though not at all sure.

Tasmira's Task

OUT OF SIGHT of the caves, the pine wood opened to a lush alpine meadow filled with willow, carpets of yellow dryas, and springy mats of white mountain heather with its delicate bells. Kyna led them west around the base of the mountain to one of the Castleguard glaciers which they climbed to reach the Ice-field, heading north west across the vast expanse towards Cathedral and the further Twins—the higher peak pure white and its twin darkly impressive. Her high hanging valley called to her, nestled between the peaks, but Kyna knew she had to get Koko to Monk first. As they approached Cathedral, after weighing her alternatives, Kyna dropped back to talk to Tasmira, letting Inyx and Alethia lumber alongside Rakor—their joy palpable.

"Tasmira," said Kyna, quietly, "I'm taking Koko back to Monk at Cathedral, and I must speak to Grundel, but I want Rakor to go directly to the Valley. Rakor is not ready to face Grundel or Melancholia. He is far from cured yet. We still have much to work through. And I certainly don't want to get his back up, as it is sure to do in Grundel's presence. We would have to start from the beginning again."

Tasmira nodded mutely, waiting to hear what Kyna wanted of her.

"Inyx is getting old. She doesn't deal well with confrontation now. Alethia is Rakor's mate and will be torn in loyalty. I understand their good intentions—but, in the past, Rakor has been able to persuade them of anything—if even half the stories they tell are true! You're stronger willed than either of them. I need you to stand up to Rakor, to get him to the Valley. I'll send

Gorath and some of the other Brothers to you, as soon as I get to Cathedral. But you must not let Rakor persuade the Ursulas to alter our plans. Can you do this?"

Tasmira nodded again. Kyna thanked her before catching up to the others. After agreeing to the wisdom of her plans, the older Ursulas stopped briefly to watch Kyna and Koko turn west towards Cathedral. The child's eyes were radiant in her thin, pale face.

"That's going to be quite the homecoming," sighed Inyx.

"I'd love to see Monk's face when they arrive!" Alethia exclaimed, full of her own joy at Rakor's recovery. Rakor, noted Tasmira, said nothing. She wondered if he was thinking of his own return to Cathedral.

"Come," she said, turning north across the Icefield, "we'd better get going; we need to travel with the light."

They had been silent for a while, carefully navigating the Icefield's mill wells, the glacier's rounded drains, where meltwater streams plunged into deep wells in the ice, and where man or beast could be instantly lost. It was clear overhead, but cumulous clouds were already forming over the Twins. Rakor, padding along between the Ursulas, only listened with one ear to Inyx and Alethia's chatter. He was confused and surprised. He had expected to be taken back to Cathedral, and despite his betrayal, to be reinstated as Keeper. When Kyna had sent them to the Valley, he had been shocked. He realized then that Kyna was Ursula and that Grundel was The Keeper, and neither were going to step down in deference to him or Alethia.

He plodded on, only half aware of Alethia taking over the lead position, wondering what the other Brothers were thinking. Were they now loyal to Grundel? Would they ever want him to step back into the role of Keeper after what he had done—deserting them, betraying Melancholia? How angry was

Mel? Would he have to challenge Grundel? How powerful was he? Suddenly he stopped abruptly. Inyx, who had been following him closely, bumped into him.

"What," she said, annoyed, "what are you doing?"

"I need to rest," Rakor answered, slumping down on his haunches.

"What? Here—why, are you ill?"

"I'm exhausted." Tasmira who was behind Inyx, eyed him thoughtfully and then called to Alethia who was breaking trail and had not noticed that they had stopped. She came hurrying back.

"What is it?" Alethia searched their faces.

"Apparently, Rakor needs a rest," said Tasmira, snorting her disbelief.

"What is it, Rakor?" asked Alethia, knowing him too well to be convinced by such a thin lie. Rakor was never ill, never tired. He paused, collecting his thoughts, and then turned to her.

"I need to talk to Grundel. You understand, don't you? After all that's happened, I won't rest, won't be able to do anything until I speak to—."

"I'm sorry Rakor," interrupted Tasmira firmly, trying to prevent this discussion, "but Kyna said to take you to the Valley."

"Alethia," pleaded Rakor, "you're The Ursula. It's your decision. You know what's best for all of us."

Alethia shook her head. "Oh Rakor—no—I—things have changed. Please don't ask this of me. You'll see Mel and Grundel, of course, but not just yet." She turned her head away, but Rakor was not ready to give up.

"Inyx, speak to her. What's the harm in it? There's so much to straighten out. It's just a question of priorities: I speak to Grundel and then we go to the Valley. I should have spoken up when Kyna headed for Cathedral, but I was still in shock. But now I can feel my old self coming back."

"Well," replied Inyx, "I see no harm in the plan."

Alethia was torn—she knew she should stick to Kyna's directions, but Rakor sounded like his old self, and she deeply wanted Rakor and Grundel to reconcile. Their relationship had never been easy. Grundel's twin, Boris, was from the first obviously not suited for leadership. Rakor had pinned all his hopes on Grundel, and had demanded excellence from him. Alethia and the other bears found this hard to understand. It was not the bears' way to be demanding, ambitious, to seek to determine the next Keeper. In the past, they had happily left this up to Melancholia, trusting her judgement. It didn't matter who led, as long The Keeper was strong, courageous and wise—someone they could respect and follow. But Rakor was different. Alethia had always been the one to smooth things between Rakor and Grundel, although as a youngster, Grundel was both quick to learn and patient with his sire.

"Well—," she started, but Tasmira broke in.

"We're taking Rakor to the Valley," repeated Tasmira sharply, hoping to snap Alethia out of her delusions. "Kyna is Ursula until we are told differently!"

Rakor growled angrily at Tasmira's tone. "And who are you to speak to The Ursula like that?" he roared. The young female didn't flinch. It was the wrong tack to take with Tasmira, who was not easily intimidated. When she had a job to do, it was going to get done. She answered firmly.

"I'm Tasmira of the Valley, mate of Gorath, second to Grundel. I mean no disrespect, but my loyalty is to Kyna and The Keeper. It is you, Rakor, who betrayed Cathedral's trust, and stripped Alethia's role from her. She is no longer The Ursula." Rakor growled menacingly at the female's audacity. Tasmira turned to Alethia. "We trusted you, we followed you, and we gave you our loyalty. You chose Kyna. Don't we owe her that same loyalty?" Alethia bowed her head. In that gesture, Rakor saw Alethia's weakness and decided that neither Inyx nor Alethia would stop him now; and he knew that he could take the brazen young female. He rose and turned south, heading for Cathedral.

"Rakor," called Tasmira, "I wouldn't do that."

"But you are not me," he said, over his shoulder, loping away.

"Inyx, Alethia—" pleaded Tasmira, but they turned their heads away from her. She thought fast—trying to think like Rakor.

"You won't get to Grundel," she called loudly. Rakor stopped, turned his head towards her for a moment.

"What do you mean?" he boomed.

"The Brothers—they won't let you challenge him," she said, playing her last card. "There's too much at stake, and you're the least of their problems. You're so out of touch with what's happening—you think this is about you. But it isn't." Rakor growled and pawed the snow angrily. Tasmira turned briefly to implore the two females again. "You know I'm right. Do something!" Inyx and Alethia got up slowly, heaving their large, tired bodies into motion.

"She's right," said Alethia, wearily. "You better come with us, Rakor. There's so much to explain."

"After I see Grundel," repeated Rakor.

"Monk's there. With a gun," added Tasmira.

"And he'll probably shoot you on sight," agreed Inyx. "Tasmira's right—you're so out of touch, you'll just make an ass of yourself if you go now. Come on," she said, loping towards the Valley, eyeing the sky that was going grey as the cloud cover rolled in, "let's get a move on before that storm hits." Alethia followed her. Rakor looked longingly towards Cathedral, but Tasmira had kindled his own fears, his own doubts. What did they mean it wasn't about him? What did he have to learn? Perhaps he did need more information. He yearned for everything to be the way it was when he was Keeper; but there was still time.

GRUNDEL was striding back and forth across the cave floor, restless and uneasy; it was unclear now who should be The Keeper—this situation had never occurred before. Wondering where Mel was, he joined Raven out on the ledge, waiting impatiently for Kyna's return. He tried to relax, to watch just the cloud's shadow play on the Twins; but he could not calm his churning mind. Suddenly Raven spotted Kyna trudging up the mountain. Grundel had not doubted The Ursula's likelihood of success, though he knew it was not without danger. He had surprised himself—surprised at how much he had worried for Kyna's safety; how quickly she had become a part of him. He had ambivalent feelings about Rakor. He wanted him home, safe, released from SaMäel's grip, but he did not want to give up the role of Keeper. It suited him; he was good at it; in his soul, he knew he was better at it than Rakor. But what would happen if and when Rakor returned? What would Melancholia do?

"Who's with her?" asked Grundel.

"No one," replied Raven, surprised.

"Now what does that mean?" Grundel sat down heavily on his haunches.

"Want me go find out?" asked Raven.

"No, let her come, let her speak to us in her own time."

"Wait, something's on her back—looks like a child."

Grundel waited until he could see Kyna, could watch her

body movement to see if there was any suggestion of defeat, but saw none. Satisfied, he went back into the cave to wake Monk who had been given a potion by Semjaza to help him sleep. Not yet fully awake, Monk stumbled groggily onto the ledge.

"Where are they, Raven?" Monk swayed back and forth.

"Whoa, careful where you stand there, my man. They're coming. They're just below that outcropping of rock," Raven replied. Monk let out a joyous cry as Kyna came into view, with Koko on her back.

"Oh God, oh God," wept Monk, falling on his knees. As Kyna knelt down, Monk swept Koko off her back and into his arms. She clung, her head buried in his chest, weeping quietly. The others waited patiently for Monk to make the first move. Finally, he stood up with Koko, strode into the Keeper's Cave, and the two collapsed into the armchair. Koko would not look at anyone but Monk. He draped a blanket around her, rocked her, sang to her, and very quickly she fell asleep.

"I imagine that's the first trusting sleep she's had in a very long time," said Kyna. Grundel nodded. Tears streamed down Monk's face.

"What happened back there?" asked Grundel, turning to Kyna. "Where are the others?"

"Tasmira, Inyx and Alethia have taken Rakor to the Valley. We need more time with him—he's unstable, unpredictable; our work with him is not done."

"Piotr and Carth?" asked Grundel.

"They're still out there," replied Kyna. Grundel called to his Brothers in the Map Den. Half a dozen lumbered out into the main cavern.

"We need to find Piotr and Carth," said Grundel. "Take Raven with you to scout. They're out in the vicinity of the Caves; they headed down the Castleguard River. Raven, I suspect Piotr will stop well before Big Springs, and start circling. It's open ground there with no real landmarks and that will confuse the men. Be careful, all of you—the men have guns." The Brothers nodded grimly and started towards the cave's mouth.

"Wait," said Kyna, "I need Gorath and one other to join Tasmira in the Valley."

"Why?" asked Gorath, turning back, "is there a problem?"

"Rakor is not himself yet. Tasmira needs support. We're uncertain what Rakor will try as he loses power." Gorath and Grundel exchanged looks.

"I'm coming with you," Grundel said. Gorath nodded.

"I'm coming too," said Monk.

"But what about Koko?" asked Kyna, thinking that she needed to keep things simple at the Valley in order to be able to work with Rakor; Monk was not needed there at this time, even Grundel would probably change her agenda. And she was sincerely concerned for the child's health.

"We're going to stay with Mikaila for a while. I'll drop her off."

"I doubt Koko will let you do that," said Kyna, watching the sleeping child.

"Well, that's my worry. I need to know what happened. There are still gaps—terrible gaps. I won't be able to help Koko fully until I know what happened."

"We could tell you that, Monk," began Kyna.

"No! I need to hear it from Rakor! Grundel, Kyna, please!"

"But the Brothers are leaving now; they must," said Kyna. "You can't expect Koko to travel again today surely?" Monk looked down at the sleeping child, pale and fragile.

"No," he admitted, "not today. But I will come on Equus; she has offered me that privilege; and we will come early tomorrow. Don't start without me!" he said, turning to Grundel.

"All right, Monk. We have other things to do first," said

Grundel. Gorath, waiting beside him, nodded. As the Brothers left, Grundel added, "Kaare, no killing."

AT CASTLEGUARD, after Malenger left to find Slank and Payne, Vang lumbered back through the veil, transmuted into an owl and flew to the Grotto. Marmo and Mustela were still talking to the diggers, planning their own strategy and contingency plans.

"What are you going to tell the others about Koko?" asked Marmo.

"I'm not sure," replied Vang, "any brilliant ideas?"

"Why don't you just say you let her go?" asked Whistler. "You're in charge, not Malenger. You could say you were worried about her health."

"True," said Vang, "but she would go straight to her father. And the old Rakor wouldn't want that."

"Then she would have to escape," said Marmo. "There is, after all, no one at the Rivergate to stop her."

"But then SaMäel would go looking for her," said Vang, "and that's the last thing the others need."

"Then she must die," said Mustela, simply.

PIOTR had successfully kept the men near enough but not too near, for hours. He had guided them in circles until they were completely lost. Too late they realized that they had no compass, no food, and no Malenger to get them out of trouble. They had left in such a hurry that they had brought nothing with them. Piotr and Carth were lying down, hidden behind large outcroppings of granite at the edge of a stand of trees. The two men were close by, exhausted, trying to decide what they should do.

"Geez Payne, I sure don't want to give up now. We're so close," said Slank.

"We've been close for hours! The question is how do we git closer! Frankly, I'm beat and want to go home. If we don't head back soon we'll lose the light and then we'll have nothing to guide us. Where *are* we?"

Slank shook his head.

"It's just like them bears are toying with us!" whined Payne.

"Them dumb bears can't—" Suddenly Slank stopped; something was slinking through the bushes behind them. "What the hell?" He raised his rifle and cocked it.

"Don't shoot you idiot!" A voice whispered hoarsely from the brush.

"Is that you Malenger?" cried Slank.

"Yes it's me for Christ sake! Who were you expecting, the pope? Point that damn thing somewhere else," he said, as he caught up to them. He looked tired and angry.

"We got ourselves two bear, Malenger!' declared Slank, proudly.

"Ya? Well, I don't see any bear rugs," answered Malenger, sarcastically.

"No. Over there, two of them, just waitin' to be took," said Payne. Malenger did not like the sound of that—one grizzly was dangerous enough and smarter than these two idiots put together. He looked over in the direction to which they were pointing. The wood itself was not dense, but it was filled with underbrush that hindered his view, and would hinder their escape. He could see nothing of the bears.

"Two grizzlies?"

"Ya, but one's real small," said Payne. "We just haven't been able to corner them."

"No kidding; they've been stringing you along."

"No—they don't even know we're here!" replied Slank.

"Don't be a fool. They can hear a squirrel piss in the wind, and lose you in a minute in these hills, if they wanted to. They're up to something." Malenger thought for a moment.

"Geez, Malenger, they're just bears—what could they know?"

"Ya? Well, Rakor is just a bear too and he's a hell of a lot smarter than you two."

"Thanks!" carped Payne. "Anyway, Rakor is different."

"Think what you want," said Malenger, "but there ain't no such thing as a dumb bear. Ain't you heard that a bear has the strength of ten men and the sense of twelve? So you'd better start thinking how you can outsmart these two or the next thing you know you're gonna be face to face with two mean grizzlies."

"How are we going to do that?"

"Well, there are three of us now, and, if we're lucky, they don't know it. We have the advantage for the moment. Follow me."

PIOTR sat up, still panting. "What was that?"

"What?" asked Carth, not moving. He listened but heard nothing new.

"Something," said Piotr. "They're getting too close. We better decide how to get out of here. It's time we got back." As Piotr stood up to smell where the men were, two shots rang out and he dropped quickly. Carth sat up alarmed.

"Are you hit?" Piotr shook his head, visibly shaken. "The shots came from two directions," Carth said, nudging him, "north and west. What now?'

"Well, we don't want to go further south. If we head east towards the river we'll get out of their range, then we'll circle wide back towards the Icefield. Once we're past them we can easily outrun them." said Piotr, weakly. "Is there much cover?" Carth cautiously lifted his head. "Careful! I don't know how they got in range."

"Not much. We'll need to stay low," said Carth. Piotr nodded. The bears eyed each other, wordlessly. Suddenly the game had become more deadly.

"Right—ready?" Piotr nodded. As Carth lumbered out from behind the stand of trees, away from the shooters, another shot rang out in front of them, splintering the silence wide open. Carth fell. Piotr flattened himself to the ground, crawling backwards for cover. "Carth," he called, "Carth!"

"You got him! You got the big one!" yelled Slank, starting to run towards Carth.

"Stay where you are, Slank!" Malenger hollered back. "There's another."

Payne, who was poised two thirds of the way down the northern slope of a hill, heard a roar behind him and looked back, just in time to see four large grizzlies thundering down the hill, almost on top of him. He let out a yelp and galloped towards Slank. As the Brothers who had been sent by Grundel to find Piotr and Carth came over the ridge of the hill, they had seen Malenger fire at Carth. They already had a head of steam when Payne noticed them. They were bellowing in anger. When Slank saw Payne coming with the bears right behind him, he tried to cock his rifle, but his hands were shaking so hard that he could hardly hold onto it; he ran towards Malenger, shouting. Malenger tried to take aim, but the two men bearing down on him obstructed his view.

"Get out of the way! Get out of the way!" yelled Malenger.

"Jeesus, Malenger, run! Run! You won't be able to shoot them all!" Slank yelled. Piotr jumped up and ran to Carth. He saw the Brothers' rage, felt their anger, but knew Grundel would not accept the men's deaths. Piotr roared their code for 'no killing.' The bears, well-trained, halted in their tracks, practically falling over one another. They looked at Piotr, shocked. It was, after all, Carth who was shot—they did not expect restraint from his twin. Kaare shook off his anger and echoed the command.

"Chase them over that hill," he yelled, pointing. Three of the older bears hounded the men through the pinewoods, out onto the valley floor, then up a hill, dropping further and further back, until, when the men attained the crest of the hill and disappeared over it, the bears returned to the others.

Carth was bleeding from his chest, losing a lot of blood. Piotr, beside him, sat helplessly, listening to his twin's heart-rending moans. He looked up as Lunt, Aage and Inguar, older bears of Rakor's generation, returned panting.

"I don't think the bullet passed right through him. I think it's lodged in his chest. Kaare's gone to get Monk and the Ursulas. It—it looks bad," said Piotr.

"There isn't time to wait, Piotr. We need to get him to the river. Only the glacier water can stop this bleeding," said Lunt. Between the four of them, they half carried, half dragged Carth bawling in pain, over the underbrush and rough terrain to the river and plunged him in up to his chest. Carth's eyes had glazed over and he lay motionless. The others sat and waited. Piotr watched the river, watched the low clouds cast moving shadows across the mountains. No one spoke until Mikaila and Monk arrived on Equus, with Melancholia.

"How is he?" asked Mel, descending to stand behind Piotr who sat motionless, on his haunches.

"Not conscious," said Piotr, gruffly.

Monk edged into the freezing water, gingerly, with his knife.

"I'm going to dig out the bullet," he said to Piotr, who nodded mutely, "but I can't stand in this water; I'll freeze. You'll have to pull him out, just to the edge. We'll have to submerge him again for a while, when I'm done."

Monk worked quickly, while the others watched. He gritted his teeth as the knife hit bone. Afterwards, he tried to staunch the wound, but the cloth was drenched red in minutes. All of them knew that Carth couldn't lose much more blood. Again, they submerged him in the freezing water. They were all relieved when the three Ursulas arrived, flying in as owls. As they transmuted, the Brothers lifted Carth onto a bed of pine boughs beside the river.

"Will he live?" Piotr asked Alethia, crouching down beside her, looking for comfort. The forest was blanketed in darkness; snow fell softly at first then with increasing flurry; a tense silence had descended on all of them.

"We can't tell yet," said Alethia, gently. "You need to leave us here to see what we can do. Return in the morning." Piotr hesitated, but Kaare nudged him gently. The Brothers returned to Cathedral with Monk and Mikaila, leaving the females to perform their rituals. As they left, they heard the females intoning "Xexor, Xomoy, Xonor" invoking the benevolent spirits.

EARLY NEXT MORNING while dew still clung to the juniper, the Barratt willow, and the delicate pink petals of Hedysarum, a grim group gathered in the Valley of the Twins. Grundel, waiting for Melancholia, cast glances at his sire. Rakor studied the ground, reluctant to raise his head. He knew that the moment he did, he would have to tell the truth, the whole, shameful, brutal truth. And there was no way of fudging it with Koko sitting on Monk's lap beside Grundel. The females, back from their vigil with Carth, were telling Grundel and Gorath what had happened.

"Where's Carth now?" asked Grundel.

"He's with Inyx, beside the Salmon River," replied Kyna.

"How is he?"

"When we left—not good."

"Have Piotr and the others gone to join them?"

"Piotr left earlier this morning, but the others are meeting him there—they're on their way."

"As soon as we're done here, we'll join them. Is Mel there?"

"She was, but she left last night when we did."

"And Vang?" Grundel asked, changing the topic. The others shifted positions, uncomfortably. "Well?" probed Grundel. "Can he do it?"

"Of course he can," exclaimed Rakor, finally lifting his head. "He's a Brother!" Having assumed the role of Keeper, Grundel turned to Rakor, suppressing his awkwardness, his anger, his profound disappointment. Melancholia had not yet spoken to him. He knew he must remain in charge until told otherwise.

"You'd better tell us what happened. All of it—from the beginning."

Rakor looked at the younger bear in surprise; there was an undeniable note of authority in Grundel's voice. Now that Rakor was back in the familiar surroundings of the Valley of the Twins, he was torn, as Kyna knew he would be, between his ambition and his old self. There were so many memories here, entangled with Inyx and Alethia and Grundel. He felt torn in two—he could still hear SaMäel's golden voice, whispering in his ear endless possibilities; but he was beginning to experience pangs of guilt, an acknowledgement of his betrayal. And they were savage, great bear paws ripping at his heart.

The older Ursulas watched him carefully. They alone could fully feel his agony. "It's all right," soothed Inyx, "begin when you're ready." As Rakor began to speak, there was a flurry of moving air as Melancholia materialized. She stood in front of Rakor, regal and severe in a gown of midnight blue that shimmered with filaments of gold. Rakor, again, dropped his head.

"Oh Mel," he said, "what can I say?"

"Go on with your tale," she replied coldly.

Rakor's Tale

"I DON'T KNOW where to begin. It was a desire that overwhelmed me. I can hardly describe it—wanting to know what we protect." Gorath and Grundel exchanged sceptical looks that Rakor noticed. "Oh, I know we all understand what it is on one level, but this was different—this was—awareness—that it might be something of value—*value*, do you understand? I'd never experienced it before—a desire to possess something. I don't know where it came from."

Tasmira guffawed. "Oh right," she said.

"Silence!" roared Rakor, unaccustomed to the disrespect. A wave of fear swept over Koko and she clung to her father whimpering.

"Take care, Rakor," said Monk sharply. "You're not in the Caves now." The bear growled and struggled to restrain his anger at the presumption of the human.

"It was SaMäel," said Alethia, reaching out to her mate. "SaMäel put that desire in you. That wasn't you." Rakor frowned, wanting to believe her, but in his heart, uncertain. He paused.

"Continue Rakor," said Melancholia, "but omit the excuses." That jolted Rakor out of his anger—Mel had never spoken to him in that tone of voice.

"The idea obsessed me. I began to take longer and longer forays into the woods, to be alone, to think. Until one day, far from Cathedral, I came across SaMäel, sitting on a rock by a stream, idly watching me. He was laughing, and I knew instantly that he was laughing at me. I disliked him immediately, but I was intrigued. He beckoned me to sit down, and he began a story. I realize now, it was a fabrication; but it was what I was ready to hear—that Mel was keeping something wondrous from me, keeping it all to herself, for herself. It was something I had already wondered." Rakor dropped his head in shame, waiting for Mel to speak, but when there was only silence, he continued. "SaMäel was talking about the Quintessence. I longed for him to tell me where it was—a piece of knowledge I didn't have. But he wouldn't, until I struck a bargain with him. He said there was also something he desired, that we could help one another—serve one another, I think he said. But he wouldn't help me, until I agreed to a bargain. I didn't care what he wanted; I thought it couldn't be half as important as what I wanted, so I agreed."

Rakor broke off his tale. He could not look at Monk, or Koko sitting on his lap. He didn't know how to continue.

"Go on Rakor," said Melancholia, in a voice as dark and brittle as volcanic rock. "You must." Rakor took a deep breath.

"Forgive me, Monk. The bargain—the bargain was a trade—a woman, Rachel, for knowledge of the Quintessence. SaMäel staged your 'accident' on the bergschrund. He left you to die, but Rachel and Koko were saved and taken to the Castleguard Caves." Monk gasped. Koko began to cry. Monk rocked her as his mind reeled.

"All I had to do was—was threaten to kill Koko unless Rachel chose to go with SaMäel." Rakor looked away from Monk and Koko.

"What?" cried Monk. Koko whimpered.

"How could you?" gasped Kyna.

"Chose to go? What-what choice!" stammered Monk. He was shaking with anger. He wanted to lunge at the bear, to sink his knife into the bear's throat.

"You—you don't understand," pleaded Rakor.

"Oh, but we do," replied Melancholia. "You traded the path of truth and honour for a path of power. How could you be so blind? SaMäel was manipulating you, just as he was manipulating Rachel. He didn't need you. He could have threatened Koko's life easily with a rock slide or cave-in—anything to make Rachel fearful."

"What do you mean?" interrupted Monk.

"Remember, Monk," continued the spirit, "SaMäel has no means to force creatures on Earth—you *choose* to act for him or against him. He couldn't take Rachel if she didn't decide to go with him. Isn't that right, Rakor?" The bear again hung his head in shame. "His magic might be able to manipulate natural forces, but he cannot control men or creatures unless they choose to let him." She turned a stony glare on Rakor. "Why did you do it?"

Rakor didn't look up, "I know now that I was already his, long before SaMäel asked this of me." The Ursulas exchanged looks, beginning to realize the depth of their task.

"But Rachel?" cried Monk. "Where is Rachel? Is she alive?"

"She's in Abadon; at least, she was."

"What do you mean 'was'? Where's Abadon? Is she dead?"

"I don't know. But I don't know how anyone could survive Abadon."

"Why?" repeated Monk. "Where in God's name is Abadon?"

"Wait, Monk. The Quintessence—what about the Quintessence?" pressed Melancholia.

"I swear we haven't found it!" replied Rakor.

"But we did," said Koko, firmly, sitting up.

"What?" roared Rakor, forgetting for a moment where he was. "I knew something was up! You lied to me!" Koko cowered in her father's arms. Gorath, sitting beside Monk, put out a restraining paw as the man tensed.

"Control yourself, Rakor," warned Melancholia. "Have you already forgotten what The Ursula told you?" Her steely voice calmed him, and he hung his head again. "Go on, Koko."

"We found something. Mustela knew it must be important, perhaps what you are calling the Quin—Quin…"

"Quintessence," said Monk. "What did you find, Sprat?"

"Just a beam of light in the tunnel. One of the ground squirrels came upon it, when he chunked out a piece of earth. He was instantly blinded, Papa. Mustela said we needed to cover it up again, but another squirrel, Pip, was also blinded trying to cover up the little hole that let in the light."

"What happened to those squirrels?" pressed Mel.

"They—they died—horribly!" Koko covered her face with her hands, weeping. They all waited while she composed herself.

"Can you tell us how?" pressed Mel. Monk gave her a scowl. "I'm sorry Monk, but it is imperative that we know."

"It's alright Papa," said Koko, looking up and gazing into his eyes, her little hands cupping his face. "It was so strange. There they were—blind, trapped in that awful tunnel like all of us, without hope, but for a while they danced as if they were the two happiest creatures on earth. We envied them until suddenly their bodies started to shake and shake and shake. It was horrible! Horrible!" She hid her face in his chest and stayed there, her face buried in his layers of clothing. "And then they died," she whispered.

Melancholia turned to Rakor. "This is what SaMäel wanted to give you after you gave him Rachel. This would have been your fate, too. And after your death, SaMäel would have the Quintessence all to himself, to hold all on Earth ransom."

"How are we to move it, Mel, if none of us can even look

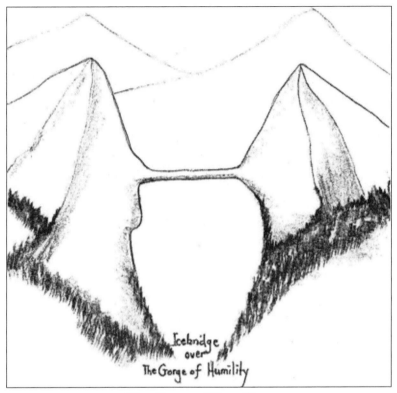

The Gorge of Humility

upon it?" asked Grundel, getting back to the practical problem.

"I'll have to think about that. It should be in a container, a shell, the *Gloria Maris*. I don't know what has happened. I should go look for myself, although I don't want to draw SaMäel's attention. Koko, where exactly did you find the light?" After Koko described the entrance to their tunnel from the Grotto, Melancholia disappeared.

"All right," said Kyna, firmly, "that's it for today. Rakor is coming with us and Koko needs rest." When the males began to protest that they needed more information, Kyna rose purposefully. "You have what you need; now we must to do our job." She motioned to the other females and they rose together. Then she motioned to Rakor; Rakor knew that Ursula look, and followed after them, but he turned back to ask Grundel where Boris was. The others exchanged awkward glances. Monk held Koko tighter. Alethia sighed deeply.

"There's so much to tell you, Rakor," she said, "please, come with us."

"Where are they going?" whispered Koko.

"They're going to the Gorge of Humility," answered Grundel, his voice stony. When Rakor heard the name, he turned back once more, and for the first time, Koko saw fear in Rakor's eyes.

"Where is that?" she asked. There was no answer. Finally, Monk muttered, *"It's not on any map; true places never are."*

THE URSULAS did not return with Rakor for many days. They took him to a narrow ice bridge over a steep and treacherous gorge high in the mountains. All along Rakor had known that one day he would face the Ursulas here. Still, his heart pounded as they climbed up the dark pine cliffs and edged their way out to the middle of the bridge of ice. The wind had scoured the ice slick. It was a place where you could not flail your arms, beat your chest, attack anyone—or run away. Any such action would certainly send you skidding helplessly over the edge. Slowly, gently, but relentlessly the three Ursulas demanded he search his heart, search for the moment everything changed. Rakor railed at his judges, with only his voice to convey his frustration. He tried to hold onto his pride, his self-righteousness, but it was a place where you must listen, not only to the Ursulas, but also to your innermost self. It was here that Rakor finally looked into his heart and felt ashamed. But there were layers and layers of denial he needed to recognize.

Gradually Rakor shook off SaMäel's wicked influence and let it slide into the depths of the chasm. When they finally left the Gorge, they didn't return home immediately, instead going deeper into the mountains, into the great solitude where nothing can hide.

AFTER the Ursulas left the Valley, Monk and Koko went back to Mikaila's cabin. First they bathed the child, a long warm bath that took off layers and layers of dirt and grime. Once, twice, three times they changed the water. Next Mikaila attacked the mess of hair, washing it, cutting it to get rid of the worst knots, gently combing out the knots left with a large toothed comb. Monk wanted to weep at the sight of the scrawny body, the bruises, the dark hollows under the child's eyes. But Mikaila just brought out more ointments and salves and massaged Koko's body, talking, singing little ditties, telling her about the bees in her yard, anything to divert the child's mind to cheerier, healing thoughts.

For the next few days, Koko wouldn't go outside; all day she stayed by Monk's side, holding his hand, or when his hands were full of logs for the fire or dishes to be set on the table, she grasped his sleeve. Monk thought it was the child who needed their closeness, but, when she said she needed a nap, he felt adrift as if his lifeline had again snapped.

BACK at Cathedral, Grundel and Gorath went to join Piotr on the Salmon River.

Earlier, as the sun rose, Piotr had started out for the clearing where Inyx watched over Carth. It didn't take him long—no one knew the area better than Piotr, and he was small and fast. In the pale dawn, he jogged out of the pinewood, to the river, expecting to see Inyx and Carth, but staggered to a stop.

Malenger had refused to let the bears get the better of him. He had not become confused by the bears' chase because he had positioned the sun and taken landmarks as Monk had taught him to do; he knew exactly where Carth lay. When he realized the bears had stopped chasing them, the three men had hunkered down in a hollow to wait out the storm. The other two, exhausted from their long day of tracking with its horrific chase at the end, slept immediately. Malenger sat, wide awake and scheming. When darkness fell, he waited for the storm to pass and the moon to rise, then roused Slank and Payne. They followed him groggily but wordlessly by the light of the cold moon.

Aroused from her thoughts and light dozing, Inyx heard them coming from a short distance away, and although every instinct told her to run, she knew she was too old and it was too late. She was alone with Carth, who had died in the night. Earlier, she had sent Alethia and Kyna back to the Valley to mediate between Rakor and the Brothers; the three knew that it was too dangerous for all of them to be away from the Valley at this critical time. Inyx was waiting patiently for the Brothers to return in the morning. With Carth's giant head in her lap, she had been listening to the night noises, the rustling and scratching of nocturnal animals, the wind, the full moon's song; she was thinking about how old time was, how softly the days fell, like ripe pine cones onto the forest carpet. She was thinking about Einar and their days together, fishing in the river, about a story he had told her of the salmon on the west coast, how on their journey home, a journey towards their death, they turned the river red. She watched the moon illuminate an old pine tree whose roots could not hold on, and so was leaning precariously out over the river like the arc of a rainbow. *Let go*, she whispered, *just let go.*

Malenger came out of the pinewood, took one look at Inyx in the moonlight, and, uncertain of Carth's condition, ordered the two men to shoot both bears.

What Piotr stumbled onto, later in the morning, were just two dead stripped carcasses, lying beside the river looking like two headless old men—the flesh scored and raw and bleeding. Then he noticed Tagore and her pack sitting protectively around them. He turned back into the woods to retch, but eventually steeled himself to sit down with the pack and wait. When Tagore heard the rest of the Brothers coming, she rose and the pack rose with her.

"Thank you," said Piotr.

"It is our duty," replied Tagore. Piotr nodded—he understood what Tagore meant; he had grown up with the stories, as had all the Keepers. The relationship between the White Wolf and The Ursula went back to the very beginning, when the first Ursula went looking for mates for her twins. It was spring, after a hard winter. The grizzly came upon a lone female wolf fighting an elk. Both animals were starving, but the wounded wolf was no match for the elk. She didn't know what prompted her to interfere, but she saved Tagore by killing the elk and offering its heart to the wolf, then dragging the carcass to a den and fending off other animals until Tagore healed. After that, Tagore joined The Ursula on her journey to find mates that would keep the line of grizzly bears strong, returning with her to the Icefield. The following year the White Wolf brought back her own mate, another white wolf willing to let Tagore lead. He understood that there was nothing ordinary about her. After that first spring journey, the White Wolf and The Ursula had an understanding. The following year the Sunados began, with Tagore becoming an integral part. In years to come, choosing the kill of the Ursula candidate represented the pure heart, courage, and protective spirit of the first Ursula, as the white wolves remember and honour her.

Piotr watched the white wolves disappear silently into the brush, and turned to face his Brothers.

Grundel had to fight fiercely with himself when he had rejoined the Brothers on the Salmon River. He desperately wanted to take swift revenge for these brutal, senseless killings; but he knew that this was not the way of The Keeper. His Brothers watched him struggle, waiting to see what he would do. They were bound to him; they would do as he asked. Finally, Grundel stood over the bodies.

"Blessed be Gaia, our Mother. Take Carth and Inyx and give them peace. May they feed their strength and their courage to all yours who need them." The others murmured the same mantra, except Piotr who said nothing. He hung his head, trying to hide his fury.

"What is it, Piotr?" asked Grundel, already knowing.

"This isn't natural—skinned—stripped—with their heads wrenched from their bodies and taken! Nothing holds true here!"

Grundel tensed, trying to control his own fury, rising with Piotr's.

"Let them go, Piotr. They are one now, no matter how they went. Think only of them at peace."

"How can they be at peace? They cannot be at peace!"

"Perhaps *we* cannot be at peace—but they are." The other Brothers silently agreed with Piotr, but they listened to Grundel, trying to curb their own anger.

"So that's it? That's all you're going to do for Carth? No fairness?"

"No. Not yet." Grundel stared at him until Piotr finally turned and loped away.

Ravenwood

Piotr

BACK at Mikaila's cabin in Ravenwood, on Angel Lake, Monk was again brooding. At first he and Koko were both intrigued by the cabin, asking about the jars, specimens, the drying plants and delicately wrought sketches. It was a busy place, filled with projects-in-progress: reed baskets started but not finished, bowls and spoons roughed out of wood waiting for a sanding, a weaving half-finished on the standing Salish loom, herbs hanging from a drying rack that filled the kitchen area ceiling, lines of bottles and boxes on shelves, carefully labelled. Mikaila had no problem finding them odd jobs to do. She showed Monk how to dip beeswax candles and he tried to settle down to make them.

"What are these" asked Monk, getting up from the table to stretch and wandering over to a shelf he had not yet explored. "These aren't specimens, are they?"

"No," laughed Mikaila, "that's my hobby."

"What do you mean?" he asked, picking up the jars, carefully labelled in her fine script and rhyming them off. "Ground juniper, roasted dandelion root, powdered bearberry leaves, juniper berries, dried cranesbill?"

"Well, when I tire of working on specimens for the museum, I like to invent new teas—these are my ingredients. You like my teas, don't you?"

"They're delicious."

"I try to combine medicinal uses with good taste. Hilda trades things I need for them—she sells my teas in Banff and Laggan. This one, for example," she picked up a small wooden box, opening its tight lid, "has chamomile and other herbs to help you sleep. Smell this."

"Wow. That smells good. Is there mint in that too?"

"Yes. Please take the box; you and Koko could both use it."

He took it gratefully, and sat back down to the table, trying again to concentrate on dipping candles. He was trying to fill every waking moment with activity, trying not to think about Rachel. But it was no good. He jumped up and headed down to the river, lost in thought.

"Don't worry, little one," Mikaila said, giving Koko a hug, "he'll be back soon."

Monk started spending more time away from the cabin, rambling aimlessly through the bush. Mikaila let Koko help her in the meadows, pressing wildflowers, taking seeds, planting them in specimen boxes, filling her day with sunshine and fresh air, slowly building her strength and healing her psyche. But Monk remained dark and restless; he seldom stayed with them for long. Koko was fearful every time he left.

Often when he returned, Mikaila and Koko would be working at the kitchen table, Mikaila singing with Koko humming softly along. This brought Monk out of his funk. He would watch them, realizing Mikaila must sing often while working because she did not seem conscious that she was doing so. The songs reminded him of some of the music the monks would sing while working—haunting arias that he felt he should know, but sung in a language he did not recognize.

"What are you singing?" he asked once. "Is it from Iceland?"

Mikaila looked up surprised and then laughed. "Oh, just something Armaros taught me as a child."

"It's beautiful. You sing like an angel."

AFTER MONK had returned one day from a rigorous morning hike through the woods, Mikaila convinced him to rest out on her porch. The noon sun stretched long fingers, massaging Monk's insides as well as his muscles. He dozed. While Mikaila worked on a basket, Koko played quietly at their feet. The sun shone, the insects droned, all was still, until the basket slipped to the ground and Mikaila startled. Shaking herself awake and jumping up, she looked around wildly. The child was gone.

Suddenly, she caught a glimpse of red down by the bee meadow. When she reached Koko, the child was sitting transfixed in front of one of the bee boxes.

"They're so busy," she whispered, smiling to Mikaila as she squatted beside her.

"Yup—making honey."

"But how? How do they know where to go and how to find home again?" her body slumped and then shuddered. "I wish I had known how to find home—then maybe I wouldn't have had to stay in that horrible cave so long." Mikaila put an arm around the little girl.

"You're home now," she said. Koko nodded, looked at her and smiled. Then she turned back to the bees, her irrepressible curiosity rising again.

"Why are they in those boxes?"

"Well, I made them a home in the box. It's just what they want and need. It's the right size and it faces south so it's warm, and it's very strong and high enough off the ground to protect them from predators."

"Not bears!"

"No, not bears." Koko peered closer into the opening.

"Don't get too close without protection."

"I can see the workers. They're busy. Where's the Queen?"

"She's in there mating with the drones and laying eggs."

"That's all drones do—right? No guarding, no collecting, no laying eggs?"

"That's right."

For a moment the child sat thinking, then piped, "I'd rather be a queen and boss everyone around!" Mikaila chuckled. "They're singing," Koko said, listening intently to the drone of the humming glade. "Like Papa's chanting."

"It sounds like it—but the buzz is created by their wings beating so fast."

"Like—like a hummingbird," said Koko, remembering a book Rachel had often read to her.

"Yes." Mikaila smiled at the child's natural inclination to draw similarities.

"Why did you build them boxes when there are so many trees?" Koko asked after a while of intent watching.

"Because I want them to share their honey and beeswax with me."

"Look!" she whispered hoarsely, "one's dancing!" She sat for a long time after that, waiting for another dance, studying the bees, watching for patterns in the hive of activity. Mikaila sat quietly beside her, watching the child's lively mind open up to the world again. Finally, Mikaila got up slowly and deliberately, putting a gentle hand on Koko's shoulder.

"Would you like to try some of my honey cake?"

The child grinned and jumped up, but then caught herself as suddenly the buzz intensified. "I don't think," she said sagely, "I don't think bees like sudden movements. So I'm just going to back up slowly keeping my eye on them."

"Good idea," smiled Mikaila. As they started back to the cabin, Koko put her hand in Mikaila's. "Do you know the scientific name for bees?" asked Mikaila, moved by the simple gesture. Koko shook her head. "*Apis mellifera.*"

When they reached the porch, Monk was awake and watching them.

"I was studying the Apis mellifera," Koko said, mimicking Mikaila perfectly and climbing into his lap to give him a hug.

"Were you indeed," answered Monk, giving her a rare grin.

"Yes, and now we are going to have some honey cake." She climbed back down and followed Mikaila into the cabin. The living area was one big room dominated by a large stone fireplace. The sleeping area consisted of two separate rooms divided off by woven tapestries of subtle colours, rather than by doors. Koko walked over to one, drawn by its multiple textures, and ran her hand down it numerous times. Remembering how many times she had done the same thing as a child, Mikaila smiled. Koko looked at her, questioningly.

"My mother made those on the loom," said Mikaila.

"Your mother? Where is she now?" asked Koko.

Mikaila paused, but when Koko looked at her questioningly she said, "She died. She was swept under the ice during the spring floods a number of years ago."

"That's sad," said the child. Mikaila just nodded. She cut the cake and placed a large slice on a wooden plate and put it on the large cedar table, pushing the baskets she had started earlier that morning to one side.

"Don't you have to finish those baskets before they dry out?" asked Koko, digging eagerly into the cake.

"It's all right. I can dampen them again."

"My Ama always likes to—" Koko stopped, put down her cake, her eyebrows furrowing, tears welling up.

"It's all right, dear. Don't lose hope." Mikaila circled the table to give her a hug. Monk, standing silently in the doorway, came to a decision.

"I'm going to rescue Rachel," he said quietly. "I'm going out of my mind. I have to try."

MIKAILA argued with Monk on and off for a few days, but he would not budge. He wanted her to talk to the angels; he needed the Watchers' help. He was convinced if anyone could get him there, they could. Although she doubted the angels' willingness to help, Mikaila finally realized that Monk would not let go of his request, until he talked with them. Knowing the Watchers' reluctance to interfere in Earth matters, she thought it would all be over quickly.

"All right, Monk. we'll go to the Hoodoos now to ask the Watchers' help, if you'll promise me to drop the whole idea if they refuse. Fair?"

Monk frowned then reluctantly agreed. He knew there would be no way of getting to Abadon without the Watchers' help.

"We'll approach Semjaza first. Armaros will be more difficult to convince."

Not long after, they were standing on Semjaza's ledge,
Monk's voice rising as he felt the subtle resistance of the angel.
Mikaila was trying to get him to lower his voice, but it was too
late.

"Abadon!" said Armaros, striding out of his quarters. "Who's
going to Abadon?" His great, stern voice glittered like the blade
of a sword.

"I am, and I'm hoping Semjaza and Mikaila will help me,"
called Monk, defiantly.

"And me, don't forget me," piped Koko, who was standing
beside him and pulling on his sleeve. The Watcher flew over
to Semjaza's ledge and gave Sem a scathing look, then turned
to Monk.

"You don't just waltz into Abadon! It's a hell pit—you can't
even imagine the dangers of the place." Armaros threw out his
arm in a wordless gesture to Semjaza, but Monk interrupted.

"I don't care. You can't frighten me. I'm going." Monk
crossed his arms as if by doing so he could ward off the dangers.

"Really," Armaros answered sardonically, "you realize you
would have to navigate The Burning Sands, pass through the
Rain of Fire, cross the River of Blood just to get to the iron walls
of the city, which are guarded by warrior angels—and that would
be the easy part compared to the moat filled with flesh eating
fish, a floating oil vat that at a touch SaMäel can turn into flame,
and the shadows in the city of Dis that will suck your life spirit,
not to mention what you'd meet inside the castle, should you
miraculously get that far. Abadon is SaMäel's realm—there, all
his powers are at their height. I'm sorry, Rachel does not deserve
to be there, but rescue is out of the question. Mikaila is not
going, nor, I imagine when he comes to his senses, is Semjaza."

Before Semjaza could respond, Mikaila jumped up and stood her full height, eyes flaming. Up until that point, she had not considered going, but no one was going to make that decision for her.

"And who are you to say what I can and cannot do?" she retorted. Armaros swallowed a quick retort, took a deep breath and regained his composure. When he spoke, his voice had softened.

"Don't be foolish, Mika. You don't know the place. The very idea is impossible. It's madness." Standing face to face, two brilliant golden figures, the resemblance dawned on everyone, except Mikaila herself.

"But it's *my* madness, and I will do as I please!"

"I—" Armaros began, then turned suddenly on his heel and flew over to his quarters. Mikaila swirled to face Sem. He put his hands calmly on her shoulders, looking deeply into her glittering blue eyes. For a moment, Mikaila softened, drowning in the pools of his penetrating gaze.

"Have you ever dreamed of flying?" he asked lightly.

"What?" She tried to pull herself out of the quicksand of her mixed emotions. "What has that—?"

"Do you dream of flying?" he insisted.

"Yes—all the time. But what does—?"

"Those aren't dreams, Mikaila; those are your shadow wings beating the night air. Surely you know by now."

"Know what?"

Semjaza drew a big breath, threw a look over to Armaros' hoodoo and made a momentous decision. "He is your father."

Mikaila gasped.

She swung to face him as Armaros stepped out onto his ledge. The look on his face was unreadable. Dumbfounded, Mikaila gaped at Armaros, then Semjaza, then wildly around at the others. She gasped again for air. Suddenly, she whistled for Equus—she needed to get away, there was not enough air on the hoodoo ledge. She couldn't tell whether she was about to rage or cry. For a moment, she thought she could feel her dream wings preparing for flight, but she shook her head of such nonsense. Wings! Didn't he think she'd know if she had wings—even shadow wings! Equus flew onto the ledge. Semjaza began to say something, but at the sight of her withering look, let Mikaila go, watching her mount silently.

Flying was one of the enchantments Semjaza had given the horse, but Mikaila seldom used it, unless it was necessary. Reading her thoughts now and realizing the woman's need for solid earth under her, Equus flew down from the ledge, and thundered into a canter, galloping tirelessly through the rough terrain, sure-footed in his muscular stride. Mikaila clung to his back, feeling the vibrations of his thundering hooves pulsate through her body. *I won't think, I will not think.* When they arrived in Ravenwood, Equus dropped her off at the edge of her clearing, gave her a loving nudge, and then moved away to graze.

Mikaila halted, as if seeing her home for the first time. How she loved this spot—the rough hued log cabin with its sloping roof, the worn path to the workshop, the gardens, berry bushes, to the left the path to the lake and behind the cabin, the bee meadows. She entered the cabin slowly, walked over to the mantel piece and picked up an old photograph of her mother standing in her work clothes outside the door of the workshop—a strong figure, tall, serious, eyes bright, but her sensuous mouth warm and almost smiling—taken by the Scottish botanist before he left the mountains. He had inscribed it 'to the future.' Mikaila looked again at that almost smile—as if someone had said something as the camera clicked—and her mother's hand reaching back to her shoulder as if someone stood behind her in the doorway—Armaros? Was this really a photograph of her parents? Again she struggled for breath. Wrapping a wool blanket around herself, she stumbled outside.

Mikaila threw a look over to the workshop, but instead took the path through the brush to the edge of Angel Lake. The water was rough and spoke to her in a familiar, noisy lapping. The cedars that overhung the lake with great arching umbrage, shielded her from the wind. She gazed out to where the lake ended in a fast flowing creek, and the water spilled over the rocks, a foaming green and white. She walked down to the end of her dock, staring hard at the distant mountains, willing them to tell her what happened—Armaros and Mother? It explained a lot—her suspicion of wings, and her attraction to Sem. She silenced these thoughts out of habit. But that let her rage and her loneliness back in, and she railed at the water and the mountains, weeping bitterly for her mother and a voice of comfort, explaining, caressing.

When her energy was spent, she emptied her thoughts, letting the warm, Healing Wind coming from the hoodoos do its magic. Soon, she was asleep, huddled on the dock, with nothing in her mind but the sounds of wind and water.

The next morning Makaila trudged to the nearest meadow by foot. She wanted work to centre her, ground her, to help her regain her balance. She opened her sketchbook resolutely, determined to think of nothing but drawing gaillardia for the entire morning. Much later that day, when she was hunched over the bee houses collecting honeycomb, still working hard and trying not to think, Monk and Koko returned, hoping to be welcomed. Koko put on her bee-hat with its drooping veil and her protective gloves, then tiptoed up behind Mikaila, trying to surprise her. But before she could, Mikaila spoke without turning around.

"Hello Koko. If you have your protection on, come closer, I want to show you something." Koko stopped, baffled.

"How did you know it was me? I didn't make a sound!" Mikaila turned around and smiled wryly; here was another skill she needed to acknowledge.

"It's a—a gift."

"What do you mean—eyes in the back of your head?"

"No," Mikaila laughed, "each of us has an aura—like a thumbprint—that is unique. Lots of people sense them but without substance; I can just—see them."

"Behind you?"

"Well—it's hard to describe. An aura is made up of many facets—colour and texture, but also emotions and scents—you don't have to actually see all those things." Koko was quiet for a moment, thinking.

"What's my aura like?" she finally asked.

"It's lovely—the loveliest I've known. That's how I knew it was you. It's a rich golden colour like a golden fall day and it smells of pine and mint and it feels like the gentlest breeze over warm blue water." Mikaila did not add that there were tints of darkness in it.

"Really?"

"Really."

"I wish I could see yours."

"It takes practice—try looking without your eyes."

Koko closed her eyes. "Well, I know what Malenger's looks like—it's hard and mean and smells of dung!" Mikaila sat back on her haunches, putting her hands out to the little girl standing defiantly in the sunlight. Her own emotions had been in turmoil all day, but it grieved her to see anger in Koko—so much fear and loathing in one so young.

"You must let go of your anger, little one. It will do you harm."

"But you're angry, aren't you, with Armaros?"

"Sort of," Mikaila answered honestly, "but I'm trying to release it. My anger's covering other emotions. But you'll lose your golden aura, if you let anger or hate consume you." When the little girl looked troubled, she gave her a hug and drew her towards the bees. "Come, look what the bees are doing."

The Plan

THE BROTHERS were in the Keeper's Cave. Carth and Inyx's deaths had unsettled them; they were restless and edgy. There was the unmistakable scent of revenge in the air. The Brothers, with Kyna who arrived that morning, were working on a plan to move the Quintessence. They had been at it off and on for hours, but no one plan seemed complex enough to work. Everyone's temper was on edge.

"But any plan we think of won't be enough to fool SaMäel!" Gorath argued. "How can we outsmart SaMäel? It just isn't possible."

"We couldn't even outsmart Malenger," grumbled Kaare, and then regretted it when he saw the hurt in Piotr's eyes.

"Then we must think of another course," said Grundel, casting Kaare a severe look, which silenced him. "If we can't outsmart him, perhaps we could—."

"Could what? We've been through this so many times!" snorted Gorath.

"Well, give me a minute!" Grundel snapped. "Your pessimism is not helping. Whether we like it or not, we have to move the Quintessence."

"But there are too many angles to sort out all at once, too many—" railed Lunt, one of the older bears.

"Maybe that's the answer," interrupted Piotr beside him. His Brothers perked up. He had been silent for days and they were all worried about him. The youngster had lost his energy, his sense of humour, and the exuberance that always found a way out of predicaments. They needed him.

"What is? What did I say?" asked Lunt.

"Maybe the way to outsmart SaMäel is to get him working on so many fronts that we could distract him away from the Quintessence," said Piotr. Lunt patted the young bear on the back. He didn't yet understand the idea, but he was delighted that Piotr was suddenly with them again. He beamed at Grundel, as if he had thought of the idea himself.

"You mean creating a host of other problems for SaMäel to solve?" asked Grundel.

"I was thinking more like diversions," said Piotr, "but yes, a number of diversions to draw him away from the Caves, while we move it."

"Ok," said Gorath, "but that's just one problem. *Where* are we going to move it? Where on Earth will SaMäel not be able to find it?"

"Well," said Kyna, catching Grundel's eye, "perhaps we could combine these two problems. Perhaps we could look like we're taking it somewhere, have SaMäel follow, but really move it somewhere else."

"That might work," Kaare piped up, not wanting to lose Piotr's involvement.

"But it doesn't solve the problem of where! Isn't *where* our biggest problem?" insisted Gorath.

"They're all big," grunted Grundel. The other bears nodded glumly.

Suddenly Melancholia materialized, then Rakor appeared as a great grey owl and transmuted back, followed by the other Ursulas, who also arrived as owls and did the same. The other bears backed away, uneasy.

"I think you're on to something," said Melancholia. "Diversion is a good idea. I agree, Gorath, that where we take the Quintessence is crucial. I believe that there is nowhere now on

Earth that SaMäel would not find it."

"Does that mean you're going to take it to another dimension?" asked Piotr.

"You forget that I am a spirit; I have no substance; I could not take it anywhere."

"Then we're doomed!"

"No, Piotr," said Rakor, giving Melancholia a studied look. "You just didn't listen carefully. Mel said that there was nowhere *now* that we could hide it."

"What does that mean?" asked Lunt, shaking his large head, not getting it at all.

"I suspect that it means we need to move the Quintessence in time, not place," replied Rakor.

"Yes, you are quite correct," answered Mel. "It would take SaMäel a very long time to search all time and place. It might give us another millennium."

"But how? We can't change time!" said Piotr, his eyes widening.

"I suspect that Melancholia can," said Rakor, turning to face her.

"With some help from the Watchers and, of course, Toholinagi—yes," she replied.

"But Mel just said she couldn't take it anywhere. Who would do this, if she can't?" asked Gorath, confused, "the Watchers?" Melancholia shook her head and turned slowly to face Rakor.

"I would like to do this," said Rakor, quietly. "I would like to redeem myself in all your eyes, if I could." The Ursulas exchanged glances, nodding their heads, endorsing the idea.

Grundel and Gorath also exchanged looks—but they did not yet trust Rakor. Was this another ploy to gain power? Rakor did not miss their exchange.

He said, "You have every reason to doubt me. I do not yet deserve your trust. I can only tell you that I will do this; I will travel back in time to where Mel and the Watchers send me to secure the safety of the Quintessence. It is the only way that I can repair the damage I've done; the only way you will ever trust me again."

Melancholia watched the bears carefully—there were mixed reactions.

"The plan is not without danger," she said, "we cannot guarantee Rakor's safe return. In fact," she hesitated and then continued, "in fact, we need to send two of you—in case something unexpected happens." The Brothers searched one another, wondering whom she meant.

"Do you have someone in mind?" asked Grundel. "I'll go."

"I appreciate that Grundel, but I do have someone in mind. I seldom interfere in your plans, but this is a special circumstance." The bears nodded solemnly, each one wondering if it would be him. Melancholia looked over them all, her gaze finally stopping at the smallest one.

"Piotr—we need you," she said. Piotr stood up resolutely and nodded his consent.

"But why?" exclaimed Kaare. "He's the—youngest!" He was about to say smallest, but they all knew how Piotr disliked attention drawn to his size. The other bears were all noisily agreeing, upset by the spirit's choice—wasn't it bad enough that Piotr had just lost his twin? He was depressed. Surely she could see that he needed time to recover.

"We need Piotr's particular skills to do this," replied Mel, simply. The Brothers wondered how Piotr would have the physical or emotional strength to do what would be required of him; they grumbled between themselves.

"This decision is not your concern," said Melancholia sternly, calling them to her with her dark, penetrating eyes. The bears fell silent. "You need to think of your diversions. Only Rakor and Piotr will know where they are going. And Grundel and Kyna, of course."

Just then Monk, whom they hadn't noticed standing in the entrance, barged into their midst. "Well, here's one diversion," he announced. "I'm going to Abadon!"

With a mighty rush of air, the Watchers flew in behind him, and for a few moments there was bedlam as everyone released their own private fears in a barrage of raised voices. Grundel roared for silence and turned to Monk, but before he could speak, the man stepped into the cave and spoke first.

"I know the Quintessence is paramount. I know you don't want anything to jeopardize your plans to move it. But I'm going to rescue Rachel—now." He spread his empty hands wide before them all. "How could I fail her again?" He looked around the room. "Won't anyone help me?"

The bears all turned to look at the Watchers who were still standing in the entrance to the Keeper's Cave. Mikaila, who had just arrived with Koko, pushed past them and marched over to Monk.

"I will," she said, recklessly. "Apparently I have wings to get us there!" She threw a defiant look at Armaros.

"You don't just waltz into Abadon," Armaros said, wearily.

"So you said," replied Mikaila. There was an awkward silence, broken by Melancholia.

"And I will—I can guide you, if nothing else."

"But you've never been to Abadon!" Semjaza blurted out, surprised at the offer. "How will you guide them?"

"Because you will teach me."

"Melancholia," said Armaros, sternly. "Why? First Rakor, now Abadon? It is not like you to be rash."

But," replied Mel, "these are strange times, and we are all entangled, even you. SaMäel has terrorized the Icefield, kidnapped Rachel, held Koko ransom, enslaved others, killed remorselessly, and now threatens the life of the planet. We have no choice. He must be stopped."

"Don't get me wrong, I'm very grateful. But isn't this beyond Cathedral's domain?" asked Monk, picking up Koko who was pulling on his sleeve.

"No," Mel answered, "not at all. SaMäel must understand that we will not allow him to dominate our sacred places or hold us ransom in any way. Besides, Rachel deserves a much, much better fate." Koko put her arms tightly around Monk's neck.

"Speaking of fate, shouldn't we find out how Vang's doing?" asked Gorath.

WHEN Malenger, Slank and Payne returned with the bear skins, Malenger told the two men to guard the Rivergate, while he entered the Castleguard Caves alone. He had a high, sharp whistle that he used to call Rakor, which he now blew. With a rush of wings, the owl swept in, picked him up, turned and flew down the tunnel. They could hear the wailing even before they reached the Eye. When the owl dropped Malenger on the floor of the Grotto, the animals were all wailing around a small fire.

"What on earth is happening?" cried Malenger. Vang tried to look nonchalant.

"It's the child," he said.

"What do you mean? Where is she?"

Vang nodded towards the fire. "Dead. The others insisted on cremating her. They said it was the way of humans." He kicked at the fire, picking up a small bone and started to gnaw on it. Malenger looked at him aghast, but could not help sneaking a look in the fire to see what remained of Koko's small white bones.

"Oh my gawd," groaned Malenger, "SaMäel will kill us! He told us to keep her alive."

Vang shrugged, seemingly nonplussed. "SaMäel kills out of rage or necessity, or," he said, looking Malenger coldly in the eye, "for sport, like some men. Which do you think this will be?" He had smelled the bear skins the moment the men had brought them back to the entrance. Malenger shrank away from that stare. Usually Rakor looked around him instead of at him, even turning his head away to talk. This deliberate ignoring, Monk had taught Malenger, was a bear's way to avoid confrontation when you were in his space. He remembered that Monk also said that a direct stare from a bear meant certain confrontation. Don't misconstrue this behaviour for poor eyesight, Monk had warned him, bears see and hear as well as any man. It was their sense of smell that was extraordinary—a bear could tell your age, sex, and what you had for breakfast just by sniffing you out, often from miles away. Malenger never knew whether or not to believe him, but he wasn't taking any chances and tried to avoid this hard cold stare.

"What will we tell SaMäel?" Malenger said, looking towards the exit, wondering if he should make a hasty retreat.

"I have no doubt that you will come up with one of your strategic ideas," Vang said, taking a step towards the man, the smell of dead bear overwhelming him.

"Well," Malenger said, scuttling to put the table between them, and to change the bear's focus, "you better tell them to put out the fire and get back to work."

The animals hurried to do so, and then scurried back into their tunnels. They had decided it would be best for Marmo and Mustela to hide just inside their tunnel to listen to what was transpiring in the cavern. They didn't know when Vang might need their help.

Slank and Payne, who had stretched and hung the hides to dry near the caves' entrance, returned to their post. In the Grotto, Vang and Malenger tiptoed around one another for a while. They updated the map, Vang quietly seething about the bears; Malenger dreading SaMäel's next appearance. But eventually the man's curiosity got the better of him.

"So what happened exactly?" Malenger finally asked, throwing a furtive look at the remains in the dead fire.

"I was just going to ask you the same question," said Vang, turning away his head, barely able to contain his anger. Malenger stared at Vang; something had changed.

"What's with you, Rakor?" he asked. But before he got any further, they both heard the sound of mighty wings beating through the tunnel. Malenger gasped and recoiled, stopping only when his back scraped against the rock wall, as SaMäel entered in dragon form. The dragon wings rose mightily, touching the top of the Grotto; fire snorted out his nostrils, and his golden eyes whirled.

"Where is the child?" he demanded. Malenger clung to his corner, trembling. SaMäel turned to Vang. "I am in no mood to be trifled with, Rakor. Just get her."

Vang took a deep breath, and in as gruff a voice as he could muster, he growled, "She's dead."

Suddenly, it seemed like SaMäel's golden body was all in flame; it glowed, it sparked, fire breathed out his nose and mouth, scorching the walls and cavern ceiling. Malenger cowered in the corner; Vang watched the maps crackling in the heat. "You will destroy everything, SaMäel, if you continue," Vang roared. SaMäel returned to his angel form, but with the same mighty wings, the whirling golden eyes, the same hot breath. Vang knew that the terrible angel was just barely controlling his anger. But it was all illusion and the papers settled back to their place on the table.

"What do you mean?" SaMäel said, his voice dangerously quiet.

"She died. She—couldn't survive the conditions."

"Then why didn't you improve her conditions?" SaMäel roared.

"I tried, but I was too late."

"Where is she?' SaMäel gazed wildly around the room.

"We cremated her."

"Damn! Damn! Damn!" ranted SaMäel. "I promised Rachel I'd bring Koko to her. How can I keep Rachel if the child is dead? She has no reason to stay!"

"Don't tell her," muttered Malenger from the corner. SaMäel turned his rage towards Malenger, enjoying the familiar pleasure of watching the vainglorious man cringe and cower.

"Yes, that would be your response," drawled SaMäel, contemptuously. "You are a worm." Then amusement crept into SaMäel's voice. "And how do I explain not bringing the child?" Malenger felt that the moment of danger had passed and grew braver. He sat up.

"Blame it on the child, of course," replied Malenger with a smirk of self-satisfaction. "Say she was too scared to come with you. The mother will respect the child's concern. You could even look sympathetic. That is, if you have no traitors in the City of Dis who would unmask you?"

"You always go too far, Malenger. One of these days it will destroy you," said SaMäel, flicking his wrist, "go be a bat." Instantly, Malenger lunged around the cavern, flapping his arms, until SaMäel, annoyed, threw a spell. Changed into a bat, Malenger flew towards the tunnel.

"Won't he—" began Vang, staring after the disappearing bat.

"Oh, never mind him! What is your progress, Rakor?" asked SaMäel, striding over to the table and the maps.

"The same."

"That's not what I want to hear."

Vang was surprised and relieved when SaMäel left as suddenly as he had arrived. He's still angry, Vang thought, but apparently weightier matters were now claiming his attention. The bear heard the great wings beating up the tunnel. As the dark angel prepared to exit the caves, a bat flew out a side shaft, right in his face. SaMäel grabbed it and sent it flying out the mouth of the cave. The two men at the entrance flattened themselves against the rock wall as SaMäel transmuted into a dragon and roared out of the cave. Malenger awoke on the ground, a fair distance from the entrance, with an intense pain in his chest and the familiar feeling of having been inside a dark void, but with no memory of what had just happened.

Back in the Grotto, listening to the sound of the beating wings retreating, Vang stopped for a moment, thinking about Rachel and what she must be enduring: to be imprisoned by that wicked creature, to have no hope of escape. How, he wondered, did she endure such loneliness, such despair? He longed for a way to tell her that Monk and Koko were alive. But there was nothing to be done; his job was to continue deceiving SaMäel for as long as he could. He would see the Ursulas tonight and would ask them; perhaps someone could get a message to Rachel.

He tried to turn his thoughts away from the skins of Inyx and Carth hanging near the Rivergate or, he knew, anger would overwhelm him.

Reds

SAMÄEL flew from the cave in a rage. His massive dragon body shook with anger; he gritted his teeth, holding back his rising, burning bile. Those bungling idiots were ruining all his plans. Payne and Slank shrank at SaMäel's hell-bent screech and watched in fearful awe as the dark angel flew straight into the eye of the sun, his breath flaming as he rose. They winced at Malenger's howl of pain as he hit the earth.

The dark angel, magician, dragon, entered the skies over Abadon somewhat in control, having spent the worst of his anger on the ascent and fiery passage through the sun's portal, but he still radiated fury. He swept over the Burning Sands and then through the Rain; he was the only being anyone knew who could pass through the Rain of Fire unsheathed. When they saw his dragon shape, the two Seraphim at the Gate opened the heavy iron doors wordlessly. Further along, at the imposing iron palace, the condors and vultures perched on the wall turned their heads away to avoid SaMäel's whirling golden eyes.

Cerberus, a three-headed guard dog, bounding towards him from the Seraphim quarters of the outer court, stopped, dropped, and lay whimpering, his serpent tail between his legs. SaMäel looked around absently for his lion and leopard, but they were nowhere to be seen. *Cowards* he thought. Back in angel form, he strode through the castle, as the inhabitants discreetly stayed out of his way.

In the inner court, at the centre of the castle, a series of hot pools were surrounded in palm trees, smooth flat rocks, exotic ferns, crimson calla lilies. The pools descended in a cascade of gentle waterfalls. Soft, exotic music wafted around the room played by women on intricately carved instruments. The place was warm, mist-filled, and inhabited by Rara Avis, a great flightless bird, twelve feet tall, with a massive hooked beak, who stalked silently through the mist, guarding the women who waited to serve SaMäel.

At first glance, the women of SaMäel's seraglio appeared strikingly beautiful, with silky long hair of many shades, radiant skin, and elegant, graceful bodies dressed in diaphanous gowns, but on closer scrutiny, their eyes were glazed and blank. The women turned their heads to watch SaMäel, and for a moment, their eyes intensified with desire and possessiveness.

Rachel's quarters were off this centre conclave. Her rooms were guarded by a she-wolf who now lay passively in front of her door. Rachel was free to wander through her spacious rooms and the seraglio, but beyond that her guardian would not allow her. The she-wolf, whimpering for affection, leapt to her feet when SaMäel came into view, but the dark angel ignored her, striding past Rachel's door and into his own opulent quarters.

He needed to think. He had promised Rachel he would bring Koko to her, and now the child was dead. Those idiots! His rage returned and he struggled to gain control. He expected as much from Malenger. He had found him as a cat finds a mouse—something to toy with, but no fun in the end, too easily manipulated, too paltry in imagination. All the man could think to desire was money—such a bore. But SaMäel expected more of Rakor; Rakor was different; Rakor understood the game: he wanted power, secret knowledge. SaMäel gave these things to him gladly, eager to find a worthy opponent. He had used some of his more sophisticated ruses to pull Rakor in, to set him up for eventual destruction. Except for the slowness of progress in the caves, Rakor had done nothing to taint SaMäel's admiration—until now.

In the past, SaMäel had not spent much time on Earth. He had fallen there once, long ago, as Angel Glacier revealed— the day he fell from Paradisi¤. Not a memory on which he wished to dwell—although it was a place he was drawn back to, periodically. His imprint was still there, outlined by the hanging glacier which filled it. For a time, the bears had intrigued him. Once in a while, when bored, he would wander into Semjaza and Armaros' hoodoos to enjoy their company. He sometimes missed the pair; Semjaza was charming and amusing, and Armaros was an intelligent conversationalist. Later, there was Armaros' earth mate, Faida, who intrigued him with her sophisticated self-mastery, but who was too old for his taste. He had made a mental note to return to appraise the daughter in the future to see if she had inherited her mother's fascination.

SaMäel was on Earth to do just that, the day he first saw Rachel. It was spring, an unexpected warm day when he had appeared in the skies over the Icefield. He had decided to take a quick look around—survey the area. He spotted movement by a river and flew closer to investigate. A woman had stripped down to a light shift, her radiant skin glowed a honey brown, her long dark hair just washed was still loose, drying; she was leaning over—sketching an elegant arc in the blue expanse— washing clothes in the clear cold water. Few Earth women aroused SaMäel, but this one did. It took him a few minutes to realize that this was not the woman he had come to see. This was another, smaller, darker one. Presently he noticed a girl child skipping along the shore near her. A plot slowly formed in his mind.

Long ago, he had tried to lure the Keepers away from their

duty, but could never make them bend to his will. He had almost decided the bears were incorruptible. But he had decided to give it one more try, a grander plan: to corrupt the line of Keepers instead of one individual—flaming Einar's desire for Inyx, working on Galina's weakness, playing havoc with the natural process, shaping Rakor. And all had gone according to plan. He had Rachel and soon he would have the Quintessence: Earth itself. The winnings of that grand game were finally at hand.

He was so close—so deliciously close—except for those damn, bloody idiots! He could kill them both—but he knew he still needed them. He clapped his hands, and a seraph came running.

"Get the banquet ready in the Hall—I'm starving. And entertainment! Tell the seraphim and women full dress. I'll suffer nothing mediocre tonight. And pour me my drink." He was surly and abrupt, but the seraph, Dagon, had anticipated his wants and was standing ready with carafe in hand.

"Shall I inform the Earth woman?" Dagon asked smoothly, pouring SaMäel a glass of dark amber liquid, lightly steaming.

"No. I'm tired of her bloody holier-than-thou attitude. She's like having the Virgin Queen at our party. Serve her in her quarters." Dagon nodded and bowed out.

Rachel, thought SaMäel angrily. He had had more than enough of her frustrating resistance—so far she had foiled all his moves. Nothing he did convinced her to trust him, to turn to him. How long had it been? No woman had resisted for so long. How many times had he sat across from her and watched her weave—all those things for the child. A trade—he'd give the things to Koko and she, in return, would dine with him. But he could not tempt her further.

What was it about her, he wondered, that fascinated him?

She was beautiful with her lush, raven hair and large brown eyes, her perfect proportions, her disarming smile—of which he hadn't seen enough! But he was surrounded by beautiful women with charming smiles. No—something else captured him. That first time—down by the river—she seemed the very centre of the universe; the calm peaceful centre of a chaotic universe. Yes, he admitted to himself, that was it—her peace. It radiated from her, even here where she did not want to be, devastated by her loss of a husband she would not talk about, separated from her child, still her inner peace, her sense of knowing where she belonged and her profound happiness in that knowledge radiated from her. Sitting across from her, he sometimes felt the peace he once had on Paradisi¤, and was grateful to her for reminding him of it, even if it was involuntary. Only to himself would SaMäel admit his envy of her. And it made him all the more committed to breaking her. But her ability to resist was formidable—and wearing.

At first her resistance had been invigorating and amusing, especially when there were glimpses of her mental strength collapsing from the constant struggle, the subtle deprivations, the relentless temptations, the lack of natural daylight and routine. Yet she held on. Perhaps it was time for her to partake in the seraglio's vapours—although she had been able to resist even that drug so far. Surely now she was at a breaking point. If he could give her what she wanted most—*Damn!* he thought, remembering Koko.

Dagon started his task with the Commanders, knocking on their doors and poking his head inside.

"Astorath!" he called sharply at the first room, "full dress tonight. Tell your men." Unlike SaMäel's opulent rooms, the commanders' rooms were more comfortable then the barracks of the Seraphim, but still simple as befitted a warrior. There was a bed and cushions were allowed, although most commanders shunned these unless they had a female guest. In front of the large hearth were a wooden table, chairs and two loungers. They had few decorative possessions, but these were exquisite and rare. A closet held their armour, tunics and their Reds. To one side was a privy.

"Look alive, Anmael," Astorath said, rising from his lounger by the fire. When the other seraph didn't move, he poked him with the butt of his spear. "Didn't you hear? The Dragon wants us in Reds tonight." *Reds*, he thought, *never a good sign.* Astorath went to his closet and drew out a blazing red tunic, his matching cloak edged in gold and leather sandals which laced to his knees.

"SaMäel," muttered Anmael, gazing into the fire, "why did we follow him?"

"Oh don't start that again," barked Astorath, throwing his clothes on the bed and starting to undress, but when he turned to look, Anmael hadn't moved. He strode across the room and hefted Anmael to his feet, then added, "You know why— because he was perfect."

Anmael turned around, his blue eyes blazing, but his voice was gentle, almost resigned, "No, Astorath, we were wrong. The One is perfect. All else is naught."

"Oh bloody hell—wake up you fool—or SaMäel will have your head!" He pushed Anmael towards the door.

"Should I wear my armour then?" muttered Anmael as he padded off to change.

RACHEL was relieved when Dagon entered her room with a tray of food. She had gambled that SaMäel would eventually grow weary of the novelty of her presence at his evening revelries, if her company was not entertaining. The party evenings in the Hall were debaucheries, drunken orgies, with SaMäel fuelling the fire of everyone's raw, unfocused passions. They revolted her. She held on fiercely to her image of a simple supper with Monk and Koko. She could hide her anger, but not her contempt—her silence at dinner spoke loudly of her judgement, although she knew it was dangerous to judge others here. The other women had pleaded with SaMäel to leave her in her room, so as not to spoil their pleasure. SaMäel heard their condemnations, but wanted her there; he enjoyed his displays of power.

Lately, in yet another attempt to appeal to her, he had acknowledged her discomfort and, although he still insisted on her appearance at dinner, let her retire early. He still believed he could convince her that her life would be better if she would just give herself over to him. Although frustrated, SaMäel still found her fascinating. Her will was stronger than any female's he had ever brought to Abadon. But he would wait only so long before he tired of her acts of avoidance, however artful.

Rachel found the game she was forced to play exhausting—*everything* was a chess game with SaMäel. In the beginning, she sought knowledge of Abadon's inexplicable rules through the other women, but most of the time they wouldn't even acknowledge her—every action spoke of their hopelessness, their loss of integrity—turning erratically from daily indifference to nightly lust and mindless risk-taking. They spent their days lolling around the pools, in a kind of isolated limbo, as if they didn't really exist, waiting for the evening and a violent release from the deadening boredom of their lives here. She had been shocked to discover that they were there by their own choice, and that they could, if they wished, leave at any time. At least, that's what they said. Somehow, SaMäel had broken their spirits. She had quickly realized that even if they did speak to her, they had nothing to tell her—nothing that would help her. All they thought about, all they wanted was to stay in

SaMäel's good graces. Although she desperately tried to believe it could not happen, she realized that if SaMäel broke her will, she could end up one of these lost women, or worse.

It hadn't taken her long to realize that the mist rising from the pools had a euphoric effect, so she avoided the area as much as possible—she needed to keep her wits about her. She had noticed a rune over Abadon's Gate when she first arrived that Dagon had told her meant: "Abandon blind hope—all who enter here." When she asked him why anyone would want a motto like that, he replied it was a message to SaMäel's enemies. But by the look on their faces, these women too had lost hope for any independence, integrity or real warmth. For all its luxury and passion, Abadon was a cold, hard place.

Rachel did not know if she should dare hope—a rescue seemed so impossible. Who would risk such a foolhardy attempt? Even if Monk were alive, which she doubted, how could he possibly get here? And yet, she did hope. When despair crept into her mind, she just looked into the other women's faces. She could not, would not give up, not while there was still Koko—back in the caves, alive. Alive.

Rachel had quickly understood that SaMäel's motivations and actions were directed only by his own needs and desires. He would bring Koko to Abadon not to please her, but to create some new, cruel game. She realized that it was probably better for Koko to stay in the caves, however lonely and dreadful for the child; but she also knew that if SaMäel wanted to bring Koko to Abadon, then he would do it. Rachel was so lonely, so desperate to have her child with her that when SaMäel suggested it, she leapt at the chance.

Today, wordlessly watching Dagon deliver plates of steaming fish and vegetables, she had dared hope that the food had been brought to her room because Koko would be joining her.

But, as the food went cold, no one had come; not even SaMäel. Now, trying to eat something, her throat so dry she couldn't swallow, she wondered why he had not brought Koko to her. *What had she done?*

Preparations

BACK ON EARTH, everyone was crammed into the Keeper's Cave. They had arrived just before a severe snowstorm had blown over the mountains and descended upon the Icefield; all day, while the storm raged just beyond the entrance, they had been inside, planning. Mikaila had draped a tarp over the mouth of the cave to shield them from the wicked wind and Monk had made a roaring fire and had lit candles he had made and brought from Mikaila's cabin. The bears had watched with amusement; they neither felt the cold nor feared the darkness like the humans. The remains of food sat on the table, long forgotten. Vang had already transmuted back into owl form and was obviously anxious to get going before he was missed back at Castleguard.

Finally, Grundel stood upright, addressing the group. "All right, Vang has to get back. Are we agreed?" Everyone nodded solemnly; there were a myriad of emotions lighting their faces: fear, weariness, excitement and apprehension. "Let me briefly summarize: Vang and the others in Castleguard will continue to feign that nothing of significance has happened, until given the signal. Gulo will keep us in touch with what is going on in the Castleguard Caves." Gulo nodded. "Raven, Took and I will appear to be taking the Quintessence to the Barrenlands, but we will instead meet up with Neva and Nanuk at Ram Ridge along with the Yukon bears. It's time to share information. They are not going to like what I have to tell them this year, but who knows how long it will be before they will be sharing the problems of the Corridor."

"I never thought I'd say this," said Kyna, "but I wish we were concentrating on our task of keeping the Corridor free, instead of all this rubbish!"

As Grundel nodded, Kaare blurted, "Do you really have to be the one who goes this time? Couldn't one of us go in your place? The Keeper will be needed here."

"I would prefer to stay, Kaare, but if I don't go, SaMäel will be suspicious, and that would undermine all our plans. It is imperative that he believe that I'm taking the Quintessence away from the Icefield. The Ursulas will be in charge — Kyna at Cathedral and Alethia at the Valley, and will be responsible for getting news to us via Aquila and Winda. Monk, Mikaila and Mel will go to Abadon and rescue Rachel," continued Grundel.

"What about me?" piped Koko. "Can't I go too?"

"No Sprat," said Monk, his hand patting her knee, "remember what I told you. You must be very brave. Everyone must be brave and do the job required of them. We need you to stay here with Kyna. You are the only one with intimate knowledge of the Castleguard Caves. Kyna needs you to advise her. It is very important Koko; can you do this?"

"Yes," said Koko, sadly, "but I'd rather rescue Mama."

"I know." Monk hugged her. He had already asked Mikaila, should anything happen to him, to take Koko to Hilda Creek and Rachel's mother. He was torn between his love for Koko and his love for Rachel. But Koko was here, surrounded by love and protection, while Rachel was alone and without hope unless he tried to save her. He didn't dare imagine what she was suffering.

"I will also need you to watch for me, Koko. You will be my Raven." Kyna smiled kindly at the child. Koko looked shyly at Raven, who winked at her.

"Vang, with the Furtive Folk help, will get the Quintessence out of Castleguard," continued Grundel. "And then Rakor and Piotr, with the Watchers' help, will take the Quintessence to its new resting place. If we are successful, somehow we will have to deal with SaMäel's reactions. I know we haven't even discussed that particular problem, but we'll just have to cross that bridge when we come to it." Everyone sighed; it seemed an enormous task, even impossible. Armaros shook his head—how had they talked him into this?

"Timing, of course, will be crucial," concluded Grundel. "No one is to do anything until you get directions from Kyna." He looked at them all sternly. "Any questions?"

"What about the rest of us, Grundel?" asked Tasmira, gesturing to the Brothers. There was a note of annoyance in her voice that both Grundel and Kyna caught.

"You know your duty: to do whatever is needed to protect the Icefield. This hasn't changed." The Brothers nodded, but there was a swift exchange, a hooded look between Tasmira and Gorath.

The enormity of their tasks descended on everyone in the cave. Slowly they all turned to look at Melancholia, hoping, now that Rakor was back, that she could tell them the future, the outcome of their plans. She was present but not really with them, Grundel was thinking, for he too had turned to her. It's as if she's here but not here, he thought, as if our chatter were no more than the sound of bees moving among the flowers.

"I know what you are thinking," announced Melancholia. She spoke slowly, deliberately, as she always did, but she was shimmering in and out of vision. "I wish I could answer the question paramount in everyone's mind, but I can't—it all depends on you." She paused, but they waited, needing more. "Yes, there are many variables, many contingencies—but hear me—I believe that what you are attempting is possible. And I trust your courage and your great love." Melancholia had not yet told anyone that her fractured vision had not mended with

Rakor's return and that it was getting harder and harder to hold her earthly shape.

Suddenly a loud growling erupted at the entrance and the tarp was ripped down — in leapt Tagore and her pack of white wolves. The male bears scrambled to their feet. Tagore seldom ventured to Cathedral; she was an ally of The Ursula and frequented the Valley of the Twins, but had little contact with the Brothers. She remained at the entrance, her magnificent eyes gleaming in the firelight, eyeing each member of the group. Most of the Brothers had never heard Tagore speak, except on the wind, howling to her pack.

"We are prepared to help," she growled, turning and bowing to Kyna. "What can we do?" An electric murmur raced around the room. Kyna thought for a moment.

"We can't say right away, Tagore, but we do know we could use your help. Perhaps for the time being you could warn me, here at Cathedral, when SaMäel is coming. You sense him before all others. This in itself would be a great help."

Tagore nodded. "We will signal like this," and she gave a sign to the wolves, who threw back their heads and gave a very distinct high howl that would travel far. When Kyna nodded, Tagore turned around and the pack left as suddenly as they had appeared.

"Well," said Grundel, shaking his great head at the unexpected appearance, "we'd better get to it; we'll take the next few days to prepare for our tasks." Vang nodded, beat the air, and gliding silently on owl wings, disappeared out the mouth of the Keeper's Cave.

MELANCHOLIA, Monk and Mikaila were sitting on the grass below the hoodoos, with Koko on Monk's lap as usual. All morning Semjaza had been instructing them on the devils of Abadon.

"Burning Sand, Rain of Fire, River of Blood, Cerberus, lion, leopard, and—and something else, not to mention vultures and condors and what was that other twelve-foot creature? Semjaza— you must come with us—we'll never keep all of this straight!" Monk moaned, unable to retain everything Semjaza was saying.

"Thank you, but I think not," replied Sem with exaggerated politeness.

"But you're a seraph!" exclaimed Mikaila. "You were of the Order of Seraphim—Mother said so. You can be a fiery serpent—like SaMäel. Why would you be afraid? We need you!" Semjaza laughed—his light, mocking laugh.

"Afraid? Oh yes, I'm afraid. You don't understand the hierarchy of this power, Mikaila. You cannot begin to understand. Suffice it to say that SaMäel was a Prince of the Order of Seraphim; I was not. He is much more powerful than I can ever dream to be. My help would be limited—like Mel's."

"Do you dream of being powerful, Semjaza?" Koko piped up. They had a tendency to forget about her, curled up, seemingly half asleep. Now everyone turned to her, and then back to Semjaza. The angel drew a deep breath, thinking through the complexities of the question, and its answer.

"Not really. Power is a deceptive thing. It distorts your perception; it pulls you off the path of truth; it robs your peace." He paused. "But in all honesty—sometimes I wish I were more powerful than SaMäel, so I could undo what he does."

Koko nodded, "Me too." Monk gave her a hug.

"But that kind of thinking can also make us fall into a trap— the trap of power, only to find out, too late, that we have succumbed to its lure. And that we have deserted all that's good in our lives—."

"Like Rakor," Koko interrupted scowling. She had not forgiven him.

"Yes, like Rakor."

"Is that why you won't go with them to rescue Mama?" she asked. Semjaza found her questions disarming. Her world was so simple, so marvellously clear: if someone needed to be rescued, you rescued her.

"I haven't ruled out the possibility entirely, Koko. I am merely pointing out the complications."

"Good," she said, solemnly, "because I don't think they can save Mama without you." Monk and Mel exchanged glances— no one could have made a more convincing argument. But as much as Semjaza admired the little girl, it was Mikaila who finally convinced him. Semjaza loved her. He had always loved her. He had tried to hide these feelings until she was old enough to understand them fully, to decide for herself what she wanted. That day on the hoodoo ledge, when she found out that Armaros was her father, Sem had realized that she had feelings for him. Now, after reminding himself of all the dangers in Abadon, he realized that he could not let her go into so much danger without his protection.

"All right, all right, I'll go. Armaros will stop speaking to me, SaMäel will never forgive me, and I will pay through all eternity—but I will go." He smiled ruefully at Mikaila. Koko clapped her hands.

"Good," said Melancholia.

"Ok, o-kay!" exclaimed Monk, enthusiastically thumping his knee. "Now, we're getting somewhere." It was the first time that he believed this mad rescue might work.

"You will need your mother's black dress, Mikaila," said Sem, thinking out loud.

"Whatever for? I've never worn that."

"For Abadon's banquets. Trust me, just take it."

"It's not fair," wailed Koko, suddenly feeling excluded. "I

want to go too!" Semjaza could see tears welling up in the little girl's eyes, and took pity on her.

"Believe me, Koko, that's the last thing you want. Abadon is no place for any creature, especially children. You've suffered enough. And you already have done more than your share."

"But I could do more," she whispered. "Can't I help more?" Semjaza couldn't resist her spunk.

"All right, perhaps I can find something more for you to do. Will you come with me?" Semjaza held out his arms and she went to him shyly. Lifting her lightly, he flew up to his hoodoo opening.

"What do you suppose that's all about?" asked Monk.

Mikaila smiled, remembering her first time in Armaros' hoodoo. "She's about to have a rare treat. One is not often invited into such a dwelling. An angel's home is full of wonder." They stretched out to wait in the warmth of the lingering fall sun, listening to the hum of insects, the sweeping wind in the pines, and the background roar of the waterfall.

When the two returned a short while later, Koko was holding an exquisite obsidian box, her face bright with happiness. The lid was inlaid and sparkling with precious gems—topaz, jasper, gold, banded agate, amethyst—worked with angelic skill.

"His house smells of lemons, lovely lemons and something else?" She looked inquisitively at Semjaza, "oh yes—jasmine! I love jasmine!"

"Koko is going to assist me with the enchantments that will help protect you in Abadon. Right Koko?" asked Sem. The child smiled and with seriousness far beyond her years, she carefully put the box on the ground, sat down in front of it, and opened the lid. First she handed Monk an ancient bronze medallion with strange markings hung on a gold chain.

"For you, Papa."

"This allows you," explained Sem, "invisibility. When necessary you will wear it around your neck. But like all enchantments, it has limitations. It lasts for one day from sunup to sundown. Then you must take it off and put it in a dark place to heal. If you want to be visible you simply take it off. It will not work at night." As Monk reached for it, startled by its tingling hardness, Armaros strode out of his hoodoo and flew down beside them with another much larger obsidian box.

"Why Armaros," said Semjaza, grinning, "what have we here?"

Armaros glowered at all of them. "Put away your trifles, Sem. Your enchantments won't do much good in Abadon; these fools are going to need Hermes wings and sheaths." Koko reluctantly closed the lid to her box, and turned to Semjaza, tears welling up again.

"He doesn't mean that, Koko. He means he has something too. Don't you Armaros," Semjaza said pointedly.

"Yes, yes, of course. I'm sorry, Koko, I didn't see you there. I've come to add Hermes wings to your marvellous box." Armaros threw Semjaza a scathing look behind the child, who was beaming once again.

"Hermes what?' asked Mikaila, not at all afraid of Armaros' look, knowing it was just for show, knowing it was just his way of saying he was worried.

"Think of them as rubber boots and a raincoat—except to be used for Burning Sand and Rain of Fire," answered Armaros.

"Excellent," said Monk, "this gets better and better."

Mikaila was not so sure. The more she grasped the dangers, the more she wondered what she had rashly agreed to.

"You don't have to go," said Semjaza quietly, reading her look.

"Yes—I do. It could just as easily have been me whom SaMäel took—and I would be hoping against hope for rescue. What else would keep you going in a place like that? The rescue attempt needs all of us and even then it will be a miracle if we succeed."

Koko, who was listening, patted Mikaila's knee, in an imitation of Monk. "Don't worry," she piped, "everything will be fine. You'll have Armaros' gifts, Sem's enchantments, and Mama will be helping from the other side and she's very clever."

"Right," said Semjaza, smiling, "so let's get back to your box, Koko."

MEANWHILE, back at the Keeper's Cave, Tuktu and Raven were making last minute preparations, plotting their course to the Barrenlands. Grundel, Kyna and Alethia were busy charting a schedule—everything hung on timing.

"The most important timing is when to let slip to SaMäel that I'm not at Cathedral," Grundel noted. "Once that's out of the bag, SaMäel throws a wrench into our plan."

"So, first we need to get everyone in place," replied Kyna. "Rakor and Piotr near Castleguard Cave, but not too near because they must not be seen; Monk and the others waiting at the portal to Abadon, and you started on your way to Ram Ridge to lead SaMäel in a grand chase—you have to delay him long enough for the others to complete their tasks. When everyone is in place, and Vang gets the Quintessence to Rakor, Vang needs to let slip the news."

"Are we forgetting anything?" asked Grundel. "I have this hollow feeling in the pit of my stomach that we're forgetting something."

"If we are, it's not for lack of trying," answered Alethia.

"We've been at this for days. Let's just get going. The sooner we start, the sooner it's done."

TASMIRA and Gorath had taken the familiar route down Cathedral's outwash glacier to the river where presently they were fishing, but also arguing.

"What harm is there in thinking ahead, of thinking about contingencies? Can't you think for yourself?" retorted Tasmira, angrily, slapping at but missing a fish hovering in a dark pool.

"I just don't think we should do anything more than we've been told," continued Gorath, stubbornly shaking his great head. Tasmira took a deep breath, calmed herself, plunged her paw into the pool and grabbed the fish, winging it over her shoulder where it dropped onto the grass, its tail wildly thrashing, searching for water. Then she turned calmly to Gorath.

"It's not like you to be so submissive. Doesn't it occur to you that Grundel and Kyna have too much to think about? It won't hurt will it?" she pleaded, wading out of the water.

"No," hesitated Gorath, chewing thoughtfully. "It's just—."

"What?"

Gorath stopped chewing and swallowed. "It's just that Grundel and Kyna have stressed not acting on our own."

"They have just stressed not acting *before we're told*. That's different," she argued.

"Then why don't we tell them—let them ok it?"

"Precisely because they have too much to think about already."

"And because you think they may say no."

"Look Gorath, they want to keep things simple. I agree—but up to a point. We are dealing with a complex mind. SaMäel can see through us so easily. Why not take a step or two further, out of character, something he won't expect?"

"Isn't that what we are already doing—isn't that the whole idea of the diversions?"

"Yes. I just want to be sure that we at least get the plan off the ground! If anything goes wrong in the handoff between Vang and Rakor, the whole plan fails. C'mon Gorath—use some initiative! Do you really need Grundel to tell you everything? This is harmless—isn't it? It won't hurt anyone, will it? And it might help."

"All right. But we keep it as simple as possible—agreed?"

"Agreed." Tasmira walked back to the fish, put a paw on its head and tore out the belly, eating it with renewed vigour.

That night no one slept well. Gorath tossed and turned in a deep hollow. Grundel paced the Keeper's Cave, his Brothers watching him. Despite the animals' foreboding, it was a night of exquisite beauty. Tasmira lay on her back watching the lovely northern lights shimmer and glow in great dancing columns—lime green, pale yellow and red. Mikaila and Monk watched the magical dance from the Ravenwood porch, wordless. Thankful, Melancholia stepped out onto Cathedral's ledge to bathe in its mysterious light. Overhead the kaleidoscope bands of light flamed, faded and flamed again, twisting and twirling, radiating like ribbons of spirit, messages from the universe of hope and light and ecstasy.

The Day of Execution

THE BEARS gathered at Cathedral for last minute instructions. Snow-laden clouds drifted across the mountaintops. Snow already falling on the south-western slopes, pushed by westerly winds, blew up and over the northern ridges. Cold winds funnelled through the passes. Grundel, waiting on the ledge, his snout high in the air, realized with a start that they were running out of time—winter was almost upon them. He turned to Kyna, but before he could voice his concern, she answered.

"I know. I know." She'd already felt her body responding to the cold, had felt the overwhelming impulse to den. "Let's get this done, so we can return to our normal lives," she said, quietly. "After this, the problem of keeping the Corridor open and safe is going to seem straightforward."

They were waiting impatiently, nervously, for Melancholia. It was to begin. Semjaza had helped the Furtive Folk with a plan to secure the Quintessence in a form that the bears could carry. Neither Mel nor the angels could transport through the rock of the underground tunnels—it was too dangerous. One miscalculation and they would be entombed in the granite forever. The Quintessence had lain deep in the Castleguard Caves, encased in its protective shell, for millennia. The essence of water and light, it took different forms depending on who was looking at it and their understanding of it. Out of its shell, it appeared to most as a frozen waterfall backlit by light, which no one could look at directly without being blinded and then overwhelmed. What puzzled Melancholia was that Mustela and the others had found the Quintessence out of its shell. They had decided the safest plan would be for Semjaza to teach

Mustela and Marmo an enchantment for the blinding liquid
light, so that they could put it back in its magic shell, the
Conus-Gloria-Maris. This he had done. Now the small animals
had to do their part, their very dangerous part. Melancholia
silently hoped the shell would be somewhere near the Quintessence. This morning, she had gone to tell Vang to send Slank
and Payne on an errand to the settlement, and to tell Mustela
to begin the digging.

The cave was full of restless bears. Kyna gave a sigh of relief
when Melancholia returned to Cathedral.

"All right," said Mel, holding up her hand to silence the
murmuring bears, "it's begun. Rakor and Piotr, you need to start
out now. Wait for Vang in the woods northeast of the Castleguard Caves, just where the river takes a sharp turn north." The
two grizzlies nodded and took the Spiral. The others watched
them go, then turned to Mel.

Tasmira grunted to Gorath and they went out on pretext to
feed. Crossing the Castleguard meadow, they didn't notice
Mikaila who was working, waiting for Semjaza; but Mikaila
noticed them. She wondered why the pair was headed to
Castleguard. She watched the bears make their way to the
woods beside the caves, trotting just inside the forest. Then
Semjaza arrived with Equus, and Mikaila felt her heart race
and her breath come quick and hard. She chided herself, determined not to let this happen. Semjaza was an angel; she was
human, at least raised thoroughly human, despite Armaros. It
just wouldn't work. Besides, she liked her life, her freedom; she
didn't need an angel—as old as time—telling her what to do.
But the hand she held up to wave still shook at the sight of him,
and she couldn't help smiling, suddenly shy, when he turned
his full loving gaze upon her.

"It's time," he said. "Here's Equus—we need to get there

quickly." She climbed on Equus' back and it jumped into flight, beating its wings in unison with Semjaza's.

On Cathedral's ledge, the others were gathering: Monk, Koko, Raven. Tuktu was in the Ancient Wood waiting beside Toholinagi; now that the time had come, she was anxious to get back to the Barrenlands. Grundel wished everyone luck, then, after rubbing muzzles with Kyna, his party started out. Semjaza and Mikaila arrived in time to wish them a safe journey. When the angel and Mikaila entered the cave, they found Monk packing for Abadon. He looked ashen and grim. Stealing a glance at Mikaila, Semjaza noticed that she too was pale and tense.

"This would be a good time to change your minds," he said lightly, "if you so desire. There is no shame in it. I could do this myself."

"And with me," said Melancholia.

"I'm going," Monk said and picked up his pack and slung it over his back. He called to Koko and gave her a hug. The child pulled away from him reluctantly, and then ran to Kyna, throwing her small arm over the grizzly's neck for support. She stood there silently, her eyes wide, trying to be brave.

"Me too," replied Mikaila, although when she tried to smile at Semjaza it came out more like a grimace. Her stomach was turning over in fear and anticipation.

"I know you just packed them, but I need to see what is in your packs," said Semjaza. Mikaila and Monk exchanged puzzled glances but decided not to ask questions. They quickly unpacked while Semjaza checked for Hermes wings, sheaths, food, tools. He wanted to shift their focus from their fear to their task. It worked. When they were done repacking, they hoisted their packs confidently over their shoulders, straightening to let them settle on their backs. Both were accustomed to travelling long distances with full packs and the weight seemed to brace them for what lay ahead. *Good*, thought Semjaza, *because this is the farthest they will ever travel.* Before she left, it struck Mikaila that perhaps she should mention to Kyna that she had seen Tasmira and Gorath headed towards Castleguard. There was something odd about their behaviour.

TASMIRA and Gorath were crouched down in thick brush just outside the Castleguard caves when Vang came to the Rivergate to send Slank and Payne on an errand. He had already convinced Malenger to go out trapping for the day. The bears watched as Slank and Payne disappeared over a ridge towards the settlement. Vang took a deep breath and then headed back inside.

"Do you think Vang and Rakor can be trusted?" whispered Tasmira.

"We have to trust them," replied Gorath.

"I wish *we* were doing this instead."

"Let's just keep to this plan—we will be in enough trouble as it is."

"Don't worry so much. This is a precaution, that's all; no one will be upset with us." Gorath nodded; he wanted to believe Tasmira. He always thought that he was better suited for Keeper than Grundel. Perhaps this would give him an opportunity to prove that to the others. A challenge was not out of the question if Grundel failed.

THE SNOW CLOUDS had passed and the sun was slowly rising to its zenith as Malenger, comfortably astride his horse, headed down a trail through the spruce wood. It had stopped snowing and the wind had died down. As he descended into the valley and the day grew warmer, he stripped off his outer parka and stuffed it into his pack. In a moment of genius, he had devised a cunning new trap, something so out of the ordinary that the

Furtive Folk could not go around it, would not even detect it —
at least for a while. He had set the first trap when he realized
that he was short on the fine gauge wire that tripped the whole
device, and that he would need to go to Hilda's. He didn't mind
today; he also needed supplies: tea, sugar, flour for bannock.
'Screw Rakor,' he thought, 'and his bloody demands. All he does
now is give orders.' He was taking his time, enjoying the ride,
the sun on his face, the sense of freedom, and the solitude.
Because it led to the settlement, one rarely saw any animals on
this trail, so his rifle was stuffed in his saddlebag. But he
clutched it automatically when he heard a noise coming up
behind him, startling him out of his reverie.

"What are you doing?" he roared, as Slank and Payne came
into sight.

"What?" said Slank, who was also enjoying the day's ride.
"I thought you were supposed to be trapping. We're going to
Hilda's for supplies."

"Both of you?"

"Why not? It's a good day for a ride." Slank watched as
Malenger's face took on its accustomed sneer and look of contempt. He hated that look.

"Who's looking after the caves?"

"The bear. What's the problem? The animals won't get past
Rakor."

"Don't you think it's just a little suspicious that Rakor sent
all of us out today? When has he ever done that?" Malenger
spat on the ground. "You two are useless." Taking no chances
of being swindled of his share of the treasure, Malenger
whipped them around and the three men rode hard back to
Castleguard, Slank cursing his oversight.

BACK IN THE CAVES of Castleguard, Vang called to Mustela who came running down the tunnel.

"How's it going? You don't have much time."

"Almost there, I think," Then she turned around and raced back down the tunnel. The largest and strongest of the Furtive Folk were digging courageously at the bend where they first encountered the liquid light.

As Mustela arrived she spoke firmly, "Stop. Wait now for me." Just before they broke through, Mustela performed the enchantment, with Marmo's prompting.

"All right, the rest of you stand back and for goodness sakes don't look until we tell you." The two animals broke through the rock and a light shone through the opening, but it was duller than last time, as if coming through a veil. When the opening was large enough, Marmo and Mustela stepped through. Inside was another large cavern. At one end, what looked like a frozen waterfall glowed as if a light shone from behind it.

Mustela and Marmo knew that what they saw was an illusion. They needed to find the shell, the *Gloria Maris*, which could contain the liquid light, the life force. Looking around wildly, they finally spotted a large cone shell beside a pile of rock rubble. There were odd shaped bones lying nearby that they couldn't identify. The shell was very beautiful—with an elongated but perfectly straight body and elegant whorl at the top; the inside was a silky smooth opaque white; the outer colouring was like a fine net thrown over gold and silver. They reached for it gently and then approached the waterfall, still fearful of what this day held for them.

Melancholia had told them to place the shell at the base of the glowing waterfall, and Semjaza had given them the strange words to chant so that the Quintessence would flow into it. They couldn't see how this great frozen waterfall could flow anywhere, let alone fit into this shell, but despite their doubts, and against what their senses were telling them, when they did as instructed, the glowing ice flowed smoothly and perfectly into the shell. They drew out a pouch the Watchers had given them, put the shell in it, and drew the long straps tight. Between the two of them, they carried it out to the others who were waiting. Silently they all marched to the main cavern where Vang was waiting. He took the pouch wordlessly, gave them all a quick nod, transmuted into an owl and flew out the tunnel to the entrance.

Back in his bear form, upright and carrying the Quintessence in his giant paws, Vang came out of Castleguard's Rivergate into the opening in front of the caves, just as Malenger, Slank and Payne rode over the ridge of the hill. Vang gasped and froze. The men, sliding off their horses, called out to him. The bear threw frantic looks around him, but no one moved, not wanting to give themselves away, waiting for him to act. When Vang didn't respond, Malenger called again, angrily. Vang started towards the men, then veered suddenly and bolted. The men leapt after him. In the shadows, Gulo, hiding unbeknownst to the others, followed Vang stealthily, keeping a wary eye on the three men who were quickly closing the gap. Vang was trying desperately to get the pouch around his neck so he could run faster. Tasmira started to shout out to Vang to shape-shift, but Gorath stopped her. For a moment he considered doing nothing. To let Grundel fail. But something prodded him, a voice inside him that sounded a lot like The Ursula. He sighed, and then laughed at himself.

"C'mon," he said, loping after the others, "we need to overtake Vang. We need to cause a diversion, lead the men away from him." Tasmira nodded, keeping up with him, thinking quickly.

"I'll stay out of sight until we're further away," she replied, "then the two of us can appear, but we'll go in opposite directions and they'll have to split up. That'll give us a better chance to escape them later."

"All right, but stay out of rifle range," said Gorath.

The three men were getting dangerously close to Vang, who had been awkwardly running upright as he tried to put the pouch with the Quintessence around his neck.

"What's he doing? What's that pouch?" yelled Slank.

"Damn!" said Malenger dropping down on one knee and taking aim with his rifle. He had a clear shot because Vang was still out in the open. For a moment Gorath and Tasmira froze. But before he could shoot, Aquila sky bombed him and as the man was looking up, Gulo leapt out of the bushes, growling viciously. The wolverine had little chance to escape all three men, but he knew what he must do. With a mighty leap, he sank his teeth into Malenger's neck, splitting the jugular vein, refusing to let go until he felt Malenger go limp—and his own hatred drain out of him.

Slank, running behind Malenger, dropped to his knee, raising his own rifle. As Gulo looked up and leapt, Slank shot him through the heart. The wolverine dropped at the man's feet. As the two men watched, the surprisingly small body contorted and then lay still. Aquila screeched, dove and dug her claws into Slank who knocked her off with the butt of his rifle. But before he could do any more harm, she flew off. Her last glimpse of the scene was Gulo's fur shimmering in the sunlight.

"That pelt is mine when we get back," said Slank, turning to Payne. Malenger was already dead when Slank reached down to feel for his pulse. Tasmira and Gorath had skirted around them, deeper in the woods, looking back only once when they heard the shot, and caught up to Vang.

"Take owl shape now, Vang, it will throw them off. We will divert the two men. Malenger is dead."

"Dead—how—you?"

"Gulo. I think he's dead too. Can you carry the Quintessence in your owl shape?" asked Gorath. Vang nodded. "Keep out of sight until we lead them away, and then get to Rakor as quickly as possible." Vang nodded again, numbly; he was badly shaken. "*Now* Vang, they're coming. Tas—get out of sight."

Gorath roared to get the men's attention and then changed direction, the two men hot on his trail. He ran to a rocky stream bed, and charged down its gully, while Tasmira stayed just inside the wood. The two men had enough trouble running on the rocks and loose gravel that they could neither use their weapons nor look around to notice Tasmira. When the two men started to catch up to Gorath, he ducked into the woods, and then both bears appeared in front of the men, picking up speed, careening to avoid becoming a target.

"Which one?" yelled Payne. "I can't see the pouch!"

"Split up! Split up!" hollered Slank as the bears headed off in different directions, Tasmira racing across the shallow stream and into the woods on the other side, Gorath into the nearer woods. They headed southeast and west, away from Vang's northern destination.

Vang leapt up after they had gone, and disregarding Gorath's suggestion, put the Quintessence around his neck, and remaining in his bear shape headed for Rakor and Piotr. He felt stronger, safer, in his own shape. He was headed for the big bend in the Sunwapta River, where it took a northerly turn, but first he had to cross an outflow glacier. He lumbered across the ice silently, casting nervous glances skyward, expecting SaMäel to explode out of the sky at any moment. At the bottom of the glacier, he turned north west, following the Sunwapta River until he spotted two bears waiting for him around the bend in the river.

"What happened," asked Rakor as Vang loped up, "was that a rifle shot?"

"Gulo attacked Malenger and then the other men shot him." Vang hung his head; he couldn't help feeling it was his fault, as if somehow he had failed.

"Are they both dead?" asked Piotr.

"I don't know, but I'm guessing yes. Gulo got to Malenger first and then the men shot the rifle at him point blank. The three men were together—how did that happen?"

"Never mind that now. Are you all right, Vang—can you return?" asked Rakor. Vang nodded. "Good." He turned to the smaller bear, "Piotr, we should go."

Just then Aquila swept down, back beating her wings, and landing beside them. She said, "I come from Kyna—she does not want you to return to Castleguard, Vang."

"Any message for us?" asked Rakor. Aquila shook her head. "Then we're off." Rakor and Piotr took the Quintessence, patted Vang on the back, gave a brief farewell, and loped off. Vang sat down with a resounding thump.

"Does she know?" asked Vang, avoiding eye contact with the golden eagle.

"Kyna? Yes, everything."

"And Gulo?"

"I tried to use my—," began Aquila haughtily, but when she saw Vang's stricken face, she stopped. "He's dead. It wasn't your fault, Vang. You did your part. Kyna is not upset with you; but the Furtive Folk have left the Cave, and she doesn't want you to face SaMäel alone. You are to return to Cathedral."

"It wasn't supposed to go that way."

"Put it behind you," urged Aquila, flapping her wings.

"Gulo made his own choice—you know how he hated Malenger. We need to go." Vang didn't move.

"But because of me he's dead."

"He was protecting the Quintessence as much as you," Aquila said impatiently. "C'mon Vang, get a grip, The Ursula needs you." Duty was ingrained in the Brothers; Vang got up slowly, trying to shake off his lethargy, and lumbered heavily off after the eagle who kept a wary eye on him over her shoulder.

WHEN Tasmira and Gorath each decided that they had drawn their man far enough away, they picked up speed, disappearing into the land they knew so well, leaving Slank and Payne scratching their heads, lost in unfamiliar woods without Malenger, each other, or the wherewithal to get home again. They might have died there if it had not been for SaMäel. He returned to Castleguard to find Malenger and Gulo dead, the caves empty, and the two men gone. He circled over the area to see if anyone was still around, wondering if the two men had stolen the Quintessence. It seemed very unlikely; the two of them were too incompetent, too bungling. Where was Rakor? He swept over the area, his great wings beating with powerful strokes. He spotted Payne first, swooping down and picking him up unceremoniously, carrying him by his collar, just over the tops of the trees, looking for Slank. Payne was too terrified to even scream, until SaMäel dropped him beside Slank, then Payne cursed SaMäel long and loud.

"Shut up Payne," said SaMäel dismissively, eventually tiring of the man's rant. "Where's the Quintessence?"

"The what?" asked Slank.

"The treasure," replied SaMäel, impatiently. "What happened?"

Terrified of SaMäel's wrath, Payne and Slank interrupted

one another repeatedly, trying to tell what happened. SaMäel stood, his arms crossed, his hand on his chin, listening intently.

"Are you sure it was Rakor who came out of the cave with the bag around his neck?"

"Yes," said Slank, "of course."

"Well—pretty sure," interrupted Payne. "They're hard to tell apart."

"And there was no one with him?"

"Not until the other one showed up," replied Slank.

"And then we had to split up," added Payne.

"Did either of you see the bag, once you split up?"

"Uh—well, no, not really—he had it around his neck, in front, on his chest. And we never caught up," replied Slank.

"Was there any time that he was out of your sight?'

"Not until we lost them," said Payne.

"Yes—there was," corrected Slank, remembering. "At the very beginning, for a short time when he ducked into the woods and then two bears appeared."

"So, Rakor could have given the pouch to someone in the woods. In fact, neither of the two bears were necessarily Rakor. The two bears you chased could have been a diversion."

"A diversion?" Slank dropped to his knees. "All that for nothing?"

"And now Rakor and everyone else is gone?" asked Payne.

"Was that the treasure—in the pouch?" gasped Slank.

"I suspect it was."

"Damn! What now?"

SaMäel gazed past them, "Now we find Rakor."

AFTER Aquila told her what happened at Castleguard, Kyna realized that if Vang wasn't at Castleguard, SaMäel would come looking for Rakor at Cathedral. Her first concern was for Koko.

She had been discussing the problem with Bighorn, out on the ledge, when the child, who had been sitting cross-legged beside them watching arctic terns, suddenly jumped up and patted her on the back.

"Kyna, Kyna," she said, "is that Winda?"

Kyna looked up and nodded. "Good. I asked her to speak to Nagi." Winda alighted in front of them with a grand flurry. "He's willing," she said, tucking in her wings neatly.

"I think it would work, Kyna," urged Bighorn. "SaMäel pays no attention to Nagi, and he won't be looking for the child." Kyna nodded thoughtfully.

"Me—what about me?" Koko asked, suddenly fearful. Kyna turned to her, gently.

"Koko—do you trust Melancholia?"

"Yes."

"Nagi is a spirit like Mel. He wants to protect you. He will hide you inside."

"Inside what—?"

"Well, the tree that he is."

'A—a tree?" Koko's eyes widened. "That's impossible!"

"Nagi is a special spirit, what we call a portal."

"No. No, I don't want to do that," she replied stubbornly, shaking her head, crossing her arms and planting her feet as if she expected to be whisked away.

"We would never force you," said Kyna gently, "but SaMäel must not find you. Remember, he thinks you are dead. And it is best if he goes on thinking you're dead—for now." Koko puckered her face and continued to shake her head vigorously.

"You would be the first to see Rachel and Monk when they return, and—" added Bighorn. Kyna shook her head at Bighorn, interrupting.

"Do not manipulate her," she said.

"What do you mean?" asked Koko, ignoring Kyna and turning to Bighorn.

"Well, that's the portal they will come through from Abadon. Well, it is," said Bighorn, turning to Kyna. "And I'm not manipulating her; I'm giving her a reason to overcome her fear."

"Really? That's where they'll come?" Bighorn nodded his great rack of horns.

"Well," said Koko, turning back to Kyna, "is this what Papa would want?"

"I can't say for sure, but I believe so. He wants you safe, and Cathedral is no longer safe for you."

"But if it's a-a portal, won't SaMäel come through it too?" Koko's body trembled at the thought.

"There is that possibility, but in all the eons that Melancholia has known him, he never has. He prefers the sun's portal. It is a matter of pride with him—no one else can stand the heat."

"How does he?"

"Because he is a dragon and dragons are born from fire. But think now about Nagi."

"All right then," said the child, subconsciously stroking Kyna's lush fur as if for reassurance, "I'll go."

"I think this is a wise decision. I want Bighorn to take you now, if you are willing. We will come for you as soon as it is safe." Kyna smiled warmly at Koko's trust in her.

Koko reached up and spontaneously gave Kyna a hug—she loved the way Kyna smiled, not only with her mouth but with her face, her whole body, her gentle soul.

"Climb up on Bighorn now, and he'll take you down the mountain and across the Icefield. Are you warmly dressed? It's cold on the ice—best get some gear on first." Koko did as she was told, pulling on her woollen sweater, coat, mittens, wool hat, wrapping her face in a woollen scarf, and then grabbing hold of Bighorn's rack to steady herself on his back, lying flat to wrap her arms around his thick neck to get down the mountain.

Once they were across the ice bridge, Bighorn told her to sit up and hold on by putting pressure with her knees, for balance. Noticing her tense silence, he tried to relax her by telling her about Toholinagi.

"They say, 'In his highest boughs the gods sleep, and in his roots infinity rests.' You are very fortunate—whoever knows how to speak to Nagi, whoever knows how to listen to him, learns many truths. He tells the story of who we are. He has a long memory, much longer than ours, and he is writing our history in his rings—in the luminous wooden pages of his trunk—all the good years, the peace and happiness, and the bad years, the sickness, the years of hunger and suffering. We are all there—Carth and Inyx and Boris too."

Bighorn made his way gingerly down Entrance to the Ancient Wood. He stopped for a moment, to let Koko get her bearings and draw a deep breath. The trees in the grove were small, gnarled, blunted by centuries of unforgiving wind. Finally, Bighorn stopped in the centre of the wood, in front of the oldest tree, the portal, Toholinagi.

"And now you'll be here, Koko, written into our history."

Koko watched wide-eyed as Toholinagi swirled into a great cone to accommodate her. She watched as the thin limbed branches whorled outward, the trunk grew and stretched, and a warm golden glow shimmered from inside, like Monk's lantern inside their cabin in the night valley.

"Are you ready?" asked Bighorn. Koko nodded wordlessly, trusting Kyna and Bighorn, as only a child can trust the animals. "He'll take you in, then. Put your hand on the trunk, close your eyes, and think inside the tree."

"You're not coming?"

"Honestly—you won't need me at all." Koko gave him a big hug, reached for the tree, closed her eyes tightly and took a deep breath—when she opened her eyes, there was a clear, sharp smell of spruce and a soft golden light filtered down into the hollow centre of the tree.

"Where am I?" she whispered.

Inside. It was a deep, resonant voice—no, not a voice, a thought inside her head.

Would you like to sit down?

"Yes."

Then imagine what you want to sit on. Koko remembered the little wooden chair that her father had made for her long ago and suddenly it appeared in front of her. She felt Toholinagi chuckling.

"What's so funny?"

You may have anything you want. Is this what you want? Koko began to get upset until she tried to sit and noticed that she had outgrown the chair. She laughed too and then pictured the most wonderful chair she could imagine—covered in material as soft as down, with overstuffed arms, a high back that encircled her, and a long seat so she could stretch her legs straight out in front of her. And suddenly it was before her.

"Oh!" she squealed and climbed on, sinking into its luxuriant warmth.

Hungry? The voice asked.

"Yes."

Well, imagine what you want to eat. Koko imagined her mother's bannock, smothered in wild berry jam with a cup of hot cocoa to go with it. *Now imagine something to put it on.* She imagined a small table, and to her delight, it appeared beside her laden with her food. Toholinagi let her wolf the food, like a little pup.

"Now what?" she asked, feeling bolder.

How about a story?

"Oh yes. I love stories!"

Well, let's see, what shall I tell you—perhaps a bear story?

"Yes please!"

This is the story of Arctos and the first Ursula. Melancholia and I were alone in the mountains for a long time. But when the animals started to move closer to the Icefield—the furtive folk, the bears in the Valley, the sheep in Sunwapta, the eagles on Chaba—Mel realized that watching would no longer be enough. There were problems to be solved, individuals to help, young to be rescued from the dangers of the Icefield. She needed a companion who could act in this new world. So she went to the gods and explained her problem; they asked her what kind of a companion she needed. Melancholia thought deeply and then answered: someone strong and courageous and pure of heart. The gods searched the area and finally brought her Ursula, from the Valley of the Twins, while she was still a young cub and eager to learn. For many seasons Melancholia and Ursula were content, but as Ursula aged, she became aware of Mel's immortality, and she realized that her own life would not last forever. Mel laughed when Ursula raised the problem.

"That's easily solved," Mel said, "I will ask the gods to make you immortal too." But Ursula did not want an alien life.

"No," she said, "but I can give you offspring to take my place." Mel went back to the gods who decided Ursula was right. A god came to her in the guise of Arctos—a great male bear; three times he visited, and each time Ursula subsequently bore twin males. When they were old enough, after they had been taught what they needed to know as Keepers, Ursula left them at Cathedral with Melancholia and went back to the Valley and far

beyond, searching for mates who would keep the line strong, courageous and pure of heart.

"Is that why Kyna is called The Ursula?" asked Koko.

Yes. It was Ursula who understood the path all Keepers walk.

"Except Rakor," replied Koko, flatly.

Rakor has paid and will continue to pay for his betrayal. Koko was silent, still struggling inwardly with her hatred and fear of Rakor.

"Thank you for the story." She was silent for a little while, and then she asked, "Can all trees talk?"

Yes, but most don't.

"Why?"

They have no need.

"What do you mean? Don't they care about things?"

Oh yes, but they believe that what will be will be—and so they accept things as they are—silently.

"Accept what things—like?"

Like forest fires and lightning and infestations—they accept you humans—even with an axe in your hand—without complaint, believing that there will be renewal and reclamation.

Koko thought hard for a while. "Renewal—you mean new baby trees? But that wouldn't save yourself from being cut down."

And yet the forests thrive. Just think, Koko. Animals and humans carve their trails and make their homes in forests, but when these creatures leave, the forest reclaims the ground—and surprisingly quickly.

"But not the same trees. Not the ones cut down."

No. But do you know how old this grove is? Koko shook her head. *Seven hundred years old.* Koko whistled, like Monk, through her teeth.

"These scruffy little trees? Oh—I'm sorry!" she cried, her hands flying to her mouth.

No offence taken — we are a scruffy lot! Nagi chuckled.

"They must have lots to say saved up." Koko yawned widely, and sank lower in her chair. "I'm going to sleep now. May I have my blanket, please?"

Koko, already half asleep, reached down and pulled up a long forgotten wrap, the quilt Rachel had made for her second birthday when she moved to her own cot. Instantly, as children can, she sank into a deep sleep. Occasionally she woke, briefly, to eat, and then slept again. Sometimes she cried out in her sleep; sometimes she wept. Nagi watched over her, soothing her nightmares. Gradually, the broken pieces inside of her started to mend.

At Cathedral, Kyna stood on the ledge, waiting for Vang. After the golden eagle told her how upset Vang was, The Ursula wanted to greet him, to let him know that no one blamed him. She watched him climb the Face of Fakara so dejectedly that she worried if he didn't put more effort into it, he would fall off.

"All done?" she said, as he reached the ledge. He nodded mutely and sat down, looking out over the Icefield.

"Good job, Vang." But he shook his head.

"Not so good."

"There was nothing else you could have done. Nothing could have said would have made those men doubt that you were carrying what they thought of as their treasure. You had to run; it was your only choice."

"And Gulo?" Vang asked.

Kyna dropped her head, silent for a moment. "We have him. At least the men won't do what they did to Carth and Inyx."

"Are Tasmira and Gorath back yet?" asked Vang, wanting to change the topic.

"No. What happened? What were they doing at Castleguard?"

"I don't know, but thank goodness they were. Has everyone left?"

"Yes, and I've sent Winda to tell Grundel that they must travel faster and be more watchful. Vang," said Kyna, changing her tone, "you realize that our problem is that SaMäel will now be looking for Rakor, instead of Grundel."

"Rakor, oh no! I hadn't even thought about that!"

"Well, that's my job. What I need for you to do is to stay out here where SaMäel can see you, and continue to pretend that you are Rakor. You will have to let on that The Keeper and the Ursulas overpowered you. That way, SaMäel will go looking for Grundel." Vang gave her an admiring look.

"You're good, Kyna. We're lucky to have you as Ursula, especially now."

Kyna ducked her head in embarrassment. But privately, she was worried that Tasmira and Gorath might have alerted SaMäel to the whole idea of diversion. She and Grundel had decided on other modes of protection for Vang for just that reason—both Gulo and Aquila had been hidden outside the caves—but they had not foreseen all three men showing up at once. She had mixed feelings about Tasmira and Gorath and what they had done, although it had saved the plan, for now. She decided that she had to treat them diplomatically; she needed her two strongest bears even if they were acting too independently. She wondered what had prompted them to be there; she suspected their ambitions were urging them to act on their own. They might cause trouble yet. Suddenly, they both heard Tagore's wolf pack howling. Kyna quickly stepped inside the Keeper's Cave, leaving Vang exposed.

In Abadon

EARLIER THAT DAY Rachel had heard the raucous, whooping laughter and wild screams coming from the dining hall. SaMäel was either in a very good or very bad mood. But where could Koko be? Surely even he wouldn't take a child into that maelstrom? She was pacing her quarters, wringing her hands, trying to keep control of her mind, a rein on her imagination. Anger, despair, fear all tumbled chaotically. There was nothing she could do at this point—she needed something to take her mind off possibilities until she had more information. She gazed longingly out to the pools—is this how SaMäel had made the others dependent on the vapours? It would make things so much easier to bear. She paced the room endlessly, back and forth. Finally, she threw herself onto her bed and fell into a fit-ful sleep, exhaustion overcoming her fear. Days passed with no sign of Koko.

It was late morning before she dragged herself out of bed; she could hear an unfamiliar commotion out in the pools; someone had arrived. When one of the Seraphim brought her food, she asked what was going on.

"A visitor!" said the Seraph, smiling.

"Oh? With SaMäel?" she asked, hoping it was Koko. "Who?" She tried to keep her voice light.

"Semjaza, a Seraph who lives on Earth. We've missed him," he said simply. "And he has brought his Earth mate," he added as an afterthought, "the women are not pleased about that!" He laughed and set her tray on a small table.

"Is SaMäel with them?"

"No, he left earlier this morning."

"Thank you." An Earth woman? But Rachel's emotions were so exhausted that she could not raise any excitement. She was instead overcome with despair for Koko.

MONK, Semjaza, Mikaila, and Melancholia had arrived on Abadon through Toholinagi's portal, landing on the edge of a bleak little wood of wizened hemlock trees, under a scorching sun. Beyond the wood was desert. They could see the Burning Sands and the mist from the Rain of Fire in the distance. Monk and Mikaila immediately felt their nerve deserting them; their knees turned to jelly, their bodies trembled uncontrollably.

"Oh my God," said Mikaila, turning ashen, "what have we done?"

"Just breathe deeply—well, as deeply as you can without scorching your lungs," said Semjaza, "this is the first defence of Abadon. The weak of heart turn back here. Remember your purpose; concentrate on what you came for, on Rachel." Monk drew deep breaths, coughing hoarsely against the searing air entering his lungs. He closed his eyes and pictured Rachel and felt his body calming. Semjaza watched Mikaila closely to see if she could handle this treacherous place.

"Mikaila, put on your Hermes wings and sheath; you and I are going to enter the Gate."

"What do you mean," interrupted Monk. "We're ALL going to enter the Gate."

"No, Monk, that won't work. The Seraphim will let me in, and I can get Mikaila in as my mate if she is willing. But I cannot get you in at all. You will just raise the alarm. You and Melancholia must stay here and wait for us to bring Rachel out. If we are not back by midnight tomorrow night, you will have to decide what to do."

"You must be kidding! I can't stay here and just wait!"

"You must," said Melancholia. "You must trust them." Monk looked back to Semjaza who stood resolute.

"Look," Monk said, pulling out his chain, "I can wear my invisible thing."

"Not in the castle," replied Sem. Monk paced, trying to control his conflicting emotions.

"Tomorrow night? Why wait so long?"

"Because SaMäel takes his time; he'll want to entertain us; he'll be in no hurry for us to leave now that we are here and we will need time for the rescue."

"Surely we can't hide here?" Monk gazed around wildly at the small grove and its poor protection.

"Mel can, and that's what the medallion is for. Put it on." Semjaza waited until Monk did this. "Now rub it. There's nothing I can do that SaMäel can't undo, but he isn't suspecting trouble here, and he has his hands full, so I think the spell should do the trick. It will wear off by night, and then you must take it off and hide. Put it back on in the morning; by the second evening we should be back." Semjaza turned to Mikaila. "Will you come with me as my mate?" She nodded. "Can you do this? Be very certain."

"How can I possibly be certain? I couldn't have predicted my reaction if you had explained a hundred times what landing on Abadon was going to be like." She turned to Monk. "All I can do is my best. Is this good enough for you?"

"Yes," replied Monk.

"Then I'm ready." Rubbing the medallion, Monk was slowly disappearing before their eyes.

"All right? We can't see you," said Semjaza.

"Well I can see you," Monk muttered dejectedly, his voice floating eerily on the air.

"Take heart, man. We'll be as quick as we can possibly be.

Come, my dear," said Semjaza, smiling, taking Mikaila's arm, "I think I'm going to enjoy this." At the edge of the desert, Mikaila stopped to put on the Hermes wings for her feet and the sheath Armaros had given her, then stepped warily out onto the sand. It was unbearably hot, further on it flamed red.

"Just flutter your feet and you will hover above the sand. That's it. Now just walk normally. You've got it! The Burning Sands get hotter as we approach the city. When we get to the fire, you'll need to hover a little higher." Mikaila scowled, working hard to keep herself from pitching forward while she looked ahead. As flames rose from the sand in front of her, her heart seized and she had more difficulty breathing.

"Take my hand," said Semjaza, "you're all right." He wanted to sweep her up and carry her across the desert in his arms, but if anything happened to him, she needed the experience, the belief that she could cross it herself. Mikaila took his hand gladly, clutching it in a death grip that made Semjaza smile. He couldn't help admiring her courage. As she beat her Hermes wings harder to gain more height and pass quicker over the Sands, she felt the first sizzling drops of fire on her sheath. The outer protective covering acted like a coat of rain, but it was terrifying being enveloped by fire and her heart leapt to her mouth repeatedly. She involuntarily closed her eyes fearing being seared, but almost lost her balance. Semjaza grabbed her elbow and held her straight until she recovered. From underneath the sheath, she breathed through damp gauze covering her mouth and nose against the hot smoky air. Still, her lungs burned. Just when she thought her nerve would fail her, the Rain of Fire stopped, the air cleared, and the great wall of the City of Dis came into view. Semjaza stopped to let Mikaila recompose herself.

"Let me do the talking," he said. "And please don't take offence at anything I or the others say. I must go along with their lurid banter or they will be suspicious."

"All right," replied Mikaila slowly, wondering what on earth he could mean, but knowing that her life was in his hands. Semjaza helped her off with the wings and sheath, and she stuffed them into her pack. "Am I presentable?" She smoothed her hair nervously.

"You are beautiful," replied Semjaza, simply. Mikaila felt her heart melt for the second time that day, and her face flushed red. *'Must be the heat from the Burning Sands,'* she thought, trying to shake it off.

"We will be stopped at the Gate by the Seraphim. With a little luck they will not suspect anything and they will allow us through. But before they do, they will try you—they will instil fear and awe, in order to see through you. They will try to dazzle you with their power—it's what they do naturally. You must not back away, nor open your mind to them. Do not reveal our plans. Look into my eyes so you'll know what to expect." Mikaila realized that she had seldom looked, if ever, deeply into Sem's piercing cobalt blue eyes. She looked then, knowing she must do this, but she could not keep her deep love out of her gaze. Semjaza gasped. "Mikaila," he uttered, "Mikaila." And he clasped her to him. "Listen, when they look at you, think of me. Think of me." And he shook her a little, fearing for her.

"The city is full of miserable shadows—ignore them; they are beyond the ability to harm you if you keep your spirit strong. If they feel you weakening, they will prey upon you, trying to drain your life force to feed their own. When we get to the castle beware Cerberus and the others—but I will remind you of this when we get there. For now, keep your focus on rescuing Rachel. Ready?" Semjaza raised an arm in greeting as the seraphim waved at them from a distance. Suddenly the sky was full of large, black, beating wings and great hooked beaks. Mikaila ducked instinctively.

"Condors," said Semjaza, "checking us out." When the lead bird recognized Semjaza, it gave out a loud cry and they turned en masse, heading back to the castle. The angel turned to her, waiting for her reply.

"Ready," said Mikaila, drawing a deep breath.

As they crossed the brief distance to the River of Blood, a great metal drawbridge descended making a terrifying clamour as it clanked and shuddered and came to a jolting halt against the ground. Mikaila clutched Semjaza's arm tighter.

"Don't worry—it's all show. No one sneaks out of Abadon. Even Rara Avis, deep in the castle, hears the drawbridge. This is a good sign—they have recognized me and are prepared to let us through."

"Strange that the bridge has no sides, considering the River of Blood," said Mikaila, fearfully, stepping onto the curved wooden plank. She was looking down into the river's murky depths. It was deep red, almost black in places; in others it was a brilliant, alarming red. The blood ran sluggishly and she could see movement within it—large, ponderous fish rose to the surface with gaping mouths.

"That's so you can be easily pushed into the river if you are trying to escape," said Sem, absently. He was studying the seraphim, trying to figure out who was on duty guarding the bridge.

"Oh great," replied Mikaila, shuddering, thinking of their planned escape with Rachel.

"Breathe deeply, Mika," said Semjaza, using her mother's nickname for her. "Let's take this one step at a time."

Suddenly, in a blaze of golden light, the two seraphim flew across the bridge to greet them. Their wings were layered like translucent dragonfly wings, haloing each seraph; yet they beat the air powerfully.

"Semjaza—welcome!" cried a tall, golden, dazzling angel, alighting and folding in his wings. "What took you so long?" The other angel alighted gracefully in front of them, embracing Semjaza warmly. Mikaila eyed them critically. The two seraphim were similar yet different. One had a mass of golden locks that he tried to tame with golden clasps. He had a high forehead and laughing mischievous eyes; his golden tunic was somewhat dishevelled as if he had just come from bed or a skirmish; the other was perfectly tailored, golden cuirass, tunic, laced sandals, not a seam out of line; his smooth golden hair lay tidy and subdued down his straight back. Both were magnificent—elegant yet muscular, radiating an immense strength. Though not, Mikaila thought to herself, as strong or beautiful as Semjaza.

"And who do we have here?" The first seraph turned his penetrating gaze on Mikaila, who cringed inwardly, feeling him trying to penetrate her mind. She looked past his golden glowing and fell into his piercing blue eyes; then Semjaza squeezed her hand and she stood up taller, closing her mind. Under that ruthless stare boring into her, she thought of Semjaza, and saw the likeness. She smiled. The angel was disarmed and then charmed.

"Don't tell me, *this* is your seductive distraction, your par amour, your earthly delight?" Mikaila blushed deeply. "Oh, and modest, too. How quaint! Zaza, you devil, how dare you not bring this enchanting creature sooner! Come my dear—let's take a look at you." And the angel took her hand and twirled her about. His touch was the touch of feathers on the wind.

"Behave yourself," said Sem, lightly, "and I will introduce you. Astaroth, Anmael, allow me to introduce Mikaila, daughter of Faida, whom you will remember as Earth mate of Armaros."

The two angels bowed formally, but Astaroth, noticing that Sem had not used 'mate' in his introduction of Mikaila, gave her a big wink as he raised his head and, taking her hand, kissed it with an infinitesimal brush of his lips.

"You are as beautiful as your mother and will be the toast of the evening, my matchless, magnificent Mikaila, but if you tire of this oaf's attention, I will be at your service," and Astaroth bowed deeply again. Then the welcoming angels turned their piercing attention away from Mikaila and back to Semjaza.

"Well, the women will be both delighted and disappointed I fear," said Astaroth, crossing his arms and studying Sem. Semjaza knew what was coming.

"Are you going to invite us in or leave us out here in the heat until we roast?" he scolded, smoothly changing the subject.

"Of course, of course," the two chimed, but not yet moving out of the way.

"SaMäel will be most pleased. He has missed your company," said Anmael.

"As he tells us far too often," add Astaroth, rolling his eyes. "Apparently we have neither your wit nor your grace."

"You flatter me, I'm sure, but I will happily accept the compliment and hope to see you both at the evening meal where I will do my best to entertain."

"Now you see," said Astaroth, nudging Anmael, "that's just what SaMäel means—all grace." They bowed again elegantly and stepped aside, but there was a hint of mockery in Astaroth's eyes. Semjaza put a hand on the small of Mikaila's back and guided her gently but firmly past the Guardians of the Gate. She tried to smile, but not too prettily, conscious of Astaroth's lecherous gaze. Her attention quickly shifted back to the narrow bridge and the hot, pungent odour of blood. The angels flew over them and began to turn the great mass of metal wheels that opened the Iron Gate.

"Anmael is much quieter than Astaroth," Mikaila said softly when they were through the Gate and it had closed behind them, followed by a great clanging as the Guardians raised the drawbridge. She did not know how well angels could hear.

"You liked him better, I think," replied Sem.

"Yes."

"Not surprising, Anmael is of a gentler nature than Astorath." Mikaila waited for him to elaborate, but their attention was diverted by the maze of narrow deserted streets that confronted them inside the high iron walls. The streets were framed by tall gloomy buildings, and appeared to be arranged in a spiral; they were travelling uphill in a tightening circle. Suddenly, through the grimy windows, Mikaila became aware of grey shadows gliding past.

As the shadowy figures sensed their presence and started oozing out of doorways, Semjaza reminded her to keep her focus and spirit strong. She shuddered as the shadows attempted to edge their way between them. They smelled greasy and the brush of their arms was like a net of spider webs. Her focus evaporated as the shadows began to penetrate her mind with their darkness and loneliness and envy.

"We are almost to the Blade—an interior corridor that cuts through the spiral; however, it is a sharp ascent. Would you prefer to take this shortcut?" offered Sem. Mikaila nodded mutely, her skin crawling as the number of shadows increased, drawing closer. She closed her eyes and focused fiercely on Rachel, but she could not get the dark shadows out of her mind.

"Take my hand," said Sem, watching her intently, "we need to increase our pace." Semjaza realized he had to prevent the shadows from separating Mikaila from him. His force was so strong, he could easily ward them off, but Mikaila was not able to keep them from beginning to feed, weakening her. He knew she could do it, but first she would have to conquer her fear.

"They can't harm you unless you let them," he said, gently, "think of them as a cloud, blow them away, don't let them build up." Mikaila was breathing hard, her face ashen white, her energy draining, but with the force left to her, she did as Semjaza advised, and slowly the shadows began to disperse like cirrus clouds in a high wind.

"Excellent," beamed Sem, "we are almost to the entrance."

In an endless wall of dreary brown and grey stone, an unobtrusive door appeared, one exactly like every other door they had passed. Mikaila looked around for some kind of marker, to see how Semjaza recognized this particular door, but saw nothing until he pointed to a small mark engraved in the centre of the door frame: an upside down V.

"A key?" she asked, unsure if it was just scratching.

"Yes—the Blade—for the Guardians." He opened the door and ushered her through, closing it quickly before anything could follow them. The corridor was narrow, less than six feet wide, with an earthen floor. Along the walls at a height of about seven feet, globes of light glowed every ten metres or so.

The grade was steep and it wasn't long before Mikaila was breathing heavily.

"Are you all right?" asked Sem, turning back to her when he heard her call out. She was leaning over, trying to catch her breath.

"Yes. I just find the air in here hard to breathe."

"We'll be out soon—take my hand."

Moments later an exit loomed in front of them. The door opened to reveal a green lawn running up to an elegant wrought iron gate in the high wall of an imposing castle. They were finally on top of a hill; the sky had cleared, the fog lifted and stars shone overhead.

"When did it turn night?" asked Mikaila, bewildered.

"It is always night over the castle," replied Semjaza, "it's the way SaMäel likes it. Another line of domination and defence." The gate opened and they were ushered into the castle compound. As they stood before another grand entrance, Semjaza reminded her of what to expect inside: Cerberus first, then the lion and leopard, then the she-wolf. He was heading for the castle when Mikaila who had not followed called to him.

"Wait, Sem, can we stop here for a moment longer?" Mikaila didn't want to admit to the terrible trembling inside of her. She didn't know where she could draw the courage and strength needed to face what was inside the castle. Semjaza stopped and turned to her; when he saw her stricken face, he drew her to him, enveloping her in his reassuring arms. She collapsed into him, wanting the day, the task, all of it to be over, longing for her cabin beside the emerald lake.

"Look," he said, raising his eyes to the stars, "make a wish." Mikaila looked up and let the cool night air clear her head and fill her lungs. The stars were brilliant, but unfamiliar.

"But these are SaMäel's stars," she said, not letting go of him.

"No, that's the best thing about stars. No one owns them."

"True." Mikaila closed her eyes and made a wish. When she opened them, Sem was still looking at her. "What?" He bent down and kissed her lightly.

"Ready?" he said. She nodded, startled by the wild beating of her heart.

MONK and Melancholia were waiting in the hemlock grove. They had watched Semjaza and Mikaila until they passed into the

Rain of Fire; they heard the great clanking of the drawbridge, and then they settled down to wait. Well, Melancholia settled down; Monk remained intensely agitated, barely able to contain his impatience. He feared Semjaza would be intimidated by SaMäel, or worse, harmed by him. He desperately wanted to be in the rescue party, to see Rachel, to know her state, to rescue her himself. He paced the grove until even stoic Melancholia, who could not see him but could hear him, was annoyed.

"Monk, for goodness sake, you'll wear yourself out. Sit down."

"I can't. I can't stand the suspense. Maybe you could pop in there and see what's happening?" Melancholia had considered doing just that, but had decided she could not leave Monk alone. In his present state, it was impossible to predict what he might do.

"Please be patient."

"But Semjaza might not be able to do it! How do we even know he wants to? What's Rachel to him? I should have gone!" He was starting to show the negative effects of Abadon: frustration, growing anger, distrust. "He's not forceful enough; SaMäel will be able to manipulate him!" Mel's light laughter surprised him. "What? What's funny about that?"

"My dear man, you know very little about angels if you think that Semjaza isn't forceful enough. Do not be fooled by his mild manner. If anyone can outwit and out will SaMäel, it's Semjaza. Now, please, calm down. Sit. Think positively."

"How do you know that I'm not already sitting?" he asked wryly and slumped down, his back against a tree, and tried to imagine what Semjaza and Mikaila were doing.

INSIDE THE CASTLE, Semjaza and Mikaila entered a small courtyard with a beautiful garden, but with high windows on either side of the stout walls. Lovely faces peered from each of them.

"Murder holes," Semjaza said, when he noticed her staring at them. "This deceptively lovely courtyard is meant to trap his enemies." He smiled charmingly at the golden seraphim who burst from the inner massive carved oak doors, swarming their guests, exuberantly welcoming them, obviously curious about Mikaila. Cerberus came bounding over and drooled from his three large mouths, banging his serpent tail against everyone's legs, until Dagon sent him howling out of the yard with one cruel word. Mikaila strove to remember the word, but it was so foreign to her that she couldn't keep it in her head. The lion and leopard strolled over more leisurely, eyeing them, growling deep in their throats, until Semjaza spoke to them and they quieted. Still, they brushed up against Mikaila, to get her smell, memorizing her scent.

Mikaila kept a tight hand on Semjaza as another pair of angels approached and led the way past the guard room, then the hallway with its high painted ceiling, to the centre sanctuary where the women and Rara Avis were now waiting. It was a large area; to the left was an open courtyard full of exotic plants and a running stream with delightful waterfalls enclosed on the women's side by large glass doors.

"How is it daylight in here?" asked Mikaila, confused.

"Illusion. It's all illusion," replied Semjaza, squeezing her hand tucked under his arm.

Mikaila looked around for Rachel, but she wasn't there. She wondered how she could find out where Rachel was being kept, or if indeed Rachel was here at all. Surprised by mounting feelings of jealousy, she was watching the beautiful women fawning over their "Zaza" when she heard Rachel's name mentioned.

"So which of the lovely ladies is favoured by SaMäel these days?" Sem quietly asked the angel nearest him. "I don't want to make any faux pas."

"Oh none here," the angel replied. "His latest is Rachel, an Earth woman, and the lady keeps to her rooms." He nodded towards Rachel's rooms where the she-wolf languished.

"Why does the wolf lie at her door?" asked Mikaila innocently. The Seraph eyed her suspiciously, but Mikaila smiled sweetly in reply.

"Let's just say it is for her own protection."

"In that case no one will mind me paying my respects to a fellow Earth woman," said Mikaila, who startled them all by marching over to Rachel's door. The she-wolf jumped to her feet and growled threateningly. Mikaila forced down her fear, and turned back to Semjaza. "Sem, dear, is there something I should do or say, to let myself past the lady's guard?" she asked, trying to keep her voice light and devoid of fear. Semjaza smiled inwardly at her courage and wits, not to mention the endearment. He liked the sound of that.

"Dagon," said Semjaza, turning pleasantly to the angel. "Please let Mikaila into the lady's quarters, she wishes to pay her respects."

It all happened so quickly, the Seraphim were taken off guard. Dagon could see no reason to deny Mikaila's request. Since SaMäel was not present to direct him otherwise, he commanded the she-wolf to stand aside. The wolf was clearly not pleased, but responded, shifting a mere foot in protest, to let Mikaila by.

Closing the door quickly so the she-wolf would not slide in behind her, Mikaila scanned the large, spacious rooms, noting the high windows, the art work, elaborate floor loom, the Persian carpets, and the Japanese silk panels.

"It's rather opulent and a little chaotic, not my style at all; but SaMäel does not understand the concept of homespun," said a voice from behind the loom. Mikaila spun towards the voice.

"Rachel!" Rachel stood slowly, unconsciously letting the wool in her lap fall to the floor.

"I know you," she said, her voice hollow and inexpressive, "but I've forgotten. I've forgotten almost everything here— everything except Koko." Mikaila was shocked by Rachel's appearance. The few times Rachel had visited her mother, when Koko was a baby and ill, Rachel had been vibrant, charged with energy. This woman was like the shadows Mikaila had just witnessed. Her loss of weight made her seem taller, more ethereal. Like those other women out there in the seraglio, Mikaila thought. There were shocking white streaks in her lush, black hair.

"Are you alright, Rachel?" Mikaila decided to be as direct as possible. She knew her shock was written on her face.

"I'm not a shadow yet, if that's what you're thinking."

"I'm sorry—I was just taken by surprise. I didn't mean to be rude." Mikaila blushed deeply. Rachel seemed unmoved.

"I don't even know how long I've been here. It's always night, you see, except in the courtyard which is always day— and nothing is regular. I eat when I'm hungry, sleep when I'm tired, and appear before SaMäel on demand. I've lost count of the banquets and I don't know if even they are regular. Some things are apparitions designed to wear me down; like you, perhaps. Are you an apparition meant to wear me down? What do you want?"

"No Rachel! I'm real! I'm here with Semjaza."

"Semjaza—am I supposed to know this name?" she asked sceptically.

"Yes. No! It doesn't matter. Surely you remember me? I'm Mikaila. My mother helped you. I have good news for you. Perhaps you should sit down. We don't have much time."

"You perhaps don't have much time. I, on the other hand,

have infinite time, and I prefer to play these games standing," she said coldly.

Mikaila had not known what to expect, but she was least prepared for Rachel's disbelief and indifference. She was suddenly very unsure how to proceed, how much to tell Rachel — what, in fact, to tell her. Would mentioning Monk just make her more sceptical? Rachel, she remembered, believed Monk was dead. It seemed so long ago now.

"Listen, Rachel, Koko is out of the caves. We staged her death and now she's with the bears — ."

"Bears? What bears?" Rachel's face went grey with fear. Mikaila's mind reeled with the amount of knowledge she needed to tell Rachel.

"I don't have time to explain that now, just believe me that Koko is safe, and she needs you. SaMäel thinks she's dead. He can't hold you here if he can't threaten Koko. We're going to try to get you out. SaMäel can't force you to comply now by threatening Koko, but we still have to get past his defences." Mikaila sensed that her time was running out and was talking quickly, furiously thinking what exactly Rachel needed to be told. "To be frank, I don't know what state you are in — after all, you've been here for over a year — "

"A year — !" Rachel sat down hard. Mikaila moved towards her, but stopped when Rachel looked up at her coldly.

"It is imperative that SaMäel goes on believing Koko is dead and that you think she's alive and in the cave. Do you understand?"

"How do you know about the cave?" Rachel asked, her suspicion growing. Mikaila ignored her and raced on.

"Then we can use your knowledge of what he believes is her death as a trump card. Ok?" It all sounded wild and improbable even to her own ears. Rachel sat thinking for a while, unresponsive.

"Is there anything you can tell us about this place that might help us get you out?"

"Perhaps—if I truly believed you are who you say you are. You have no idea how many lies I've been told; how many ways my hope has been shattered. If you are SaMäel's latest trick, it is a good one. Now I need to rest." Rachel sat down, picked up her fallen wool, and resumed her weaving.

"What proof do you need, Rachel?" cried Mikaila, alarmed.

"If you are who you say you are, then I'm sure you will think of it," Rachel answered from behind her loom.

The door opened, and Dagon entered, with SaMäel hard on his heels. SaMäel started towards Rachel, and then caught sight of Mikaila in his peripheral vision.

"Well, well, well," he said, stopping suddenly and turning to her, "so the mother's daughter is all grown up and Semjaza got to her before I did." He walked around her, clucking his tongue. Mikaila felt him undress her with his wicked eyes. "More's the pity. Rachel, my dear, are you acquainted with this Earth woman? She comes from your neck of the woods. Her mother was very beautiful until her untimely death—drowning in the Chaba River I believe—a woman wise in the ways of plants and their medicinal use."

"Faida?" Rachel rose slowly. "Faida was your mother. Now I remember. She saved Koko—twice."

Mikaila saw an opening and took it—despite the risks.

"Yes, I remember you, too, now. You brought your baby to see my mother—such a sweet child. Is she here? She must be—what—six now?" Mikaila scanned the room, as if expecting the child to leap out from behind a Japanese screen.

"No." Rachel's voice went icy. She turned to SaMäel. "No, she's not here at the present, but I am expecting her momentarily."

Subtly, before he lost control of the situation, SaMäel changed the topic of conversation. He was content that neither woman appeared aware of Koko's death.

"It is a lovely diversion to have you and Semjaza visit us, Mikaila. We have planned an evening's entertainment in your honour. Haven't we Dagon? Come my dear," SaMäel said, reaching for Rachel's hand, "I want to introduce you to Semjaza."

Mikaila did not miss SaMäel's use of the word 'diversion'. She hoped that Monk and Mel were still hidden in the hemlock grove, and that all was going as planned at Castleguard.

EVERYTHING, HOWEVER, was not going as planned, and Kyna was wondering how long she could wing it. When SaMäel alighted on Cathedral's ledge, both she and Vang trembled—so much depended upon this one deception—and the bears were not trained, not practised in the ways of deception. Theirs was the path of truth. And yet, thought Kyna waiting inside, it seems all we're playing at these days is deception. How had Rakor trapped them here? Surely, she thought, there is another way. But she knew there was no time to think of an alternative for Vang in this moment; all they could do was to continue the deception already begun.

"Well Rakor, I hardly expected to find you here of all places; what on earth brings you to Cathedral? And what has happened to my brother-in-arms? Have you deserted me?" SaMäel positioned himself boldly, leaning up against the serac of Arctos, draping a careless arm around its neck. Vang bit back an angry remark about disrespect, while SaMäel smiled ingratiatingly. "Perhaps you should tell me a story?" Vang was not fooled by the light tone. He hung his head and waited.

"Come, come Rakor—it's not like you to be hangdog. It

does not suit you. Just tell me what happened." A story, thought Vang desperately, yes, I can tell a story.

"It was the Ursulas, SaMäel. They're shape-shifters, too. They sent Malenger and the others off, and when I returned, they ambushed me. No one—*no one* can stand against three Ursulas—three, there were three," he insisted when SaMäel seemed unmoved. SaMäel shook his head in disappointment.

"And this is the best you can do? I thought you had more in you. Well, never mind. Just tell me where the Quintessence is." Vang hesitated, wondering how much to tell. But he had little time to hesitate before SaMäel would grow suspicious.

"The Ursulas took it—and gave it to—to Grundel."

"Grundel? Where is he—here?" SaMäel looked towards the cave's entrance.

"I don't know! They don't trust me! They tell me nothing. I saw the Brothers leave, that's all I know." SaMäel studied the bear intently.

"I see," he said finally. SaMäel turned his head and looked down the mountain. Vang followed SaMäel's gaze. And they both saw a single set of new bear prints up the mountain, and many different prints down. Rakor's misinformation, for SaMäel didn't doubt that it was misinformation, puzzled and infuriated him, but he set it aside for now.

"And who is at home in Cathedral," he asked lightly, turning back to the cave's entrance. Vang looked wildly at the cave, not wanting to endanger Kyna. He lumbered awkwardly in front of the cave's entrance.

"No one of significance—a couple of young Brothers of no consequence—"

"And me of course," said Kyna, coming to the entrance and to Vang's rescue. She nudged Vang aside. "How can I help you SaMäel?" SaMäel nodded in admiration at her cool composure, her control, her aura of power. He also noticed that there was no invitation into Cathedral in her remarks.

"Alethia is it, Rakor?"

"Kyna," she answered, coolly.

"My apologizes, Grundel's mate, of course. What brings you to Cathedral?"

Kyna thought quickly but carefully after each of SaMäel's seemingly benign questions, knowing there would be black pits into which she could fall, to the detriment of everyone. What had Inyx taught her? Ah yes: deflect whenever possible. Keep your position of ascendency.

"I belong at Cathedral," she said icily, "what brings you?" SaMäel smiled, appreciating her skill. Damn, he thought, but these bears were surprisingly worthy opponents.

"My dear," he said, trying to soften her, "I'm just here visiting. I was hoping to see Grundel. Will you invite me in?" Kyna held her ground.

"I apologize, SaMäel, but The Keeper and his Brothers are engaged elsewhere." She turned to Vang. "There's just our poor company. As you can see, Rakor and I are abandoned here, together. But I will tell Grundel when he returns that you wish to speak to him."

"Surely this isn't the way you treat an old friend, Kyna. The Keepers have always been the most gracious of hosts!" SaMäel feigned shock, wondering what she was protecting inside the cave.

"Well, you are certainly welcome to join us on the ledge while we bathe in the last of the day's light," said Kyna. She stood up, moved away from the entrance and lay back down, as if to make room for SaMäel. In the gesture, the dark angel realized that there was nothing of value in the cave, for a female would never leave anything she valued unprotected. Then where was Grundel?

Suddenly he felt a blinding headache coming on and his patience ran out. The game no longer amused him. He needed the information now. To make his point, he dramatically transmuted into a dragon and let out a wild belch of fire into the cold air over the Icefield. But Kyna, controlling fear as she had been taught, did not flinch. Vang trembled but did not bolt, taking strength from her courage.

"I will not be toyed with, Kyna! Tell me where Grundel is!" SaMäel raged. Kyna gave him a withering look.

"You may intimidate others by your transmutations, SaMäel," she said quietly but sternly, not even rising, "but surely you forget that an Ursula, too, can transmute at will; I am not impressed. It is not your concern where Grundel is. However," she added sweetly, "I will certainly let him know that you paid your respects, when he returns." Kyna knew that she was taking a great risk, infuriating SaMäel, that he was unpredictable and brutal when angered. But her own anger had been aroused, and she was holding steadfast. Vang secretly cheered her on, impressed at her skill and courage. Alethia had chosen well. He pretended to cower under her dominance, lowering himself to her, in supplication. SaMäel, wanting to incinerate both of them, let out an oath of frustration and left.

As he flew out over the Icefield, SaMäel reviewed his options. The cold air cleared his head. He beat his wings, sweeping gracefully over the hanging glaciers, the cirques, the icefalls, marvelling at their beauty, at their ability to conform. The bears might be frustrating but the game was entertaining, and he hadn't had this kind of amusement for a while. He was beginning to enjoy himself, again. So what if it took a little longer to get the Quintessence, he thought, he was in no hurry; he might as well enjoy the hunt.

The bears had the Quintessence—of this he was fairly

certain. How they had managed to acquire it was thought for another day. Today he needed to focus on its location. He was confident that it was not at Cathedral. It was unlikely that it was hidden with animals other than the bears—he glanced over to the Heights of Chaba, then Snow Dome—but not impossible. More likely, it was with the bears. Where would Grundel go? He hovered, making a slow sweeping circle of the Icefield, finally settling on the mountains of the Twins. Yes, he thought, I might as well check the Valley first, before retuning to the feast at Abadon.

Engelmann

ARMAROS was in charge of leading Piotr and Rakor carrying the Quintessence to another portal that dwelled further away in the Sacred Grove. They needed to use this portal not only because they didn't want traffic around Toholinagi while Koko was there, but also because it was the only one old enough to go back so far in time. They were hoping that SaMäel wouldn't notice them. They were also betting on the fact that the dark angel had forgotten about this long unused portal; that he was watching Vang not Rakor; that he was searching for Grundel not Piotr; and that he was distracted by Semjaza's visit to Abadon. Armaros hoped it would be enough. He joined the two bears at the big bend in the Sunwapta River after Vang departed for Cathedral.

"I'm sorry to hear about Gulo," Armaros said, touching down beside them on the pebbled edge of the river. "He was a ferocious loner, but courageous." Piotr and Rakor nodded mutely. "Are you ready?" When the two nodded again, Armaros again led the way. They were in a wide valley, a u-shaped glacial trough with hanging valleys along its edges. Now that it was fall, the glacial river that ran through the valley on its way to the sea was bluer, less clouded by silt; dark evergreens covered the mountain slopes down to the river's stony edge. They travelled the rocky river bed silently for many hours, and at last came through a pass and over a rise, just as the sun broke through cloud. Piotr stopped, arrested by the scene before him; Rakor, snorting his annoyance, almost ran into him.

"Look," said Piotr, nodding to the mixed forest at their feet. The forest, green all summer, lay transformed. The trembling aspens shimmered in the light soaked land, ephemeral, their leaves a radiant gold; amber tamaracks stood ready to shed their needles.

Rakor's mouth dropped. "I've been so preoccupied, so underground in the caves, I hadn't noticed—the season changes—we're running out of time." Piotr nodded.

They followed the river until they came in sight of an alpine meadow of heather and willow, strewn with mounds of rock rubble. Beyond, they could see an old growth forest. It was dense, dark, and as they entered, Piotr could feel a presence. Armaros led them deep into the forest, through pines dripping with old man's beard, draped with large nests of witch's broom and pine dwarf mistletoe. As they neared the centre, overhead the sky lightened, until finally they entered an ancient aspen grove with its smooth white bark and lovely translucent leaves. In its centre stood a gnarled, spiteful looking spruce. Armaros motioned for the bears to sit. The aspens trembled and whispered as if there were a wind.

"Before I wake Engelmann," he said quietly, "be prepared. This is one ornery old tree—the great granddaddy of Earth portals. No one has broken his sleep for a hundred years. He is not Nagi; you will have to convince him to take you where you want to go."

"How will we do that?" asked Piotr, alarmed by the greenish white glow emanating from the venerable tree.

"We can only do our best, Piotr," Rakor interjected calmly. He lowered his dark haunches to the ground. "But wait a few minutes, Armaros. I need to think." Piotr sat down beside Rakor, glad his sire was in charge, grateful that Rakor seemed back to his old self, confident, in control. After a few minutes, Piotr, obeying his body, got up and wandered about, looking for an ant ridden log to upturn. He was surprised by the intensity of his hunger. He realized he could eat anything—anything at all. His hunger was barely satisfied when Rakor called him back.

"Should you tell Piotr now where you will take the Quintessence, Rakor?" asked Armaros. Back at Cathedral, when asked, he and Semjaza had given Rakor, Grundel and Kyna many options, but none had felt right to the grizzlies. At first the bears thought that if they went back far enough in time, before the last glacial age, before the changes that the glacial age had wrought on the landscape, they could place the Quintessence in another valley or gorge that later would be filled with a glacier, like the Icefield had been. But they decided that this was too obvious for SaMäel. Where, they wondered, would SaMäel not look? The life force had to stay on Earth.

Armaros and Semjaza had then given them endless examples of places on Earth that were difficult, even impossible to find: places like Alibay, a city so ruinously sad even it had forgotten its own name. Or Abaton, a town of changing location. Armaros said that though not inaccessible, no one had reached it yet and visitors headed for Abaton had been known to wander for many years without even catching a glimpse of the town—a fitting fate for SaMäel. But, Kyna asked, if SaMäel couldn't reach Abaton, how could they? At this point, Semjaza had looked at Armaros. "We could send it to Altruria," he said. The angels passed knowing looks.

"Altruria?" asked Kyna, watching the two closely. She did not appreciate where their thinking was taking them.

"Altruria is a large island continent in the Southern Ocean. Its exact location is not known by most."

"Then don't we have the same problem?" Kyna asked.

"Some angels know this place. The country is thought to represent the kingdom of Heaven on Earth. They are a strict Christian people. It is a place SaMäel despises—the people are frugal, vegetarians, non-drinkers. It might be the last place SaMäel would look."

"But the Southern Ocean!" said Grundel. "How could we protect it?"

"No," said Melancholia, appearing, "the Quintessence must stay here."

In their hearts, the bears knew the spirit was right. Kyna believed there was a simple solution just waiting for them to discover. They had thanked the angels and let them go. The bears alone must find the answer. It was Kyna who suggested they look at the dream map for clues. Staring at the odd markings for hours produced no answers, just endless questions. They were considering asking Winona, Rachel's mother, to interpret the map, when suddenly Melancholia pointed. There on the map at Angel Peak was a small symbol they hadn't noticed before.

"What's that?" she asked. The bears stared hard.

"It's a bear symbol like the one at Castleguard," said Kyna slowly.

"Perhaps we have misinterpreted the first one," said Mel.

After much deliberation, the bears came to a decision. Rakor was now rehearsing the plan in his own mind, deciding what he needed to tell Engelmann. But first it was time to tell Piotr. He turned to the younger bear.

"We have decided to put the Quintessence underneath Angel Glacier."

"What?" roared Piotr. "That's absurd! Angel Glacier is the one place near the Icefield where SaMäel always returns!" The aspens murmured loudly.

Armaros looked over quickly to Engelmann who stirred in his sleep, his top branches waving as if moved by a wind; the angel started to say something, stopped, and turned his attention back to Rakor. Angel Glacier is a devious plan, he thought — brilliant in its simplicity — so bear like.

"Yes," Armaros replied, putting a reassuring hand on Piotr, "but whenever SaMäel is at Angel Glacier, his mind is always preoccupied with other matters."

"Exactly," said Rakor, standing up, "and he is always preoccupied with the one event that he can never get over, producing an emotion he cannot master completely — anger. We are betting that his anger blinds him. Besides, Piotr, even if it crosses his mind as a possibility, SaMäel will think we wouldn't dare put it right under his nose. We are, after all, just bears. And he is the great SaMäel. Trust me, this I know."

Piotr looked at Rakor, and, noting his sire's deep resentment, realized or perhaps believed for the first time that Rakor's desertion of Cathedral had not been voluntary and was now causing him great pain.

"But do we dare?" asked Piotr, contemplating possible consequences. "His anger, if he finds out, will be so intensified—that we tricked him at the very site of his downfall!"

"Should it happen at that point, it won't make much difference," replied Rakor. Armaros nodded in agreement.

"And that's only the half of it, right Rakor?" Armaros said.

"What?" asked Piotr, sensing the energy passing between the two.

"Well," said Rakor, "we have SaMäel distracted in this time, right? But he also has to be distracted in the new time frame, so we can hide the Quintessence without his knowing. Grundel and Kyna think that SaMäel was never more distracted than the day he fell from Paradisi¤."

"You're joking! Right?" Piotr looked wildly back and forth between the two. Rakor shook his great shaggy head. "Well, I'm NOT going back to the centre of that day!" blurted Piotr. "That's madness! You know the stories: the sky cracked, the mountains roared, the earth shook worse than an earthquake, and seraphim fell like giant boulders out of the sky. Weren't there hurricanes and a tsunami?"

"A pretty good distraction, don't you think?" said Rakor. Piotr slumped to the ground, burying his head in his paws. When he regained some courage, he looked up at the angel. "Were you on Earth then?" Armaros nodded. "Well, what was it like? Are the stories true?"

"As true as stories can be."

"Great."

"Come on Piotr, we chose you because of all the Brothers you are the most adventurous, the most courageous," argued Rakor. "You think quickly; you've been in tight places before. We can do this. We just need to focus on the task and let the chaos around us fulfill destiny—we don't have to pay it any attention at all. In fact, the more we ignore it, the quicker we'll be done."

Piotr thought about what Rakor said. He had been in difficult spots; he had managed to think his way out—until Carth. His confidence had been badly damaged that terrible day. His trust in himself shattered. He had not yet mended from the loss. Armaros noted the expression on the young bear's face, and tried to ease his pain. "None of us is perfect. Not even angels save everyone. We just do our best, making whatever contribution we can."

"We know how you feel about Carth," added Rakor. "You must not blame yourself. It wasn't your fault. If anyone is to blame, it's me—listening to that deceitful creature. But let's put the past behind us and do this thing we are being asked to do. I had my doubts too, but Angel Glacier is the wish of Grundel and Kyna. Mel agrees. Isn't that enough for us?"

Piotr sat up. He had made a promise to The Keeper. As mad as it sounded, he was going to get the job done.

"Okay," he said, "where do we start?"

Rakor let out a sigh of relief. "We start by convincing Engelmann," he replied.

There was a great groaning, the ancient tree bent down menacingly towards them, until Piotr could touch the peeling rough grey bark and feel the tingling prickly needles against his face. He crouched instinctively.

Of what? said a deep resonating voice inside his head. Piotr jumped back. Rakor held his ground, then bowed deeply.

"This is a great honour," he began.

Yes, yes, but what do you want? asked Engelmann gruffly. Rakor threw Armaros a questioning look, but Armaros just shrugged.

"We need a favour," Rakor began again.

Engelmann

So I heard. So every tree in the Sacred Wood heard, said Engelmann sarcastically.

"I'm sorry, we didn't mean—"

Are bears always this loquacious? Engelmann spat out contemptuously.

"Loquacious?" queried Rakor, turning to Armaros.

"Verbose," replied Armaros.

"Verbose?" asked Piotr.

I heard. You need to go to Angel Glacier…blah, blah, blah.

So many words.

"Don't mind him," whispered Armaros to Piotr, "he has too much time on his hands." Piotr snorted loudly.

"Angel Glacier, the day SaMäel fell from Paradisi¤," said Rakor formally, scowling at Piotr and then Armaros, whom he thought ought to know better.

The day SaMäel fell? Engelmann fell silent for a moment. *Well, you made a good case to Piotr. However, he is obviously the brains of the party—it's a fool's mission you're on—outsmart SaMäel, indeed!*

"Will you do this, Engelmann? Our need is great," pleaded Armaros.

Ah, my dear Armaros—will you be with these two at Angel Glacier when SaMäel falls? That should prove advantageous to these two, but dangerous for you—

"But you haven't answered my question," replied Armaros, amusement creeping into his voice.

Yes, yes, Engelmann said, waving his branches. *Listening to the three of you sweat over this was amusing, even if I was annoyed at first for being wakened—unceremoniously. If I was less trusting, I would think you deliberately let me wake myself in order to overhear these two. However, I am old, there are few amusements left to me. So, Piotr, put your hand on my trunk, close your eyes, and think inside the tree.*

UNLIKE MOST of the bears, Piotr and Rakor had made a few journeys with Nagi to more remote parts of the area when necessary, but they were still not prepared for Engelmann's centre. The great heart of the tree was three times Nagi's size—a deeply engraved wood, draped heavily from its high rafters with nanny's beard, a greenish grey hanging moss, and lichens; its floor a spongy carpet of mountain heather and reindeer moss of musty scent. Piotr thought he spotted an orchid and thought of Boris. On the interior walls of the tree were strange but beautifully carved runes in languages even Armaros could not decipher. To the back of its centre were shadowy passageways to other rooms that spoke of the tree's great age and past glory when it was the greatest portal Earth had known. They stood silently for a few minutes, taking it all in.

I know what you're thinking, Armaros.

"Pardon my bad manners, Engelmann, but I have never seen it so—so empty."

Yes, well, its users departed didn't they? And a long time ago.

Armaros remembered when he and Semjaza had first arrived at the Icefield, before SaMäel had fallen, before the old gods had passed on. Engelmann was the hub of great activity, allowing the spirits to travel earth and beyond unimpeded by time or space. In those days the old and new worlds were full of spirits and their sacred places. Gaia was well protected. Now, few were left. Time, erosion, and human encroachment had unwittingly destroyed most in the old world and even here they were quickly disappearing. After the gods were gone and SaMäel had fallen and Paradisi¤ had taken control of the Wind Gates and their portals, everything had changed. The new angels were not like the old gods; Paradisi¤ was not interested in protecting Gaia in the same way. The angels stayed out of her affairs unless it involved damage by SaMäel for whom they felt embarrassingly responsible and whom they tried to monitor. Engelmann broke into his reverie.

Have these two travelled before?

"Yes, but not in time."

Few have travelled in time. One does not travel time lightly. Few can withstand the strain. Not even great distances to other realms are as difficult. They'll need some trial runs—a few shorter trips back in time.

"Good. But not to Angel Glacier—we don't want to create any disturbance that will give the plan away."

True. But it should be close by so their bodies become accustomed to the relationship of distance and duration.

"Well—let's vary the trial site so no pattern is set up for SaMäel to follow, should he notice the disturbances in the time continuum."

Of course.

"Wait!" blurted Piotr, urgency in his voice. "I can't do anything until I feed. Rakor—aren't you—don't you—" Rakor suddenly realized what Piotr meant. His own hunger roared loudly. All the Brothers had been so intent with The Plan that they had not noticed that fall was slipping away, that it was past time for feasting. Suddenly Rakor felt like he could eat anything in his grasp.

"He's right," he said gruffly, "Piotr and I must feed first." When Armaros raised his eyebrows, Rakor added, "Now."

No need to leave. Tell me what you want.

Piotr, in his hunger and fatigue, pictured a gentle hillside, southern exposure, late summer, covered in sweet ripe berries, elderberries, black berries, bearberries, soapberries to fatten on, and pine nuts at his feet; marmots, moles and voles scampered through the grass and, at the bottom of the hill, he envisioned a black creek alive with salmon. Instantly it was all before them. The sun shone on the hill, in glorious rays radiating from high in the ancient tree, throwing a warm and peaceful glow to the cavernous centre of the portal. Piotr didn't question the mirage, he just dug in.

Rakor?

"This is more than sufficient for both of us, thank you."

Take your time. It is best that you are well fed and rested for what lies ahead.

Rakor nodded, wondering suddenly how the other Brothers were doing. He wished he could warn Alethia.

THE BROTHERS were aimlessly roaming the area around the Icefield. At Castleguard they stopped, stricken, when they saw the skins with the heads of Inyx and Carth stretched dried in the sun. Most of them could only turn away, but Gorath approached the frame cautiously and loosened the taut straps with his teeth until the skins fell to the ground. He picked them up quickly—there was no emotion pronounced in his face or countenance, neither pity nor anger, just firm determination. There was no one to stop him; Slank and Payne were hiding out in Malenger's cabin.

Some of the bears, disoriented and directionless, feeling a deep gnawing hunger had wandered over to the Valley of the Twins, seeking diversion, but the females, too, were short tempered and unsettled. They did not want males, in their current condition, around the youngsters, and had driven them off. Kyna and Alethia both realized that the lack of the fall feast was becoming a serious problem—confrontations and incidents were mounting. There was little that could alleviate the tension, even though the bears were eating voraciously—but they needed meat and for that they had to wait for Grundel. During the Feast, bears gorged their bodies, satisfying primal hunger, preparing for months of abstinence. Kyna would have gone ahead to endorse the Feast, if she were not worried that Grundel or Rakor might need the Brothers at some point. If the bears feasted, they would then go to their Long Sleep, and it would be difficult to rouse them until spring. Even if they could be roused, in their winter stupor, they would be useless.

Vang trotted into the Keeper's Cave, where Kyna was pacing, after SaMäel departed. "There are Brothers fighting on the Icefield," he said, "and it looks serious."

"Did you watch the direction SaMäel took?" asked Kyna, more concerned about SaMäel's destination.

"Looked like he was headed for the Twins."

"Of course. Come on, Vang, get those who are still around, break up the two on the ice. And tell them all to eat something! We're paying Alethia a visit." Vang nodded, renewed with purpose.

SAMÄEL, after stopping to pick up Slank and Payne, had dropped them off in the Valley of the Twins in front of a covey of caves. As he flew over the valley, he noticed females staying close to their dens, but this was not an unusual occurrence this time of year; he knew that they became more territorial as winter set in.

Still, he decided to test if they were hiding something from him. He knew that if he stood between a female and her den she would not find him a threat, would not assume that he was trying to muzzle in on her territory. That is, he thought, if the cubs were not in the den, and he didn't get between the sow and her cubs outside the den. He alighted in front of a sow that was munching bearberries near the mouth of her cave. She looked up, glancing to see where her cubs were, then returned to eating. SaMäel nudged closer to the cave — still no response. When he stood in front of the cave's mouth, she lifted her large head, stared at him through her small, beady eyes, and waited for him to move on. He did, trying a few more dens, but the other females took no more notice of him than she did.

It's not here, he said to himself. *It can't be. But where's Alethia?* The sun was beginning to slide down behind the mountains throwing long shadows and still he hadn't found her. Sitting down on an outcropping of granite, SaMäel decided to call it a day. It was then Alethia and Tasmira with five cubs in tow lumbered out of a wooded area. SaMäel flew towards them, taking them by surprise, alighting directly in front of them. The bears tried to ignore him, to go around him, but he moved to block their path.

"A lovely day, my dears," SaMäel said. Tasmira snorted her annoyance.

"What are you doing here," she said, pawing the ground, staring at him directly.

"Control yourself," Alethia replied quietly, nudging her forward, "just keep going." But SaMäel fluttered annoyingly over their heads. With every direction they moved, he countered.

"What is it this time, SaMäel?' said Alethia, sharply.

"Is that any way to greet your old friend?" SaMäel began, light-heartedly. But when the two bears were unmoved, he changed tactics. "Fine. I will be on my way as soon as you tell me where the Quintessence is. You stole it from me and I want it back." He was trying to provoke them, but they were not about to play this game. The bears refused to answer and after sending the cubs up trees, sat down on their haunches, prepared to wait him out.

"Oh look, here come Slank and Payne with more persuasive methods," countered SaMäel. Alethia rose and turned swiftly behind her. Slank and Payne came out of the woods, shepherding a couple of sows and their youngsters with their rifles.

"Have you fallen this low?" retorted Alethia, turning on SaMäel. "This can't be your style." The hair on her neck ridge bristled.

"My style, my dear, is anything that works. Slank is very resourceful, don't you think? Now, perhaps, you will give me my answer." The taller man, Slank, jabbed a young cub in the ribs with the butt end of his rifle to move it along. When the females growled menacingly, Payne scurried to hide behind SaMäel, but Slank let off a warning shot.

"Next time, I shoot you," he snarled, coming up beside SaMäel. He had slipped easily into Malenger's role.

"My dear man," said SaMäel, "what an idea, but next time there is a false move, shoot one of the cubs."

"My pleasure," said Slank, sneering, moving towards the bears and putting his rifle up against the head of one of cubs who looked back stoically. A deep, menacing, communal growl grew from the females. Slank backed off, drawing closer to SaMäel and Payne.

"Now, where were we? Ah yes Alethia, you were telling me where the Quintessence is."

"The what?" asked Payne.

"The treasure, you ass!" replied SaMäel, impatiently.

"We know nothing about any Quintessence," Alethia stated coldly. "We have stolen nothing from you."

"Well, someone has and Slank tells me it was grizzly bears. Still, I am prepared to be reasonable. Give me back what is rightfully mine, and I'll tell Slank not to shoot."

"For goodness sake, SaMäel, we know nothing!" Alethia exclaimed.

"And if we did, we would hardly tell you!" Tasmira spat out, unable to control her anger.

"Tasmira!' gasped Alethia.

"False move!" yelled Slank, jumping to conclusions and lifting his rifle, but before he could take aim, the females rushed the men, not stopping to consider their own danger. At the same time, Kyna and the Brothers came thundering over the rise behind them. The men froze, not knowing which way to turn as the air filled with sonorous guttural growling. The men howled in fear. Sighing in exasperation, SaMäel moved quickly.

"Shall I?" he said, grabbing the men by their waists.

"Yes! Yes! Hurry!" yelled Slank.

Before the bears could trample the men from both directions, SaMäel flew up, hauling them high into the air. Beating his massive wings, he propelled them into an adjacent alpine valley, dropping them unceremoniously onto the snow covered ground. Then he stepped back and glared at them.

"What the devil did you think you were doing?" he snarled at Slank.

"You said—"

"Oh never mind!" SaMäel paced back and forth, deep in thought. "The sows obviously don't have it. That leaves Grundel. So where is he?"

"What is Quin-quin," began Payne, standing up, only to sink knee high into the drift. Puzzled, he looked over to where SaMäel effortlessly walked on top of the snow.

"Quintessence," finished Slank, wading through the powdery snow to an outcropping of rock. Payne followed.

SaMäel looked at them contemptuously, missing both Malenger and Rakor. He ignored their question. "Somehow we must find Grundel," he said, more to himself.

"Well, he shouldn't be too hard to track. We should start at Cathedral," said Slank, prepared to bide his time. 'Quintessence' sounded important, sounded wealthy, and now that Malenger was dead, there would be even more for him.

"Yes," SaMäel agreed, surprised by Slank's initiative. "But it will be dark soon. We'll start tomorrow."

"Was that thunder?" asked Payne fearfully, looking over his shoulder. Slank thought it sounded like an avalanche—he was deathly afraid of avalanches. Cursing loudly, SaMäel picked them up again and flew off, as the grizzlies thundered over the mountain ridge.

After SaMäel dropped them off at Malenger's cabin beside

Wild Wood Creek, the men felt some relief to be between sturdy walls, but all night in their dreams they were chased by angry, stampeding bears.

A Rescue

AFTER ridding himself of Slank and Payne, SaMäel headed southwest to the Icefield. Something was clearly not right. Before he reached Entrance, Tagore started howling again; that bloody wolf was getting on his nerves! He glanced over to Snow Dome as he ascended the Icefield and noticed Bighorn and a couple of other large males moving across its eastern slope. With its entire summit area covered by snow, there was no reason for the bighorns to be on the mountain — there was nothing to eat on Snow Dome — there was only snow covered rock and ice. *I suppose they're watching for me too,* he muttered to himself.

Although SaMäel was on his way to Cathedral, he didn't expect to see the bears yet. Hovering over the Icefield, however, he could just make out a small dark movement on the northern edge of the ice. The Brothers must be headed back. Soon he was circling and then landing on Cathedral's ledge. He surveyed the surrounding area, entered the cave's mouth, then stood gazing around the empty cavernous room. No one appeared from within. He noted the eerie silence: no sign of the human or raven, nor did Melancholia materialize when he called to her. In fact, there was no movement in or around the cave at all. He returned to the cave's entrance, deep in thought, his elegant wings breathing on the wind. He shook off his dark musings, leapt powerfully off the ledge and flew over to the Heights of Chaba, only to find no sign of the eagles. He flew over Mikaila's empty cabin on Angel Lake on his way to the Watchers' hoodoos. Perhaps Armaros could explain the absences. But at the hoodoos, there was no Armaros either.

SaMäel sat down on the Watchers' ledge, puzzled. He whistled for Equus, Mikaila's powerful pony, watching her appear as if by magic out of the snow and ice—as if she rose out of the glacier itself, watching her race swiftly across the Icefield, her strong hooves barely touching the ground. SaMäel vaulted lightly off the ledge, landing beside her, stroking her silky coat, wishing she could tell him something… anything.

"Where is everyone," he asked her. "Where did everyone go?" But the Cayuse wild horses from Xeni are strong, fast and silent.

Suddenly he realized it was late; lambent shadows played hide and seek off the hoodoo walls; he realized he was starving and, after such a disappointing day, in need of some compelling entertainment. He decided he had better get back to Abadon before Semjaza and Mikaila left. Perhaps they knew what was going on. Giving a great roar, he leapt into the waiting, empty air, flying recklessly into the eye of the sun.

"Well Astaroth," said SaMäel, alighting on the bridge in front of the City of Dis, "any visitors, deserters, tergiversators today?' The Seraphim had quickly lowered the heavy drawbridge when they saw SaMäel emerging from the smoky clouds of the Rain of Fire, hoping that he was in a better mood than yesterday.

"No sir, all quiet on this front," Astaroth answered, grinning broadly.

"Good. Pass the word that no one is to open the Iron Gate tonight except by my direct order. Understood?"

"Yes, sir."

Semjaza and Mikaila had spent the day with Rachel, with Dagon fussing around the edges of their conversation. SaMäel had instructed Dagon not to leave the three of them alone. But it could not be helped when he was called away on an emergency—one of the women in the enclave had attacked Rara Avis with a heavy pole and broken his leg.

"She will be severely punished," explained Rachel in a monotone. Mikaila exchanged glances with Semjaza, shocked at the lack of emotion in Rachel's voice. "I suppose you find that callous. Well, you grow accustomed to the violence of this place. Rara receives the brunt of the women's frustrations. I can see how he gets on their nerves—stalking around in the mist—with his great wide eyes and relentless silence. But they never get away with it; Rara is a favourite with SaMäel.

"They're forced to choose between leaving and punishment. And if they stay, they must choose their own punishment. If they are too lenient on themselves, SaMäel has them thrown out for cowardice. And they never seem to have the will to leave—they linger in Dis, becoming increasingly haunted souls, barely living shadows. In the end, the ones who will do anything to stay are always harder on themselves than SaMäel would be—at least that's what he tells me. They want to show their remorse to please SaMäel."

Mikaila turned her head away, not wanting to hear any more, but Rachel continued. "Lashings. They choose lashing—no one is forced to leave if they choose lashing. She will be punished tonight, but not before SaMäel is finished humiliating her in front of everyone. He also takes a perverse pleasure in that."

"Rachel," said Sem, putting a light hand over hers. Rachel looked down at his hand oddly, as if it were an alien object. "I know how hard this place has been on you. But try to believe us, to trust us. We will get you out of this horror—tonight if possible." Rachel let out a hard laugh.

"How—you won't even get by the she-wolf."

Mikaila reached under her long skirt where she had deep inside pockets and pulled out a soft leather bag full of powders and herbs.

"First, we have a little something to quiet the four-legged beasts of the castle—a few mushrooms and herbs to insure that they have a long, deep sleep."

"Well," admitted Rachel, "that will help, if you can get to them." She looked dubious.

"And I can get us out of the castle and through the City of Dis via the Blade," added Sem. Rachel shook her head vigorously, not wanting to believe.

"But what about the rest—what about the iron gate with its guards; what about the bridge, river, sands, rain of fire—and then what? How will we escape the condors, the warrior angels, *SaMäel* when he comes after us? And even if we could miraculously escape them, how do we cross a universe—how do we get home? Home!" For a moment Rachel's face crumbled with confused desire, then a great shudder wracked her body and she put her head in her hands to weep dry hard tears.

"You can't know," she whispered hoarsely.

"No, you're right—we don't know what you've suffered. But we are going to get you home. Please, will you let us? Will you help us?" Sem took both her hands. After a long pause, she gave an almost imperceptible nod, enough for Semjaza and Mikaila.

"Ssh now, here comes Dagon," said Mikaila as the door to Rachel's quarters opened. She jumped up and said loudly, "Will you show it to us Rachel, it sounds lovely; no need to be modest." And she headed over to the loom. "Look Sem, here it is. And here's—ah Dagon! There you are. We were wondering if we may impose on your hospitality—we're famished!" Semjaza had also risen and wandered over to the loom to inspect Rachel's work. Dagon searched each of their faces but found nothing suspicious.

"My apologies for the delay. We had to see to Rara."

"Is he all right?" asked Mikaila.

"He will be, thank you. Now let me call a servant to get you something to eat."

THAT AFTERNOON passed pleasantly enough. When Rachel excused herself for a rest, Semjaza insisted on giving Mikaila a tour of the castle, while Dagon went happily back to his business. After touring the castle with its bewildering number of levels, spiralling staircases and twisting corridors where they would suddenly come across the leopard or lion who eyed them suspiciously, they finally stepped outside into an eerie afternoon darkness. Mikaila looked up at the ghostly moonlight, trying to identify the stars, wanting but failing to find something familiar, recognizable, trustworthy.

In the outer courtyard, Semjaza showed Mikaila the quickest route out of the woods and to the castle entrance, marking it with a discreet charm so that she could follow it, and insisted that she memorize the directions out of the maze of the city.

"Just in case something happens and we get separated," he insisted. "You will have to take Rachel through the wretched city. The Blade only opens for the Seraphim." He shuddered inwardly remembering how quickly Mikaila had weakened around the shadows.

"Don't worry," she said, noticing his concern, "first of all, we are not going to be separated; I intend to stick to you like a burr. But if—*if* something unforeseen happens, the shadows won't bother me now that I know what they are. And I can take care of Rachel; I will get her to the Gate. But we will wait for you there—I have no means of getting us by the Seraphim."

"Oh my dear," grinned Sem, "you are mistaken, you have plenty of means."

"Oh no—I would never attempt to sweet talk those two!"

"You might have to. Speaking of seduction—I wonder where SaMäel is—I'm surprised he disappeared. I thought he'd be all over us today."

"Then I'm glad he was called away this morning." Mikaila shuddered as she thought of those golden, whirlpool eyes.

Semjaza drilled her, making her repeat the directions a dozen times. Finally, when she refused to do it again, Sem relented, putting his arms around her and holding her close. Under the stars, in Semjaza's arms, watching his wings flutter in passion, she thought she felt her own wings rising. Semjaza saw their outline, and smiled, but said nothing.

"What was it like—mother and Armaros' relationship?" Mikaila asked, breaking into his thoughts. He hesitated and then spoke warmly.

"Magical. He loved her from first sight. They were so well suited—strong, practical, fascinated by the natural world. He entered her life so gently she hardly noticed and then he was there sharing all her joys and hardships."

"Why didn't they tell me?"

"That was Faida's decision. She wanted you to have a choice in the life you led." He waited, but no more questions followed. "We should return now and dress for supper. SaMäel will be back soon, that I can guarantee. He always returns for the evening banquet and its entertainments." Mikaila shook off her thoughts and returned to the present predicament.

"You haven't said when we will make our move."

"We'll have to play it by ear. We wait for an opening. I won't know when—until it happens. You both know the signal?" Mikaila nodded. "You must be prepared to leave on a moment's notice."

"As long as it's before Monk shows up."

"The One preserve us! I've forgotten about him—I imagine Mel is having a hard time holding him back. Well, we'll have to cross that bridge when we come to it. Have you prepared the potions for the animals?"

"Yes. Rachel has them." They fell silent for a few minutes; each wondering if it was time to tell Rachel that Monk was alive.

"I think Rachel is just coping," Sem said aloud.

"She doesn't need any more shocks just yet," agreed Mikaila.

In mute agreement, Semjaza offered his arm, and they turned back to the castle.

AT SUPPER Mikaila stayed close to Sem. The banquet hall, a majestic room that rose on all sides to a great glass dome revealing the night stars, glittered with a chthonic light of hundreds of black candles flickering on the two long mahogany tables, in the wall sconces, and on the intricately carved mahogany side tables doubly reflected in the large gilded mirrors above them. Escorted by the Seraphim, the women entered the room, wearing long shimmering gowns and bejewelled hair. Then they all waited, standing in two long rows, for SaMäel's entrance.

Mikaila was glad that Semjaza had insisted she bring her only evening dress, inherited from her mother — a dress Faida had bought on one of her rare journeys to the city to deliver flora specimens. It had been the only dress in the cabin in which Mikaila was raised, her mother preferring practical work skirts or homespun pants. The dress was a singular extravagance, seldom worn except for special evenings with Armaros — a sophisticated black satin gown, simple, elegant — like her mother. And it had only taken a few small adjustments to make it fit perfectly. Rachel had offered to put up Mikaila's long blonde hair for her, but Mikaila declined, preferring to wear it down; but she had accepted a few of Rachel's pearls to adorn it.

Semjaza gazed in admiration when he came for her, and smiled lovingly; then tucked her hand under his arm and squeezed. She knew from the look in his eyes that she was more than presentable. Like the other Seraphim, Semjaza was dressed in a golden, belted tunic that came to his knees, topped by a deep crimson cape edged in gold. A striking pair, they arrived last in the hall and stood at the end of one of the lines. She smiled shyly at the woman beside her on the arm of Anmael, a tall, red haired beauty who eyed her through luminous green glazed eyes. Mikaila was looking around curiously, noting the marble walls reaching to the great dome window, the exquisite tapestries which hung in archways all along the length of the Hall and partially hid the elaborately carved side doors, when, with a flutter of fanfare, SaMäel made his grand entrance.

Mikaila hardly recognized Rachel when she entered on SaMäel's arm. She wore a silver gown of many layered silk, embroidered with gold thread, which fluttered behind her like wings; her dark hair was swept up and elaborately dressed with strings of tiny gleaming jewels. With the many layered gown disguising her thinness, and her face made up to emphasize her large dark eyes and full mouth, she was hauntingly beautiful. They were an exquisite study of opposites—the powerful golden angel and the dark, delicate Earth woman.

SaMäel spoke briefly to Anmael about the state of Rara Avis, and then nodded appreciatively to Mikaila, motioning for her and Semjaza to follow him and take seats at the head table on the richly carpeted dais at the front of the room. The first thing SaMäel did after gesturing for everyone to sit was to pour tall glasses of an amber liquid from one of the many carafes waiting on the table.

"My dear," SaMäel said, handing Mikaila a glass and raising his, "to your grace and beauty. You are very like your mother." He clinked glasses, gave Semjaza a large wink, and downed the entire contents of his glass.

At Mikaila's elbow, Sem whispered, "Slowly, slowly." She took a sip and her eyes widened as the smooth liquid first tingled then soothed her lips, tongue, and throat. Moments later it surged through her body, generating warmth, filling her with euphoria, making her smile.

"So, you like my little home-grown concoction?" asked SaMäel, smiling back. Mikaila turned to him and instantly began to lose herself in his bewitching eyes.

"It's—it's…" she was at a loss for words.

"Potent—very, very potent," finished Sem, taking her glass and putting it down on the table.

"Oh, don't be a spoiler, Zaza!" SaMäel chastised, mischievously.

"What else is on the menu, SaMäel? I'm sure you are full of surprises this evening," replied Semjaza, changing the focus. SaMäel tore his eyes off Mikaila and shrugged.

"Well—I certainly wouldn't pass up this opportunity to show off!" He laughed gaily, clapped both his hands and a long line of servants dressed in royal blue, wearing white gloves and carrying massive trays over their heads, entered and swiftly deposited the trays all along the length of the table. From under their lids were revealed: roasted pheasant surrounded in mouth-watering asparagus, stuffed red peppers, nuts and fresh herbs; tureens of paté, fragrant cheeses and long loaves of warm bread. Everyone immediately started eating, all except Rachel, who bowed her head and said grace silently. The women rolled their eyes at the seraphim who looked uncomfortable. SaMäel ignored both Rachel and the others' discomfort and dug in.

Midway through the meal, Semjaza leaned over to whisper to Mikaila, making it appear that they were exchanging pleas-antries, but he was instead cautioning her. Looking over at Rachel's plate and noticing her food and drink were hardly touched, Mikaila realized that she had better follow her exam-ple, or she wouldn't be in any condition to flee when Sem decided the moment to escape had come.

After many courses of gluttonous eating, SaMäel clapped his hands and called for entertainment. Musicians entered flamboyantly through every door of the Hall, accompanied by exuberant dancers, tumblers and jugglers, surrounding the guests in a flood of vibrant colour, movement, and song. The evening became progressively more raucous, with SaMäel on

Mikaila's left pouring her more of the wicked amber liquid, and Semjaza on her right deftly diluting it with water. Suddenly, SaMäel clapped his hands again and the musicians, dancers, jugglers all disappeared from the hall, while waiters swiftly removed the remaining dishes. There was an air of excited expectation, a sense of impending drama. Mikaila looked around—everyone's eyes were shining dangerously; the women seemed to be holding their collective breath. Out of the silence that had fallen, SaMäel stood up slowly and spread his hands to include everyone. He seemed to grow in stature and radiate light.

"Now," he said, "for a little diversion. I understand we had an accident here today." His merciless eyes roved the room until they fell on one of the bejewelled women. Mikaila realized it must be the one who had harmed the ancient bird, Rara Avis.

"SaMäel, please," pleaded Rachel, quietly, her hand on his sleeve. "Not now. Not this. You have guests."

"No, no, my dear," replied SaMäel, impassively removing her hand, a cold cruel note rising in his voice. "This will be amusing—you'll see. Our guests will be most impressed with our democratic system of justice." The dark angel proceeded to the front of the head table and nodded to Dagon. SaMäel's first commander opened a side door and a group of seraphim entered with Rara Avis, who limped pathetically into the room.

"Surely someone could explain how this happened?" SaMäel said, pointing to Rara. He scanned the room, but no one would look at him, preferring to gaze at their hands or wine glass or one another. "Come now—one of you has acted like a hooligan, a depraved brute. What has Rara ever done to you but protect and guard you?" He waited menacingly. "Can you not even own up to your cowardly act? Look at him," he said, pointing dramatically to Rara, his voice rising, "who has done this?" He glared at the woman willing her to respond, but when she didn't, he nodded to Dagon. "Bring her here."

Dagon and another seraph strode to where the woman cowered in her chair and gently but firmly helped her up. Mikaila could see that the woman could not stand on her own, so great was her shame and dread. They made their way slowly the length of the great hall. The other women from the enclave turned their glances away from the beseeching looks from the wretched woman. The green-eyed beauty was watching Mikaila's reaction, knowing that no one could help the woman now, if they didn't want to be included in the punishment.

Mikaila turned to see how Rachel was reacting, but her place was empty.

RACHEL had slipped out a few moments earlier and had raced down to her room, brushing aside the she-wolf who whined and growled at her, stripping off her gown and grabbing her travelling clothes. Now, she swept up Mikaila's herb mixture and some tantalizing raw meat she had stolen from the kitchens earlier, mixing them hurriedly together.

In the late afternoon while everyone was dressing for dinner, Rachel had waited until the servant who fed the beasts had come into the enclave with the animals' evening meal. She had drawn him into her room, given him a glass of wine, and insisted on feeding the animals herself. After some convincing, the servant had gone back to the kitchen, more than willing to let someone else do the dangerous job—no one could predict what mood the beasts would be in. The cats were known to bite the hands that fed them. But Rachel had not fed the animals, reserving the food and the sleeping potion for later. During full banquets the animals guarded the inner castle. No one was allowed in or out. If they could incapacitate all four of them, they could escape the first line of defence—the castle itself.

She put the food down in front of the she-wolf, who ate it hungrily. Cerberus soon came bounding over and wolfed his helping. Rachel led him back to his favourite resting spot near the pools before he succumbed to the drug. She watched the she-wolf nervously—the drug was taking longer than she anticipated and the wolf glared at her. It growled as if realizing what was happening, then suddenly fell to the floor. Rachel was even more nervous about feeding the lion and leopard; she had always avoided the large cats as much as possible. They leapt eagerly towards her when they smelled the long overdue meat. But she didn't want them eating it here where the other two animals would soon be deeply sleeping. It would look immediately suspicious for all of them to be asleep together. She took a deep breath and spoke harshly to them. Still, they leapt at her hands.

"Wait!" she ordered. The two cats stopped for a moment, surprised, and in their confusion, Rachel quickly walked down the hall to their accustomed spot near the front entrance. The cats bounded along beside her, growling in frustration. She hastily put the food on the floor and stepped aside; the two cats stopped, looked at her warily, sniffing the food suspiciously. Rachel held her breath, glancing around nervously.

Inside the Hall, Mikaila turned to Semjaza, who was gripping her arm painfully.

"I said now," he repeated firmly in her ear.

"Now?" Mikaila could hardly believe it. Her attention was riveted on SaMäel, who had focused all his awesome treachery on the woman. Everyone was captured in his malevolence. All except Semjaza.

"Yes—now."

"But—." She turned her head to watch what was happening. SaMäel had his back to them, but was interrogating the woman who muttered something Mikaila couldn't hear. Then SaMäel asked the woman whether she wished to stay or leave. When she muttered something incoherent, SaMäel said, "Speak up—they can't hear you."

"Stay," she whispered hoarsely.

"You realize you must be punished?" The woman nodded.

"And what do you think is fair punishment for your barbarous behaviour?" Mikaila could hardly hear the response, it was so weak, but she thought she heard, *"lashings?"* And she heard SaMäel exhale a sigh that made her shudder. The others were leaning in towards SaMäel, mesmerized by his cruel, whirling, golden eyes. SaMäel gestured benevolently to the others. "Do your fellow Abadonians agree?" They all nodded wordlessly, as if hypnotized. "Then so be it," and he nodded to Dagon who handed him a whip as the dark angel stepped off the dais and into the centre of the floor between the tables. He moved effortlessly, like a cat, raising his whip, an expression of regret and disappointment on his face, although his hands spoke otherwise. The sleek long line whipped out with a crack, the woman crying out before it even hit her.

Semjaza pulled Mikaila to her feet, held her under her arm and, calmly, smiling and nodding at the others who ignored him completely, drew her through a side door. Rachel was waiting for them.

"But—" sputtered Mikaila, her head still pivoted towards the room, "shouldn't we help her? I can't believe we—" Rachel shook her ferociously.

"Snap out of it, Mikaila. No one can help her now. On Abadon, when SaMäel wants revenge, he takes it. Save yourself if you can. Here." Rachel shoved her travelling clothes into her hands and started to undo the buttons of her gown.

"What are you doing?!" Mikaila clasped her gown to her.

"There is no time for modesty. Just change—quickly. Semjaza will turn his head. We're running out of time." She stripped Mikaila of her dress, yanking on her shirt and long skirt. Mikaila stuffed her sheath and Hermes wings and a knife into her pack and then quickly folded in her mother's dress, not wanting to leave it in this foul place.

"Are the animals fed?" queried Semjaza. Rachel nodded, helping Mikaila on with her pack, and then pointed to the she-wolf who was fast asleep in front of her door and to Cerberus who was snoring from three heads near the fountain. She hoisted her pack and they ran down the eerily empty corridor towards the front door. The lion and leopard were thankfully asleep across the entrance; but they slept so lightly that Rachel feared they might wake, and wondered if she had given them enough of the concoction. Semjaza didn't wait to find out; he stepped over them gingerly and pushed open the heavy oak doors. The great cats growled in their sleep, but didn't wake. The women followed Sem through the courtyard, glancing nervously up at the murder holes, but everyone was at the banquet. Outside the unfamiliar stars were coldly brilliant.

INSIDE, SaMäel, having taken his disappointment and wrath of the day out on the woman, turned triumphantly to Semjaza and Mikaila, daring them to challenge him. But like so many others that day, they were just not there. As he turned to Rachel, the others followed his gaze to her empty place. The whip in his hand shook with his renewed fury, and he lashed it into the open air.

"Find them!" he roared. "Bring me Semjaza!" Sem heard the Seraphim coming as they entered the streets of Dis. He had hoped they would have more time; now all he could do was delay the angels so Mikaila and Rachel could escape. He clutched Mikaila and she came to an abrupt halt; then drew her into a dark alley.

"Listen to me and please don't argue. I'm going to hold off the Seraphim. You must get Rachel across the bridge."

"The bridge? How? How can I get her past the guards?"

"You know how."

"What about you? I'm not leaving without—" Sem crushed her to him and then held her at arm's length.

"Trust me—I will meet you back home. Do not wait for me in the meantime." He looked over to Rachel. "Do not let any of them wait for me. I can handle myself here, but I can't protect you or Rachel now. Do you understand?" She nodded mutely. "I want you to hide here in this alley. Can you see the Blade door?" The women nodded. "When the Seraphim have gone through it after me, you are to make your way through the city. I can hold them off for a little while. Run like hell—you won't have much time. Ignore the shadows; they are the least of your worries. SaMäel can't keep you now, Rachel, but you need to get across the bridge. There is help on the other side." He flew up and over to the Blade door; they could hear the beating of many wings. He opened the door, waiting until he was sure the angel warriors had seen him.

Rachel followed Mikaila who was madly conjuring up the map of the city in her mind's eye, grateful for the dozens of times Semjaza had insisted she repeat the directions. They raced through the dark streets, Rachel struggling to keep up with Mikaila's long legs, trying to ignore the growing number of shadows aroused from slumber and now following them. Rachel began to slow down, flailing her arms to keep the creatures away from her; suddenly she stopped and collapsed on the ground.

"I can't do this, Mikaila. Go. Save yourself. I've no strength left. I can't resist these—these—besides, SaMäel will never let me go. I'm endangering you and Semjaza and Koko. I don't know what I was thinking." Mikaila raced back, driving the shadows away, and grabbed Rachel's arm, pulling her to her feet.

"I'm not leaving you too! Keep close—don't let these wretched creatures get between us. Koko is safe. We're going to the Gate." She kept a firm grip on Rachel and kept them moving together. Rachel let Mikaila pull her along, numbed by the swiftness of the turn of events, exhausted from the mental games with SaMäel, doubtful they could free themselves without Semjaza's help, slapping ineffectually at the shadows who hovered all about her.

Mikaila was furiously trying to figure out how to open the Gate and get past the guardians. She no longer feared the shadows. Somehow, knowing they were the creatures once enslaved to SaMäel, who had been banished from the castle but had no will to leave Abadon, made her pity them more than fear them. She was more afraid for Rachel—she was practically carrying her.

Turning a corner, through a peep hole in the wall, they saw the River of Blood gleaming in the moonlight. The Gates were before them. The two women gazed hopelessly at the formidable sight. Suddenly Semjaza burst through the Blade door, turned to lock and hold it with an enchantment. Then he leapt into the air, released the drawbridge and swept them up and over the Gates. The bridge clanged and rattled and crashed down across the River. Semjaza set the women down on the bridge.

"Start across the bridge, but if I tell you to, run!" he said, turning to face the Guardians who had been surprised. Mikaila started to protest, having no intentions of leaving Sem behind again, but Rachel, with escape suddenly in sight, tugged savagely on her arm until she moved.

"Is there a problem?" Semjaza asked calmly, turning to the fuming Guardians of the Gate.

"What the hell are you doing, Semjaza? You know the protocol—everyone goes through the Gate!" The seraph stamped his foot in anger.

"Sorry, Forcas, slip of memory. I will, however, remember next time."

"Call the women back," snapped Forcas. "SaMäel said no one was to leave tonight without his permission. And I have had no word."

The other Guardian was looking suspiciously at the women. "Wait a minute. Isn't that the Earth woman?" he asked. "What are you doing with her?"

Suddenly there was a great thrashing and banging at the Blade door as the warrior angels came sweeping out, shouting to the Guardians. The two guard angels grabbed Semjaza. He looked up to see where the women were—they were half way across the bridge. He knew the angels couldn't physically stop the women without permission, but fear could drive them into the River.

"Run!" yelled Sem. Rachel, who was in front, hiked up her skirt and dashed across the bridge. Mikaila looked back, only to see condors and vultures swooping down over the Gates. She reached into her inner pocket and pulled out her knife, determined to fend them off. But the bridge was narrow, high, treacherous, and in her struggles, twisting and turning to avoid the wicked beaks and claws, she lost her balance. Tumbling over the edge, she fell towards the River of Blood. Monstrous fish rose to the surface, mouths gaping open.

"Mika," Sem called frantically, struggling to get away from

the angels, "use your wings!" It was a moment of faith, of belief, of trust in herself. Mikaila felt her wings, as she had always felt them, shadowy but strong. She closed her eyes and thought of Sem's sinuous wings beating golden over the Icefield at dusk, of their long, steady strokes, and, as if in slow motion her direction changed and she flew up just before the river engulfed her. She turned towards Sem, slashing her knife at the birds. Semjaza was surrounded by astonished Seraphim, including SaMäel, but Semjaza was pointing across the bridge to Rachel who was putting on her sheath, a knife glinting in her hand. Mikaila flew up over the bridge, tore off her pack and pulled on her sheath. Glancing once at the angels, she swept up Rachel, and headed for the grove, forcing herself not to look back.

Rachel was so light that Mikaila thought she must have hollow bird bones. She was amazed at her own strength, and deliriously happy at finally admitting her wings. But her happiness was shadowed by concern for Semjaza's fate. What would SaMäel do? How did he take revenge on other angels? She understood that SaMäel was letting the women go—for now—but this was not over.

SAMÄEL sat in the shadowy Hall, twirling his glass on its fine stem. He was scowling—the day had been a disaster—but not at all an ordinary disaster. He could feel mischief in his bones. What made Semjaza rescue Rachel—and why today of all days? Were there connections he was missing? What had happened to the Quintessence—did those two bungling humans know something he didn't? Where was everyone from the Icefield? When he heard the clanging of the drawbridge, he jumped up and flew swiftly to the Gate. His Seraphim were just exploding out of the Blade. The guards held Sem. He watched Mikaila fly up—yet another surprise today—but put up his hand to stop the Seraphim from pursuing the women.

"Let them go. But Astorath, I want you to follow them — tell me where they go and who accompanies them. Oh, and Astorath, once she is in the portal, give Rachel a taste of what is in store for her." Astorath nodded, and disappeared. Out of his troop of seraphim, SaMäel had a small elite group that he called to him now, his golden eyes twirling.

"Bring our wanton guest to the castle, then prepare to leave in two hours."

Semjaza watched over his shoulder as Mikaila carried Rachel, hoping she could manage the weight. In the distance he saw a shimmering and knew it to be Mel waiting for the women. He glanced over to SaMäel, but the dark angel had already turned to fly off. Then the Seraphim surrounded him and Semjaza was escorted to the castle.

MONK had slowly become visible as the evening drew on and the invisibility spell wore off; he was now just inside the grove, still out of sight, but pacing aggressively, waiting impatiently, waiting for the first glimpse of Rachel. After they had heard the ruckus at the Gate, Mel kept a close watch on him. He was cursing himself for not using the invisibility spell to his advantage and entering Abadon when he had the chance. Just when he was about to throw off all caution and storm the Gate, he saw an odd movement in the sky ahead of him.

He cried out when the women came into his line of vision. However, coming across the burning sands in twilight, Rachel did not see him, so intent was she at not falling, nor causing any disturbance for Mikaila. She had her eyes closed and was unconsciously holding her breath. Mikaila flew over Monk, to the middle of the grove of hemlock trees where they would be nearer the portal, lowering Rachel gently to the ground beside

Melancholia. In wonder, Rachel had just opened her mouth when she heard someone running towards her and turned fearfully, expecting SaMäel. When she recognized Monk, she let out a sob and fell to her knees, burying her face in her hands. Monk stopped abruptly, looking in bewilderment at Rachel then at Mel and Mikaila. He had so many questions that he didn't know where to begin.

"Rachel," he said, kneeling in front of her, putting his arms around her, "what's wrong—look at me."

"I can't," she moaned, "I'm afraid if I do I'll wake from this strange dream and be back in my nightmare."

"This is no dream."

She slowly raised her head. "But you're dead and Mikaila flew and—what is that?" She pointed to Melancholia whose shape she could just make out in the strange aura of light, and then fearfully looked behind her at the burning sands. "And where is SaMäel? Why didn't he follow us?"

Monk gently raised her to her feet, embracing her, but she stiffened and offered no response. She had spent too long in Abadon avoiding SaMäel's touch.

"I don't know, but I don't think we should stay to find out. This is Melancholia—I'll explain later, but she'll get us back home. We need to leave now." Monk looked around. "Where's Semjaza?"

"SaMäel has him," said Mikaila, bitterly. "Sem insisted we leave. But what will happen to him? How can we abandon him when he risked so much for us?"

Melancholia said, "We must get the others home first, then we'll think about what to do about Sem. For the time being he can hold his own with SaMäel. I promise I won't leave him here." She glanced around—sensing an angel presence, but not, she thought, Semjaza. "Come," she said, "and remember to keep your eye on Polaris. No talking in the portal." The others looked at her questioningly, but they knew there was no arguing with that tone. They made their way back to the portal and disappeared through it, Astaroth slipping in with them.

Stella Polaris

BACK AT THE ICEFIELD, inside the portal, Koko was wide awake and restless. Toholinagi watched her sympathetically. The child had much healing to do. He hoped that the rescue had gone well; he wasn't sure how much more she could bear. *Look up, Koko,* he said gently, wanting to keep her mind off her fears. Koko gazed up into the darkness of the inner tree and suddenly saw stars—thousands of stars so close she felt she could touch them. *See the brightest one?* Koko nodded. *That's what everyone is waiting for. Keep your eye on it—when it reaches its zenith everyone will focus on it.*

"Why?"

Well, let's see—Grundel and the others are using it to guide their course north. Portals use it in the same way, so I will use it to bring your parents home. They all need to keep their eye on it to help direct their journey; and Rakor and Piotr are using it to guide them back in time.

"So we're all looking at the same star, right now, together?"

Yes. Koko was silent for a few minutes, wrapped warmly in the thought.

"But why this star?" she asked suddenly. Nagi chuckled—the child was irrepressible.

Ah well, this is Polaris, Stella Polaris, the pole star. It is the most fixed point in the night sky.

"Wait a minute! I know that star, that—that's the North Star!"

Yes, that's another name.

"And Ama says it belongs to—" Koko hesitated, racking her memory then she looked up and saw the shape of the dipper

"—the Little Dipper!"

That's right. We call it Ursa Minor or Little Bear. But it has many names, often the name of gods or goddesses—Arcas, Hesmut, Shesemet, the Raging Mother— Koko giggled. *Nikisuiituq (Niki sweet TOK), Throne of Thor, the Tail of Light, the Guiding One—*

"That one makes the most sense," interrupted Koko.

Yes, many use it to steer their course. My favourite name is Drag-Blod.

"Drag-Blod?" Koko giggled again.

It means The Fire Tail. See how Polaris is the tip of the tail or the handle of the dipper as you call it? Watch, and I will connect the stars and show you Little Bear. In the night sky overhead, Nagi first intensified the dipper that Koko was familiar with so it glowed brightly, then he overlaid the shape of a bear.

"Ah!" said Koko, her eyes widening. "Now I see it!"

Some believe that Ursa Minor can bestow eternal life. Now, do you see the front two stars of the dipper? Koko nodded. *Shall I tell you a story about Little Bear and these two guard stars?*

"Oh yes, please!" said Koko, forgetting her fears for the moment.

You know that there are two dippers?

"Oh yes," replied Koko seriously, "the Big Dipper and the Little Dipper."

We call them Ursa Major or Great Bear and Ursa Minor or Little Bear. The Bears endlessly wheel around the northern sky dome as if trying to escape the hunter—

"Like our bears and SaMäel."

Yes—it is rather. Well, Great Bear is not only bigger but also brighter than Little Bear and, in her old age, Great Bear grows greedy and wants to steal Polaris because it is the only star of Little Bear's that matches her own brilliance. She tries many tricks, but Little Bear outsmarts her. Finally, when Great Bear decides to try to overpower Little Bear, it is the courage and loyalty of the guard stars Kochab and Pherkad that prevent her. Great Bear has never given up and pursues Polaris endlessly, but Kochab and Pherkad are vigilant and never tire.

"I hope Grundel has a Kochab and Pherkad!"

Don't worry—he does. Are you watching Polaris now? Koko nodded. *Keep your eye on it, something is happening.*

INSIDE THE PORTAL, Melancholia had even a stronger sense of the hostile presence, but she was intent on focusing on Polaris and getting everyone back to Earth. She didn't like the look of Rachel who was increasingly grey with fatigue. The portals were demanding; the darkness a terrible void; it pressed against one and yet had no boundary. It was this duality, its infinite presence and infinite absence, that created the overwhelming fear—the fear that one wouldn't escape it. Only by holding on to Polaris when all else disappears could one successfully navigate the portal. Mel wasn't sure that Rachel was mentally strong enough, especially coupled with a hostile presence. She had no doubt that it was one of SaMäel's warriors sent to recreate havoc, but there was nothing she could do, and to reveal his presence would only increase the woman's fear. Either way, in the portal, each of them would have to deal with this presence alone. Mikaila, on the other hand, was flushed with excitement and seemed larger than life. Monk stole a look and hardly recognized her. As everything went black, he grabbed Rachel's hand, and they all held onto Polaris.

Rachel struggled with the image—Polaris was slipping away much too quickly. She felt the invisible presence, heard his mocking voice telling her that SaMäel would never let her go, telling her that Monk would never be able to love her as he once had. Rachel weakened, losing Polaris, and for a moment floundered in the deep dark abyss. But then Astorath made a grave error, telling her that Koko would be forever resentful of Rachel deserting her in the cave. By trying to instil doubt and guilt in Rachel, he had given her something, not Polaris, but something stronger, more fixed in her heart and mind, to focus on—Koko. Koko had been her Stella Polaris, her fixed point, for a year and not even the black void could deprive her of the image, the memory of Koko. Suddenly she felt Monk's hand in an iron grip and they were rolling together onto the cushioned moss floor of Nagi; Koko gave a joyous whoop and flung herself towards her mother.

Rachel spread her arms and Koko fell into them crying "Ama" over and over. Rachel just rocked her, letting the child release her pent up emotions. Koko laughed and cried. Rachel's face, too, was quickly streaked in tears. Finally, she held Koko away from her, noting all the changes in the child.

"You've cut your hair," she smiled, but silently noting how pitifully thin Koko was, how dark the circles under her eyes, how rough and bruised her hands and arms and legs. Monk, seeing what Rachel was seeing, was thankful that she had not seen Koko when she first came out of the caves—half dead.

"Yours is longer." Koko tugged at a loose strand and then gently fingered the strings of jewels still in Rachel's hair. "What are these?" Rachel yanked them out, flinging them into a corner, letting her long black hair fall over her shoulders. Koko clasped her arms around her mother's neck and buried her face in her thick, sweet smelling hair. Finally, Rachel looked up at Monk and he helped them both up and over to a chair. When they were sitting, Koko sat up and clasped her mother's face between her hands.

"Was it horrible, Ama—in Abadon?"

"Yes," answered Rachel. "Was it dreadful in the caves?" Koko nodded, unable to speak. "We'll talk of it later, little one."

Monk saw that Rachel was deathly pale—he turned to Mikaila, but before he could say anything, Mikaila put a light hand on Rachel's shoulder. Rachel couldn't help wincing.

"Rachel," Mikaila said softly, "Monk and Koko have been staying with me. I know you want to get things back to normal as soon as possible, but would you be so kind as to share your family with me for a few days longer—before you return to the settlement?"

Rachel was uncertain how to answer—her emotions were in such turmoil. She could still feel the hostile presence and all it represented; she feared that nothing would be normal ever again. She dreaded having to talk about her experience. It would take a long time before she could tell Monk everything. And until then, it would lodge between them, separating them almost as completely as Abadon had separated them. She wondered how, if ever, she could be free of SaMäel.

Monk, rubbing her back, gently shook her out of her dark thoughts.

"I'm sorry." Her eyes welled with tears. "Please try to understand, I'm not ready to be touched. I—I'm finding it hard to make the simplest decisions." Monk lifted his hand, his face contorted with grief, and anger at SaMäel.

"No need for apologies," answered Mikaila. "Will you permit us to make this decision?" Rachel hesitated. In Abadon she had discovered the difference between solitude and loneliness. She had known solitude in the mountains, had always known the feeling of losing oneself in the magnitude and majesty of the mountain landscape—of becoming one with everything. She was not afraid of solitude. But the loneliness in the presence of others that she experienced in Abadon was different.

And the fear of losing herself to SaMäel's power had been terrifying. She had fought alone against his mighty power and now was still afraid. She was not ready to be with Koko with just Monk to protect them; she felt too vulnerable. But how could she tell Monk.

"Let's stay for a few days, Ama," Koko piped up. "I want to show you the *Apis mellifera*—and my specimens and Papa's beeswax candles!" The child's enthusiasm heartened Rachel. She looked up at Monk, reading agreement in his eyes. Perhaps with Mikaila and the Watchers nearby she could begin to find some measure of security and peace.

"That would be lovely, Mikaila. Thank you. I'm not ready to—to face the settlement yet."

They exited the portal into a moon drenched night. Mikaila whistled for Equus and the roan horse emerged like a phantom out of the darkness.

"I'll take Koko with me so we can prepare the cabin; then Equus will return for you two," she told Monk, who nodded. She patted his hand and said quietly, "Take heart—it'll just take time."

Back at the cabin, Mikaila laid blazing fires, and pulled out a cot for Koko, setting it in front of the living room hearth. Koko changed for bed and happily dove into the pile of quilts. She was sitting, hugging her knees, trying to keep herself awake, when her parents arrived. Bounding over to them, she tugged her mother's hand, drawing her around the warm, inviting room, explaining the on-going crafts, proudly displaying Monk's candles and her own carefully pressed flowers.

"And tomorrow I'll show you the *Apis mellifera!*" Koko exclaimed, as Rachel gratefully sat down. Rachel smiled and hugged her, drawing the child up into her lap and holding her for a long time.

As it grew late, and Rachel grew paler, Monk suggested, "Now Koko, I think you should show your mother where she is to sleep." Koko obediently walked over to one of the two rich tapestries and drew it back.

"In here, Ama. Come see the fire we laid for you." Rachel and Monk thanked Mikaila and followed Koko into the room. It was a comfortable size with a small fireplace and a large window heavily draped with a tapestry to hold back the wind that in winter howled to be let in. A bed dominated the room, heaped with quilts and pillows. There was a small homemade chest of drawers and a night stand with a porcelain wash bowl filled with water.

"Shall I tell you the story of the wash bowl?" piped Koko who did not want to go to bed, did not want to let her parents out of her sight.

"Tomorrow, dear," answered Monk, gently from the doorway. "Now I think we all need sleep." Koko nodded, gave them each a hug and left the room for her cot. But the fires had not yet burned down when she tiptoed back and crawled up the bed between them and snuggled down under the quilts, a small hand on each of their cheeks.

AFTER GRUNDEL led Tuktu and Raven down Entrance to the Sunwapta valley, and skirted wide of the outfitter's camp, he followed the river, looking for the mountain pass. Scanning the dark slopes and blue shadowed valley, he spotted the wide gravel river bed, which he followed through the scrub and brush until he found the steep animal trail, worn, but to Tuktu's surprise, spongy underfoot. The late fall storms that often sweep the pass had not yet started, so they made good time to the summit despite the sharp ascent, coming easily down the gentler far side.

They scrambled up glacier draped mountains with great

waterfalls that seemed to drop from the very peaks. They loped steadily over the craggy Tangle Ridge where streams accumulated and cascaded over the steep cliffs forming Tangle Falls. From here, Grundel led them down a steep precipice which Took was barely able to navigate, until they reached the wide white shingle flats of the river valley. The river was gaining size and momentum as tributaries fed into it, to form the great river that ran all the way to the northern sea.

Grundel led Tuktu and Raven around the mile-long patch of quicksand that once had been a site of disaster to an ancestor and which remained etched in The Keeper's memory. A rock slide forced him to wade through muskeg, searching for the trail. Just as he began to think he had gone off track, he spotted the Endless Chain Ridge, a high grey massif that marched across the landscape. They followed its fir clad lower slopes for many hours. The tributary they were following met the muddy, turbid main river after plunging through a deep elbowed canyon that they traversed on the high side. They skirted wide again at Jasper House, following an ancient animal trail, until Grundel suddenly veered at the Indian River ford, and headed northeast. He was taking Took and Raven to the meeting place with the Yukon and polar bears. He was hoping to get there before SaMäel found them. After their meeting, Took and Raven would leave for home on the Barrenlands.

Except for a couple of close encounters with lone hunters, the animals' journey was without incident for the first few days. They woke in the early dawn before the moon had disappeared or the mist had risen from the river, hiking until noon, stopping for the heat of the day, and then resuming late afternoon to journey well past nightfall. They rested again in the darkest hours. In the mornings they came upon lakes so still that the mountains with their fir slopes were perfectly reflected. One

Tangle Falls

could mistake which was real, which the image. Then the sun would rise and a long wind down the Corridor would lightly ruffle the surface, erasing the illusion, leaving the dazzling light glimmering on the water.

One morning they woke to so deadly a calm that not a leaf rustled, not the thinnest branch moved. The lively chorus of birds had stopped mid-note from a rustling in the dead leaves, very close. Grundel turned to Raven who flew up to a low pine branch. Through the trees a large cat appeared, haughty, elegant, with little black tufts at the top of her ears.

"Purdina," squawked Raven. There was a light note of mocking in his voice, but also, thought Grundel, a note of fear. The lynx looked up lazily at Raven, licking her lips, then sat down with Grundel to give him her news. She departed as silently and quickly as she had appeared. Raven was happy to see her leave.

The bird was talkative that morning, Took noticed, flying above their heads, giving endless advice, until Grundel told him sharply to be quiet. In the heat of the day, they rested. A woodpecker rattled and drummed rat-a-tat-tat, chickadees scolded, insects droned. The air thickened uncharacteristically humid as clouds built up into towers of darkening trouble. Grundel wakened.

"Thunderstorm coming," he said to no-one in particular. Tuktu looked up from her grazing. When they found an overhang of rock to wait out the storm, Raven swooped in to join them.

But most days were clear and the grizzly kept them at a steady pace, knowing how far they had to go, his mind busy with contingency plans should SaMäel appear. He had taken this route many times, a path carved deeply into the memory of all the Keepers, but he saw it anew as he watched for places that might protect them from SaMäel's wrath.

The weather held and except for the occasional swarm of gnats or cloud of biting flies that they escaped by plunging into the river, their going was pleasant. They made their way through richly timbered valleys speckled with golden-needled larch, forded shallow pebbled streams, climbed high passes with narrow rock ledges until even Took became accustomed to navigating breath taking precipices and easing down the slopes of mountain runnels. They passed aquamarine lakes and marshy ponds noisy with wild fowl preparing to migrate; they slept in alpine meadows with the last of the blue larkspur, snowy valerian and golden arnicas, listening to the trembling aspen leaves, already turning gold.

Tuktu found plenty to graze on, except in the high rocky passes, while Grundel fished for speckled trout in the deep emerald lakes and clear, fast flowing streams, gorged on berries or overturned logs full of ants, or dug out rodents. It was fortunate that food was plentiful because there were times when the Keeper's hunger would overpower him. Raven scavenged for both of them, looking especially for fat rich pine nuts for Grundel.

The night air was cold and became colder as they moved north, coating the bushes and hardy alpine flowers with light frost needles until the flush of morning sun burned them off. Each day the snow seemed to creep lower down the mountains.

ON A HIGH BLUFF, Grundel stopped, gazing thoughtfully at a flock of honking geese heading south in their familiar V formation, knowing the bears should be feasting, should be preparing for winter and the Long Sleep.

When they left familiar territory, Grundel periodically sent Raven ahead to scout out the lay of the land or to ensure that what he thought he remembered was accurate. With a sharp eye, Raven saved them from a few muskeg-filled bogs that would have slowed them down. They kept on track with the help of Polaris, keeping it in their sight as soon as evening revealed it.

NEXT MORNING Grundel woke to the sound of shrieking wind. A storm roared over the peaks and pelted them with hard crystals of rain. Though they were sleeping under an outcropping of rock, the driving wind found them, driving the pellets into their eyes and noses. They looked around for better protection, but finding none they huddled together, their backs to the wind.

"We should reach Ram Ridge soon, Grundel," said Took, "what happens then?"

They had run parallel to the Great Rocky Trench for the last while, and Took was anxious to turn east towards home. The great wide open plains were calling her.

"Hopefully we'll soon rendezvous with Neva and Nanuk, and the Yukon bears."

"Funny that we haven't seen anything of SaMäel yet," piped Raven, "I wonder what that means?"

"I've been wondering the same thing," mused Grundel, and Took nodded. Grundel looked down at the sack that he had tied around his neck. Inside were maps, but SaMäel would not guess that right away.

"I would rather encounter him before we reach the others. I don't want to draw them into this."

"Will we go further today?" asked Raven.

"I think we will wait for the worst of this storm to pass. We've made good time."

SaMäel and the seraphim had spent the last three days scouring the Mountains, but it is a great land mass, full of ragged peaks, deep valleys, gorges, a million places to hide. When SaMäel realized the complexity of the land, he sent for all the seraphim. The angels were now in formation, spread out in a line, making their way north. The animals did have one advantage, though; SaMäel was convinced Grundel would be travelling with his Brothers, so he was looking for a group of grizzlies.

The rain muffled the beating of wings, but Grundel still heard it. The angels flew over them, disinterested in the lone caribou. Tuktu was actually blocking their view of Grundel who was pushed up against the back of the rock outcrop with Raven.

"I thought we wanted to encounter them!" whispered Raven.

Grundel said, "We do, but not quite yet. The longer we delay them, the longer Rakor and Piotr will have to hide the Quintessence. Rakor said he would need three weeks before they would be ready to travel in Time. I expect them to be travelling now. We must continue to hold SaMäel's attention today."

"Don't we have to get it first?"

"I wouldn't worry about that; they'll be back."

GRUNDEL waited until noon when the storm had passed; as the sun broke through the clouds, he led the others north. Later in the afternoon while they were scrambling over a high pass they noticed SaMäel sitting on a log beside a small tarn; there was a skiff of snow on the ground and the few tamaracks had turned a deep bronze. He waved them over to him and let them drink from the bracing water, eyeing the bag around Grundel's neck, before questioning them.

"It's getting late, Grundel, shouldn't you be home, bedding down for the Long Sleep?" Grundel said nothing. "Come, come, let's not play any more games. Just give me what I want and I'll be on my way." SaMäel smiled graciously, but no one answered his smile. Raven looked around nervously for the seraphim. Tuktu stamped and pawed her hoof impatiently.

"See—even your stalwart companions want to be on their way." Greedily, SaMäel eyed the bag, imagining the power inside it. "You must be tired of carrying that."

"What I have is of no benefit to you, SaMäel," said Grundel slowly and deliberately.

"I'll be the judge of that!" snapped SaMäel. Angered by Grundel's lack of fear, he rose to his full height, whirling his golden eyes and beating his wings. But although Raven scuttled under Grundel's legs and Took stepped back, lowering her rack, Grundel didn't budge. Suddenly they were surrounded by beating wings as the seraphim in all their glory swooped down upon them. Took and Raven collapsed in fear, but Grundel held his ground.

"It's a good show, SaMäel, but we both know that you cannot make me do anything I do not wish to do." Grundel grunted to Tuktu, turned and padded across the alpine meadow. Took rose slowly and followed after him, watching SaMäel nervously over his shoulder. Raven cautiously flew behind him. When the trees in front of them burst into flame, Raven flew up and Took turned to stampede away, but Grundel stopped them with a roar.

"Stop!" he said, "Look how the trees do not change, do not burn down. It's not real—it's an illusion. We can walk through that fire unhurt."

"But we're not going to—right?' replied Raven, hopefully.

"On the contrary, Raven. We must." Grundel started through the flames, willing himself to stay calm, to not react to what he felt was hot, searing, smothering fire. Raven rolled his eyes at Took and flew up over the fire. The caribou took a deep breath and, trusting Grundel as she had for so long, followed him. Her mind was a confusion of hot and cold, of flame and the smell of burning pine, but she glued her eyes on Grundel and kept going. Before she was through the grove, the fire stopped as suddenly as it had started. As they cleared the meadow and started down the slope, Raven glanced back at SaMäel who was back sitting on the log, deep in thought.

"What will he do now, Grundel?" asked Raven, landing on Grundel's shoulder.

"I don't know. Probably his same old tiresome tricks—try to instil doubt and fear and, if that doesn't work, he'll try to appeal to what he assumes is our greed and ambition, and if that doesn't work he'll prey on our desires. And all along he will wear us down, trying to set us against one another, discouraging us, making us feel hopeless."

"It works on the humans," said Raven.

"Somehow he understands humans, knows their emotions, can predict their responses and behaviours. He gets to them."

"But it doesn't work so well on bears!" Raven giggled nervously. "Right?"

"Except Rakor," added Tuktu. Grundel grinned grimly. He was going to miss Tuktu's clear headedness, her quick intelligence and stark honesty, when she returned home.

"Rakor's case was an aberration! He wasn't acting like a Keeper!" defended Raven. "SaMäel doesn't get to Grundel or Kyna, does he Grundel?'

"No. He can't seem to grasp our way of thinking. But it's going to get trickier because I can't send him back to the Icefield. If he doesn't think he can persuade me, he might go back to find someone who he thinks he can, or to bring Slank to do his dirty work for him. Although I'm pretty sure he doesn't want to bring those bungling idiots at this point. He's proud enough to think he can do it himself. On the other hand, I can't make it too easy or he'll suspect I don't have it and go looking elsewhere."

Grundel wandered off to find something to eat. Tuktu, out of the corner of her eye, had been watching a dark speck in the southern sky slowly getting larger and she turned now to get a better look.

"What is that?" she said. Grundel looked up, his snout bleeding berries. "Is that Aquila?"

Grundel stood tall and waved madly while Raven cawed loudly and flew up until Aquila spotted them. She alighted on the ground in front of them.

"Did you see SaMäel," she said breathlessly, "he's—"

"Yes, we know. What's the news?" pressed Grundel.

"Rakor and Piotr have left—they will need the day. Monk and the others are back—apparently Mikaila can fly—" "

"Really?" said Raven. "Now there's a story I want to hear!" Aquila flapped her wings in agitation. "Don't interrupt."

Raven looked contrite. "Sorry," he said.

"Where was I?"

"All safe?" asked Grundel.

"Not quite. The others all got back safely but SaMäel has Semjaza under guard in Abadon and no one knows what's happening to him. Armaros is with Rakor and Piotr, so Melancholia is trying to find out what's happening to Semjaza. Any message for Kyna?"

"SaMäel has just discovered where we are and made his first bid for the Quintessence. We will do our best to hold him here for the rest of the day. How are the Brothers?"

"I won't lie, Grundel—they need to feast and to sleep. Tagore and her pack are waiting to join in the kill."

"Tell Kyna to do as she sees fit. I hope to speak to the northern bears tonight and then I'll be home as fast as I can."

"One last thing—it's time Winda and I head south. Do you still need us?"

"I would appreciate it if you could just stay until I get home. We still might need you. It could make all the difference." Aquila nodded.

They stayed with the great eagle while she hunted, fed and

rested briefly, admiring her powerful launch for the flight home, watching as she again became a small dark spot on the horizon.

"Ok," said Grundel, rising, "last leg. Let's see how far we get before SaMäel reappears."

Ram Ridge

NEVA AND NANUK were waiting for Grundel at Ram Ridge, strong ivory polar bears silhouetted against the darkening mountain. There were grizzly paw marks on a prominent pine tree alerting Grundel that the Yukon grizzlies had also arrived, but had gone hunting. Neva and Nanuk were old friends that Grundel had known since he had made his first trip north, with Rakor, as a youngster. They settled down to catch up. It wasn't long before a large honey brown grizzly strode out of the wood with a young female in tow. Grundel had met Tawl before on earlier trips, and had always liked him. The Yukon bear was outgoing and confident; if he had one flaw, though, it was his pride. He was quick to take umbrage; still, Grundel was pleased to see that Tawl had become the Yukon leader. After the grizzly proudly introduced his offspring, Zara, they settled down to business.

As Grundel took the bag from around his neck, the sky lit up in a blaze of fire as SaMäel appeared. Tawl growled menacingly, but before anyone else could move, the polar bears had leapt at SaMäel. He flew up, barely out of their long reach.

"He's just a fallen angel—don't waste your time," said Grundel, pulling out a map from the bag and spreading it out on the ground. "The light is fading; soon we'll not be able to see at all. We must do this now." Inwardly he wondered where the rest of the seraphim were.

"How did you do that?" asked SaMäel, floating back down close to the polar bears, visibly impressed. "I thought your bodies were completely relaxed. I've never seen anyone move so quickly from a relaxed position—well, except me."

"You like that, do you?" smiled Neva. "Relaxed readiness—a trait acquired by sitting at breathing holes in the ice, hour upon hour, waiting for food to appear. We could never sit there with our bodies tensed for that long, but we would starve to death if we couldn't move swiftly on a moment's notice." Grundel growled, aware that SaMäel was attempting to flatter and distract the polar bears, to put them off guard. SaMäel turned to him.

"Don't be jealous, Grundel, I was getting to you. What else is in your bag?"

"Nothing."

"Bah! You expect me to believe that? You'd better give it to me so you can get on with your business here."

Grundel looked up at the darkening sky; it was dusk; the day was over. He shook out the other contents, and turned the bag inside out.

"Satisfied now, SaMäel?" Tossing the empty bag carelessly behind him, Grundel turned back to the map.

"Then where is it?" SaMäel roared. When Grundel ignored him, the map suddenly went up in flame, whirling on an updraft. As the other bears gasped, jumping away from the flying flame, Grundel swiped at it with his paw and caught it.

"It's just an illusion," said The Keeper. "Come." The others cautiously gathered around as he deliberately spread the map out on the ground again. SaMäel fumed, spitting fire. The bears chose to ignore him, intent on their own concerns. Finally, discouraged, the angel flew off. Grundel silently hoped that he had delayed long enough. He turned his attention back to the map. If they couldn't imagine a way to keep the Corridor open and safe for the animals, it didn't matter what SaMäel did—they wouldn't survive anyway.

His first task was to show the newcomers how to read his

map. They were accustomed to a simpler form, drawn in sand, and were intrigued by the portable map made by Monk.

"Here is our Corridor," Grundel began, pointing out a long snaky line that started in the north and ran all the way down to the southern edges of the Mountains; the Corridor along the valley floor that all the large mammals and many smaller animals used to traverse the Mountains. "The activity around the Yellowhead Pass has died down; the men left. It looks like they have abandoned the idea of a northern railroad. Just a few outfitters, hunters and guides remain in the area around or north of our Icefield.

"But the climbing is increasing—groups come into our area now just to climb a mountain and then leave. They have not yet discovered our Icefield; although I don't think we have long. There are a few homesteads in our area, here at Hilda Creek and here on Angel Lake. But these humans don't present problems for us. The section from Banff to Jasper House is becoming more frequented and that will be a problem. But the bulk of human activity is still around Banff, staying close to the railroad for now, and the railroad is headed west. Still, lots of animal migrations cross that valley and will have to cross the railroad. It's dangerous from what we hear from the Yellowstone bears."

"We've heard some horrible stories about the humans," said Zara, the female youngster.

"She means the new humans," added Tawl, "the ones in charge of the railroad."

"Individually, the white humans are unpredictable. Some of them are predators and some aren't; but acting as a group, they're ruthless. Unlike the brown humans, most have no sense of the great chain, aren't even aware of Gaia. They're mass-killing wolves. If they don't like you, they just get rid of you. And they don't just hunt for food. They hunt for what they call 'trophies'—pieces of animals—heads, antlers. Sometimes they will skin the coat off the animal but discard the rest. It's gruesome and pathetic. The Corridor is becoming increasingly dangerous.

"I suspect when their curiosity is aroused, they will head north and it will be towards the Jasper House area, since it is already inhabited by them to some extent and there's the Stoney Trail. Jasper House is a supply depot—they seem to need their human comforts. But it's hard to tell—I'm not sure how much longer men will stay there as the activity seems to have shifted. The main thing to remember is that when humans do travel, they travel the Corridor. It will be only a matter of time before they reach your lower territories."

The northern bears studied the map thoughtfully.

"We're not worried about the brown humans, we've lived with them for a long time—it's these newcomers," replied Nanuk.

"And they're starting to enter the northern interior from the west coast," Tawl added. "What can we do to prepare?"

"You need to explore alternative routes away from the main Corridor because the humans will certainly use it and hunt it relentlessly."

"That's easier said than done!" retorted Zara. "The Corridor is essential to us. Couldn't we just scare them from using it? From what you tell us, they can build trails anywhere." Grundel eyed the young grizzly, noting her strength and will.

"Unfortunately they have weapons we cannot compete with. That strategy is not working for us, or the southern bears." In his mind's eye, he saw Boris lying in a heap.

"What else, then?" asked Neva, who had grown restless. The moon was rising. It was time to move on.

"Teach your offspring to stay away from the humans even when they're curious."

"How long do you think we have, Grundel?" asked Tawl.

"Hard to say. But we'll keep you alerted to any movement north."

"How can we thank you?"

"No need. The southern bears are sharing their information with us. We're all in this together. Somehow, we have to think of a way to keep the Corridor open and to manage the humans. One day, with its fragile landscape, the Barrenlands might face an even greater challenge."

"We know," replied Nanuk. Neva nodded, rising heavily to her feet.

Tuktu, who had been listening closely, rose with the bears. "I will pass all of this on to the Council," she said, turning to Grundel. "We can't bear to think what will happen if a rail-road cuts across our migration path. Bad enough that we have to endure the brown human hunt, but these others are a nightmare."

"Perhaps together we can minimize the danger. It was good to see you, my friend," said Grundel warmly. "Please give my respect to your mother and the Elders." He turned to Raven. "You're free to return home now, Raven. You have more than paid your dues."

Raven looked into the familiar faces of Neva and Nanuk and Took. He thought about his homeland, the Great Plains, the river of caribou, the rising hills in the northern reaches with their midnight sun. He thought about the extended family that he had not seen for a long time, and was momentarily homesick. But it passed. More urgently, he realized, he needed to know what happened to Monk and Rachel, how they would rescue Semjaza; he wanted to see Mikaila fly, and to hear Piotr and Rakor's tale of travelling Time; he wanted to be there to defeat SaMäel and to rejoice with the others when the

Quintessence was safe or to mourn and commiserate together if it were lost. It would not be enough to hear all this from far away.

"Grundel, I'd like to come back with you, if you agree. I'm not ready to leave." Grundel looked at him surprised, but Took laughed.

"I'm not surprised, Raven. I'm finding it hard to leave too. Too many loose ends!" she said.

"I would enjoy the company on the return trip, Raven," replied Grundel, "it's up to you." Raven settled on Grundel's shoulder.

"Well, we're off then! I'll have many a story to tell when next we meet, Took!"

"I'll look forward to that, Raven." Tuktu laughed. "Good bye, Grundel!" She tossed her head and leapt into motion, anxious to be home.

"Keep in touch, my friend," called Nanuk as the polar bears turned and raced off after the caribou.

BACK AT CATHEDRAL night had fallen. Kyna was sleeping in the mouth of the cave, her head resting on her crossed paws, when the brilliance of the full moon woke her. She tried to turn her head away, to find her dream again, but the moonlight was insistent. She lumbered to her feet, shook herself fully awake and started down the path of light. She crossed the ice bridge and loped across the Icefield, keeping up a steady pace. Something gnawed at her, though it was not hunger. At the top of Entrance, she saw Tagore, sitting intently on an outcropping of rock, alone, alert. Kyna approached behind her, but the White Wolf did not turn. She threw back her head and let out a long, lonely howl.

"What is it, Tagore?"

"Something's coming—listen for it."

Kyna squatted beside her, patiently contemplating the glacier, its crags and masiffs, its milky green tarn at its base shimmering in the moonlight. She was aware of Toholinagi's presence and the bittersweet fragrance on the night air, rising from the Ancient Wood. For a long time, all she heard was the moaning and pinging of the ice, and occasionally rock or ice falling and clattering across the glacier, until, almost imperceptibly, a sound like distant thunder rolled down the mountain Corridor, intensifying. The ground shook as it swept past them.

"Gaia stirs." Tagore got to her feet.

"Good," replied Kyna. Tagore nodded, then trotted off.

Piotr's Tale

PIOTR and Rakor had finished the feast Engelmann had prepared for them and lay down for a restorative nap. Engelmann
didn't argue; he knew they had to be rested to make their long
journey and succeed at their dangerous task. They were travelling back in time, further than anyone had ever travelled
through Engelmann's portal, back before the first glaciation.
The spirit would not have let any other species attempt such a
leap, but he was convinced the grizzlies were mentally and
physically capable. And Armaros would be with them. So
Engelmann waited while they slept, slipping back easily into
his own time. Later, as the bears were waking up, Winda
arrived. Engelmann swirled into his cone to welcome her.
Rakor shook himself and stood. Nodding to Piotr and Armaros,
Winda turned to Rakor and said, "Kyna sent me to get a report
on your progress."

"Tell her we're just leaving," replied Rakor, "and that we'll
need the full day. Grundel must keep SaMäel occupied." He
paused for a moment then asked, "Is Vang all right?"

"Yes, he's with Kyna," the young eagle said, looking around
curiously.

"Has SaMäel been there?" asked Rakor. Winda had begun
to wander around the portal. "Winda!" She came fluttering
back.

"Sorry, yes, he seems to have accepted the deception that
Vang is you."

Rakor nodded, satisfied that all was well. About to exit,
Winda suddenly turned back, remembering.

"There's one more thing—Kyna wants you to give the

Quintessence to Piotr until you get there. You don't want trouble in the portal where you can do nothing to help yourself. This bag with a shell full of stones is for you to wear. If SaMäel figures it out and catches up with you in the portal, he will expect you to have the Quintessence. You are to enchant Piotr's bag, Armaros, so it can't be seen. If you would," she added quickly, remembering Kyna had said to be sure to ask Armaros, not to order him.

"SaMäel can disenchant it," replied Armaros, dubiously.

"Yes, but Kyna thinks it might give all of you some extra, valuable time." Rakor nodded, seeing the wisdom in the move, and took off the bag around his neck, handing it to Piotr. When Piotr had it securely around his neck, Armaros cast his spell and the bag with the Q vanished—but not the weight. Piotr felt it chaffing his neck though nothing could be seen. It was an odd sensation.

After Winda left, Engelmann opened the skylight so they could all keep their eyes on Polaris, the North Star.

"It's a long trip, Piotr," said Rakor, "keep your eye sharp and the bag steady. All set?" Piotr nodded, stealing his nerve. Suddenly he felt himself swept up in a maelstrom, a whirlwind of darkness. He heard a high wailing sound—as if all the everyday sounds from all the days and years were whipped together on the wind. Finding it hard to get his breath, he could no longer sense Rakor or Armaros near him; in fact, he could sense nothing and the nothingness stretched out before him, endlessly. He began to panic. Then he remembered to look up—to keep his eye on Polaris. But, nothing was there but tumbling, twirling darkness.

Use your mind's eye, Piotr.

In the dark void, Piotr made a desperate effort to remember, to imagine Polaris as he saw it last. He clung to the image, gasping for breath, trying to hold on to his sanity in the chaos that enveloped him. Just when he had given up hope of ever escaping the whirlwind, the motion slowed and he felt himself tumbling head over heels. Suddenly he was rolling down a short incline with Rakor beside him. When they finally came to a stop they just looked at one another in awe.

"Do you think we could find a short cut home?" asked Piotr. Rakor gave a great guffaw and the two of them burst into mad laughter. Rakor grasped for his bag. "Do you still have it?" he asked, sobering. Piotr looked down as the bag became visible around his neck.

"Was it supposed to do that?" he asked, surprised. Rakor shrugged.

As Armaros flew down to them, a great crack filled the air, and they found themselves in a world they didn't know. It was much warmer, lush with vegetation; no snow could be seen on the jagged mountains. Above all, was the chaotic clashing noise with great claps of thunder and shafts of lightning.

"The first thing we need to do," said Rakor, trying to focus on their task amid the chaos, "is to find our bearings. Do you see anything familiar, Piotr?" The two bears peered through the growing dusk, turning around and around, but found no familiar landmarks. Everything had been displaced. There were no glaciers, no Icefield, just great green valleys and ragged mountains.

"Nothing," whispered Piotr, in awe, "nothing at all. Can you smell anything familiar?"

"Only the burning." Rakor ducked involuntarily as a great dark mass fell near them.

"What was that?" Piotr asked, shuddering.

"A falling angel. Come, we have only a short time," said Armaros, herding them out of the way of the falling warrior who was groaning bitterly, "you are south of Angel Glacier, but not far. Soon the sheer volume of impacts will create another whirl-wind; one you will not be able to survive; we must hurry."

"Has SaMäel fallen?" asked Rakor, staring at the gasping heap of armour, spear, and splayed body. Other dark masses were crashing nearby; the earth shook as a number of mighty warriors fell.

"Not yet. But there's not much time. Mark the portal—there's the Engelmann—do you have your bearings?" The bears looked around carefully then nodded. "Good. Now follow me." As Armaros led them over unfamiliar ground, Piotr and Rakor tried to ignore the battle cries, the great clashing heavens, the moans of the falling bodies, but their hearts leapt to their mouths every time a warrior shook the earth.

It grew darker; the smell of burning grew stronger. They picked their way through the darkness lit only by the brilliant flashes.

"Is that lightning?" asked Piotr, fearfully.

"No, it's the beginning of the firestorms caused by the clash of angel spears, but it is still far away," replied Armaros. "Look, we are almost there."

The bears were unconvinced when Armaros announced that they had arrived.

"How do you know? There's no glacier, no lake, no scree, no rubble, nothing, nothing familiar. Not even the mountains look the same."

"Trust me—look carefully—there's Sorrow Peak, there's Angel Peak where SaMäel will fall and Angel Glacier will eventually fill in." Piotr scrunched his eyes, focusing on the mountain, imagining what should be there with his mind's eye.

"Oh—I see it now!" said Piotr, breathlessly, "but the mountains look so different."

"The last glaciations haven't left their mark yet," interrupted

Armaros impatiently. "Piotr, your main task is not to be seen. I can't predict what will happen if you are. The angels will regain consciousness shortly. SaMäel will fall—and soon. There's something we need to tell you now. I'm taking Rakor back to the Icefield. He's going to put the Quintessence back in the Castleguard Caves."

"What?" Piotr looked at them both astounded. "Isn't that risky? Won't SaMäel figure that out?"

"It's all risky," replied Rakor.

"Why the change in plans?"

"It's not a change," answered Armaros. "Angel Glacier is another diversion. We wanted to make sure that no one, no invisible angel, was listening in the portal. SaMäel has already searched thoroughly at Castleguard. He thinks it has been taken from there to somewhere else. We're hoping it will take him a long time to look everywhere. And only Rakor, Grundel, Kyna, you and I will know the truth. It will keep the others safer."

"Then why have we bothered to go back in time?" Piotr asked, dreading the trip back.

"As soon as we enter a portal, it multiples the choices—makes it a tremendous task. The day of the battle is our best distraction. SaMäel can never go back to that day without experiencing tumultuous emotions. And we can make some slight changes that might confound SaMäel if and when he does figure out that we have travelled in time. You are still to bury the contents of the bag on Angel Peak as planned. It's just not going to be the Quintessence. But, if anyone sees you, they'll think you've buried it there.

"I have to hurry now. I'm sorry I can't stay to help you. Semjaza and I rescued SaMäel when he fell and took him to the Hoodoos to recuperate. Pay close attention to our route, Rakor, because you might have to return on your own. We will meet

Piotr at the portal as soon as possible, but whatever occurs get back to your time as quickly as you can, even if you have to leave the other—understood?" The bears nodded. "Piotr, give the Quintessence to Rakor, and remember to hide your decoy deep and high up so when the glacier retreats it will remain hidden for the longest time possible. Can you find your way back?" Piotr nodded, exchanging bags with Rakor.

"Rakor, you must take the Quintessence deep into Castle-guard. Past the central cavern, go as far as you can into the first tunnel on your right, place the Quintessence there, then return half way and say the spell Semjaza taught you that will bring down the roof of the tunnel on the back portion. But be careful—you don't want the collapsing tunnel to bury you too. All set?"

The bears nodded again, but they were just managing to quell their terror of so many unknowns.

"It's getting so dark," said Piotr.

"That would be the dust cloud obscuring the sun. It will be dark now for a long time. It is the beginning of the long winter," answered Armaros.

"Long winter?" asked Piotr, not liking the sound of that.

"An age of darkness until the sky clears again. Piotr, you'd better climb out of the valley—you need to position yourself—I suggest behind that outcropping on Sorrow Peak. Wait there until we remove SaMäel. I'll give you a signal when you should make your move. I will look up, but just once—don't miss it. Now, exchange bags." Piotr felt for the bag; it had a strange effect on him and although it had filled him with a sense of exhilarating energy, he was more than ready to give it to Rakor. Rakor took it, carefully hanging it around his neck, giving his own smaller, lighter bag to Piotr.

"Maybe you should render Rakor and me invisible," suggested Piotr.

"I would if I could, but it's not possible this far out of your natural time."

"Be careful of the shale slopes, Piotr," warned Rakor, giving him a last look. Piotr didn't need to be told, but he nodded. It was the only fearful thought they exchanged.

"All right—let's go," Armaros said, and flew up with Rakor and disappeared. Piotr looked around, drew a deep breath and started for Sorrow Peak.

PIOTR heard SaMäel's fall from a great distance. Horrified, he scanned the sky until the angel appeared, grotesque in size, flaming, falling at an incredible speed. It was the uncontrollable descent of a great and terrible dragon, wings stretched trying to break his fall—he was flailing, roaring, tearing at the empty air. Piotr covered his ears as SaMäel's roar of anger and frustration and fear reverberated through the mountains. As SaMäel smashed into Angel Peak, his agonizing cry of pain sent out shock waves. Piotr clung desperately to the rock of the mountain. The dark angel was the last angel to fall and for a moment there followed an eerie silence, then the faint sound of a dull roar.

The beginning of the tsunami on the inland sea, thought Piotr, remembering what Armaros had told him, *not much time left*. He searched the sky for signs of the Watchers, not wanting to move until they had taken SaMäel to the hoodoos. A few of the warrior angels had made their way to SaMäel, but they were all in terrible condition, unable to help him. The dragon had disappeared and in its place was a broken angel.

Armaros flew over Piotr without showing any signs of recognition, but the small bear backed further under the ledge where he was hiding, fearful that if Armaros could find him that easily, others could too, now that they were regaining consciousness. Semjaza and Armaros lifted SaMäel and flew off slowly. The other angels just sat in the depression SaMäel had rendered, while Piotr's anxiety grew. Soon, Armaros was back, herding them down into the valley into a protected spot, moving ceaselessly between them, offering aid and comfort. Piotr didn't take his eyes off him. When he glanced up once, Piotr knew it was time to act. He moved slowly, deliberately, hugging the mountain, not wanting to draw attention to himself. Only one pair of eyes surreptitiously watched his steady progress. When he reached the spot, he started digging.

ARMAROS waited at the portal for Stella Polaris to rise. He sensed Semjaza's anxiety in Abadon and wondered what was happening; but he could do nothing for the moment. He had just arrived and was waiting for Piotr. Time was running out. The roar of the tsunami had increased dramatically; the hurricane force winds were lashing and lifting trees. When he loped up to the portal, Piotr was showing signs of acute trauma.

"Where's Rakor?" the young bear asked.

"Put it out of your mind, concentrate on Stella Polaris. I'll explain when we get back, now follow me," he said sternly.

"But—."

"Now Piotr! Before we lose the chance." The young bear gave one last look around and then followed the Watcher into the portal. Engelmann sent them immediately through the long, black void and they made it back to Earth without incident. The young bear tumbled out onto Engelmann's moss floor, profoundly grateful to be back in his own time, but he lay where he landed, exhausted beyond anything he had ever experienced. Dreading what Armaros had to say, Piotr finally rolled to look at the Watcher.

"It's done," said Armaros, "but Rakor did not survive."

"Why?"

"There was an earthquake. He didn't escape—the cave."

The young bear was stunned into silence. He just wanted to lie down and not get up, but he knew he still had his duty to perform. Despite being devastated, Piotr thanked Engelmann before leaving the portal. After the chaos of the angel's battle, the world seemed perfectly calm and serene. The sun radiated a healing warmth. The aspens, drenched in light, trembled in the wind. Piotr breathed deeply. This was the world he knew. For one glorious moment he lay down on the good earth and smelled its rich familiarity. He was just opening his eyes when he heard another great beating of wings. SaMäel alighted in front of the portal.

"Going somewhere, Piotr?" SaMäel drawled, with an ugly grin on his face.

"You can just give that to me," said SaMäel, holding out his hand. Piotr rose, and felt for the bag still hanging around his neck.

"It's not what you think—not what you are looking for, SaMäel," began Piotr.

"Enough!" snapped SaMäel. "Give it to me."

The bear tried to remember what Mel and the Watchers had taught him. SaMäel was an angel, the most powerful of all angels, but he couldn't harm him directly. Fear, one's own fear, was what usually killed. He knew he didn't have to give the bag to SaMäel; that he could refuse—but what for—the bag did not contain what SaMäel so desperately wanted. One way or another SaMäel would find that out shortly. He might as well give it to him now.

In greedy anticipation, SaMäel couldn't help grinning, until the empty bag was put in his hand. He felt it, shook it, peered into it, his brow becoming more and more furrowed, and his eyes beginning to whirl. Piotr was surprised at how long it took for the dark angel to realize that it was not the Quintessence, as if he could not accept the truth. This was one too many disappointments; one too many betrayals. In a towering wrath, SaMäel transmuted into a dragon and breathed great surges of raging fire at the bear. Piotr cowered, trying to steel his gaze at the dragon, to let him know he was not afraid. *It's not real,* Piotr told himself sternly, *it's not real.* But it sure felt real; his fur singed, his face burned, he felt himself collapsing, but he chanted it like a mantra, trying to hold on, *it's not real. It's not real.* Finally, SaMäel realized the bear was not going to succumb.

"You will pay," roared SaMäel, "you will all pay!"

After the dragon departed roaring uselessly, Piotr collapsed and Armaros, who had remained in the portal, not wanting SaMäel to realize he was helping the animals, picked up the bear and flew him to Cathedral. He flew directly into the cave, where many of the Brothers were already congregating, waiting to hear the news. He grunted heavily as he released him on the floor. The Brothers crowded around.

"Well?" said Kyna, coming out of the Map Den and looking down at Piotr motionless on the floor. "What happened?"

"They were successful, Kyna," Armaros reported. "Rakor was magnificent. You should all be very proud of him." There was a resounding whoop of joy throughout the cave.

"Where is—?" began Kyna.

"Is Piotr dead?" blurted Kaare, staring wildly at his youngest Brother.

"No—traumatized—but not dead. SaMäel attacked him just after we arrived back."

"Why? Why then?" gasped Kaare.

"SaMäel saw him outside the portal with the bag around his neck. But when he discovered it was empty, he let out his frustration. Piotr resisted him valiantly."

"Where is Rakor?" asked Vang, dreading the answer.

The angel looked at him with pity. "As I told Piotr, Gaia shook the earth and Rakor didn't escape the collapse of the cave." Kyna saw the grief starting to numb the bears and acted quickly.

"Raven, inform The Keeper." For a moment they all looked down at Piotr, motionless on the cave floor. They wondered what he would tell, when he told his tale.

The Long Sleep

Hilda Creek

WINTER was upon the land. Snow shrouded the forests; the lakes were stilled; there were few travellers to the mountains. All hung in suspension, hushed, muted, silent. Koko crouched beside Kyna out on the ledge. A light snow was falling.

"There are things I don't understand, Kyna," said the child, nuzzling up to her to keep warm.

Kyna smiled wryly. "Me too," she answered, "but what did you have in mind?"

"I don't understand why Rakor trusted SaMäel and got us into this mess. Papa says that Rakor was taken in by SaMäel.

Papa says I should forgive him in my heart."

"And what do you think, Koko?"

"I-I don't know. I'm still angry at Rakor, but I think he was changed by SaMäel's words. Sometimes in the cave, he would be kind to us, then SaMäel would appear and he would be mean again. What's wrong with SaMäel anyway? Why is he like that?"

"Well, I think Rakor was convinced by SaMäel's words too, but that's not the same as trust. Trust is something deeper, something you feel. It's not found in words, it's revealed in a being's whole conduct, what they do, how they react, how willing they are to live in harmony with others. SaMäel's conduct is not trustworthy; he sees the world from one fixed point of view—his own—and thinks that the rest of us are simply here to serve him. That's why no one can ever trust him."

"Then what happened to Rakor? Didn't he know better?"

"Yes indeed, but as Monk said, he was drawn in by SaMäel's lies, convinced of things he would never have believed or accepted if he had thought them up himself."

"I don't understand that."

"Rakor let himself believe that he trusted SaMäel, even though he knew better, because he was mesmerized by the glitter of false power—like light on water."

"Light on water—oh—here one minute, gone the next?" Koko asked.

Kyna nodded. "And impossible to grasp."

"What's so great about power?" the child asked sleepily, yawning, curling up, soothed by Kyna's warm thick fur, her body warmth, her calm breathing. Before Kyna could answer, Koko was asleep. Ahead, in the storm, Kyna heard great wings beating; she drew the child closer to her, shielding and hiding her.

Everyone except Semjaza, who was still in Abadon, and

Vang who had been sent to the Valley of the Twins to be out of SaMäel's sight, had returned and were gathered in the Keeper's Cave to celebrate their victory and mourn Rakor's death. Even Tagore had appeared. And although the feeling in the cave was of unity and companionship, no one could stay long; they all needed to make up lost time—the bears needed their final feast; the eagles were preparing to migrate; the Furtive Folk needed to burrow deep into the earth to escape winter's blast; even the humans needed to get in their supplies and hunker down for the winter. But first, they all felt a stronger need to celebrate their joint success, to acknowledge each other's courage and resourcefulness, and to mark Rakor's passing. They applauded his success, acknowledged his return to responsibility, and grieved his death.

The noise level had risen steadily in the cave as different parties arrived. In the midst of shouts of relief and joy, there was suddenly a howl from Tagore. The room fell silent and moments later SaMäel swept in, giving only a cursory glance to Kyna curled up seemingly asleep on the ledge.

"What? A party and you didn't invite me—even you Armaros? Where's Semjaza—oh yes, visiting us in Abadon. I do hope you won't miss him; he might be there for a while— the women do love him so." SaMäel glanced behind him at a sudden movement. Kyna entered with Koko.

"So, little Koko is not dead—interesting." Kyna stepped in front of the child, protectively. SaMäel's gaze swept the room until his piercing blue eyes alighted on Rachel who instinctively clutched Monk's arm.

"Relax, Rachel, I'm not here for you. I was tiring of you anyway." He continued around the room until he reached Mikaila, who gave him a steely look in return.

"My dear girl, do not worry about Semjaza; I would hardly

hurt the one being who doesn't bore me to death — what would I do for eternity? Just don't expect him back any time soon." He eyed her. "You could, however, join us." Mikaila said nothing and his glance continued around the room until it fell on Grundel. There was a discernible tightening in SaMäel's body, a suppression of anger.

"Well Grundel, you made it back home safe and sound I see. I suppose you are all feeling very smug. Well, enjoy the moment. We're not done yet." The bears in the cave all gave a low menacing growl. SaMäel began to feel his anger rising, but instead of giving them the satisfaction of thwarting him further, departed.

GRUNDEL was not alone in worrying about what SaMäel would do next. But Melancholia told him to set his worry aside for now and to focus on drawing the Keepers together and preparing the feast, so they could finally settle down to their Long Sleep.

Tagore, as with the Sunados, had arrived to play her part in the bears' fall feast. The ritual feast was introduced long ago by Melancholia and the first Ursula with the help of Tagore in order to prevent an uncontrollable hunger in the male bears when they woke in the spring. That raging hunger endangered new born cubs. There had been a time when the females had to fight the males for the life of the cubs. All the males could see in front of them was food; not even their own young survived such intense hunger.

It was Tagore who had realized the problem. Although the bears ate heavily in the fall, filling up on ants, small rodents and pine nuts for their protein richness, and it had allowed them to survive the winter, this was not enough. Tagore had persuaded Melancholia to encourage the bears to eat more meat before the long sleep and to store some for the spring. She and her pack had even provided the first feast—killing prey the wolf knew could not survive the winter because of old age or a weak state. It was a gesture that turned quickly into ritual. She was waiting for him now, to lead him to the kill her pack had made.

The other animals scurried back into their homes while the bears feasted, content with their own shelters stocked with food for the winter, to curl down deep into the warm earth, and to rest after the hectic flurry of summer activity. The female bears returned to their comfortable dens in the Valley of the Twins, to prepare for the next generation and their long winter labours.

Rachel and Monk had accepted Mikaila's offer to remain with her over the winter, grateful for help with Koko; realizing that this time Mikaila needed them to divert her attention away from Semjaza's fate in Abadon until Melancholia and Armaros could act.

They all assumed that SaMäel had retreated back to Abadon.

BUT SAMÄEL was not ready to retreat. Even as the sheep hunkered down for the winter, the bears feasted, the Furtive Folk slept, the humans rested in their winter cabin with healthy wood piles and larders full of food to see them through the winter, and all felt that life was finally getting back to normal— SaMäel stalked the Icefield, unsatisfied.

He had stopped in a small clearing in the wood at the western toe of Cathedral and was sitting motionless on a rock, thinking. He was searching for clues, any clues, going over and over the same information: those two bungling idiots knew nothing, Malenger was dead, the Quintessence wasn't at Cathedral, Grundel didn't have it; it wasn't with the females in the Valley;

nor with the Watchers. Monk and Rachel certainly didn't—
they wouldn't jeopardize Koko for anything now. Rakor must
have had it and then in the maze of diversions it was lost from
sight. But how and by whom? He had seen Rakor at Cathedral.
Gorath and Tasmira were plainly a diversion, Grundel was a
diversion, Rachel's rescue was, in part, a diversion. Did he have
his eye on everyone? Even that last trip of Piotr's was a diversion—wasn't it? His bag was empty. SaMäel knew that some
part of the puzzle was missing, some bit of knowledge that
would reorganize all his information and make it fall into a recognizable shape. What were they not telling him? Who was the
missing piece of the puzzle?

In a scuffle of wing and raw flesh, a young golden eagle,
feeding in preparation for the migration ahead, descended from
the blue sky into the clearing with fresh prey in her great yellow
talons. She landed effortlessly and began to tear at the flesh
with her hooked beak. The smell of hot blood filled the air.
Vang had just returned from the Valley and, like the others, was
preparing for the Long Sleep. But as he had missed the feast,
he was foraging for a last protein rich meal. Smelling fresh
blood, he loped unsuspectingly out of the wood and into the
clearing. SaMäel looked up.

"Rakor?" SaMäel said out loud, unconsciously, his mind
folding in on itself. Winda looked up from her prey, still young
enough to want to show off her knowledge.

"Vang," corrected Winda, turning back to her meal.

"Who?" SaMäel's voice was deadly.

"Rakor's twin."

Suddenly, pieces fell into place—the deception in the
Castleguard Caves; Vang standing in for Rakor, while all the
diversions distracted him, and Rakor was—doing what? And
where? SaMäel had last seen the bag near a portal but because

it was empty, he had assumed that Piotr had been another diversion. He had thought Rakor couldn't have been involved because he had seen Rakor too recently at Cathedral. But that must have been Vang. The bag was empty. Piotr, he suddenly realized, could have already been through the portal, with the Quintessence. With Rakor? He stopped, arrested—*a portal! The Quintessence could be anywhere! Hell's bells*, he thought, *not just anywhere, but any time*! SaMäel, his breath flaming, let out a long, terrifying, dragon roar. Winda flattened herself against the ground. Vang's legs gave out as his blood ran cold. Rachel in Mikaila's cabin heard it and clutched Koko to her. Kyna heard it deep in her den carrying the next generation. Grundel, half asleep in the depths of Cathedral, heard it and it haunted The Keeper's Long Sleep.

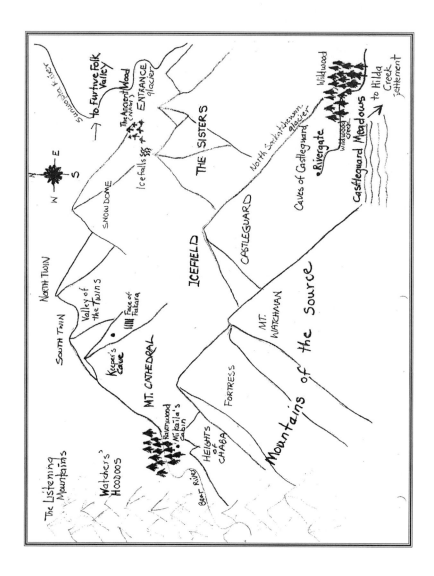

Brief Descriptions of Characters

Pronunciation key: capitals indicate the stressed syllable

The Spirits
MELancholia: the spirit of Cathedral, created by the gods to watch over the Quintessence
ToHOLinagi: a spruce tree, spirit and portal to other worlds
ENGelmann: a spruce tree, spirit, and eldest of Earth's portals

The Keepers—a race of grizzly bears created by the gods to help Melancholia protect the Quintessence. They live in the caves of Mt. Cathedral.
The male twin bears (The Brothers)
RaKOR & Vang—Rakor is the former Keeper (leader)
Aage & INguar
KeDAR & Lunt
GRUNdel & Boris—Grundel currently The Keeper
GORath & Kaare
Piotr & Carth
The females
The Ursula—mate of The Keeper, and leader of the female grizzly bears who live in the Valley of the Twins.
INyx (Einar's mate): former Ursula
aLETHia (Rakor's mate): current Ursula
Candidates for Ursula: KYna, TASmira

Yukon grizzly bears: Tawl (the leader) & Zara (Tawl's offspring)
Bighorn sheep: Bighorn, BAsho. Bighorn is the leader of the mountain sheep who also help protect the Icefield at Snow Dome

Golden eagles, from the Heights of Chaba: aQUILa, WINda
From the Barrenlands:
Tuktu: (took-too) a caribou, once saved by Grundel
Raven: bound to Grundel for an evil deed carried out on the Barrenlands
NEva & NaNUK: leaders of the polar bears

Humans

Monk: a wilderness guide who once studied to become a Jesuit priest but gave it up and found his refuge in the Shining Mountains
Rachel: A Stoney trail guide and Monk's wife
Koko: their daughter
Faida: An Icelandic woman, a hermit & biologist, who immigrated to the Shining Mountains
MiKAila: Faida's daughter
MALenger: A wilderness guide, trained by Monk, who works for SaMäel
Payne & Slank: Malenger's joe-boys
Hilda Van Buren: owner of an outfitter and trading business at Hilda Creek, a small settlement on the Stoney Trail between Banff and Jasper House. The settlement consists of Stoney guides, their families and Hilda.

Fallen Angels

The Watchers: SemJAza, ARMaros, who live in the hoodoos of the Listening Mountains, are angels, Seraphim from Paradisi¤, who fell because they mated with daughters of men.
Warrior Angels: SaMäel: Ruler of Abadon, the greatest of the Fallen Angels. He and the Seraphim of Abadon are the warrior angels who fought Paradisi¤ and were expelled.
Other Seraphim of Abadon: DAgon, AStorath, ANmael, FORcas

In Abadon:
The lost women of Abadon
Rara Avis, an ancient flightless bird who protects SaMäel's seraglio
A leopard, lion, she-wolf, two-headed dog, condors and vultures that protect Abadon

Other Animals
Marmo & Whistler: hoary marmots who live on the scree slopes above Furtive Folk Valley. Marmo is the leader of the Furtive Folk.
TaGORE: a female white wolf, leader of the wolf pack that is tied to the Ursula
GUlo: a fierce and solitary wolverine
MusTELa: an ermine, a leader of the Furtive Folk in the Castleguard Caves
Equus: a Cayuse wild horse from Xeni, descended from a mix of native wild horse, French Percheron and Spanish Barb—getting a rare combination of speed and endurance

The Line of Keepers

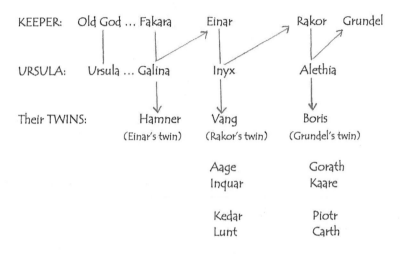

KEEPER: Old God ... Fakara   Einar   Rakor   Grundel

URSULA: Ursula ... Galina   Inyx   Alethia

Their TWINS: Hamner   Vang   Boris
             (Einar's twin)   (Rakor's twin)   (Grundel's twin)

                 Aage   Gorath
                 Inquar   Kaare

                 Kedar   Piotr
                 Lunt   Carth

Legend

... many generations